SOUL
FORGOTTEN

Laura Winter

To my dear @lexa.
Thanks for printing this entire manuscript and texting me play by play updates as you read.

I miss you.

1

Girl

Not dead. At least, I don't think so.

I'm not sure how long I sat in numbness, completely swallowed by a blinding white light. My mind was as blank as my vision, silence ringing in my ears. Or maybe that was actual ringing.

The loud, high pitched shriek slowly faded as the rest of my body settled and feeling tingled through my limbs. I stared up at the night sky, color returning around me despite the blurry vision. My lungs and throat burned as I took a breath. My mouth might have been dry, but I definitely knew the metallic taste. Why had I been screaming?

As the trees came into focus, I felt my heart pick up in panic. I couldn't remember why I had been screaming. In fact, I couldn't remember where I was, or what I was doing. But even worse, I couldn't remember *who* I was. What could have happened to make me forget my own name?

I squeezed my eyes shut, trying to steady my breath. I couldn't have a panic attack now. I needed to focus and figure out what the hell was going on. I needed to be logical here.

Senses; the metallic taste and burning throat must be from screaming. The smell of fresh air and sweat swirling around me was just as concerning, especially because the sweat was me. Well, the muggy air might have had something to do with it, but for some reason I didn't feel hot. *Focus.* If my legs were sore and I was this sweaty, had I been running? And how did I end up on the ground?

Underneath me, my fingers tangled in the slightly overgrown grass, uncomfortable and sticky under my sweating arms. Wait, not just sweat. My left arm stung from my palm to my elbow, throbbing with each pound of pain from a headache radiating around my entire head.

I focused my energy on lifting my heavy arm. If the moon hadn't been so bright, I might have thought it was just a trick from the shadows. But this was unmistakable.

Blood, and a lot of it. I watched it run down my forearm and drip from my elbow onto my clothes and the grass underneath me. Even in the dark, it seemed too deep a color to be blood, but there was a lot of it. Maybe it was the blood loss and the headache making me see things.

A million more questions ran through my head but I shoved them down. I was already using too much of my energy to keep from shaking. I had to focus on getting the answers of my situation, but it wouldn't help if I kept adding more questions rather than staying under control. With a few breaths to build energy and confidence, I pushed my back off the ground to get a better look at my surroundings.

Shit.

I regretted it immediately. Not ten feet in front of me was a man's body. His jeans were ripped and charred, his body contorted in a limp pile, bending in ways a body should not be bent. For a brief moment, I didn't feel scared. No, I felt relief; relief that he was dead, blood pooling from his head and seeping into the cracks of rock underneath him.

What kind of person am I to be relieved he's dead?

Fear rolled back through my body. Was I running with him? From him? Was I chasing him?

Had I killed him?

I gripped my hands into fists to keep from losing my control. With no memories, I wasn't going to find the answers in my head. I had to use what I could around me to put the pieces together.

I scanned the immediate area, locating a backpack just out of reach from me. I leaned over and pulled it closer, careful not to move my left arm too much. My best guess was that the pink and blue checkered bag was mine. At least, that's what I had to tell myself to keep hope alive that I'd find answers somewhere.

Inside the floppy compartment, I pulled out a map that looked like it had been ripped from a large book. It was in good detail, the layout of a town and forest with a small gap in the trees. Maybe that's where I was now. But the scribbled red circle between the town and forest edge caught my attention. There weren't any structures or clues as to what could be there, though; just empty space. Could that have been where I was going, or where I was running from?

I kept digging through the bag, pulling out an extra set of clothes, a worn book titled *The Magicians*, a big key on a thick chain necklace, and an iPod that was clinging to life.

1:45 A.M. August 18.

The screen shut off as it died.

Still no real answers, but the best shot I had to figuring things out seemed to be the red circle on the map. If I wanted to figure out the answers to my questions, I had to work with what I had. Besides, with no memories and people around to help, I had to find the answers myself.

As I put my hand down, bracing to stand up, I felt something cold and smooth press into the palm of my hand. I picked up a shiny black marble... well, half marble. The object was split perfectly down the middle, no imperfections visible. Somehow, that wasn't the first question in my head. How could something so small be so cold? In the middle of summer?

If there was another half somewhere, it wasn't close by. The grass might have been hiding it, but I wouldn't be able to find it at night anyway. I shoved it into the bag and slung it over my shoulder, looking back at the man's body. Whatever was going on, I wasn't going to figure it out here; and I definitely didn't want to be caught in the middle of the forest with a dead man and no memories.

My only option was obvious. I oriented myself on the map and headed toward the red circle near the town of Forest Hills.

The map led me to the bottom of a long and winding driveway that looked like it hadn't been used in years. And right where the red circle had directed me, I spotted a small cabin tucked within the dense trees of the forest. It was dark and hard to see as I cautiously approached, confused and losing hope as it looked like the roof had caved in from a fallen tree.

What the hell was I getting myself into? It wasn't likely that I would have run *from* this place, but why would I be running toward it? The cabin itself certainly looked uninviting, even from afar, but up close it looked like a disaster. The weathered wood creaked as a slight breeze rustled through the trees, causing my heart to pound harder in my chest. Despite my nervousness, I had to get closer. If I had any other clues as to what was happening to me, I would have turned around, but this was my only hope.

I stepped onto the porch, surprised that the weakened wood was stable under my feet. I would have guessed that my weight would have snapped the rotten boards, but they barely creaked with my steps.

In front of me and looking out of place compared to the rest of the house, the door appeared brand new and clean. I frowned. Just a second ago, I could have sworn it looked just as rotten as the porch. I must have just been exhausted, and I'm sure the shifting shadows and trees were making me see things. I moved to the left, carefully stepping along the boards to peer into the broken window. There weren't any lights on inside, and no matter how much I tried to focus, I couldn't see anything but blackness. I doubt anyone would be awake this early in the morning, nor living in such a run-down cabin to begin with, but there should have been some light coming from the broken roof and full moon.

If it was empty, there wouldn't be any harm in staying inside just to keep out of the open. I walked to the front door, prepared to reach for the handle, but froze.

Where is the doorknob?

I leaned closer, a gentle hum from the wood pulling my attention. Carefully, I pressed my hand against the door to balance and held my ear to the wood. Underneath my touch, I could feel a soft vibration from underneath the surface. Then, somewhere inside the door, I heard a latch click, echoing around the empty forest as the door edged open slightly. Despite the darkness I had just seen through the broken window, light spilled onto the porch around me. And not just moonlight; artificial light.

"Hello?" I called, trying to look inside without actually moving forward. The door responded, opening further, as if it was inviting me to walk inside.

This is definitely the part of the movie where you die.

But somehow, I knew that wasn't true. There was a strange nagging in the back of my mind, but I couldn't quite grasp what it meant. I should have actually believed I was going to get murdered or something worse by going inside. It should have terrified me that there wasn't anyone on the other side of the door to open it, but it wasn't fear I felt. It was... familiar, almost comforting. I felt like there was something about this cabin I should have remembered, but the harder I tried to focus on the thought, the more it slipped away.

I continued into the house without another worry. The living room was bright, clean, and organized. A small couch rested against the left wall, a mirror hung just to the right of it, and a kitchen table just beyond that. After seeing the outside of the house, I never would have guessed the inside would look this nice. But if all these lights were on, how could I only see blackness through the broken window? A window that was very much *not* broken now that I was looking at it from the inside.

As I looked to my right, a light flicked on and illuminated a hallway. It extended deep into the cabin, with one door on either side and another at the end, all with the same design as the front door. But the hallway looked far too long for such a small cabin, especially when the outside looked like it could just barely hold the living room I stood in. And I could have sworn the roof had caved in from the outside, but it was perfectly intact; nothing broken or damaged, and definitely no tree through the ceiling.

I shut the front door behind me and placed the checkered bag on the couch, still studying my surroundings. Everything was clean and dusted, so someone had to have been here recently. The only clutter in the entire space was a pile of papers on the table. Maybe I could figure out who this cabin belonged to and why I was coming here. I started to head for the kitchen table, but as I passed the mirror, I froze at the reflection.

I didn't recognize the tall girl staring back at me, but she made all the same movements I did. I ran my hand through my ponytail, spinning violet-red hair between my fingers. And looking even more unnatural than my hair were the fiery, almost glowing blue eyes that stared back at me. They probably seemed so bright next to my black shirt that was soaked in sweat and clinging to my torso. Blue jeans stuck to my figure, shaping down to a pair of Converse sneakers, all of which were splattered with blue ink.

Holy shit.

That wasn't ink; that was blood. My blood.

I shifted my arm to look at the cut, trying not to panic or hyperventilate. Most of the blood was dried, but there was still pain and tenderness around the wound. I focused closer on the cut, studying my forearm in the light. If I didn't know any better, I would have thought it looked like a lightning strike. The cut originated in the middle of my palm and traced up to my elbow, little slivers of blue extending from the bolt that split in two halfway up my forearm.

How could a cut like that happen?

I shook off the image of the dead man that flashed through my head and refocused on the reason why I had walked over here. On the table, I shifted the papers that were neatly stacked, picking up the ID that was sitting on top. I twisted the driver's license with my right hand before pulling it closer to my eyes. The picture looked like the face I had just seen in the mirror; my face. How could I forget what I looked like? Was it because the eyes in the photo were green?

Clara Rivers.

If that was my name, it didn't feel right, but if I couldn't remember what I looked like, how could I remember my name? And why did none of this trigger any memories?

I sighed and studied the details of the girl on the ID. Clara was eighteen today, and six feet tall, with this address listed. Maybe that meant I really did live here.

Strange as it felt, this had to be me, and as much as I wanted that to trigger some sort of memory, I still felt empty. But not completely empty; I could feel something just out of reach, as if it was right on the tip of my tongue. Whatever it was, I wasn't going to figure it out by just standing here.

The papers were mostly school documents with Clara's name on them. *Your name. You are Clara.* I was going to have to remember that. I was enrolled at West Hills High School, starting my senior year on August 28th. At least that was something.

I took a breath. "My name is Clara Rivers. I'm eighteen years old and I'm a senior at West Hills High School." I rolled my eyes. "Oh, and I have no recollection of my past, no idea why I woke up next to a dead man, and I have a cut on my arm that bleeds blue blood."

Seems like a solid backstory you got there. That won't raise any red flags.

Hm, sarcasm. At least that felt natural to me. If only that would help me remember something of actual value.

2

Clara

After chugging two glasses of water, I decided to finish touring the cabin rather than just sleeping on the couch. It still didn't quite feel right calling it *my* cabin, mostly because I couldn't remember anything about it. The bedroom located on the left side of the hallway was decently sized, furnished with a desk and a bed that looked so damn comfortable I thought about just finishing the tour in the morning.

The room across the hall was some sort of training room, with padded walls and assortment of training equipment. Though my guess was that I wasn't the one lifting the weights because they were ridiculously heavy. But if there was only one bedroom, who could have been using them? It seemed like I was the only one living here, though it was strange that my parents would let me live alone. Well, maybe it would make sense if I could actually remember them in the first place.

I stood outside the third room, looking at the handle-less door. It didn't respond to my touch like the front or other two doors had, and it wouldn't budge despite my forced attempts at entry. I dug around the bag I had found to see if I missed something that could help me open the door. Clothes and a book weren't going to do much good, but what about the key on that necklace chain? My excitement was short lived when I realized the key wasn't going to open a door that didn't have a visible lock. I turned the bag over and shook it to see if I had missed anything.

The half marble dropped to the ground and bounced a few times before finally settling on the flat side. As I leaned down to pick it up, I heard the mechanism inside the door click and open.

Interesting. Had the marble really just opened the door? Could this place be magic? Maybe that book was trying to tell me something, because magic went against everything normal... at least I think. Though blue blood and no memories should have been enough to throw my logical brain out.

I picked up the marble and shoved it in my pocket before stepping inside. The lights in the room flickered and finally illuminated an impressive, two-story library. There were ancient papers and leather-bound books scattered everywhere, cluttering the desk and lining every wall, even resting on a spiral staircase that led to the second floor. For a living room that was kept so pristine, I was surprised to see this kind of mess in such a beautiful library.

I closed my eyes and breathed in, letting the charming yet musty smell of books calm me. *Magic. This place is definitely magic.*

Forget the long hallway and collapsed roof; the cabin I had seen on the outside was absolutely not a two-story building and couldn't have been deep enough to hide this room. Whatever was going on, I was meant to be here. Even if I couldn't remember what was going on, this place felt familiar. I felt drawn to the cabin, and the library even more. There had to be something in here that could help me get answers.

But before I could tackle the books, I needed to sleep... and I desperately needed a shower. If the sweat wasn't enough to disgust me, the dried blood was going to make me sick. I made my way back to the bedroom and tried to ignore the call of the empty bed again. A towel was already folded over the side of the tub, and all the shower supplies were already inside. I kicked off my shoes, expecting the tile to feel cold against my feet, but it actually felt warm.

I peeled the rest of my clothing off and turned on the shower to the hottest setting in a natural twist of my hand. *That's good. I have a habit.* I turned to look back at the mirror and frowned. Did I have a tattoo? I twisted to get a better look at my side, the tree a familiar shape... the book! The tree printed on the cover of the book was painted into my side, curving around my hip and stretching tall onto my ribcage. There was no denying that bag was mine now.

I moved the shower curtain and stuck my hand in the water only to yelp and pull away as the water burned my skin. Maybe I was wrong about that habit. I adjusted the handle a little more and waited for it to cool down, but it still burned. I played with the settings for a few minutes, and by the time I finally found the right temperature, I was one twist short of turning off the shower. The water should have been freezing cold but it still felt warm against my skin. Maybe the pipes out here in the woods were screwed up.

I don't know how long I stood in the water, trying to carefully clean my left arm and watching the blue blood run down the drain. I had been right when I stood in the mirror in the living room. The lightning bolt on my arm was jagged and intricate, weaving in slivers from its origin on my palm to the inside of my elbow. Still, I had no idea how it had gotten there.

I turned off the water and dried off, dabbing my arm to keep the wound from re-opening. Under the sink, I found a first aid kit and used it to clumsily wrap my arm. First aid was definitely not my strong suit because I nearly fainted trying not to focus on the blue blood that seeped through the bandage. I needed a shirt to cover this up so I wouldn't pass out.

I shuffled back into the bedroom, hesitating as I stared at the bed. Folded neatly on the foot of the bed were a stack of clothes that hadn't been there before.

"Hello?" I shouted. "Is someone here?"

I wrapped my arms tighter around the towel as the house around me made a strange creaking noise. Other than the wind blowing outside, everything was quiet.

I thought I already lost my mind. I must be exhausted. That's the only reason I hadn't noticed the clothes when I walked in. I slid my arms through the long sleeve and pulled on the oversized sweatpants, thankful for the feeling of comfort. I searched around to find a place to throw the rest of my dirty clothes besides the floor.

The closet was just as magic as the rest of the house, lined with shirts, pants, and jackets that would last me an entire year before I needed to do laundry. There wasn't a hamper, though, so I just dropped my bloodied clothes on the floor. The house creaked again, making me unsettled, but I couldn't locate the exact source. It wasn't the floorboards, and the sound seemed to come from everywhere at once. But with an old-looking cabin on the outside, it was probably just the wind playing tricks.

Finally clean and dressed, I sat down on the bed and looked around. With each passing moment, I was more convinced this place was magic. There was no logical explanation as to what I had seen tonight. No amount of exhaustion could have played the kinds of tricks on my mind that I was seeing. I mean, the cabin was supposed to have a tree branch taking up the living room, yet it was perfectly intact. Even without memories, there was something about this cabin that felt comforting, aiding the nagging pull at the back of my head that I was close to learning something about myself.

It would have to wait for tomorrow. I dropped onto my back and pulled the covers up to my chest. The questions spinning in my head were starting to slow, but only because I couldn't fight exhaustion any longer. I closed my eyes and sank into a deep sleep.

3

Clara

I woke up late afternoon the next day, aching and still tired despite sleeping in so late. I should have been more unsettled to fall asleep in a mysterious cabin, but it was feeling more and more like this place was mine. By the time I made it to the kitchen, there was already a full table of fresh food. If I hadn't just accepted that there was something magic happening in here, I would have freaked out. Whatever magic was inside the house, it almost seemed like it was looking out for me. And if I had any doubts, after I was done stuffing myself, I looked away from the table for just a moment and turned back to see it cleared. Maybe one of the books in the library would help me figure out how the house could do that.

I spent the next week digging through book after book, trying to find answers to the millions of questions in my head, but by the day before school, I didn't have nearly as many answers as I wanted.

Even though I still couldn't remember who I was, I had gathered enough background information that I felt somewhat better about my situation. That background came with a lot of headaches, though; real ones that were brutally painful and made me nauseous, and I was pretty sure they didn't just come from all the reading I had done.

First, I had further confirmation the bag was mine. I read *The Magicians* from cover to cover and was so in love with the book, I concluded that the tattoo on my side was perfect. The iPod had a library full of music, each song more amazing than the last. My forgotten self had some great taste in music, and made equally amazing playlists. If only there was a method to her madness in naming them, because most of them were just a string of characters or emoticons that had no relationship to the songs within.

The second answer, something that was actually helpful, was printed in a book on the third step of the stairs, four deep in the stack. It was the only numbering system I could keep track of without losing my place in the library or accidentally re-reading books. The title, *Spatium Liminal*, was written in Latin; a language I recognized but couldn't read. Some of the pages had handwritten translations of passages, crammed into the small margins.

I pieced together enough to understand there was a place called The Complex that housed special objects of power. On your eighteenth birthday, if you passed some set of Trials created by the leaders, you were granted permission to enter a place that housed these objects. You could then pick an object, and if that object determined you were worthy of its power, you could receive some of the energy from it. But there was also a risk that the object would reject the individual, leaving them without power, but no other information was available on what happened after.

Could that have been what happened to me? I might have been rejected by some object and lost all memory as a result. But that didn't explain why I was running away, how I got the cut on my arm, or how that man died.

The whole power thing was confusing until I was halfway through a shelf of books on the first floor. As I set down another stack of books on the desk, something caught my eye. Sticking out of the locked drawer and barely visible, I saw the corner of a notebook page. The drawer had a physical lock, unlike the doors in this place, but where there should have been a key hole, there was only a hollow, circular hole. I tried everything; the key, any round object I could find lying around the library, and even the half marble that fit perfectly, but nothing worked. Eventually, I just wiggled and pulled the paper out.

The handwriting was neat, and after making my own notes about the books I was reading, I knew it was mine.

I can feel the Blue Star power source calling to me. I hear the voices speaking, and they aren't just from the people who's thoughts I can read. The voices are coming from the Blue Star, pulling me closer to the deep and bitter cold. I should be frightened, but it's getting easier to slip into the feeling of it; easier to give in and harder to get out.

The Trials are nearing and I have to keep distancing myself from the people around me. The headaches are too strong, and my outbursts are getting more violent. I'm going to get caught soon because I can't control them anymore. Earlier, I set the furniture flying into the walls. But I can't let anyone know I have these powers before The Trials, especially because they didn't come from a power source. I don't know how to do it, but I think I would rather the Blue Star take me if it meant the headaches would go away. For now, music is the only thing that keeps me grounded.

I don't understand how I can have these powers without a ceremony; without passing The Trials. Why is a power source that has never shared its power with anyone calling to me like it is? I don't know what it means, but I am losing myself more and more. I can feel my mind slipping into the cold. What will happen when it comes time to choose?

-F

As if I didn't already have the issue of missing memories, now there were power sources, a Blue Star, and telekinesis and telepathy to deal with? On top of headaches? It was my handwriting on the note, but who was 'F'? And if 'F' didn't trigger any memory, which name was fake?

Something must have happened from The Trials, or maybe someone found out about my powers before the ceremony. Maybe it was that man who was dead in the clearing. That might explain why I was running away, but had I used my powers and killed him? Was I the kind of person who killed others?

If any of this was true, I needed to blend in with the world and find out what was going on. If I had run from The Complex, it was possible they would come after me. Clara was probably the fake name, and the school registration papers were a way to help me in a new life so I could hide from them until I had answers. That meant I would have to go to high school, try to control the mind reading and telekinetic powers I had, and do my best to appear like I hadn't just lost eighteen years worth of memories. How hard could that be?

Happy first day of senior year.

4

Nate

"Nate, why the hell are we walking to school? I could have slept for another twenty minutes," Glitch groaned. He hopped over a fallen tree, his backpack slapping against his back. I don't know why he even had one since he never carried any books or supplies in it. Still, he was the smartest kid in school, even if he never opened his textbooks or took notes. He was that kid.

I shrugged. "Because it's our first day of senior year and we always walk to school on the first day. Keep the tradition going."

I watched him toss a branch across the clearing. At six-foot, two inches, Glitch was just an inch shorter than me, but more than made up for it by being strong as hell. I was plenty good at pushing a little weight around in the gym, but Glitch made me look like I was lifting toothpicks. He put most guys our age to shame.

"Dude," he shouted from ahead of me. "Rumor is they found a couple dead bodies out here last week. Some guy had his head split open and had literally all the bones in his body broken. They didn't release details on the other one."

"Gross. How do you even know that?"

"Miss Bonner's always listening to the gossip. I tried to glitch out here to see what all the fuss was about, but they had already cleaned everything up."

Glitch could teleport, which is what we called glitching. Over fall break a few years ago, we had been playing video games in his basement when suddenly he was gone. He reappeared a minute later and started to freak out. He had been thinking about getting a snack and suddenly found himself standing in front of the fridge. I gave him the nickname because it looked like a video game glitch when he left and came back.

He was probably just relieved to know he wasn't the only one with weird, unexplained powers. I had my own version of traveling, but mine involved dropping into shadows and sliding along surfaces as one. I could either become a shadow or hide in one, which was always more fun because I could hide and play pranks on Glitch, popping out to scare him when he walked by. Though, unlike Glitch, I couldn't remember the first time I had used my power. I had never showed anyone what I could do, but I vividly remembered doing it when I was just a little kid.

"Seriously, man," Glitch said, popping up in front of me. "I could get us to school in an instant. It's late August and hotter than an armpit out here."

It's not that I enjoyed the heat any more than he did, it was just our tradition to walk, no matter how sweaty we got. It's not like we were trying to impress anyone. No one in our small town was interested in hanging out with us outside of school anyway. We liked it better that way.

"Hell no. I'm not going with you. Glitching makes my insides twist. Besides, you can't stick the landing for shit and I always end up on my ass or throwing up."

As Glitch laughed, the toe of my shoe kicked something small in the middle of the clearing. It was dark, almost black, but had a subtle blue tint to it. I reached down and picked up the half marble, turning the surface over in my palm. For something that had been sitting in direct sunlight, it wasn't hot. In fact, it almost felt like picking up an ice cube. I just shrugged and shoved it into my pocket. The smooth surface was enough to make it a nice trinket on my shelf at home.

Glitch pulled his shirt off his chest and fanned himself. "Can we at least walk a little faster so I can get to the air conditioning sooner?"

I laughed. "Is the famous Glitch-in-as-the-bell-rings nervous he's going to be late for the first day of school?"

"Race you there?" he asked, faking a running start. Though I knew what he meant.

"Not a chance, you always win."

Glitch grinned, raising his eyebrows. "I know, that's why I do it."

I rolled my eyes as I started to slide into a shadow. "Fine. Give me a head start."

"Nop-"

He was gone before I had completely sunk into the darkness. We met up just outside the trees to the parking lot, along the route we would take if we were walking. He was leaned up against a tree, scanning the shadows to make sure I didn't pop out and scare him. By the time I arrived at West Hills, the parking lot was nearly full. Students were lounging around the entrance, catching up with all their friends they had sworn they were going to hang out with over the summer but never did. Half of them flaunted their fake tans, claiming they got them on the beach or on some fancy vacation while chatting up a hot pool boy while others talked about their distaste for the start of school. I was thankful Glitch and I had an endless supply of new video games and a working air conditioner to keep us cool and entertained all summer.

We hurried up the steps and opened the doors to the familiar smells of paint and hopelessness. They always claimed a new paint color would make the place feel like an 'inviting learning environment', but in reality, they could barely afford to paint one hallway so they just refreshed the same ugly tan and called it good enough.

Helpless and confused freshmen ran around the hallways, struggling to open their lockers and scrambling to find their classrooms. It was always interesting to see how much smaller they seemed to get as we got older. I'm not sure we were that size since fifth grade.

I left Glitch at the water fountain to observe the chaos as I popped open my locker, tossing in my notebooks, extra clothes, and shoved my old sweatshirt in the back.

Glitch leaned against the locker next to mine, still looking out into the crowd. "Rumor mill says there's a new girl."

Only here five minutes and he's already heard the gossip. As social outcasts, I'm not sure how he figured these things out so quickly.

"Dude, there's a whole mess of girls in the freshman class. Why do you even care?"

"No, man. New girl in our *senior* class. No one's heard of her or seen her around. Maybe she was home schooled."

I shrugged. "Well, maybe she can help the volleyball team finally beat East this year. We're on a losing streak."

There were two high schools in Forest Hills, East and West. Of course, the rivalry ran deep in the only sport that mattered around here: girl's volleyball. It didn't make sense, but we weren't big enough to have football teams, and none of the other team sports in town were good by any means. The winner was usually the team that sucked the least, but volleyball seemed to be the only competitive sport we had so everyone showed up for the event. Stores in town even refused service to fans of rival high schools. It was ridiculous, but we got a late start at school that day to improve game attendance so I didn't really question it.

"Well, maybe we can finally get you a girlfriend just as weird as you," he mocked. I punched him square in the shoulder, not holding back. "Ouch."

"Shut up and grab your books for once in your life. The poor girl is going to have enough of the school gawking at her like she's an alien. Not many people choose to move here."

The small town of Forest Hills wasn't kind to strangers, and its high school students were just as bad as the adults. Once, students bullied a kid so badly about his slight country accent that he transferred out in a week. Luckily for Glitch and I, we took our share of bullying throughout middle school. Most of them got bored with bothering us, especially after we hit our growth spurts sophomore year. This girl was going to be in for a tough first day transition.

As the warning bell rang, we made our way into Mrs. Roberts' history class. Glitch hopped over a few desks and slid into one in the back row, snagging the one next to his just as Eliot and his on-again, off-again girlfriend Ashley were trying to sit. Apparently they were on-again today because Ashley stuck up her nose and pulled Eliot back to the middle rows. I dropped my backpack next to my desk and slid in while Glitch kept his on his back as the final bell rang.

"Welcome to history, and congratulations for getting the worst class in school out of the way first period."

Nothing like getting Mrs. Roberts' class first thing in the morning. If anyone hated high school more than the students, it was her. She had gone off to some big college and grad school just to end up back in the same town she grew up in teaching high school history. She constantly reminded everyone in not so subtle ways that she thought she was too good to be here. Her apathy and sarcasm was just one of the ways she coped with it.

"Unfortunately for you, I do keep attendance at the beginning of class. If I have to be here on time, so do you," she said in a monotone. She made her way to the podium and started reading off names as everyone responded with their best enthusiasm.

"Nathaniel Beckett?"

"Nate, please," I corrected for the third time in as many years. She never seemed to care. She continued on without acknowledging my response. Glitch snickered, but I knew his turn was coming.

"Oliver Hood?"

This time, I was the one holding in a laugh.

"Glitch, please," he groaned.

"That's not a name, Mr. Hood."

I knew Glitch hated his name. He never knew his parents, but Miss Bonner had raised him using the name he was given. He always asked why he had to go by a name when the people that gave it to him weren't around for it. I didn't have a good answer to that, and Miss Bonner gave up trying to explain. There weren't any answers as to what happened to them, or why they left, but she was always there for him. He knew he was lucky to have her, and besides arguing about his name, didn't fight about much else with her.

"One more time, Ms. Rivers?"

Mrs. Roberts had reached the end of the list by the time I started paying attention again and was giving one last call to... wait, who had the last name Rivers? I looked over to Glitch who mouthed *new girl* to me. Yikes. She was already going to get crap from the students as a new girl and now she was going to be the new girl who was late to her first day of class.

Just as Mrs. Roberts turned to her desk, the door creaked open and an unfamiliar student slid through the opening, remaining close to the wall. The entire room turned to stare at the tall girl with purple-red hair in a long sleeve shirt as she walked to the front of the room. She didn't look at any of the students and headed straight to Mrs. Roberts, headphones still stuck in her ears.

"Ms. Rivers," Mrs. Roberts said, eyeing the girl. "I don't take kindly to lateness in my class. I don't get to sleep in, and neither do you."

"Ma'am, they printed my schedule wrong. I thought I was in calculus first period," she said, lowering her head as she stuck out her right hand. I could see the schedule and yellow excused late slip from our calculus teacher. Her gray long sleeve hung loosely from her arm as she lifted it, shifting nervously in her stance as her eyes darted around the room.

Mrs. Roberts' cheeks turned a bright red. "Find your seat, Ms. Rivers. And take those headphones out when you're in my class," she snapped, trying to recover.

I looked around and saw every student had their eyes locked on the new girl with long sleeves on in August, one of the hottest months of the year. I felt bad staring as she walked toward the back of the room, but I couldn't look away. Here was this beautiful new girl who I had never seen around town before. News usually traveled fast if someone new moved in, but if she had been living here for a while, I should have seen her somewhere around town.

She settled into the seat next to me and I felt a cool breeze follow her as she dropped her bag next to the desk. For a minute, I could have sworn her hair was changing color, but I was even more mesmerized by the bright blue eyes shining underneath the hair she had covering her face. She hesitated, but eventually pulled out her headphones and stuck them into her bag that was already stuffed full of papers. As she sat up, she tucked her hair behind her ears and tried to sink into her desk, probably because she knew everyone was watching her.

Mrs. Roberts' voice startled everyone as we jumped in our seats. "Since you are all being disrespectful to our new student, let me introduce Ms. Clara Rivers."

5

Clara

I sat down in the back of the room and reluctantly pulled my headphones out before stuffing them into my bag. I tried to pull my knee up into the desk to make myself smaller, but I couldn't fit so I just curled my shoulders in. I could feel everyone staring at me, and their thoughts confirmed it as they came flooding in, mixed together in a garbled mess.

She looks like a weird kid. Who let her dye her hair purple? How is she in a long sleeve? She is so tall. I hate these students so much. I wonder if she's good at volleyball.

Hell no. I am not letting a new girl steal the thunder here. "Aren't you the one who moved into that creepy cabin at the edge of town?"

The thought and voice belonged to a girl who looked to be several inches shorter than me, her blonde curls bouncing as she swung around to glare at me. What had I even done to deserve that? I had just walked into class late, that's all, and it wasn't even my fault.

A common thought passing through a lot of minds labeled the girl as 'Queen Bitch Emma'. I tried not to let out a laugh and just remained silent. I wasn't about to cause another disruption, even though I wanted to snap back at her. Instead, I glared at her for a split second before turning my attention to my desk, poking at the scratches and carvings previous students had made in the surface.

"Don't mind QB over there, new girl. She's just mad her fake tan didn't make her a better volleyball player."

I turned to see the blond boy two seats down from me leaning so far forward in his desk to look at me that I thought it would tip over any second. Emma turned a brighter shade of orange as she blushed, the class erupting in laughter.

"Settle down, students," Mrs. Roberts groaned. Her eyes locked on the boy. "Keep the juvenile business to a minimum, Mr. Hood."

The boy rolled his eyes and set his desk back down, still looking at me as Mrs. Roberts started to hand out the syllabus.

"Thank you," I whispered back to him. I was actually kind of relieved he had distracted QB from my glare because she was pretty pissed about it.

He smiled and winked back at me. *Oh, she is totally Nate's type.*

Nate must have been the boy sitting between us as his eyes darted to him. I glanced toward the dark-haired boy, catching his stare and his stray thought.

How are her eyes such a bright blue? He turned away, embarrassed that I had caught him staring. I smiled to myself and turned back to grab a syllabus from the kid in front of me.

I tried to pay attention as the teacher read the syllabus word for word in monotone, but everyone's thoughts were distracting. I started to build up a wall around my mind to block them out. It was oddly reflexive; something that had kind of happened out of habit. Maybe this was something I could do before I lost my memory.

As it quieted down in my head, I watched all the kids passing notes to each other while the teacher wasn't paying attention. The kid who had stood up to Emma was Glitch; I had heard Nate's thought come through before I had blocked him out. He and Nate must have been best friends because they were teasing each other quietly, trying not to be noticed. I stifled a laugh when I saw Glitch pass Nate a note that was written in large enough letters for me to see.

She's totally your type. Nate crumpled the paper quickly, his cheeks turning red.

"You'll do a project in groups of three. Pick any of these topics, one group per topic. Get both approved by me by the end of class."

As soon as the teacher finished her sentence, the class erupted into chatter. Great, first day group project and I'm the new girl who has no idea who she is. And I'm pretty sure everyone already hates me.

Just when I thought all hope was lost, I looked up to see Glitch standing right in front of my desk, staring down at me.

"M'lady, my best friend and I are in need of a third member to join our quest through senior year history. Would you be so kind as to take a plunge into the depths of mediocrity with us?" He spoke in some medieval mixed with southern accent and looked at me expectantly, eyebrows raised.

Ugh, Glitch. You are the worst. Nate's thought came through and I held back another laugh. It was hard trying to focus on multiple things at once while still blocking thoughts. Trying to have a conversation by only responding to spoken words would be a whole new challenge.

"Sir, I would be honored to join your group under two conditions. First," I said, raising my finger. "Never use that accent again. And second," I continued, raising another finger, "never call me m'lady."

Glitch's face lit up in a smile. "Great. Also, my best friend Nate here thinks you're cute." And with that, he spun around to go tell the teacher about our group.

Nate groaned and put his forehead into his book, his thoughts spinning in embarrassment. I did my best to distract him, because even if it was funny to watch, I knew how uncomfortable that must have been.

"I'm confused. We didn't pick a topic."

Nate lifted his head back up, surprised that I was talking to him. "Oh, well, Glitch always picks the Spanish Inquisition if it's an option. Have you ever seen the Monty Python sketch?" I nodded. This version of me hadn't seen it, but somewhere inside me I felt like that was the right answer. Why was it that memories like that came back to me so easily yet I couldn't remember anything that was actually important? Nate continued. "He's slightly obsessed with it and always picks the topic if it's an option. On the bright side, all the research is done so we just have to change the format to fit the requirements." *Great, those are my first sentences to the cute new girl; talking about my weird best friend, Monty Python, and the Spanish Inquisition. Yup. I'm going to die alone.*

I had to stop focusing on his thoughts if I wanted to keep my cover. Or I just needed to stop laughing at all the funny things that went through Nate's mind.

"I'm Nate, by the way."

I had been so distracted with his thoughts, I must have forgotten to respond. Forget Queen Bitch, I was going to be Queen of Awkward Silences.

"I gathered from your friend there. I'm... Clara, if the awful, full senior class introduction wasn't clear. How'd he get that nickname?" I asked, trying to change the subject to distract from the pause I had before saying the name I had almost forgotten myself.

Nate shrugged. "He claims he can magically make a video game glitch so he can win. Or, at least keep himself from losing." *Teleporting, video game glitching... same thing, right? At least our cover story hides his real powers effectively.*

Holy shit, Glitch has powers? I ignored my nervously pounding heart, trying to think of some comment that didn't sound like I was responding to his thoughts.

"So, does he?" I asked, raising my eyebrow.

"Does he what?" he asked.

"Have *magical* powers to win video games?" I emphasized the word, hoping to pick up a clue. At least if I could pretend to poke fun at the whole situation, it would draw suspicion away from myself. Could these two be from The Complex if Glitch had powers and Nate knew about it?

"Controller trick," Nate answered with a smile. "I looked up his Internet history." *Actually, new girl, my best friend and I have these weird powers that no one else seems to know about. But don't worry, we're not crazy.*

I laughed with him to hide the feelings of nervous excitement I had inside. Nate had powers too. First class, first day, and I've already found two boys who have abilities like me. Maybe I wasn't the crazy one after all. As far as I could tell, they weren't from The Complex, or at least didn't know about me, but that seemed too convenient. What were the chances I'd run into them here without trying?

"I leave you for three minutes and you've already given away my biggest secret?" Glitch asked as he walked back up, poking Nate in the shoulder before looking at me. "If you have some sort of power over him and you steal my best friend away from me, I'll make us dress up and perform the sketch in front of the whole class. See if you make any more friends after that."

Friends? I have friends? I felt my face get warm and looked away. I could feel the headache starting to build in my neck so I played with the key necklace that I had thrown on this morning. It helped me focus on what I needed. Answers. If these two had powers, maybe they could help me figure out my own, but the first day of school probably wasn't the best time to announce my weird abilities. I needed more information about my previous self before I went around telling people what I could do. Besides, I didn't know if I could trust them yet. I glanced up to see them exchanging weird looks.

Dude, talk to her. I'm trying to set you up, idiot. That thought was definitely Glitch who was not so subtly nodding toward me.

Stop embarrassing me. Shit, she's looking at us. Nate lowered his head, his cheeks turning red again.

"So, what class do you have next?" Glitch asked, looking over my desk to read my schedule upside down. He spoke over the bell that started to ring. "Oh, English next, then you'll have PE and Calculus with Nate. Make sure you come sit with us at lunch; we'll save you a seat."

"Okay, thanks," I replied, smiling as I picked up my things to walk out the door. Behind me, I could still hear them talking in the back of the room.

"Dude, she is so cute. Open your mouth for once," Glitch groaned. Actually, it almost sounded like he smacked Nate's arm somewhere in there.

"I know, man. I'm just nervous. She's totally out of my league. I don't understand why she's talking to us."

6

Nate

I spotted Clara sitting at the bottom steps of the bleachers, headphones stuck in her ears again as she flipped through a worn book. She had probably already picked up her gym clothes and put them in her locker. Luckily, that's all we ever did on the first day of class.

She didn't notice when I walked up so I gently tugged one of her headphones out. She looked up at me and smiled, her bright blue eyes shining. "So, English is the greatest class here. Can you really just read whatever you want as long as you reach a page count by the end of the year?"

Clara tossed the book back into her bag. I couldn't see the title as it settled with the crumpled papers inside, but I could clearly make out a tree on the cover.

I sat down next to her and laughed. "Yeah. You'll have to do a few book reports. Glitch found a loophole and does all of his reading with comic books."

She raised her eyebrow, surprised. "Wow. The teachers here really don't care about anything, do they?"

"Oh, absolutely not. They are just as miserable here as we are."

"So, does that mean this is going to be one of those typical movie PE classes where they make everyone play dodgeball? Like, the jocks pick on the weirdos while the teacher pretends not to notice?" Clara asked. She pulled her foot up on the seat and rested her chin on her knee to look at me.

"I wish. I'd bet money on us weirdos flipping the script on them all. I wouldn't mind getting a few shots in," I said, pointing to a few individuals before gesturing to the entire class.

Clara gasped, holding in a laugh. "Weirdos? Speak for yourself. Just make sure you save that one for me."

I followed her finger down to Emma. A few of the volleyball players had gathered and were practicing their serves over the net while QB tried to coach them. Well, that would imply she was trying to help them. Really it just sounded like she was bossing them around.

I shrugged. "Just don't do too much damage. If QB can't play in the rivalry game, you'll have to answer to the whole town."

"Your town is weird," she said, rolling her eyes.

Says the new girl with purple hair and a long sleeve on in the middle of summer. "So, why did you move here?"

I could tell that question made her uncomfortable. She hesitated, pulling her knee in tighter as the air around us got cold. Her key necklace, stuck between her chest and knee, tugged at her neck, leaving a red mark underneath. Yikes, maybe that was a touchy subject between her and her parents.

"Sorry," I blurted. "You don't have to answer that. I won't ask any more questions." *Shut your big mouth, Nate. This is why you don't talk to cute girls out of your league. Serves you right for only hanging out with Glitch.*

"No, really, it's okay," Clara said, trying to reassure me. "I just... haven't really been asked about it yet. I needed a new start; maybe to be a new person. It's just tough being new." There was a sadness in her voice as she frowned. Maybe something bad had happened at her old school. But before I could say anything to break the uncomfortable silence, she perked up and put on a huge smile. "Truth is, I ran out of ice cream and root beer and had to brave the supermarket in town. Next thing I knew, I was here."

"Let me get this straight. You wanted a root beer float and somehow got sucked into public high school? That sounds like a horror movie."

"Or maybe I wanted to see the psychological effects of toppling the social hierarchy that these girls are so obsessed with. Think of it like an experiment."

I laughed, but when I caught a glimpse of Clara's face, I almost thought she was serious. No, she was staring at me, like she was trying to look into my soul. Wow, brilliant and confident enough to own her uniqueness. That was definitely my type. She broke her gaze away just as a volleyball bounced between us and settled into the seats. Clara picked it up and tossed it between her hands before looking directly at me, a mischievous smile growing on her face.

"Ready for this?"

I raised an eyebrow. "Uh, I'm not sure how to answer that."

"Are you gonna toss that back any time soon?" Emma shouted from the other side of the gym, a smirk on her face. I'd have bet good money that she had aimed to hit Clara with that ball.

Clara didn't acknowledge her, still keeping her eyes locked on me. "Case in point. We have identified the leader of the social hierarchy, codename QB. After observing and gathering the appropriate data, I have developed a testable hypothesis. Now, I perform the experiment."

Clara stood up, with one headphone still in, and tossed the ball into the air, preparing for a serve. Her shirt slid up slightly as she swung hard with her left arm, and I could have sworn I saw part of a tattoo on her side, but there was no time to focus on that. She connected with the ball and sent it screaming over the net, cutting between two players who were about five seconds late on reacting. Emma's face went from shock to anger in an instant. She stuck her nose up and tried to ignore the whispers breaking through the stunned silence of everyone in the gym.

But Clara wasn't bothered by it. She turned back to me, a smile growing on her face. "Analyzing the results, I draw the conclusion that her social status is effectively threatened by my demonstration. Also, I've ruined all my chances of becoming popular." She spun her loose headphone around her finger, studying my reaction. All I could do was try to pick my jaw up off the floor.

"You know you're going to have to try out for the team now."

Clara shook her head. "Not a chance. I like to leave the people wanting something they can never have." She sat back down on the seat and stuck her chin back on her knee, reveling in her demonstration.

And I couldn't stop staring at her. She was beautiful, brilliant, and unafraid, even now when she tried to make herself smaller by curling into herself. How could a girl like this exist in a town like Forest Hills? And why the hell was she still talking to me?

Her blue eyes darted to me as she furrowed her brow. "What?"

"You're kind of a badass," I replied with a smile. And somehow, that word was still an understatement. I was so out of my league.

But then, she took me by surprise. She lifted her hand and offered me her loose headphone and iPod. "I just march to the beat of my own drum."

She's Out of Her Mind. blink-182.

I looked back up at her as she laughed and winked at me.

7

Nate

The bell rang, sending the students into a frenzy as they raced to the lunch room. According to the dumb social norms of West Hills, you had to claim your table the first day of school because that's where you were stuck the rest of the year. Glitch always cheated and used his powers to get to our regular small table in the corner and out of the way of everyone. Our lowest social status made it pretty clear no one would sit with us for fear of being an outcast for the rest of their high school years. Glitch chased off a few freshmen who didn't get that memo as we walked up.

Clearly, Clara didn't get that memo either because she slid into the chair next to Glitch without flinching. I wasn't about to get caught staring at her again so I sat beside her instead. Being in her company was enough of a stretch. I didn't want to ruin whatever it was that made her think we were cool enough to hang out with.

"Aw, you didn't want to sit next to me?" Glitch asked, tossing a fry at me. He made a few weird faces while Clara wasn't looking, trying to see if I had made any progress with her.

Normally, I wouldn't care about his antics, but for the first time, I was actually interested in this girl. And she was sitting with us, a new record. I shot him a glare and shook my head, mouthing *stop it*, even though I knew that wouldn't do much good.

"No, I just wanted to stare lovingly into your eyes for thirty minutes," I jeered.

"Down, boys," Clara said, looking between us as she rested her elbow on the table and held her head up. "I didn't come to school to be an awkward third wheel. I've got enough things to worry about today without getting involved in that."

A million thoughts ran through my mind. Pretty, smart, and funny? How was she real? Glitch leaned back in his seat, looking smug. I knew exactly what was running through his mind; *she's totally your type.*

I just shrugged. "You missed it, Glitch. Clara knocked QB's royal crown off during PE."

Glitch shot forward in his seat, smacking the table with his palms and causing both Clara and I to jump. "I demand to know what happened, C. Did you peg QB in dodgeball and take your rightful place on the throne? Please tell me you did. I need to climb the social ladder somehow and Nate's holding us back."

Clara went back to poking her food. "Thrones aren't really my style, sorry. But they probably wouldn't mind burning me at the stake," she replied.

"Burning at the stake? I can get on board with that."

I looked up to see Emma standing in the empty space at our table, her eyes locked on Clara. Her entourage stood behind her, all glaring at Clara too.

Before any of us could react, Emma launched her smoothie across the table and down Clara's shirt. Glitch tried to jump up but was caught off balance as Eliot pushed him back down into his chair. I clenched my teeth, disgusted that Emma and her friends laughed at the mess they had caused. I couldn't do much, but I could at least help Clara. I dropped out of my seat and pulled some napkins off the table to help clean up the sopping mess in Clara's hair and lap.

"Really, QB?" Clara snapped, clenching her fists. "Threatened because someone finally proved you aren't actually good at something?"

"Don't, she's not worth it," I muttered under my breath. Clara shot me a look, her eyes blazing blue, but seemed to listen.

"I guess you shouldn't have started a fight you couldn't win," Emma snapped back.

"She can kick your ass and you know it," Glitch growled. He stood up again, shoving Eliot who knew he had only gotten lucky the first time. That was a fight Glitch would easily win; he had about twenty pounds of muscle against Eliot.

I turned back to Clara and pulled her out of the seat, shivering slightly as I touched her freezing cold and sticky hands. As much as I wanted to see her take down Emma, now wasn't the time.

"Come on. I have an extra shirt in my locker."

"Fine," she growled quietly, still keeping her eyes fixed on Emma. But when she didn't budge, I grabbed her shoulders and physically spun her toward the door and away from the growing crowd of onlooking students.

Emma still didn't want to back down. "I told you she wouldn't fight back," she chided from behind us.

If I hadn't been pushing Clara out the door with most of my strength, she might have turned back around and Emma would have been flattened in ten seconds. Clara was easily twice her size, and I bet her fist would cut just as hard as her words. I glanced back briefly, watching QB twirl around in her victory just as Clara pushed out the door and into the empty hallway, but a growing commotion behind us caught my attention again.

I turned to see Emma lying flat on the ground as the girls around her tried to hold in their laughter. Glitch broke that silence, howling hysterically at the girl. Karma. The only unfortunate thing was that Clara had missed it. I hurried into the hallway to find her leaning over the water fountain, holding her hair over the stream of water to try to wash out the strawberry bits still stuck in the strands. I opened my locker and pulled out my extra shirt, handing it over to her as she stood up.

Clara frowned. "You wouldn't happen to have a long sleeve, would you?" she asked, wringing her hair out over the drain.

"Sorry, you're probably freezing. Is a sweatshirt okay?" I asked, feeling slightly embarrassed that I hadn't thought that through.

"Yeah," she said with a shrug, staring off into the distance. "I'm not cold, I just have a scar. I don't need any more attention right now."

I could tell she had already said more than she wanted, but she was distracted. I traded the shirt for the oversized sweatshirt in the back of my locker and offered it to her. "I'll wait out here while you change."

I felt horrible as she took the sweatshirt from my hands, holding it carefully so she wouldn't get it wet. She offered a sad smile before slipping through the bathroom door. Just a few seconds later, Glitch came bursting out of the lunch room, still laughing uncontrollably. He swung our three backpacks over his shoulder, hurrying over to where I was standing.

"Dude, you missed it! QB tripped on a chair when she tried to gloat and completely ate it in front of everyone. C totally got her payback. That will hands down be the best part of high school," he cheered. His smile faded as he looked around. "Is she okay?"

I shook my head. "I doubt it. She didn't deserve that, and definitely not in front of the whole school. She's in there changing into my sweatshirt," I replied, nodding toward the bathroom.

Glitch's shoulders sank. "Wait, that oversized gray blob you have stuffed in your locker? That thing is old and nasty. You've ruined your chances with her now. She's never going to talk to us after seeing that thing," he groaned.

Clara opened the bathroom door, holding her wet shirt in her left hand. Glitch had been right about the sweatshirt; it was old, stained, and had several holes in the neckline, not to mention the sleeves missing most of their stitching. But, somehow, it looked really good on her. More than that. It was perfect. She pulled her purple hair out from the collar, her necklace chain snagging on a knot. It was almost like she was moving in slow motion in front of me.

Glitch pulled me out of my trance as he grabbed my shoulder. "I take it all back. Nate, you look terrible in that sweatshirt, but Clara actually pulls it off. You're just going to have to give it to her permanently." He turned to face her, slightly bowing as he held out her backpack. "M'lady, this fine gentleman here will escort you to Calculus, and I will see you after school."

Clara took her bag and just stared at him like he was from another planet. He was off faster than he had come in. In a daze, she looked up at me. "Damn, he really knows how to lighten the mood. Does it ever get old?"

"Ugh, don't tell me you're actually falling for that bull," I groaned. Clara laughed and threw her bag over her shoulder, sending her key necklace bouncing. I just rolled my eyes and tugged her sleeve in the direction of class. "Come on."

8

Clara

I sighed in relief as the final bell rang. I had barely survived my first day of high school. Well, the first day for this version of me. I sat back and waited for the crowd to leave the room before I made my way out, keeping my head low so I could avoid seeing other people stare at me. It was enough torture to have their thoughts running around my head. Before I made it to the door, I picked up two thoughts and sighed again in relief. Nate and Glitch stood on either side of the door, waiting for me to walk into the hallway. I threw up my mental walls to keep from getting distracted, a last ditch effort to survive the final moments of school.

"How do you already know my schedule better than me?" I asked, locking eyes with Glitch. I knew it was one hundred percent his doing.

He grinned. "Oh, C, you're in too deep now. The volleyball team hates you and Nate likes you. There's no going back, even if you try. Stuck with us, friends forever."

Nate turned a bright red and tried to punch Glitch who jumped away just in time. As much as I was enjoying the silence of staying out of their heads, I really wanted to know what Nate was thinking. But I couldn't risk the headache that was growing in the back of my skull. I didn't want to find out what previous me had meant about causing outbursts with them. Having one in public was definitely not a good thing either.

"Why do I even keep you around?" Nate asked, rolling his eyes as he adjusted his backpack back over his shoulder. I couldn't help but be distracted by his movements as he ran his hand through his hair, trying to shake off the embarrassment Glitch was causing.

"I make everything a million times more entertaining," Glitch replied as we started walking out. "You'd never survive without me, but now I have a little competition, don't I?"

He tried to tug at my backpack strap but I smacked his hand away. "You know, I've only been here a day and already gotten myself into more trouble than the two of you combined have committed your entire life. I think you're better off surviving without me." I instinctively pulled my arms around my chest.

"Hey, leave no man behind," Glitch said. I raised my eyebrow and he corrected himself. "Or woman."

Nate rolled his eyes. "Glitch actually gets into a lot of trouble, but he blames it on me then runs away so I'm forced to clean up his mess."

I looked up and caught Nate staring at me again, as if he was trying to study my reactions to the conversation and figure me out. Maybe he really was interested in me. But, sorry to disappoint; I'm trying to figure me out too. I just smiled and played along. "You're telling me I could have blamed everything on you today? I really could have used a scapegoat. Then you could have taken the brunt of that strawberry smoothie and not my hair." I pulled a strand in front of my face to smell it, turning my nose up at the smell of yogurt. I hadn't gotten everything washed out in the bathroom earlier and it had started to crust around the ends of my hair.

"Yes! I like this girl," Glitch cheered, poking Nate. "Good choice, man. We're definitely keeping her around." He reached around Nate and high-fived me. I made sure to slap his hand with my right, still not ready to tell him about my giant scar and the powers that potentially caused the injury. Or the powers that let me know that they were also hiding their own secret abilities. I don't think any of us were ready to deal with that, especially if I had no idea how to answer any of their questions about my past. I finally had people to talk to. I couldn't ruin that.

They walked me home even though I was pretty sure it wasn't along their path. I was just thankful to be out of school and have a normal conversation with people rather than talking to the walls of an empty house. As Glitch rambled on and on about the history project and other topics that weren't really that interesting, I couldn't help but stare up at Nate walking next to me. I might not have known much about myself, but I knew I definitely thought he was cute. Did the previous version of me have crushes? If Nate was my type, who would be her type? Were we even similar?

I studied his outfit, admiring the put-together style without really trying. I think I was more excited that we were both fans of Chucks, though his were much more worn than mine after I had scrubbed mine clean of the blue blood from the previous week. He had to be at least a couple inches taller than me, filling out his shirt that was clinging to his back as he sweat in the summer heat.

I turned my attention back to the sweatshirt he had given me, squeezing the ends of the sleeves in my palms. Ever since I had come to in the clearing, I had felt cold, and the heat never bothered me. Even if I looked strange wearing the sweatshirt in the middle of summer, I was thankful I hadn't been forced to wear his shirt or keep my stained long sleeve on. In my distraction, I had revealed that I had a scar, but that didn't seem to bother him. Maybe that was a good sign that he really didn't know who I was. Unfortunately, that also meant he didn't know about The Complex or my past. I wouldn't have been disappointed if he had some answers to my future. So far, that part was going well.

I was a little bummed when we finally made it to the bottom of the hill, not quite ready to say goodbye. Still, I had a lot of work to do in the library. The sooner I found answers, the sooner I could tell them what was really going on with me and how I knew about their powers as well. I waved once I was halfway up the hill.

Glitch enthusiastically returned the wave. "Nate will meet you here tomorrow morning!" he shouted, nudging Nate in the process. Wow, Glitch was definitely flirting with me *for* Nate. Must be nice to have a best friend like that.

I smiled and walked a little further, ducking behind a tree so I was still within earshot.

"You're not going to come with us?" Nate asked.

I held my breath. *Come on, Glitch. Don't crash it. Maybe he'll finally get the courage to talk to me again.*

While being shy and nervous was kind of cute, I really couldn't understand why he thought I was out of his league. I should have been the one begging for company.

"Hell no, man," Glitch replied with a laugh. "I'm not getting in between whatever spark it is that you two have. Did you not see she couldn't take her eyes off you this entire day?"

Shit. So Glitch had seen everything. Still, he was content to be the wingman and help us both out.

I heard them both head off and I skipped the rest of the way to the house.

9

Nate

I dropped into the shadows and made my way home, enjoying the cool feeling of darkness. I was sweating profusely under my shirt, and I hoped Clara hadn't noticed the stick of my clothes. Somehow, she spent the entire walk with her hands shoved into the sleeves of her sweatshirt and didn't look like she was roasting. Lucky.

I slid out of my shadow and face planted into my bed, completely exhausted. For first days of school, today had been pretty good. As embarrassing as Glitch was, I'm not sure I would have ever gotten the courage to talk to Clara without his help. And for whatever reason, she still wanted to talk to us; perhaps a first in my entire life. And though it was great to have another friend, there was one part of our lives we couldn't include her in.

Glitch and I had never heard of anyone with powers or abilities, which meant we kept that part to ourselves. It's not like we saw people running around and flaunting their supernatural skills every day. It wasn't really that hard to keep our secret, though. Miss Bonner wasn't one to hover and usually just made sure we weren't getting into serious trouble. My parents were never home, so I didn't have to worry about anything either. Mom was somewhere on a research project and had been gone for most of high school doing whatever it was she did. Dad, on the other hand, dropped by every few months thanks to his government job. I probably wouldn't see him again until closer to the holidays.

I sat up on the edge of the bed and felt something cold pinch into my leg. I reached into my pocket and pulled out the half marble I had found this morning. Even after spending the day in the August heat and even longer in my pants pocket, the surface was still cold. I flipped the marble over to the round side, narrowing my eyes as a swirl of blue flashed under the surface. But as I looked closer, I could only see black. Probably just a reflection of light in the surface. Well, as strange as it was, the perfectly halved marble was still a decent trinket. I put it up on the bookshelf and left to shower.

After finishing some homework and making dinner that would last a few evenings, I made my way back upstairs to get into bed. Just as I plugged in my phone, the screen lit up with a text from an unknown number. I clicked open the icon and smiled, realizing there was only one person it could have been.

Hi, it's Clara. Glitch stole my phone at lunch and got my number, which means he sent me yours too. Anyway, I wanted to thank you for today. And for the sweatshirt. Lifesaver.

I laughed to myself. Glitch was playing the matchmaker role seamlessly. He probably had a million moves lined up for us, saved up over the years of not getting to use them. I pictured his smug face in my mind as I replied.

Anytime, C. I'll pick you up tomorrow morning at 7.

I sent the message before realizing how quickly I had responded. Glitch used to say that there were rules about how much time you should take between text responses so you didn't look desperate. I hadn't paid attention to any of those ridiculous rules, not concerned with texting girls, so I had completely spaced. But I didn't have to sit in my dumb, teenage anxiety long because Clara clearly didn't know those rules either. She replied instantly.

I'll meet you at the bottom of the hill.

It took everything in my power not to respond and wish her a good night, but I knew Glitch would never let me live that down. In fairness, I had only met her this morning. I smiled and turned off the screen, letting the events of the day lull me to sleep.

~

I stood in the clearing; the same one where I found the half marble. A man stood in the middle, his back toward me but facing someone. I heard his laugh grow, the deep sound echoing around the trees. He lifted his arm slightly, flames dancing around his hand and growing to surround his body. In an instant, he chucked the flames forward, directing them toward a girl who now came into my sight.

Clara.

She didn't flinch, though, her head twitching only slightly as the fireball deflected away from her. But the movement revealed the blue light glowing from her left fist, creeping out of her enclosed fingers.

From the sky, a bright flash cracked on top of her, the deafening sound vibrating in my chest. I closed my eyes, the outline of lightning burned into the backs of my eyelids.

When I opened my eyes again, I was standing next to Clara, her violet-red hair plastered onto her pale skin with sweat. She turned to face me, reaching her left hand up toward my face. I frowned, noticing the blue scar that originated in her palm and traced up her elbow, outlining the same shape as the lightning I had just seen. Her fingers touched my cheek softly, but I shivered in response. Her palm was ice cold.

"You're too late," she said, pulling her hand away. Both of her arms reached toward her stomach.

I glanced down to see blue blood spilling between her fingers, dripping down to the puddle of blue blood at her feet. Her legs shook, finally giving in as she dropped to the ground. I dove forward, trying to catch her before she slammed into the ground.

My face connected with a hard surface, knocking me back down to the bed. I stared up at the ceiling, my breathing labored as I tried to orient myself. Had I really just tried to dive through my bedroom wall? My entire body was tense, pain radiating from my forehead as I let myself cool down before I tried any movements.

That nightmare had felt so real, yet nothing about it made sense. I had never seen that man before, and there was nothing about that scenario that was familiar. But even worse was that I was dreaming of the beautiful girl I had just met. Clara stood defiant in that clearing, facing down a man who looked like he wanted to kill her. Even more confusing was the fact that she had a blue scar shaped like lightning, blue blood, and powers. And there was a bigger problem.

She died.

There was no going back to sleep when my mind wanted to continue racing. I pulled up the music on my phone, searched for Clara's blink-182 album to listen to, and stared out the window until the sun rose.

10

Clara

I shot up out of bed, my face dripping with sweat. I could feel every bit of pain from that nightmare. What the hell did that mean? Panting, I tried to replay it in my head.

Fire. The man who was dead in the clearing had control over fire. He didn't say anything in the dream, but his laugh echoed through my skull. Deep. Evil.

The flash of lightning followed, blinding my eyes and burning down my left arm, leaving a solid blue scar on my skin. Just seconds before, I had been hot, but after the lightning, everything was cold.

That wasn't the worst part. Nate was there. I don't know how, or why, but he stood in front of me. My fingers lifted to my lips, feeling the words that I must have screamed in my sleep. In the dream, I told him he was too late.

And then I died.

I lifted the hem of my shirt, feeling the skin along my stomach. There was no scar there, no wound, but that's where I had been bleeding.

I sighed and leaned back against the wall. If that was how I was going to get my memory back, I think I'd prefer to stay empty. My hand and forearm throbbed as I turned my arm over, inspecting the scar on my arm. It was strange to see the same lightning strike from my nightmare permanently etched into my skin. Flexing my fingers, I tried to recall feeling from the dream. I had been holding something, but there wasn't anything in the clearing that could have fit into my palm like that. Besides, everything had been in my backpack.

Shit. The marble.

I dove over to the nightstand and pulled out the half marble, a faint blue streak of light swirling under the surface. It faded into the depths as I realized what I was holding.

This was the Blue Star; the power source I was terrified of. I had taken in the energy from the Blue Star, and I had the scar to prove it. Then, it erased my memory and broke in half.

I sat back again, my thoughts spinning. Part of my past had been revealed, but why now? What caused it?

I groaned and slid out of bed, knowing I'd never get back to sleep. I threw in my headphones to drown out the emptiness in my head and shuffled to the library in the hopes I could find something more about the Blue Star.

By the time the sun poked through the windows in the library, I was no closer to an answer than I was before. I returned back to my room in a sleepless fog, trying to get ready for the day. I hated everything I tried on, feeling like I was wearing clothes that didn't belong to me. I settled on another gray long sleeve and black jeans just to be consistent. Sadly, even my Converse didn't feel right so I threw on a pair of combat boots and decided it was good enough.

Even my hair disagreed with me. I poked and pulled at the tangled, purple mess for five minutes before giving up trying to brush it. I threw up what I could into a messy ponytail and tried to rub away the bags under my freakishly blue eyes. Staring at my dull and lifeless face, I decided to settle on looking like shit.

I stepped out of the bathroom to find Nate's sweatshirt folded neatly on the bed.

"Thanks, House," I said into the empty space. He creaked back.

It felt a little weird talking into empty space, but I think House actually enjoyed it. I started referencing him that way after the first few days since I was getting lonely. He was definitely magic, setting out food for me, cleaning up my messes, and making me lots of junk food and caffeine. Though I wish he would help me out a little more in the library, or at least point me in the right direction. Either way, I was pretty sure he was keeping me safe. I hadn't heard from The Complex, and he always made me wear the key necklace whenever I left.

He left me a donut, eggs, and coffee on the table for breakfast. There was something I was certain of; I had a craving for sugar and caffeine. I flipped the sugar jar upside down and dumped it into my coffee. Previous me must have had the same sugar cravings as me. Or maybe she was good about her diet and now I was just ruining all her work. That might explain why I couldn't lift any of the weights in the training room.

Nate was already waiting for me by the time I made it to the bottom of the hill. I felt bad making him stand in the heat since I was late. I glanced at the cute boy waiting to walk to school with me and noticed his green eyes were just as dark around the edges as mine. Had he slept just as poorly as I had? No time for staring, though. He might get suspicious. But wait, he was staring at me too.

He straightened up and faked a smile as I got closer. *She looks just as tired as I feel. Wait, you can't tell a girl that she looks like hell.*

Rude.

"I want you to be honest," I said, pausing dramatically so I could watch him squirm a little. I could get used to reading minds if they were always as fun as Nate's.

Oh crap, she's going to put me on the spot. Do I lie? Can I drop dead?

A smile grew on my face. "Do the bags under my eyes match my outfit?" I laughed and spun around, letting the key necklace swing around behind me.

Nate laughed too, distracting me from the image of him from my dream. That smile was so much better than the helpless, worried face from last night.

He gestured to his outfit. "I think they complement my shoes and insomnia pretty well."

I glanced at his worn down Chucks, immediately regretting not wearing mine. It sucked that he hadn't slept well, but at least we were both in it together. I went to move my arms and realized I was still holding his sweatshirt. I held it out for him to take back.

"Thanks again for this."

"Oh, no," Nate said, shaking his head. "You heard Glitch and I completely agree. It looks much better on you so you might as well keep it. Besides, if you keep challenging the social hierarchy, you'll probably need to keep more shirts in your locker."

His smile sent butterflies through my stomach. I didn't want him to see my cheeks turn red so I pulled back the sweatshirt and picked at a loose string on my bag. Just before the silence got too awkward, I heard him take a breath and stick his hand out toward me.

"Shall we?"

Holy shit. He wanted to hold my hand? What? Why?

Holy shit, this was so dumb. She's never going to take my hand. Nate, you idiot, you just ruined everything.

I straightened up to fight the urge to laugh, trying to figure out the best response without seeming too desperate.

His hand twitched in front of me. *I'm stuck in the longest minute of my life.*

I reached out and took his hand, wrapping my fingers around his warm grip. I could feel the muscles in his arm relax as I looked up at him and smiled.

"My fellow insomniac, we shall."

Nate's breath released as I tugged him forward to keep him distracted. I could feel his pulse pounding hard through his hand, which meant he could probably feel mine racing too.

"I listened to that blink-182 album last night when I couldn't sleep. I'm surprised you listen to them," he said, kicking some rocks on the path as we continued along.

"Really? That music is awesome. Rock and alternative are my go-to genres, followed by singer and songwriter if the mood calls for it." Wow, now I sounded like an idiot. I tucked a loose hair behind my ear and raised my head to see him smiling.

"I agree. No one really listens to alternative around here. I was beginning to think Glitch and I were the only outcasts."

I lost balance from staring at him and bumped into his hip. Damn, having a crush was the worst.

"Well," I said, trying to distract myself from that embarrassing moment, "if the purple hair didn't give it away, I think I fit into the outcast category. Have you heard of lovelytheband?"

He shook his head. "Maybe I've heard a song, but I don't know who they are specifically."

"Oh, their album is amazing. I have to be here for your first time." I bit my tongue, realizing that I stopped my sentence too short. I turned away and pulled out my iPod so we could listen. "This is my second favorite album right now."

"Then what's your favorite?" he asked, accepting the loose headphone as I started the music.

"Hush now and enjoy. I have to leave you wanting more, remember?"

There, that's how I wanted to end that sentence. I needed to remind him of the volleyball scene from yesterday when he thought I was a badass.

I tried to watch his face as he listened, not really caring that he caught me staring. Even though we only had a few inches of height difference, the headphone cord was still at its limit but he didn't seem to mind. Every time it came loose it gave him an excuse to look at me.

We got through half of the album by the time we made it to school. His thoughts were kind of garbled in my head, mixing with the music, so I figured I would just ask him about it. Though I would have to do it later because Glitch hopped off the steps and blocked our path.

"It's about damn time, you two."

I looked down to see we were still holding hands. Nate thought about pulling away, worried I didn't want to be seen with him, but relaxed when I tightened my grip.

"It was twenty-four hours, Glitch," I jeered. "Besides, I got interrupted by a smoothie and a third-wheel."

I laughed as Nate froze next to me, stuck in his spiraling thoughts.

Has it really only been twenty-four hours? Did I make a move too soon? Wait, did she just say she got interrupted? As in, she was going to make a move on me?

Glitch slid his arm through mine and dragged me away from Nate who still stood frozen in place. His hand slipped out of mine and I looked back, admiring how cute he looked when he was trying to get his thoughts in order.

Glitch laughed. "Now, the smoothie wasn't part of my plan, and I'm sure it wasn't fun, but I have to admit that it moved things along faster than my plan would have. I had a whole, three-month plan in the works."

I slipped out of Glitch's grip to go back and grab Nate who still hadn't moved. Maybe I had let him squirm a little too long.

"Stop overthinking it," I said, sliding my fingers through his as I pulled him up the steps. "You heard me right. I got interrupted. Now, let's go challenge the hierarchy."

11

Clara

By the time Friday rolled around, people had finally given up gawking at the three giant seniors walking around together. After realizing the weird, purple haired girl wasn't going to put up with their shit, they decided against bothering me. And if they had any ideas about messing with Nate, they rethought quickly since I spent most of the time holding his hand. I didn't care about anything they thought about us; I was happy. I could tell Nate was too. Glitch was ecstatic about it.

The rumor mill was still active with wild theories, though, and that didn't stop people from glaring at me. The three of us enjoyed listening to them from time to time. Glitch's favorite rumor was that I was actually a spy for the East Hills volleyball team and was reporting back all of their weaknesses so West would lose.

"I'd have nothing to report to them since you guys aren't any good," I snapped at Emma who was eavesdropping on our conversation. I grinned when her thoughts turned into a fumbling mess, thinking I had eyes on the back of my head.

Nate squeezed my hand and laughed. "Nah, I think my favorite is that you made a deal with the devil and lost your soul so you could be good at volleyball."

"That would only make sense if I was on the team. Why make that deal if I'm not going to use the skill?" I said, loud enough for the prying ears. "Although, it does sound like me to do that just to make a point and then let it go to waste…"

Glitch held in a laugh. "I'm pretty sure you sold your soul to get that sharp tongue. That's why you're cold blooded," he said, poking my arm.

I couldn't even fake a laugh on that one. What if I really didn't have a soul? Maybe that's really what the Blue Star did to me. It took my soul and memories and replaced it with this cold feeling.

Nate tensed up next to me, quickly changing the subject. "Anyway, we can finish up the project tonight and just roll into movie night. I'll get the pizza. You in, C?"

"Sure. I can bring root beer floats. What movie are we watching?"

"Star Wars, duh," Glitch gasped. He turned to Nate with a scowl and kicked him under the desk. "You didn't tell her that Friday nights were Star Wars nights?"

"Ouch, it's not my fault. I didn't know if she'd be interested!" Nate carefully dodged another kick.

Previous me suddenly got excited as a stream of movie quotes ran through my head. This version of me had never seen the movie, but I already felt like I knew it. I groaned internally, frustrated that these types of memories would come back but served no purpose in giving me any real details about my life... except that I was a total nerd before now. Eh, if it helped me hang out with Nate and Glitch a little longer, I'd wear any title.

I narrowed my eyes and pretended to force choke Glitch as he and Nate burst out into laughter. Glitch started spouting more quotes as I glanced at Nate who couldn't take his eyes off me.

Where did this crazy, amazing girl come from?

I just smiled back at him, giving my best brave face. If only I knew.

12

Nate

We finished up the history project even though it wasn't due until the end of November. At least that reduced a significant amount of homework during the semester. That rolled into movie night, which I'd consider a huge success even though I could barely pay attention. I was too busy watching Clara watch the movie. Even though she knew all the lines, it almost looked like she was seeing it for the first time. I guess it could have been her favorite movie.

Glitch headed off at the end credits, but not before his famous line to me.

"I told you she's your type," he said, winking as he walked to the front door.

"Shut up and go home," I groaned. I tried to shut the door before he could say anything else, but Glitch had a different idea.

He shouted back into the house before the door was closed. "Have her home by midnight, young man!"

I grimaced and pressed my forehead to the closed door, whispering to myself. "Glitch, you are the worst."

I walked back to the kitchen where Clara was cleaning our plates in the sink. The girl must have had an endless supply of long sleeves because she had a new one on every time I saw her. That was a pretty good sign I liked her since I could remember all the outfits she wore. It was always black or blue jeans, Converse or boots, all paired with a long sleeve. Then there was the clunky key necklace and my old sweatshirt she either wore or had tied around her waist. Oh, and those beautiful blue eyes popping behind her violet-red hair, stealing the rest of the show.

She looked up from the sink and smiled, catching me staring. I thought for a second that I saw blue ink on her palm, but before I could know for sure, she had her hands in the sleeves of my old sweatshirt, pulling it over her arms.

"Ready for a new music album?" she asked, speaking in grunts as she struggled to fit her head through the collar without messing up her hair. Funny, because it always seemed like her hair was just a bit messy on purpose.

"I have a speaker upstairs. We can use that instead of headphones," I offered, enjoying the fact that she was willing to share her music and looking for ways to stay a little longer.

"Even better!" she cheered. She skipped past me and ran up the stairs before I had a chance to tell her where to go.

By the time I made it to my room, Clara had already plugged in her iPod and was sitting on the floor against my bed. She drifted side to side, eyes closed as she listened to the music playing in the background. I sat down next to her and she leaned closer, twisting her arm around mine and grabbing my hand.

"Andrew Belle. Dive Deep. My favorite album," she whispered.

Wow. One week of knowing her and she was finally letting me listen to her favorite album. I smiled and let the music float around the room. The melody was perfect for the moment as I focused on the coolness of her touch through her sleeve. I had gotten used to the feeling, even if it still gave me chills every once in a while. I could handle that as long as she stayed close like this.

As the first song started to pick up, Clara pressed her head into my shoulder and I rested my cheek gently on top. I wanted to stay here forever. The deeper we got into the album, the more I felt her face press harder into my shoulder as she drifted to sleep.

I listened to the entire album, trying not to move a muscle as she slept on me. I could understand why she loved this album so much. It was smooth and soothing and vulnerable, perfect for Clara. She seemed to always have something new to listen to, and when she wasn't having a conversation with us, her headphones were stuck in her ears. But if that made her happy, it made me happy too.

The alarm on her phone rang just after the last song started to play, causing her to twitch. I hated that damn alarm, signaling it was time for her to leave. Plus, it always seemed to go off right when I was building the courage to *think* about kissing her. Groaning into my shoulder, she pushed off and blinked a few times before reaching over to turn it off.

"What did you think?" Clara asked. "My favorite song is Honey and Milk."

"I loved it," I replied with a smile. If that was her favorite, it would be mine too. Hell, the whole album was my favorite because I could see how much she loved it.

A brief thought passed that if I just leaned in to kiss her, I could bypass my nervous brain, but it was gone before I had the courage. Maybe I had to follow some dating rules or wait a certain amount of time before that happened.

"You're going to have to make me a playlist one of these days," she said. She sat back on her heels and tossed her phone and iPod into the mess of papers and books in her bag. For a girl who had such clean handwriting and followed strict curfews, I kind of expected her bag to be completely organized.

"You're the one with the new music all the time," I replied. "I don't think I'll have anything you haven't already heard."

"That's not the point, though. It's about making something that you enjoy; something that speaks to you and makes you feel whatever emotion you want it to make you feel." She shifted onto her knees and back to her heels but didn't stand up, fumbling with the sleeves of her sweatshirt. It kind of felt like she was stalling. Did she not want to leave? Was she waiting for something?

"Okay, I'll make you one for Monday." *Do it. Kiss her. Come on, you nervous wreck.* My muscles didn't respond to my brain's commands so I just sat there, probably looking like an idiot.

Just before all hope was lost, Clara slid forward and wrapped her hands around my neck. She lifted off her knees to lean across the space between us and pulled me into her kiss. My heart jumped through my chest with happiness and surprise. Her lips were cold, but I think the shiver I felt was just my heart pounding wildly against my chest.

As I was about to reach around her to keep her in that kiss forever, she broke away and stood up, dragging her bag on the ground behind her. I, however, remained stuck... in fact, I might have actually been frozen to the ground.

"See you Monday!" she cheered with a smile. She winked at me before skipping out the door and hurrying down the hallway.

My head was spinning and my heart was pounding so hard, I don't remember if I said goodnight or not.

13

Clara

I think I fell asleep just after the third song played because the next thing I knew, the last song was playing and my alarm was ruining it. I groaned and realized I had my face pressed hard into Nate's shoulder. He must have stayed completely still for a long time just to hold me up. Add Queen of Embarrassment to my list of titles.

I turned off the ringing and blinked to wake myself up.

"What did you think? My favorite song is Honey and Milk."

It would have been so easy to read his mind and figure out what he was really thinking, but I should probably start practicing some restraint.

"I loved it," he replied.

I didn't need to read his thoughts. His smile was too genuine for a lie just to impress me.

Glitch had warned me that Nate was a little slow when it came to social cues, but thought he'd eventually get the courage to kiss me. I wondered if he would try tonight, so I stalled to give him more time in case he was nervous about it.

Alright, who was I kidding? Of course he was nervous.

"You're going to have to make me a playlist one of these days."

I delayed longer, pressing back into my heels as I shuffled the papers into my bag so I could throw my iPod and phone inside. Hm, I should probably clean this out over the weekend.

"You're the one with the new music all the time. I don't think I'll have anything you haven't already heard," he said with a shrug.

"That's not the point, though. It's about making something that you enjoy; something that speaks to you and makes you feel whatever emotion you want it to make you feel."

I guess to me, music was how I could figure out who I was. It was all I had, and I wanted to share that with Nate. Wow, I really liked him.

He still didn't move despite my stalling tactics.

Holy shit, Nate. How long do I have to delay before you finally get the hint? I rocked a little bit while I played with the sleeves of his jacket that were just a bit too long for my arms. If he didn't make a move soon, I was going to have to break my rules and listen in on his thoughts.

"Okay," he said, finally breaking the silence. "I'll make you one for Monday."

For a brief moment, I thought that would be the moment, but he still sat there. *Alright, screw it. I'm listening in.*

Nate's thought came through as I let my walls down.

Do it. Kiss her. Come on, you nervous wreck.

Yeah, I should have known I was going to have to do this myself.

I pushed myself across the floor and lifted off my knees, wrapping my hands around his neck as I pulled him into my kiss. I could feel his heart pick up at the same time mine did, shifting my focus to his soft lips and warm touch. It felt incredible and I wanted to stay in this moment forever.

But I had already given him everything I was. He knew basically everything about me that I knew about myself, minus my powers. Music was all I had about my past, and I had just shared my favorite. I was still empty, missing the truth about who I really was... who I used to be. But this was who I wanted to be, because *this* me was completely melting in Nate's kiss.

I pulled away just before I got stuck forever, standing up to keep myself from getting sucked back in. "See you Monday!"

Ugh, what? That was the absolute worst thing to say after your first kiss. Oh, shit. Was that my first kiss? I hope so, unless previous me had boyfriends. Wait, were Nate and I dating? Was he my boyfriend now?

Oh, geez. I hope previous me didn't have this anxiety. I wouldn't wish this feeling on anyone. I turned and skipped down the hallway to avoid any more awkwardness. I think Nate said goodnight behind me just as I made it to the stairs.

14

Nate

By the seventh day in a row, it was clear the nightmare wasn't going away. It was always the same; fire, lighting, Clara. Each time I would get closer to her, but she still died. I'd watch, almost in slow motion, as she covered her stomach, blue blood spilling between her fingers. Before I could catch her, I would wake up somewhere in my room. Sometimes I dove into the wall, other times I fell to the floor. Thankfully my parents were never home to hear any of it.

Mom was off chasing her research project somewhere in South Africa. No, was it in Argentina? Wherever she was, she never had enough phone service to get in contact with me. Usually I'd get a short email when she was moving to a new location, but it was never anything special. Dad, on the other hand, was always busy with his work. I'm not even sure what he did, or what branch of the government he worked for, but it always kept him on assignment for a few months before he switched tasks.

Normal teenagers would probably enjoy the absence of parents. I knew a lot of kids at school threw house parties or got in trouble with the police. I was just forced to grow up faster than I wanted or else I'd starve.

I hadn't told anyone about the dreams I was having, not even Glitch. They were frighteningly real and painful, and for the time being, they were my burden. I mean, how do you tell your girlfriend that you've had dreams about her dying since you met the first day of school? Wait, was she my girlfriend? Should there be a time frame longer than a week before you ask that? Am I supposed to ask her on a date first?

My head spun with stupid anxiety, but there was one thing I knew for certain. That kiss. Clara had kissed me when I was too nervous to make a move, and when she did, everything made perfect sense. It was so much easier to be around her, and that kiss was proof.

I stuck my hand up on the bookshelf and picked up the half marble I had found that first day, turning it over in my hand to feel the cool surface slide across my palm. It reminded me of Clara's touch, cool and smooth, and helped me settle down after the most recent nightmare. It wasn't often that I could fall back to sleep after them, but luckily I woke up only thirty minutes before my alarm.

Glitch walked with us to school so I could only show Clara the playlist I had made for her over the weekend. It was a lot more fun than I thought it would be, featuring some of my favorite bands and songs that she might not have heard, at least more than a few times. Maybe I'd get lucky and have one she hadn't listened to before.

Clara had her arm around my elbow as we walked, bumping into me with every step. Every tap of her hip against mine sent a chill down my skin, though she didn't seem to notice her distraction as she scrolled through the list of songs. Even though she was wearing my sweatshirt, she still felt cold to me through the sleeves, though I was thankful for that chill. It was still boiling hot outside, but I never understood how she could still be in a sweatshirt.

Glitch drowned on about something in the background, but I was too busy wondering what Clara thought about my music to pay attention. I was also curious about what she thought about our kiss. If only glitch hadn't walked with us. Did she and I need to talk about it? Isn't that what you were supposed to do? Maybe I shouldn't have waited all weekend before talking to her…

"Alright, what's up with you two?" Glitch asked as he stopped in our path, nearly causing us to crash into him. I guess neither of us had been paying attention to where we were walking.

"What are you talking about?" I asked. Crap, I had been so focused on this playlist and my nightmares to tell Glitch about Friday night.

"You know damn well what I'm talking about," he replied, folding his arms as he looked directly at me. "I'm your best friend and I can tell when something weird is up with you."

While I was fumbling in nervousness, Clara spoke up. "Nate finally kissed me," she said, not looking up from the phone.

"I knew it!" Glitch cheered. "I told you he would get the courage eventually."

Wait, when had they been talking about me?

Clara locked the phone and handed it back to me, a smile growing on her face. She winked and squeezed my arm tighter, sending that familiar chill through my body.

Had she really just saved me from the embarrassment of telling my best friend that in reality I had been way too nervous to make a move? The way she looked at me with those fiery blue eyes said that she knew I was too nervous, but didn't care letting Glitch think I was the one who made the move.

How did this perfect girl exist? And what the hell did I do to get lucky enough to have her still hanging around me? Whatever it was, I'd do it a million times over again for another kiss like that.

~

I did my best to focus during the lab as Glitch and I took turns looking into the microscope, but sleeplessness was catching up with me. I think we were doing something about the life cycle of a cell, but I was pretty much useless at this point. Thankfully, my genius best friend had a clue.

"Screw it, just let me do it. You're so out of it," he said, pushing my face away from the microscope.

"Sorry," I replied sheepishly.

I felt my phone vibrate in my pocket and glanced around. The teacher was busy helping other students with his back facing us so I pulled out my phone.

Clara's text lit up the screen. *What are you doing?*

I saw you fifteen minutes ago in history which means I'm now in science lab. What are you doing?

I laughed quietly as she typed back almost immediately.

Not sitting in English.

I perked up as I heard a tapping noise at the door behind us. I turned to see Clara looking through the window, motioning for me to come out in the hallway. Glitch turned to see what I was looking at, laughing to himself.

"That girl is going to be trouble, isn't she?" he said, glancing around quickly. He gestured to the door. "Go out there. I'll say you went to the bathroom. Just be glad I actually like you two together."

"Thanks, dude," I replied, making my way into the hallway. To my surprise, it was completely empty. "Clara?"

I took a few steps down the hallway when Clara's hands reached out and pulled me into a gap between the lockers. She spun me around and pushed me against the wall, pressing her body into mine as she kissed me. I'm pretty sure I lost all motor function and forgot to move because she grabbed my hands and wrapped them around her back. I felt her hand reach around my neck and slide into my hair, pulling me closer. Before I knew it, she pulled her head away, smiling just inches from my face as I stood there, completely stunned.

"Hi," she laughed, still using her bodyweight to keep me against the wall.

"Hi. What was that for?" I asked, trying to focus on her cool touch to keep my face from getting red. Public displays always made me uncomfortable, but damn I could do that again.

Clara shrugged. "Glitch crashed our party this morning and I couldn't stop thinking about Friday night." She moved her palm to my cheek, her touch like ice. I guess I failed at not letting my face turn red. Clara laughed again. "Did I make you nervous?"

"Just a little bit. Do it again," I said, this time pulling her into me.

I'm not sure where the confidence came from, but I didn't care now. Clara made me happy, and I just wanted to hold her closer. She finally leaned back, tucking her violet hair behind her ears as she bit her lip. Now *her* face was red.

"Let's do that again some time," she said, winking at me.

In a flash, she spun on her heels and walked back toward English class.

I couldn't move for a full minute, but I finally ducked back into class without the teacher noticing.

Glitch looked at me as I slid into my seat next to him, his eyes narrowed. "Did you two just make out in the middle of the hallway?"

"What?" I asked, feeling my cheeks flush again.

He rolled his eyes with a grin. "Yeah, that's what I thought. Who are you and what have you done with my awkward best friend?"

15

Clara

I know I should have told Nate about my powers, but after two weeks it felt like I missed the chance. Then another week passed and soon it was early October. I couldn't say anything now, especially because I didn't want to ruin what we had. How do you even tell someone that you can't remember the first eighteen years of your life?

But if anyone would have understood, it was Nate. So why couldn't I bring myself to tell him the truth? Maybe because there was still the chance he'd look at me differently. How can you trust someone who can hear all of the secrets in your head? I guess I could have been blowing all of this out of proportion, but at this point, it was easier to keep quiet than try to explain myself. It's not like there was an explanation for all the questions he would have.

For the time being, I enjoyed what Nate and I could share. When I was with him, I could ignore the nagging emptiness I felt about my past. I was no closer to an answer for my missing memories, The Complex, or the Blue Star. Months of research in the library felt like a waste now.

By the middle of October, people had pretty much stopped paying attention to me entirely as I became just another social outcast with Nate and Glitch. Everyone had turned their focus back to the ridiculous volleyball rivalry match. Nate tried to explain the charm of the game, but the only positive was a late start at school.

If the teachers had any ounce of care before this week, they definitely didn't on Friday. They did make attendance mandatory if you wanted to go to the game, but most of the classes were arts and crafts or free reading.

If I had been given the choice, I would have stayed at House.

Waking up with a headache was unpleasant enough, but I knew it could only get worse. If previous me had left a note saying I couldn't control my powers when I had a headache, being in a gym full of people was the worst situation to be in.

Somehow Nate and Glitch convinced me to brave the day. We pushed our desks to face each other while the students in front helped Ashley make posters for the gym. Mrs. Roberts had left for a bathroom break over twenty minutes ago, and I'm pretty sure she forgot about us or just fell asleep in the teacher's lounge.

Did I do something wrong? Why isn't she talking?

Nate's thought came through as my wall slipped. I glanced over to see him staring at me, a concerned look on his face as he studied my hands. I absentmindedly tugged at the sleeves of his old sweatshirt, my headphones still stuck in my ears to distract me from the pain of the headache. I found more comfort in Nate's sweatshirt and playlist than in my own stuff. A wave of nausea hit me and I tried to pull my knees up into the desk, struggling to get them to fit.

Nate reached over and grabbed my hand through the sleeve. "Are you okay?"

"Yeah, sorry. I just have a headache... there's a lot of people and it makes me nervous for the noise," I replied, sliding my desk closer so I could lean my head on his shoulder. The music was loud enough, so I'm sure he could hear me playing his favorite song.

Mason Jar. Smallpools.

"Don't worry, C," Glitch chimed in, throwing a paper airplane at me. "I bet the game doesn't go more than thirty minutes. You really messed with QB's head that first day. Now the whole team sucks and it's your fault."

I caught it and threw it back. "Well, I was the one who ended up with a smoothie in the face, so I think I was the real loser there."

I reached over and poked Nate in the ribs, trying to convince him, and myself, that I would be okay. He smiled and kissed the top of my head, sending butterflies spinning in my stomach, though that might have been the nausea again. Or maybe it was the soft whisper of voices I heard with each throb of pain in my neck.

I pushed off my pizza to Glitch who was more than happy for the extra food. At least in the cafeteria I could hug my knees without getting stuck in a desk. If only making myself smaller would help. I was a walking time bomb with this headache, and everything in my body screamed at me to give up and go back to House.

Nate continued to watch me carefully, hovering in the corner of my eye. It distracted me long enough for Glitch to try to tip me out of my seat. I hopped up to keep from falling.

"Hey!"

"Come on, Nervous Nellie. Let's go find our seats," he said, nudging me. I stumbled back into Nate who balanced me, taking his side on my left as Glitch sandwiched me on my right.

If only my two bodyguards could prevent the real problem.

16

Nate

Glitch and I cleared a path through the crowd of students as we made our way to the highest row, trying to stay away from the big group of people. Clara had reluctantly removed her headphones, but with the loud speakers and screaming kids, I figured that wouldn't last long.

Even with her trying to joke, I could tell she wasn't actually okay. I wrapped my arm around her shoulders and leaned into her, letting my fingers play with the ends of her hair as she kept her head lowered. Glitch and I exchanged a glance but he shrugged it off. She'd had a few headache days like this in the past but they usually went away later. Our distraction didn't seem to work today.

And Ashley wasn't going to make the situation any better, her sights set for where we were sitting. If Clara was already in a bad mood, a tiff with Ashley was not going to end well. Eliot trailed by a few steps, looking nervous about whatever his girlfriend had in store. Maybe he was more concerned with the fact he'd have to fight off two giants now. I made sure Ashley didn't have any projectiles to throw as she stomped up and planted herself in front of Clara.

"Get out of our seats, freak," Ashley snapped.

Clara didn't look up. "I didn't see your name on them."

"I'm sorry?" Ashley growled as Eliot's eyes widened in horror.

Clara's glare turned upwards as her hands gripped the seat. "I'd rethink that ridiculous idea of yours before I shove you down these steps. I'm staying here with my best friend and boyfriend, so I think you should move along before I shove that poster up your—"

"Okay," Eliot butted in, gripping Ashley by the shoulders as he steered her away. "We'll find some other seats."

I stared in shock. Why was Clara threatening Ashley both scary and incredibly hot? Is that bad?

Oh, shit. She just called me her boyfriend.

That was the first time she had said that about us. She wanted to date me. This was real.

Holy crap, now what do I do?

"Aw, you called me your best friend," Glitch said dramatically, clutching his chest.

"You're my only friend, idiot," she said, shaking her head with a smile. As Clara turned toward me, Glitch made another dramatic gesture at me as if it would help me not freak out. She chewed the inside of her cheek. "Sorry, I know we didn't exactly talk about it, but... I just thought..."

I felt the smile creep over my lips. Screw being afraid of public displays. This perfect girl called me her boyfriend, and every part of me wanted her to be my girlfriend. I wrapped my hand around her head and pulled her into my kiss.

"Gross. Get a room," Glitch groaned.

Clara's cheeks were a bright pink as she pulled away from me, and that smile made me melt. *That* was my girlfriend; purple hair, wearing my sweatshirt, and those blue eyes that made everything else in this world disappear. A brief look of confusion flashed across her face but she wiped it away quickly with another smile as she curled into my side.

Glitch reached around us and stole the bag of popcorn at my feet. "Yeah, you're welcome for setting you up."

She elbowed him before curling into my side, gripping me tightly. I didn't mind because it gave me something better to focus on than the game. It was a nightmare out there. West was horrible, and it was almost more painful to let the game continue. After a time out and an uncharacteristic lull in crowd noise, I heard a crack of thunder outside the gym. It was loud enough to send the bleachers shaking, even with the huge number of people sitting on it.

I glanced down to the entrances as more people crowded into the gym, shaking rain off their clothes and umbrellas. I hadn't realized a storm was rolling in.

Clara seemed to perk up in attention, suddenly focused on what was happening around us as she sat up and looked around nervously. As the lights started to flicker above us, she tensed, reaching back to grab my hand. Another flash and rumbling thunder echoed around the gym, knocking the power out. As the principal tried to use a megaphone over the screaming crowd, Clara's grip tightened.

"We need to get out of here, now."

She shot out of her seat, yanking Glitch and I out of the bleachers with incredible strength. If I hadn't been prepared, she might have had enough strength to pull my arm out of socket. She shoved her way down the mass of people as she tugged us behind her. Glass shattered overhead, knocking a few lights to the ground but luckily not injuring anyone as they crashed on the gym floor.

Someone's hand smacked my cheek, knocking me off balance and deeper into the crowd. I watched Glitch being pulled away from us, caught in the mass of people heading for the east door.

Shit, not us. Clara's hand was missing from my grip. I looked around at the thinning crowd, trying to figure out if she had made it out of the gym. She was taller than most people here so if she was with Glitch, I would have seen her. No purple hair to my right either, so where could she be?

I finally spotted her as the mass of people had mostly evacuated, though even with the small number of people, the storm had almost doubled in echoing thunder. She stood near the middle of the gym, staring up at a rafter that was slowly breaking loose.

"Clara!"

She didn't react to my scream, still staring up as the rafter slid further and further down the wall. Her hands lifted, almost like she was going to try to catch the beam, but she barely had five seconds before she'd be crushed.

I couldn't let that happen, and I had a way to save her. I sprinted forward as the ceiling broke loose, tackling her and pulling her into the shadows as the rafter crashed down right where she had been standing.

As we moved through the darkness, I felt my nerves growing again. I had to save her, but that meant exposing my powers. What would she think of me now?

17

Clara

Nate's grip tightened as blackness surrounded us, the cold, empty air rushing by as he tried to find a safe place to get us out of the shadows. I couldn't focus on him at the moment, nor the fact that he had just exposed his powers to me. My head was pounding harder than it ever had before, amplified by my failed attempt at using my powers to hold up the gym ceiling. But if I couldn't keep it together just a little longer, I would risk having an outburst in the middle of a shadow.

He finally found an empty locker room, shoving me out of the depths before flying out in the opposite direction. I slid along the tile floor, my back cracking against the shower walls as Nate hit the opposite end, sprawling to the ground with a groan. I shoved my head into my knees, fighting the urge to throw up, pass out, or explode at the same time.

But beyond the echoing of my own headache and voices that were screaming at me, Nate's thoughts spun wildly, making everything worse.

She hates me. She's going to be terrified. I just showed her I had the power to control the shadows and she's freaking out. Why did this have to happen? Everything was going so well and now she knows I'm a freak.

"Clara?" he asked, his voice gentle and hesitant. I could feel him trying to keep his distance yet still check on me, worried that I was terrified of him.

The truth was so much worse.

He thought he had just revealed his powers to me, but I was the real enemy in this situation. I had known for months and not once had I told him what I was capable of. Only, I couldn't get those words out now. I couldn't even keep my own thoughts straight, let alone block the voices that were screaming in my head. The Blue Star was tormenting me, begging me to give in.

"Please, just—" I blurted, nearly shouting at the voices to shut up and inadvertently telling Nate to do so in the process. It wasn't his fault, but being this close to losing control made me dangerous. I choked down the urge to puke and curse, letting the tears of pain soak my jeans as I finally sobbed out the words. "Quiet. My headache."

I could feel him sit back in confusion, not entirely sure why I wasn't afraid of him or worried about the shadows that should have terrified me. Actually, being inside his shadow had been a relief, even if just for a brief moment. But then his thoughts turned just like I knew they would, wondering how I could be so calm after what he had done.

"Stop —" I whispered, pausing for a second. There would be no going back, now. This would be the end of normal, as if I could ever claim to be normal. "Stop thinking. I can hear your thoughts and I'm on the verge of blowing up this locker room if I can't get rid of this headache."

"What?"

It was the most painful word he had ever said to me. My heart broke, knowing it would only get worse. His energy faded from concern to anger but I had to shove him out of my head, focusing instead on keeping myself under control. Breathing steadily, I turned my attention to my surroundings, feeling the cold tile, the burn of jeans rubbing against my cheeks, and the soft trickle of water running down my back from where I had broken the pipe with my impact.

The voices slowly stopped clawing at my skull, though even their faded screams were enough torture to make me sick. I didn't need any more of that tonight, because facing Nate was potentially going to be worse than what I had just experienced.

I lifted my head, feeling my gut wrench as I saw the look of complete betrayal on his face.

"I'm so sorry," I whispered. "Please, can you give me a second to figure out what to say?"

He gritted his teeth, trying to mask his anger. "You said you could hear my thoughts. Do you have powers?"

"Yes, but it's not that simp—"

"So you knew about my powers already?" he snapped. "That's why you didn't freak out. How long have you known?"

I bit my tongue. "The first day of school."

He let out a frustrated breath as his hands gripped into fists. "Two months? You've known for two months and you never thought to say anything before now?"

I understood his frustration, but I couldn't help but feel attacked. He had no idea how vulnerable I was in this situation, and his anger was making everything worse.

"Just give me a moment to explain, please."

"You've had two months to do that, Clara. You knew I had powers because you've been reading my thoughts and lying to me for months!"

"I haven't..." I took a breath, trying to stay calm. "I haven't lied. There's just a lot to explain and it's complicated."

"It's not complicated," he shouted. "In fact, it's quite simple. We both have powers, and all of this could have been avoided if you had just told me you could read my thoughts. How do I know you haven't been manipulating me? How can I trust anything you've ever said to me if you've heard everything that goes through my head?"

"I don't listen to everything!" I snapped back, letting my emotions take over. "I can block them, but right now with this headache, I can't concentrate long enough to tell you my side of the story."

Nate growled under his breath before shouting again. "Two months. You had two months to do that instead of... this. Playing whatever game *this* is. What is it you want from me? Why do all of this? I mean, how can I trust you now when you've been lying our entire relationship?"

I fought back the sob that still very clearly jerked through my body. He was right, but he also had no idea what I was going through. Hell, I didn't even know what I was going through or who I was running from. The Complex was still just as much a mystery as the day I discovered them, not to mention the Blue Star voices constantly making things worse.

Nate sighed and rolled his eyes, impatient with my lack of answer. "I should have known this was too good to be true. That none of this, of *us*, was real to you," he snapped, standing up.

Anger surged through me. "How dare you," I growled, pushing off the ground as my fists clenched. "Don't you dare assume that it wasn't real for me after what I shared with you."

"You gave me nothing but lies."

"I gave you *everything*!" I shouted. I heard his thoughts scoff at the word *everything* and I lifted my finger at him in warning. "I did. I gave you everything I had because it was all I had to give. You might think

I've lied this whole time, but I have only ever told you one since the day I met you. My name isn't Clara."

I could see the statement startle him, but he frowned as the anger returned. "Who the hell are you?"

Glitch suddenly popped in between us, gasping in relief. "Oh, good. You're not dead. I don't think anyone saw you guys, but I guess C knows about us now." He glanced between us, realizing that Nate and I were locked in glares with our fists clenched. "Uh, did I miss something?"

"Who am I?" I growled, my eyes still locked on Nate. "That's the question I've been trying to answer for two months since I woke up with the last eighteen years of my life missing. All of my memories gone in an instant. Do you have any idea how terrifying it is to not remember your name or what you look like? So for the last two months, I've been trying to figure out where the hell I came from and why I have these powers. But despite being completely lost in this world, there has always been one good thing in my life, and that was you. I gave you everything I had, and when I say everything, I mean *everything*. So, no, I didn't tell you about my powers for two months because I had no answers for you and I was terrified to ruin what we had... the same reason you didn't say anything to me about your powers."

I shoved past him and headed for the door, pausing only briefly to finish my statement. "Don't talk to me about trust until you lose your entire past and wake up scared and alone."

18

Clara

I sat on the edge of my bed, staring at the blank phone screen. For some reason, part of me wanted there to be notifications to ignore, but I knew the truth. Nate was the only person I needed to understand what I was going through but he didn't give it a thought. He broke my heart just as quickly as he had built it up, all because he thought I was lying to him. Now he wasn't speaking to me and I had lost the only friends I had.

News reports said that while the storm came out of nowhere, it wasn't out of character for Forest Hills. The earthquakes were something new, however, and no one could explain that. Buildings across town were damaged, but the gym took the brunt of destruction.

I was pretty confident I hadn't caused the storm, but if I could launch furniture, was I capable of causing an earthquake across an entire town? If I had caused the gym to collapse when I hadn't released a complete outburst, what else could I accidentally do?

School was the last thing I wanted to deal with, but I didn't have a choice. The rest of the buildings were structurally safe so Monday resumed normal classes. Part of me wanted to just stop going altogether. It's not like I had a reason to return. School wasn't going to give me answers to my past and I sure as hell didn't want to see Nate, but if someone from The Complex was looking for me, I had to try to blend in like normal. Plus, I wasn't going to let some stupid boy ruin my life like this, even if it wasn't much of a life to begin with.

I threw on some jeans and a black hooded sweatshirt to prepare for the long day ahead of me, but when I walked out of the closet, Nate's sweatshirt was folded neatly on the bed. The last time I had seen it was when I threw it in anger somewhere in the library Friday night. Now

House was trying to get me to take it. I'd return it to him eventually, but not today.

"I'm not wearing it," I growled, folding my arms as I ignored the creaking that echoed through the room. I picked up my bag and swung it over my shoulder, turning to find the sweatshirt hanging on the door. "Seriously, House. I tried talking to him and he blew me off. I get that I screwed up, but so did he. Look, I'm already having a hard enough time trusting myself without memories. I don't need more drama."

House protested by locking the bedroom door before I could leave. I rolled my eyes and flicked my fingers, unlocking it easily. The only bonus of being so angry all weekend was the hours and hours of practice I got with my powers as I pretty much destroyed the training room with my telekinesis. At least I had figured out how previous me could lift the heavier weights.

I pushed out the front door before House could block my path with Nate's sweatshirt again. The walk was lonely, just like the first day of school. Even my music lacked its normal boost of emotion, but right now it was the only thing keeping me grounded from the headache. The constant pound had annoyed me all weekend, but now the voices were more present in each throb of pain.

As I stood outside the door to class, I watched Nate and Glitch in the back row. Nate didn't look nearly as bothered as I thought he would be, making me even more frustrated. I pulled my hood up and stuffed my headphones inside so Mrs. Roberts wouldn't see. If the music was loud enough, I could get through the three classes I had with Nate.

I kept my head down and walked inside, sliding into my desk while avoiding eye contact with my ex-boyfriend. It was easier to resist looking at him if I focused on the music, fighting the temptation to listen to Nate's thoughts. I used my newly discovered trick of changing songs without touching my iPod, scrolling to find familiar tunes to focus on instead. Every time I had the urge to listen, I pulled my arms tighter around my stomach.

God, how could he have not seen what he did to me? You didn't need mind reading abilities to understand that losing memories would scare anyone. Was it more terrifying that I had been so caught up in his whirlwind that I missed his true nature?

Maybe what was more frustrating was that I always ended up blaming myself for everything, and that wasn't fair. He shouldn't have the power to be blameless in this. The reality was that there were more important things going on in my life than Nate and my relationship. He was actually the one holding me back from finding the answers to my past. He was a distraction, helping me create this fake version of myself that didn't want to find my memories because I wanted this to be my life. I needed to figure out who I was and who was coming after me. I needed to have my memories so I could be prepared.

My mind flashed back to my notes. 'F'. That's who I needed to find; the girl who wanted to fall into the Blue Star, into the cold. Maybe I could find her in there. Maybe that's how I became… this.

I took a breath and focused on the cold feeling as it washed over me. The music faded with my headache as a cool brush of air swirled around me. I let my emotions out easily, feeling the weight of everything lift off my chest.

I felt lighter; calmer. There weren't any memories, but at least I didn't have to feel that draining emotion anymore. No more pain, no more sadness, and no more headache. This was the step forward I needed. I would find answers, one bit at a time, even if that meant submerging myself in the cold and letting the Blue Star take over. It was the only progress I had made in months.

19

Nate

Spending the weekend alone was miserable, but I didn't want to see anyone, or be forced to talk about what was spinning around my head.

Clara had betrayed everything I had given her. For months she was playing us, manipulating us to serve whatever purpose she had. None of it was real to her.

Everything about our relationship was built on a lie.

And then she had the nerve to accuse me of betraying her trust? How was I supposed to know she had powers? How was I supposed to know it was safe to tell her about my own powers when I'd never met anyone else with them besides Glitch? This wasn't supposed to happen like this.

The real issue was that I still had that damn dream where she bled out, and as much as I wanted to hate her, waking up and thinking she was dead made me miserable. I don't know why I had to see it every night, or what trick she might have played on me to make me see it, but at least the part about seeing her with powers made sense since she actually had them.

As if life had to get any worse, school was still a thing. The gym was destroyed, which effectively put an end to PE, but we still had to attend. And that meant first thing in the morning, I'd have to see Clara... or, whoever she was.

Glitch was annoyed at my silence, and even more so that I completely ignored the cold rush of air as she sat next to me. There was something different about it today, and maybe it was the fact that I was upset with her instead of head over heels obsessed, but it almost felt bitter. Pretty accurate for how I felt in this whole thing.

I turned forward as class started, catching stray glimpses of her hooded figure sitting in the desk next to me. It was pretty obvious we were both doing our best to avoid looking at each other, and once silence settled over the class, I could pick up the vague hint of music playing from her earbuds that she hadn't removed.

Why was she even attending school anyway? She didn't know who she was, and it's not like she had something to do here, so shouldn't she just be... I don't know, anywhere *but* here?

Her words echoed through my head from Friday night. *Alone.* Even if she had no reason to be here, she also had nothing outside of school.

I shoved the guilt aside, letting my anger remind me that she was the one lying. I couldn't even be sure she had been telling the truth that night. It might have just been another trick.

But life had to keep punching me in the gut. After avoiding Clara all day, I came home to another unwelcome relationship problem. My dad's car was parked outside; the crisp, black shine of a vehicle that got more attention than I did, reminding me how much I was going to hate what came next.

I pushed through the door.

"Nathaniel? About time you got home from school," he shouted from his office.

"Walking takes a bit of time, you know," I groaned. This was the last thing I wanted to deal with. My face was ready to be shoved into a pillow for the rest of the night, not rehashing arguments with my dad or explaining why my ex-girlfriend just ripped my heart from my chest and left me empty of emotion.

He stepped into the living room in his suit and tie; always intimidating. He was only about an inch taller than me, but when he dressed like that, it felt like he might have been eight feet tall.

He looked me over. "Glad to see you're okay. I heard about the school gym on Friday, and since you didn't answer your phone all weekend, I needed to check in on you."

Shit. I had let my phone die, not wanting to deal with any drama, but probably should have texted him something this morning when I finally turned it back on and saw the missed calls.

"I'm fine," I grumbled, dropping my bag to the ground as I shuffled over to the couch.

"Doesn't sound like it. Everything okay?" he asked.

I folded my arms. "Oh, right. Because after three months, you decide to come back and ask if I'm okay, but only because the gym gets destroyed. Next time I need your attention, I'll be sure to burn down the school library."

"Easy there, Nathaniel. You know I'm busy, and your mom and I are really trying to make things better for you. We trust you with a lot around here, but I get that you deserve something more from us. I just want to help."

Great, guilt. But when you don't see your parents for an extended period of time, sometimes it's hard to remember they actually have genuine feelings about you.

"I'm sorry. It was just a long day... well, a pretty crappy four days in general. I shouldn't take that out on you."

I rolled back on the couch and stared at the ceiling as my dad sat in the chair across from me.

"Well, a gym collapsing during the volleyball game will do that to you," he said, a small chuckle escaping his throat. I'm glad he thought it was funny, because I was pretty sure my ex-girlfriend had been the one to destroy it.

Then the idiotic thought crossed through my head. What if I just told him about my powers? What if I shared what really might have happened to the gym? What about sharing what happened afterward, and the heated fight Clara and I exchanged that led to us breaking up? But Glitch and I had a promise, and even if I couldn't share most of my life with my dad, at least I could possibly get some advice.

"Well, I guess that was part of it, but after, my girlfriend and I got in a fight. I found out she had been lying to me the whole time we were together... well, I guess it was more withholding information, but still. It ended badly."

"Girlfriend?" he said, leaning forward.

"Wow, please try to act more surprised about the fact I had a girlfriend," I said, rolling my eyes.

"Sorry, I just didn't know you were in a relationship," he said, a smile forming.

I cut that off before he had a chance to breathe. "I'm not anymore. Our relationship came crumbling down as quickly as the gym."

He sat back in his seat. "I'm truly sorry to hear that, Nathaniel. Do you think there's a way to fix things? Would you want to fix them?"

"It's probably too late for that, but I think that's more on her now," I replied with a shrug. She'd be way too stubborn to admit she was wrong, though. There was no fixing that relationship.

"Son, if I've learned anything in my time, it's that relationships are a two way street. You have to be willing to do your part as well, but only if that's what you really want."

Terrible advice. She's the one who broke things in the first place. "Cool. Thanks."

I guess Clara wasn't the only stubborn one. I rolled off the couch and picked up my bag, dragging myself up the stairs to go wallow in my misery a little longer. At least it was better to focus on that emotion than the enormous empty pit in my heart.

~

We had a week before Thanksgiving break and Clara and I still weren't speaking to each other. I was starting to feel the guilt pile up as she looked more and more distant every day. The more I thought about my dad's advice, the more I realized maybe I could have handled things better. But she was the one who walked away in the first place. She was the one not telling me the truth when she knew about us all along. She had to make the first move if she wanted us to work again, but it was probably too late.

Dad was preparing to go back on assignment after Thanksgiving, which was a relief. I was tired of answering all his questions about school and why I kept shouting in the middle of the night. At least I wasn't crashing into walls from that nightmare... the same nightmare that wouldn't go away.

On Thursday before break, Glitch was in a nervous fit. With our history presentation the next day, he was terrified Clara wouldn't show up or do her part. It didn't help that she had been absent the last two days.

"Okay, she just has a headache. She'll come tomorrow for her part," he sighed, setting his phone down on the lunch table.

"Wait, you texted her?" I asked.

I stopped poking my lunch and frowned. I don't know why it bothered me that he reached out, but since she hadn't talked to us in a month, I couldn't blame him for being worried.

"Yeah, and this isn't the first time I've checked in on her. You should probably care more about your girlfriend's feelings," he replied, crossing his arms.

I shook my head. "Not my girlfriend anymore. She's the one who walked out, remember?"

"Oh, you're really going to make me do this, aren't you?"

"Do what?" I asked.

"Give it to you straight since you've been avoiding the topic of Clara since you broke up. That girl was the greatest thing to happen to you, besides me, of course, and then you had to go and let her believe her worst fear," he replied.

I groaned. "I thought you were on my side."

He shook his head at me. "This is not about sides, Nate, but you know I'll always be on yours. That's why I'm telling it like it is. You didn't listen to anything she said that night because you were so focused on the fact that she was hiding her powers. Did you not realize what you did to her? She was terrified that you knowing her powers would make you see her differently; make you not trust her. The moment you opened your mouth, you did just that. You pushed her out."

"Me not trust her? She didn't trust me enough to tell me about what she could do. That's the real problem here," I said, trying to keep my voice down as my emotions built up again.

"Nate," Glitch sighed. "She lost her memory. All eighteen years of her life are just a blank space. Could you trust anyone without having any memories of who you were or why something like that happened? Even if she was working her way there, you can't blame her for hesitating. She didn't know who to trust and had no one to help her. We were lucky we got as much out of her as we did. We have no idea what that felt like for her."

Shit. For a month, I had blamed her for everything, but my dad and Glitch were right. I was the one who needed to be fixing things.

"Yeah, you messed up," Glitch said, patting my shoulder. "But you can still try to make things right, and I'll leave you with this nugget. Clara wasn't just the greatest thing to happen to you. You were also the greatest thing to happen to her."

I slumped in my chair. "How are you so good at this?"

He shrugged. "Coming from someone with trust issues from his parents left him, I know it's not easy to let someone in. But you found a way to make me feel less alone, and that's exactly what C needs right now. Make sure she knows she's not alone anymore."

20

Clara

Thursday before Thanksgiving break. Finally. I just wanted to have a week of not going to a pointless school and seeing my jerk of an ex.

I can't believe I was dumb enough to think Nate would be different; that me having powers wouldn't turn him into a self-centered ass. I had given him everything and he broke that trust in an instant. I was left to be alone.

Which is exactly what I needed today with a headache. I called in sick to school, knowing that if I was ever going to make it through tomorrow, including the history project next to Nate, I was going to need all my energy.

I shouldn't have been surprised to see a text from Glitch at lunchtime asking if I was going to be there for the project on Friday. I guess in all of this, I could at least be respectful of him. While he kept his distance, he had texted me at least once a week to ask if I was okay, especially if I checked myself out of school for a headache. I don't think Nate knew he was staying in contact with me.

I have a headache. I'll be there for the project, promise.

I placed my phone back on the nightstand and slid back under the covers to hide in the dark.

As much as breaking up with Nate was torture, I wish it didn't look like our relationship was the reason I wasn't eating or sleeping. The voices in my headache echoed with hate, begging me to give in to the Blue Star. It sang false promises of wiping away the nightmare I had every night; the one where Nate tried to catch me as I bled out from a non-existent wound on my stomach. They told me that the cold feeling in my soul would go away and I'd get all my memories back if I would just let it take control.

But I couldn't do it. I had failed once and lost everything in my head. I had lost my past, and I had to learn to trust the previous version of me who was afraid of it. She was the only thing I had left in this world, and while I'd do anything to get her back, I wouldn't do the one thing she promised not to do. I wouldn't give in, even if the voices pressed back and made me too sick to function.

Friday morning came almost instantly as I slept through all of Thursday. And that kind of sleep and rested mind gave me the perfect idea. I needed to prove that I wasn't the helpless, heartbroken teenage girl. I was so much more than that.

I straightened my hair for the first time, brushing out the tangles from the last week of not being able to run a comb through it. The new, dark purple dye was perfect to hide my roots that were growing out, complemented by a fitting leather jacket to add to my intimidation factor. Maybe this would be my final move against Nate; taking the knife he had stabbed in my heart and shoving it back into his.

All eyes turned to me as I walked in the classroom, just as I hoped. Shoulders back and fists clenched, I made my way to my desk, enjoying all of the thoughts ramble on about how it looked like I had just murdered someone.

Oh, shit. Nate might be too late. Glitch's thought rang through as he made eye contact with me briefly. He gave me a half smile.

Too late? Too late for what?

Next to him, Nate tried to catch my attention. It was a new gesture, considering he had spent the last month completely ignoring me. Is that what Glitch was thinking about? Luckily, the bell rang before he could say anything, because I was pretty sure if he had tried to talk to me, I would have stabbed him with basically every pen I had in my backpack.

Mrs. Roberts stood from her desk, getting everyone's attention. *Time to sit through the easiest day of the year.* "Would anyone like to volunteer and go first?"

My hand was raised before she had even started her sentence. I stormed to the front, Nate and Glitch following close behind. As Glitch started us off seamlessly, I put on my best act. I followed along with the jokes, acted along with the material, and even had a great back and forth with Nate. If someone didn't know that Nate and I had broken up, I could have convinced everyone that we were all still great friends. But I was just trying to get to the end of the presentation. By the time it was over, I was back in my seat and prepared to ignore Nate for the rest of eternity. Hell, since I had no one relying on me anymore, I probably wouldn't even come back to school after the break.

Nate sat down again, but to my surprise he leaned closer to me and whispered. "C, can we talk?"

I looked over at him, disgusted. "Are you serious right now? You ignored me for a month and now you want to talk?" I rolled my eyes and turned back to the front of the class.

Please, I really messed up. Will you just give me a minute?

I glared at him, furious that after all this time of accusing me of listening to everything, he was going to use that against me right now so that he could get something he wanted. I reached into my pocket and pulled out my headphones, weaving them up my shirt so they would stay hidden from the teacher, though I was pretty sure she had zoned out already.

The Blue Star voices came roaring back, promising something new. They found the gaps in lyrics, telling me that letting them in would help me get rid of the pain; get rid of the heartbreak. I didn't want them to be right, but it was true. Nate was everything to me, and he had broken my heart, but I couldn't let him see the truth of what he did to me. I couldn't be weak.

But the longer I listened, the more I wanted to let them in. I wanted to be free of the pain. I didn't want the constant reminder that Nate had left me all alone to deal with this shit. There was only one option, and it wasn't letting the Blue Star take control. I would find the answers and prove I was capable of fighting back. I'd learn to protect myself. I didn't need anyone else.

I was out of my seat the second the bell rang, but Nate must have had the same idea. As his hand reached out to grab mine and keep me from storming away, his skin burned against my palm. I yanked my hand away, horrified that I had given the Blue Star so much power over me. I had basically turned into an icicle.

Nate looked at me in confusion. *Does she have more powers I don't know about? How is she so cold?*

I spun around, afraid to admit that I had let the Blue Star get the best of me like that. I shouldn't have let them continue taunting me. I shouldn't have listened.

I made my way through the students in the hall, walking past my English class and out the main doors without anyone noticing. The voices screamed louder, gripping at my throat and making me nauseous as I walked home.

The next week was a fog as I faded in and out of migraines and sleeplessness. I felt the constant pressure of cold around my neck, tightening as I fought back against my emotions and the voices. I stopped eating completely, unable to swallow anything without immediately throwing up. How long could I fight this pain? Would I eventually cave and let the Blue Star win? At least I wouldn't have to suffer.

Between throbs of pain, I continued to dig through the library. There were no answers to my memory, no details about the Blue Star in any of the books except that it was evil. I wanted to keep searching but I was losing hope... and I was reading the same blurry paragraph over and over.

I gave up, grunting as I chucked the book off the second floor and watched it explode in a mess against the opposite wall. I slumped against the bookcase and slid down to the floor, pressing my hands into my temples as the headache roared to life again. Spots clouded my vision, even as I closed my eyes against the searing pain. Pressure built in my skull and all I wanted to do was release that torture.

Wait, that was the answer. I focused on the power inside me and shoved it out all at once. Screaming, I felt the library explode around me. Papers and books flew off the desk and out of the bookcases, littering the air and floor. But I couldn't control it now. The railing on the staircase crumpled in a loud screech, drowning out the scream that continued to escape my throat. Lights shattered above me, showering glass everywhere, but the more I tore the room to shreds, the more my headache released. The invisible, cold hand that was crushing my chest loosened it's grip and I gasped for air, rolling onto my side as I panted.

I could hear the papers settling around me now that the voices had died out, giving me something new to focus on. I swallowed the metallic taste in my mouth and opened my eyes, focusing on the library that was barely together. I lifted myself off the ground slowly, confused as to how in all of my destruction, the windows and desk were still surprisingly intact.

Holy shit. This was one of the outbursts that previous me had mentioned, only ten times worse. The entire library was in shreds, as if a tornado had destroyed the inside of House.

I threw my right hand over my mouth as I gasped. What if this had happened while I was in public? What if this was what I did to the gym. What if I really had caused the earthquake?

Something warm ran down my left arm and dripped from my

fingertips. I looked down and groaned, watching blue blood seep through my long sleeve and run down my hand. In the outburst, I had reopened the scar on my arm.

I gripped the railing with my right hand to steady myself as I started to cry. What was I becoming? I was fighting against an evil Blue Star, but in the process I had made things so much worse. I couldn't control any of it, and I was no closer to answers than I was three months ago. I was just as empty... and now I was truly alone.

I sank to the ground and curled into myself as I started to sob.

21

Nate

"Nathaniel."

My dad jarred me out of a trance as he threw more food on top of my plate. He shook his head.

"Come on, it's Thanksgiving," he said. "At some point, you're going to have to move on from her."

How do you move on from a girl you dream about every night? Or, maybe more appropriately, how do you move on when you know you're the one who messed it up and made sure your already fragile girlfriend will never trust you again?"

"Dad, you don't understand what we had. I screwed everything up and now she won't talk to me. How am I supposed to fix that?" I asked, dropping my fork as I pushed my plate away. I'm sure the knots in my stomach wouldn't agree with more food anyway.

"Son, this is just the first of many relationships you'll have. Learn from these mistakes and make the next one better."

I didn't want a different relationship. I wanted to be with Clara. I groaned and rubbed my temples. "If this is how I'm going to feel after every breakup, I don't think I'll do it ever again."

My dad laughed. "You're still young. There will be plenty of chances to move on. I do wish I could have met your first girlfriend if she made you feel as strongly as you do now. I guess I'll just have to hope you'll tell me when you find another." He stood up and started clearing the dishes. "I'm going to be back for Christmas, so hopefully you're in a better mood then."

Right. I had been so caught up in my emotions that I forgot he was leaving tonight. It would be nice to get the house back to myself. No one would be around to judge my post-breakup heartbreak anymore.

I helped finish the dishes as my dad threw his suitcases in the car. I waved him off, enjoying the crisp, November air. The familiar chill of cold was nice, though I would have much rather felt it through Clara's touch. She was probably sitting alone at home now, on Thanksgiving of all days, listening to her music so she could continue to ignore me.

Music.

I turned and sprinted inside to grab my phone. Clara had said she had given me everything, and to her, music meant everything. That's what she knew. Through all of her missing memories, that's what she always turned to. I scrolled until I found the song I was looking for and sent it.

Leave a Light on. Tom Walker.

Please, C. I know I broke your trust, but you're not alone. I just want a chance to get it right.

I should have known not to expect anything back. I sat on the edge of my bed, staring at the mass of unanswered texts I had sent over the last week. All I wanted was a chance to hear Clara's voice again, to hear her side of everything, but I knew deep down she didn't owe me that. I didn't deserve any of it because I was a selfish idiot. That guilt was going to be the end of it.

I sighed and sent one last song.

Pieces (feat. Noah Kahan). Matoma.

I'm so sorry for what I did. I get it if you don't want to give me another chance, but I'm here if you ever do.

I could have stayed glued to my phone, but I knew she was never going to respond. Not after the way I treated her. I left my phone on the bed and changed into sweats and a t-shirt to sleep, even though it was early in the night. By the time I finished brushing my teeth and had crawled under the covers, that nagging feeling was back. I could check my phone, just one more time.

My heart leapt into my throat when I saw the message I had missed five minutes ago. Clara responded.

I can't sleep.

Me either. Can we talk?

I didn't have to wait more than five seconds before she responded.

I'm outside.

I jumped out of bed and sprinted downstairs, knocking nearly everything over as I ran to the door and threw it open, almost shouting my apology.

"I'm such an ass and I'm so sorry. I should have let you explain.

You're not alone, and I want to take it all back if you'll just —holy shit, what happened to you?"

Clara stood in the freezing night air with just jeans and a light long sleeve on, not registering anything I had just said. Her face was sunken, tears staining her cheeks and hair matted in sweat around her face. But that wasn't the most terrifying thing to see. I glanced down as she lifted her left arm, blue ink staining her sleeve and dripping from her fingers onto the porch. Wait, that wasn't ink... that was blood.

Her mouth opened, but only empty air came from her throat. When she finally spoke, her voice was barely audible over the wind.

"Nate, I need help."

I dragged her inside, fighting all of the questions that spun in my mind. I guided her up the stairs and into my bathroom as she stood in a trance, her eyes shining with tears. She didn't notice as I peeled her sleeve away from her arm, blood shining against her skin. Blue blood, shaped in a lightning mark up her forearm just like in my dreams.

"Clara, how did this happen?" I asked, scooping water from the sink to help clean the cut. Her skin was cool to the touch, but not as icy as when I had touched her the last day of school.

She took a deep breath and told me everything about the last few months and what she knew, which really wasn't a lot. She talked about waking up next to the dead man in the clearing, believing she had run away from The Complex and he was chasing after her. I was just as confused as she was about The Complex and The Trials to get powers, especially because Glitch and I were in the same situation of having our powers without those things. And then the Blue Star giving her headaches and the voices screaming at her. That's why she lost control and had outbursts, which was how tonight's events had unfolded. She had nowhere to turn when she reopened the scar on her arm; the scar she got from using the Blue Star and losing her memory a few months ago, and the same one I saw every night in my dreams.

Clara's voice faded out, her gaze still distant and dull as I finished wrapping her arm in a bandage. I couldn't bring myself to let go of her hand, afraid she might never let me touch her again.

"This is going to sound creepy," I said, sighing, "but I think I've been dreaming of that night you lost your memory. I see that man—"

"Wait, what?" she asked, her fingers tensing in my grip.

"He's controlling fire," I continued. "I see this flash of light, and you're there, but then..."

"You see me dying," she whispered, finishing my thought as her right hand ran over her stomach. "Nate, I have that same dream. You're trying to help me."

I shook my head, my mind spinning again. "How can we be having the same dream?"

Clara frowned. "I don't know. They didn't start until after I met you."

Silence fell as we both tried to wrap our heads around whatever was happening to us. There were too many questions, and I finally understood why it was so hard for her to say anything to me about all of it. I wanted answers just as much as she did, but the only things we had were more questions.

I sighed and reached forward, pulling her right hand away from her stomach. "C, I can't apologize enough, but I also have no idea what to do now. You mean too much to me and I don't want to lose you. I don't want to be too late; not for this, not like in our dreams, not for any of it."

She finally made eye contact with me, her blue eyes plagued with sadness. "Do you really want to be with me? After everything I just told you, how can you look at me the same? I don't know who I am and I'm losing control."

She tried to tug her hands away but I just held them tighter. "Of course I want to be with you. It shouldn't have taken me this long to realize it, to reach back out to you, but I can't stand to lose what we had. Now I'm just worried I did too much damage to ever get back to that point. I think I should be the one asking if you want to be with me."

I started to loosen my grip but this time she was the one who didn't let go. Clara pulled my arms around her back and leaned into my chest, burying her face in my shirt. My favorite chill ran through my spine as I leaned into her, resting my cheek on her head. I could have stayed there for hours, but she finally pulled away.

"Thank you for listening. I'm sorry for the trouble tonight. I'll head home now."

Clara tried to slide by me, fiddling with her bloodstained left sleeve, but I snagged her hand before she got out the door.

"I've missed you for a month. Please, don't go," I whispered. I'm not sure I could bear the thought of watching her leave again, even if it was just for the night.

She relaxed in my grip. "Okay, but can I borrow a shirt? This one is…"

"Yeah," I replied with a smile.

I let her change into one of my gray long sleeves as I sat on the bed, watching her walk around and look at the things in my room. "So, the headaches and voices caused your arm to cut open again?"

She nodded. "I kind of screamed and blew up my library. I thought giving in would be easier. I thought I could get rid of the pain, physical and emotional."

Clara slid her hand over the speaker, leaving a visible streak through the dust. I hadn't used it since the night we broke up and nothing sounded right without her.

I sighed. "I'm so sorry, C."

"I am too," she replied with a shrug. "Maybe we should just call it even and stop apologizing? Move on with a clean slate?"

"I'm not sure I deserve that, but that would be really nice."

She smiled softly, making her way closer to the bed as she played with some of the things my bookshelf. I studied her movements, admiring her wearing my shirt. The long sleeve she had on was swallowing her, just like my old sweatshirt had. The sweatshirt he never gave back. Maybe that was her way of holding on, just like it was my way of hoping she would come back to me.

Her eyes widened as she snagged something off the shelf, turning to face me. "Where did you get this?" she asked, shoving the half marble into my right hand.

"A clearing... on the first day of school before I met you..." Slowly, the pieces started to fit together. That was the same clearing in our dream, where Clara had found herself with no memories, and the first day we started having the same nightmare. "Hold on, is this...?"

"The Blue Star," she replied, her eyes a fiery blue. She dug into her left pocket and pulled out an identical half marble, the same blue tint as her eyes shining under the black surface. "This is why we have the same dream. It broke that night and I couldn't find the other half. What if this is why I lost my memory?"

Her words spilled out in an excited mess, and I understood why. This marble could hold the answers to her past, but it also seemed to be responsible for a lot of her issues now. I watched the blue light start to brighten and swirl inside the half marble in my hand, the one she held doing the same. Did she notice the light was the same color as her eyes?

"C," I said hesitantly, watching her stare between the two halves. "You said the Blue Star is where the voices and headaches came from.

Are you sure this is a good idea?"

Clara looked up at me, a new hope in her eyes. "I've been searching for three months and had no luck. What if this is the only chance I have to figure out my past?"

I sighed, still uncertain, but this was her choice. She was the one who had lost everything, and this time I was going to make sure I helped her, however she needed me.

I nodded as she reached forward and pressed her half of the marble into mine. The blue light underneath the surface started to swirl faster, colliding and brightening as a soft glow surrounded our hands.

In a flash of freezing cold air and energy, Clara and I flew away from each other and slammed against the walls.

22

Clara

Blue light spun around me. It was like crashing waves and gentle ripples at the same time. The energy surged and danced, pulling the air through my body like electricity.

My hand twitched as I looked down to see Nate still holding my left hand with his right. We weren't in his bedroom anymore, but I couldn't say where we were except in the Blue Star. That was the power swirling around us that was terrifying and beautiful and cold.

I could feel the energy tugging at my mind, a dull ache that wanted me to reach out into the waves that ran around us. What if that was where my memories were hiding? What if I went inside?

Wait, I'm not sure you should touch it. Something feels wrong.

I frowned. I hadn't moved a muscle, but Nate's thought seemed to respond to my thought. I started to open my mouth to speak but no sound escaped.

I raised my eyebrow. *Nate, can you hear my thoughts?*

Nate spun his head to look at me, his eyes widening. He opened his mouth, realizing that he also couldn't speak. *You didn't say that out loud? How can I hear your thoughts?*

I shrugged. *The Blue Star, I guess.*

Something pinched my neck as I looked back at the waves in front of us. Part of me wanted to reach out, but that inviting feeling from earlier started to change. Instead of tugging gently, I could feel the cold grip tightening around my neck and digging into my skull. I clenched my jaw as my eyes started to water, fighting against the pain. I couldn't have an outburst right now, not when Nate was here and the Blue Star could take advantage of me.

I squeezed my eyes shut, pressing my right hand into my forehead in an attempt to relieve the pain. The tugging turned to yanking as the energy picked up like wind, trying to force me into the spinning waves around us. All I wanted to do was scream, but I had to resist.

Nate's arms wrapped around me, desperately trying to pull me into him but the Blue Star picked up yet again. I could feel it forcing us away from each other, pressure building around us and in my head. If this lasted much longer, I wouldn't be able to hold back.

Finally the energy ripped between us and tore us apart, launching us in two different directions. Nate was lucky as he flew over his bed and hit the wall, dropping down to the mattress. I wasn't as fortunate, skidding over his desk and hitting the wall just under his bedroom window.

Shit. "Ow," I growled, rubbing the back of my head as I blinked the tears away. The pain had faded into a dull ache but I could still feel the remnants of what it had been. I rolled my neck a few times, letting out the uncomfortable soreness in my muscles.

"Are you okay?" Nate asked, scrambling toward me.

"I think so," I grumbled. *I mean, shit. For getting launched across a room, I was pretty lucky to hit the wall and not smash through the window.*

Nate froze, his eyes widening as I frowned and glanced around.

"What?" I asked, trying to figure out what he was staring at. *Am I bleeding again? I have all my limbs... is there a pen sticking out of me?*

"No, I can hear your thoughts," he breathed.

My eyes widened. "Shit."

"Yeah," he chuckled. "You cuss a lot."

I rolled my eyes. "Shut up."

Nate stood up carefully, offering his hand to help me up. "So, first the Blue Star connects our dreams, now our thoughts. Where did that thing go?"

I pressed my hand into the floor to stand up but felt a sharp pinch. I turned my palm over to see the Blue Star stuck in a crease in the bandage on my hand. "Found it."

He reached forward, sliding the now whole marble out of the wrap. Black and blue light swirled underneath the surface before the blackness took over and it settled into stillness. "Hm, it doesn't feel cold anymore."

"Shit," I whispered, grabbing his right hand. I turned his palm over, running my fingers over the new blue splotch that had appeared in his palm. The scar was identical to the one I had on my left, right where we had been holding the Blue Star in the vision. I glanced up, still tracing the scar with my fingers. "Do you feel different?"

He shook his head. "Not really. Well, besides having your voice in my head now."

I shrugged. "I guess there are worse things."

"Yeah, it could be Glitch's thoughts."

I let out a quick chuckle followed by both of us laughing at full volume. Despite the unknown of what had just happened, it was a relief to smile again. It was a relief to be with Nate again. I leaned forward and rested my head on his shoulder, thankful for his touch after so long. But after all the headaches I had just gone through and not sleeping for who knows how many days, I wasn't going to be able to stand much longer. Nate was holding up a lot more of my weight than I wanted.

"You know," he whispered, shifting me toward the bed, "you're going to have to start censoring your thoughts if you want to keep me out of your head. I have no idea how to block them like you do."

He kissed the top of my head before setting me down on the bed. As we leaned back, I felt a lightness that I hadn't felt before. I still didn't have my memories, but Nate had been right to keep me away from the waves. That pain was horrible, and a reminder of what I had been resisting all these months. He kept me from falling into the cold, and I was going to need him to help me if the pain continued to get worse. The Blue Star was after something, and it had just pulled Nate into the mess with me.

I sighed as I picked up my phone, remembering the reason I had changed my mind about getting help from Nate. "Thank you for the songs. I didn't think I'd ever talk to you again."

"I just wanted to try."

"Music is the only connection I have to my past, and it's not much, but it keeps me grounded from the Blue Star. It's the only thing I can rely on… but now I have you. I can't let it take over, Nate."

He nodded. "Then I'll help you. I'll make sure you won't fall into the cold."

I smiled and unwrapped my headphones, handing him the other earbud.

Lover. Truslow.

23

Nate

I sighed and pressed my forehead to hers. "Clara, you have no idea how much I've missed you."

She scrunched her nose and smiled. *I missed you too, Nate.*

Her voice in my head carried a slight echo, but it was full of happiness. I was going to have to get used to hearing her thoughts now, not that I was mad about that.

"So, I have another song for you," I replied, picking the phone out of her hand.

Stay. Elliot Root.

I started to get up, prepared to sleep on the couch, but Clara reached up and pulled me back down to the bed. She rolled closer, resting her head on my chest.

"You can't play this song and then leave," she said, lifting her chin so she could kiss my jaw.

What should have sent a chill down my spine only sent butterflies through my stomach. Her touch wasn't cold against my skin this time, and a little part of me missed that, but it didn't matter anymore. She was perfect for me and we were back together.

Clara smiled as she squished her nose against my neck. *You're perfect for me too, you know, cold or not.*

I pulled up her favorite Andrew Belle album and shifted back in bed, letting the music play in the background until we finally fell asleep next to each other.

I woke up to sunlight streaming through my window. Had I really just slept through the night? I almost forgot what it felt like to be rested.

I shifted in bed and accidentally let the sunlight hit Clara in the face.

She groaned and threw the covers over her head.

Twenty more minutes… or hours. Whichever comes last.

I laughed and joined her under the comforter, wrapping my arm around her side to pull her closer. Even better than sleeping through the night was getting to wake up next to her. I brushed her tangled hair away from her neck, pressing my lips to her skin and enjoying the giggle that escaped as she pressed her face harder into the pillow.

I probably should have offered her sweats or shorts to sleep in because she was still wearing my long sleeve and her jeans from last night. She didn't seem bothered, her back rising and falling with her breath as my hand brushed up and down her spine.

"Stop staring at me," she grunted, her voice muffled by the pillow.

What else was there to stare at besides the perfect girl next to me? I rolled onto my back, lifting my right hand off her back to examine the blue mark on my palm. The shape was exactly like hers, but luckily it was just a deep scar and not an open cut. The blue color had the same tint as Clara's scar and the Blue Star marble that it came from.

"Are you sure you don't feel any different?" she asked, her face still pressed into the pillow. Right, mind reader.

"Yeah, I'm pretty sure everything is normal… besides your thoughts in my head. Oh, and the temperature."

Clara groaned and propped herself up on her elbow to look at me. I let out a small laugh, tracing the line on her face that had been left from the pillow. Slowly, I wrapped my fingers through her hair and tried to pull her into a kiss.

She scrunched her nose and leaned away, smiling. "Gross. Morning breath."

I groaned internally. We hadn't actually kissed since the night of the volleyball game, before we fought. I missed that… a lot.

Clara shook her ehad and reached down to her waist to adjust her jeans, but her sleeve caught my eye. Small streaks of blue blood had dried through the gray fabric.

"You bled through your bandage," I said, reaching out to turn her hand over.

"Shit, sorry," Clara said, frowning.

"Why are you apologizing? I think you should be blaming the guy who wrapped it," I replied, using her distraction to pull her in tighter.

The movement caused the covers to drag her already messy hair over her face as she laughed, squirming and giggling as she tried to get out of my grip and avoid morning breath kisses. I pressed my lips to her jaw, but that was as close as I would get as our fun was cut short.

"Nathaniel, are you up?"

My dad's voice echoed from downstairs as the color drained from my face. Clara's eyes widened as her hand shot over her mouth, barely disguising her laugh.

"Shit," I breathed, my stomach clenching as I threw the covers off the bed. "Clara, this is not funny. You have to hide."

"Oh my god, are you serious?" she asked, still unable to hold in her laughter.

I yanked her off the bed and ushered her into my closet, the only place I could think of to hide her as my dad's footsteps grew louder.

"He should be on assignment. Oh, god, he's going to kill me."

Clara folded her arms as she nestled herself in the corner. *Do you treat all your sleepover girls like this?*

I'll make it up to you, I promise.

I latched the closet door just as my dad knocked.

"You up?"

"Yeah," I replied, sprinting over to the bed to kick Clara's shoes underneath.

He opened the door as I quickly sat. "Hope I didn't wake you up. I just wanted to tell you that my assignment got changed last minute. I'm going to be here permanently." He casually strolled over to my desk and sat down in the chair.

"Really?" I replied, feigning interest. "That's great news."

What else was I going to say after that? I looked around, uncomfortable with the silence, but Dad didn't seem to mind. In fact, he was making himself at home, adjusting the papers and trinkets on my desk before leaning back and crossing his arms. God, he looked just as intimidating sitting there in his suit as he did standing, amplified by the fear of him finding the girl I was hiding in my closet.

"So," he said, breaking the silence. "How long are you going to make me wait to meet your overnight guest?"

Shit. My cheeks burned as he sat there expectantly, but surprisingly not upset. Was this the calm before the storm? I lowered my head and walked back to the closet, pulling the door open.

Clara had somehow changed shirts already, stealing one of my black long sleeves to hide her bleeding arm. She stepped out and pulled the sleeves into her palms to hide the bandage.

"Dad, this is Clara," I sighed. She started to stick her hand out but hesitated and pulled it back, drawing her shoulders tighter into her body.

My dad didn't flinch as he studied her. "I assume you're the ex-girlfriend."

"Uh, we worked things out," she replied, shifting in her stance and bumping into me. This could very well have been the most embarrassing moment of my life.

Dad half nodded. "I can see that." His gaze turned to me. "Doesn't help your case."

"Dad, nothing happened," I replied, possibly a little too quickly.

He shook his head. "But you do know how this looks, right?"

A small groan echoed in my gut. Of course it looked bad. Clara was wearing my shirt, hiding in my closet, and very obviously looked like she had just woken up.

"Yeah, I do," I replied, hanging my head. "Won't happen again."

Won't happen again?

Clara's voice startled me but I regained my composure.

Shush. I snapped back in my head, wishing I could have elbowed her without it being obvious.

"Clara," my dad said, pulling our attention back. "I wish we had met under different circumstances. You won't mind seeing yourself out now, will you?"

"Yeah," she said before frowning. "I mean, no? I'm... going to leave."

If I didn't think I was about to get in the most trouble of my entire life, I might have laughed. Clara bent down and pulled her shoes out from under the bed and hurried out the door. *Good luck. Call me later.*

A few seconds passed before the front door opened and closed, signaling my dad to finally break the silence.

"Interesting," he said. Wow, that was not the first thing I expected to hear. He uncrossed his arms and leaned forward. "I didn't picture your first girlfriend like that."

"Wait, what?" I asked, still shocked that I wasn't being yelled at.

"She's tall, and the purple hair is a new one. Just surprising to see you together after she broke your heart."

"Like she told you, we worked it out. I really like her, Dad. Can you please not ruin this?"

He held up his hands defensively. "Alright, sorry. But just so you know, you have a curfew now."

"Yeah, that's fair," I replied as he stood and walked out the door without another word.

24

Clara

House was overjoyed when I got home, setting out all of my favorite foods again. It had been so long since I had an appetite, and even longer since I'd been free of that headache.

I was about halfway through the table of food when Glitch texted to meet them at the coffee shop in an hour. I laughed to myself. Of course he'd be the first to know we were back together. He probably should have known an hour wasn't long enough for me to get ready. I shoved a donut in my mouth and hurried to the bedroom.

The bandage Nate had wrapped stuck to my arm as I tried to peel it off in the shower, regretting all the junk I just ate as my stomach churned watching the blue blood run down the drain. I cleaned it as best I could without fainting, then did a terrible job wrapping it back up. Nate was definitely a better medic than I was. I smiled as I left the bathroom, noticing that House had folded Nate's old sweatshirt on the edge of my bed. I'm not sure he was going to give me the option of leaving it ever again.

By the time I made it to the coffee shop, Nate and Glitch had already found a table in the corner. I'm not sure why they put up with me when I was late all the time, but the smile on Nate's face when he saw me melted that worry.

Glitch, as usual, interrupted my train of thought. He jumped out of his seat and picked me up in a hug, swinging me around.

"Thank goodness you're back, C. Nate's a total downer when you two fight," he cheered, giving me a final squeeze before setting me down between them.

Nate pushed a coffee in front of me, followed by the sugar jar. Well, there was no denying they knew this version of me pretty well.

"So," I said, leaning across the table to grab a stir stick. "How much do you know?"

"All of it, duh," Glitch replied. "And I have questions, but first, please tell me how awkward it was to meet Nate's dad right after you two slept together."

"Dude," Nate grumbled, throwing a straw wrapper at him.

I shrugged. "He did *technically* catch us sleeping together."

Now Nate turned his annoyance toward me. "Not helping, C." He poked the sugar jar that I was still dumping into my coffee.

I grimaced and turned to Glitch. "You had questions."

"Yes, first one. Do you have a headache right now and are you going to blow shit up?" he asked, leaning forward to look into my eyes.

I leaned away from him. "No, I'm not going to blow shit up. I don't even know for sure if the gym was my fault. But the library was pretty bad." Oops. I had completely forgotten the library back home. I'm sure that was still a disaster I'd have to clean later.

"Okay, so if the Blue Star thingy took your memory, what did it do to Nate?"

I shook my head. "I don't know, besides the scar and the telepathic connection to me."

"Wait," Glitch blurted. "You guys can third wheel me even more?"

"Focus," Nate said, kicking him under the table.

"Fine. I think this is the last big one. You said the man was already dead when you came to. What about the woman?"

My heart stopped and I felt an unfamiliar chill run down my spine. "What woman?"

Glitch frowned and pulled out his phone, oblivious to my panic. "There were two bodies found the next day."

Nate reached over and moved the coffee cup away from my shaking hands, sliding his fingers through mine. "C, it's okay. We'll figure this out."

"Nate, it's bad enough that I can't remember anything, but now there are *two* people dead." I lowered my voice, remembering I was in a public place talking about how I might have killed two people. "What the hell was I involved in?" The longer I went without memories, the worse things seemed to get.

"Glitch," Nate said, breaking eye contact with me to look at Glitch. "Please tell me you found something."

The color in Glitch's face had drained as he passed the phone to Nate who had the same reaction. They glanced at each other hesitantly before looking at me.

"What?" I asked, reaching across the table to grab the phone.

A woman's face looked back at me, her kind, green eyes sparkling in the photo. Police had identified the other body as Elizabeth Shorter, concluding that she died in self-defense of another man who was also found dead from injuries. I skimmed the details before returning to the photo of Elizabeth.

"Do you... recognize her?" Nate asked, his voice soft.

I opened my mouth briefly before closing it. I couldn't find the right words, because though Elizabeth Shorter was older, she looked very similar to... me.

"I didn't even recognize myself that night," I whispered. "I don't know if this feeling is because she looks like she could be my mom or because I actually recognize her."

I could feel how distant my voice was as I ran through the possibilities of that night. My mother and this man died because of me.

No. No matter who I used to be, I could never kill my own mother. That wasn't possible. I was running away, and the man had to be chasing me. Somehow my mom got caught in his path, and my instinct was to retaliate. Maybe some part of that nightmare was true. He was going to use his power on me too, but I fought back.

Glitch's voice broke me out of a trance. "Says here that Elizabeth was married and had a daughter. Do you want me to look into it?"

"Yeah." It was a half-hearted answer, but I needed to know. Was this my family? Would they have answers to who I was? Why weren't they looking for me? I shifted my hands in Nate's, looking to him. "Something doesn't feel right about this. I had to have run away for a reason, right? That's why I have this cover for myself. I used the Blue Star to protect myself against that man, even though previous me kept saying she wanted to fight against those voices. Nate," I sighed. "I don't know if I can trust who I used to be. I don't know if I can trust my dad, or if he even is my dad. What if I was running away from that and I'm walking into something far worse than this?"

"Look, let's just find out what we can and go from there. If you want, I'll go with you and we can just gather information."

"Found him," Glitch said as he scribbled the address on a napkin. "Richard Shorter. Lives about thirty minutes north of here."

Nate raised his eyebrow as he snagged the napkin. "How the hell did you find that so quickly?"

Glitch leaned back and shrugged. "The less you know, the better."

25

Nate

I parked the car a few houses down from the Shorter's, eyeing Clara as she wrung her hands together. She hadn't said a single word the entire drive, but I caught a few glimpses of her hesitant thoughts. I couldn't imagine going through what she felt, especially because she was right that nothing felt right, but if there was even the slightest chance she could piece together her memories, she was going to try.

She finally reached over and slid her hand in mine, still staring at the house. "It looks so normal."

"I kind of expected it to be more threatening," I replied. The house looked like a perfect, white-picket fence home you saw in a magazine. Based on what little we knew about her past, normal wasn't exactly calming. "Do you recognize anything? Could this be The Complex?"

Clara frowned. "No, but I didn't expect to." She shook her head. "This whole thing feels wrong. What if Richard isn't actually my dad? Or what if he is and he was the one I ran away from? What if-"

"If something happened to you, maybe he has answers," I interrupted. "The Complex people might be able to fill in the details. For all we know, they were helping you when the Blue Star convinced you otherwise. The voices lied to you when we put it together, so how do we know they weren't lying to get you to run away?"

She pinched her lips and looked at me. "That's a fair point, but just in case, don't let them know you have powers, okay? I don't think they know people can have powers without their Trials. It's just to keep us safe, okay?"

I nodded. "Okay, you ready?"

"Not really, but I guess we should do this."

The front gate was propped open and we walked through, carefully observing our surroundings in case we needed to make a run. The yard was perfectly manicured, the grass a perfect shade of green and free of leaves, despite the large tree to our left that was almost bare. I was halfway through planning an escape route when the front door opened.

"Finn? Is that you?"

A guy, maybe early twenties, flung the door open, pausing at the top of the porch only briefly before running toward Clara. She took a step back, but not enough before he picked her up and swung her around in a hug. As he set her down, he pressed his lips into hers in a disgustingly passionate kiss.

Clara shoved him away from her and wiped her face. "What the hell?" she shouted, adjusting my old sweatshirt back over her arms.

Yeah, I agree. What the hell?

I think I actually growled under my breath but no one heard it. The guy stepped back as I realized how much bigger he was standing straight. Broad shouldered and at least three inches taller than me. His face shifted from relief to concern.

"You don't recognize me?" he asked.

"No. Who are you?" Clara asked, taking a step back. I slid my shoulder in front of her protectively, but the guy didn't seem to notice, his eyes still locked on Clara.

"It's going to be okay, Finn. We can help you," he said.

"Help her with what?" I asked. Now he acknowledged me, looking me up and down with a dismissive stare.

"Hey," Clara snapped, getting the guy's attention as she pushed against my arm. "Why do you keep calling me Finn?"

He didn't have time to answer before a middle-aged man stepped out of the doorway.

"Aidan, is that her? Is Finnley home?" Aidan stepped to the side so the man could see us. He took a few steps toward us but stopped when he saw us retreat slightly. "Oh, Finn. We were so worried about you."

Aidan pushed his shoulders back. "She doesn't remember us, Richard."

Something about his tone felt... off. Like he was reporting?

Richard's eye twitched as he frowned. "She's had an episode, just as we feared when she ran away. Please, both of you, come in. We will explain everything."

I hesitated but Clara walked right past me, following Richard and Aidan up the steps. I hurried to catch up.

C, what are you doing? We don't know them.

But they know me. They have answers.

Despite everything in my body telling me to turn around, we followed them inside to a pristine living room, sitting on the couch as the two of them sat in the chairs opposite of us. Aidan kept his eyes locked on Clara, which only made me more antsy, but I did my best to keep a level head. Clara wanted answers, and if they were going to give them, I wasn't going to stand in the way.

Richard cleared his throat. "I'm sorry, young man. I didn't get your name."

"Nate, sir."

"Nate, I'm so thankful you've brought Finnley home. I'm not sure how you found her after all these months."

"I don't understand," I replied.

"Finnley has a habit of running off when she has an episode."

"Who is Finnley?" Clara asked, her mind spinning so quickly that her thoughts were making me sick.

"That's your name, sweetheart. This is your house," Richard replied, almost mechanically. "It's okay. You'll reorient yourself soon enough."

'F', Clara whispered in her thoughts.

I shook my head and turned back to Richard. "What do you mean by 'episode'?"

He took a breath and pressed his palms together. "Finnley has a brain tumor. Recently, her mood changes and hallucinations have gotten worse, and there seems to be more frequent and bigger memory losses affecting her. When she's disoriented, she often runs away in her confusion. What is it she believes again?"

Aidan didn't break his gaze away from Clara. "She has a recurring hallucination about a place called The Complex. Finn believes she has powers, but really she just hears voices. A symptom of the tumor and medications, unfortunately."

Aidan's look was starting to feel less like a loving stare and more like... lust? Maybe it was my anger and confusion about the situation, but the air around us was starting to feel thick. None of it made any sense. She was actually reading my mind and had telekinetic abilities. She had powers and a scar to prove it, not including our very clear telepathic connection. Were these men really that ignorant? Did she actually have a brain tumor that caused her memory loss? Or were they lying?

Clara stared blankly ahead, seemingly lost in thoughts I couldn't hear. I turned back to Richard. "We saw on the news about Elizabeth. That was her mother?"

Richard frowned. "Yes. Ellie went to find Finnley, but it seems there was a man who had the same idea. I don't know what happened, but if Finnley is having an episode and you don't approach her the right way, her outbursts can get violent."

There was the hole in Richard's story. Clara had talked about the Blue Star causing headache outbursts like the library and the note in her desk. These people were lying.

C, we need to get out of here.

That's not my name. They have the answers. I must have imagined the whole thing.

I tried to hide my surprise, not expecting her to fall for that lie as easily as she was. I needed to buy time to get her out of here, but how?

"So, Richard, I gather you are her dad," I said, glancing over to Aidan. "And you are?"

"Her boyfriend, at least when she's acting like herself," he replied, his eyes still trained on Clara. The same thick air settled around us again, but it wasn't just a feeling. I could see it, and I could see it pushing out from around his body. He had powers, and whatever they were, it wasn't working on me.

Richard stood up and pulled my attention away. "Nate, I appreciate you bringing her back to us. I'm sure you have somewhere to be now, and we don't want to keep you any longer."

I kept myself planted in my seat, trying to find a way to delay or get us out of this, but all I could think of were stupid questions.

"Actually, if you don't mind, I have a question. Cl—Finnley was so convinced that her powers were real. After what I've seen, are you sure they aren't?"

"Real?" Richard scoffed, hiding a smile as he shook his head. "She hallucinates and loses her memory. There is a simple explanation. Now, if I can show you out, it seems Finnley is getting tired and we need to get her back on her medication."

He remained standing, waiting impatiently for me to get up, but I wouldn't move. I couldn't leave Clara here with them, not when it was clear that the muggy air was part of a trick Aidan was using to keep her disoriented.

C, I need you to do something. We're out of time.

Don't you see? I made it up. The voices lie.

I couldn't keep my promise to her because there was no other way to get her out the door. I grabbed Clara's hand and sank into a shadow, watching the shock and anger on Richard and Aidan's faces as I slid out of the house. I moved across the street, pushing Clara out of the shadow and onto the hood of the car. I popped out and slammed into the car with my shoulder before rolling off to the side. I forced myself off the ground, ignoring the pain in my arm as Clara remained limp on the hood. Scooping her into my arms, I shoved her through the driver's door before jumping in after her.

Aidan and Richard ran out into the front yard, glaring at us as I drove away as fast as the car would go.

26

Clara

"Nate!"

I launched myself forward, regretting it immediately as my head split with pain. I needed to throw up, but the room was spinning so fast I had no idea where to go. I rolled off whatever soft surface I was on and landed on something hard.

"Hey, slow down."

It was Nate's voice, but there were a million echoes ringing through my head, banging against my already painful headache. He tried to get me to stand but my legs crumpled and I dropped back down to the floor. As I started to cry from the pain, Nate gathered me in his arms.

"Nate, my head. Make it stop," I said, clutching at his shirt as he lifted me up. I'm not sure where we were going, but the movement made me sick. I shoved my head into his chest as hard as I could, hoping the pressure would help. I couldn't have another explosion like the library. Not when Nate was here.

He set me down on a cold surface, and without letting me go, I felt the cold water from the shower pour over us. Nate sat still as he held me, letting the water roll over us and soak our clothes.

The pain started to die down. I'm not sure how long it took, but I slowly released the death grip I had on Nate's shirt. His heartbeat pounded through his chest and against my cheek until I could focus again. I kept my eyes closed, afraid to open them and see spots or lose control.

"I'm so sorry, Nate," I whispered.

"Why are you sorry?" he asked, his voice quiet and gentle as I focused on his heartbeat slowing down.

"I don't know what happened. Everything they said was a lie, but for some reason, I believed them. How is that possible?"

Nate lifted his hand up and held my face against his chest. "Whatever Aidan did was making you believe them. I don't know what power that was, but I could see it in the air."

"But it didn't affect you?"

"No... I don't know why, but it didn't," he sighed. "I'm sorry. I had to get you out of there."

"I know," I replied. I reached back and turned off the water but still sat there, pressed into Nate's chest as I got the courage to open my eyes. I focused on the shower curtain, confused as to how we could be in my bathroom. As I reached out to touch it, I saw three of my hand so I pulled it back.

"You know," Nate said, taking his hand off my face as he wrapped it through my fingers. "Your house doesn't have doorknobs."

I tried to hide my smile. "Yeah. How did you get in?"

"The door opened for me. I've seen enough crazy in the last two days that it didn't even seem weird."

"I think House is magic," I replied, squeezing Nate's hand. "I'm glad he likes you."

"Well, I won't say that exactly. I did carry you home unconscious. That's probably why I keep walking into invisible walls."

I started to push myself up slowly, bracing against Nate to stand up. He grunted uncomfortably as I pulled my hand back, noticing the red blood around his right shoulder.

"Oh my god, what happened?"

Nate tried to shake it off. "I'm fine. I just got it when I threw us out of the shadows back there. It's not a big deal."

"Yes it is. Come on, I think I can stand. I'll help get it wrapped."

Nate helped me up and I pulled out the first aid kit under the sink. I didn't care that our clothes were dripping water everywhere, or that my shoes squished with each step across the floor as I sat Nate down in my desk chair. I looked over to the bed and saw the stack of dry clothes House had set out for him.

Nate struggled to peel the shirt away from his gash but eventually got it off as red blood started rolling down his arm. After dealing with my bloody arm twice, it was strange to see a normal colored wound. I dried his shoulder and wrapped it as best I could. The only other practice I had was on my own arm, and I was terrible at that too.

He pulled me into his lap, kissing along my neck as his arms wrapped around my waist.

I wiggled against him, feeling the stick of our clothes. "Do you need help changing?"

"Are you offering?" he asked, his breath tickling my skin.

I couldn't bring myself to roll my eyes so I just stood up, bracing against the desk as he tried to balance me. The dull echo of my headache made everything but him blurry, but I could see how calm he looked. It was like we hadn't just run away from two people who were manipulating me and like I hadn't almost torn my room to shreds in an outburst.

"Don't you have to get home to your dad?"

He frowned. "I don't really think you should be by yourself right now."

I shook my head. "He already doesn't like me after our breakup, and now after this morning when he caught us together, I can't stay on his bad side. I'll be fine."

"I don't think you are, but you do have a point about my dad. I can't break curfew if I want to see the light of day again."

He stood up and walked over to the pile of clean clothes, laughing as he motioned for me to turn around after he caught me staring.

I made my way to the closet, balancing carefully. Whatever Aidan had done to my head was wearing off, but I still didn't feel great. I threw my clothes on the ground in a sopping mess and changed into a big shirt, sweats, and socks. As I wrung my hair on the floor, House creaked in disapproval.

"Sorry," I whispered.

I peeled the bandage off my arm, desperate to give it some air. It felt weird to wear a shirt without sleeves, even when I was home alone, but now Nate knew everything. After all we had gone through since the Blue Star, even since the volleyball game, we kept finding a way to be with each other.

Yikes, the volleyball game. All of those terrible emotions came back, but I shoved them down when I thought about that kiss. The last time we had kissed... before everything turned to shit.

I walked out as Nate was struggling to lift his arm through the sleeve of his shirt.

"Really?" I laughed. "There's an easier way to do that."

He sat, annoyed, as I pulled the shirt off and threaded it through his arms first so he wouldn't have to lift them. He held onto my hips, not letting go even after I finished dressing him.

"Are you sure you're okay?" he asked.

I placed my hand on his cheek, momentarily distracting myself as I saw the scar that I so willingly left out in the open. Nate didn't seem to mind as he pulled it away from his cheek and traced his fingers around the cut.

I sighed. "I don't think I am okay. I don't know what my dad and Aidan were up to, but now I know that I was running away from them. And probably that guy in the clearing too. I think what bothers me the most is that I don't know what side my mom was on. Was she trying to help me or catch me?"

Nate stood up quickly, letting my hand drop as he reached around my neck. He leaned down and kissed me, pulling me tighter against his body. My questions and worries melted as I relaxed into him. There were things I might never learn, but being here in this moment reminded me that I had something good again.

He pulled back, a frown on his face.

My eyes widened. "Did I do something wrong? What is it?"

"So, that guy said he was your boyfriend..."

I laughed and kissed him again, just as a text alert went off on his phone. One glance and I could see his dad was asking when he'd be home.

"You don't have to worry, Nate. Everything he said was a lie. Even if I can't remember who he was, he's not my type."

"Your type isn't tall, muscular guys who look like they are Olympic athletes?" he asked.

"Nate, you're my type. Do *you* have a type I should look out for?"

He laughed and kissed my forehead. "You've read my mind before and you know damn well what Glitch always thinks when he sees us."

27

Nate

Clara spent the weekend cleaning up the library she had torn to shreds on Thursday night. It was hard not to spend time with her after a month apart, but my dad needed help around the house as he moved back in permanently. Part of me was glad someone would be here to stay, but it was going to suck having to follow all his rules. Even harder would be hiding my powers, the new mark on my palm, and everything that was happening to Clara. My shoulder being cut up didn't help the situation either, especially as the bruise darkened around my skin.

Sunday night couldn't come fast enough. I was actually looking forward to going back to school so it wouldn't feel like a lockdown at the house. Since Friday morning, Dad hadn't asked about Clara or even referenced her, but I knew it was going to happen eventually. Maybe he was just trying to cool off after finding us sleeping together.

He set the last two plates of leftover Thanksgiving food at the table and leaned back in his chair. "So, you and this Clara girl. You never told me how you guys worked it all out."

"We talked through some stuff. I already told you nothing happened after that. We just fell asleep," I replied, feeling the embarrassment creeping up again.

He smiled. "I'm glad you both figured it out. I'd like to meet her again under different circumstances. So, tell me a little bit more. What do you like about her?"

"A lot more than her height and purple hair." I shoved a piece of turkey in my mouth, surprised I had said that to my dad.

He didn't seem to mind. "It just surprised me, that's all. I wasn't prepared to find out my son finally had a girlfriend, or that you had gotten back together so quickly, especially after seeing you sulking around for a month.

"Wow, rude that me having a girlfriend is surprising to you," I grumbled. "And if you must know, we share a lot in common. Same taste in movies, music, and our mutual tolerance of Glitch."

He chuckled. "That's a rare find indeed. But you've never mentioned her before this year. Where did all this come from?"

"We met the first day of school. She's a new student," I said. I regretted my natural reaction to shrug, feeling the pain shoot down my arm.

He leaned forward and set his fork down, looking suspicious, but not because of my arm. "Interesting. Transfer student?"

"Home-schooled. Why does that matter?" I asked, making a mental note to remember these answers so we could keep our story straight in the future.

"Just curious about her. I don't want you getting sucked in with the wrong crowd," Dad replied, studying me for a few extra seconds.

I instinctively gripped my right hand tighter, hoping to continue hiding the blue scar on my palm. "If anything, Glitch and I are the wrong crowd for her. Clara could have easily made the volleyball team and joined the popular crowd."

I should have seen it coming sooner and prepared for the motion. Dad finished his water and stood up to refill it, pressing his hand into my cut shoulder as he walked by. I winced and let out a gasp, and this time, he noticed.

"What's wrong with your shoulder?"

"Just... sore from Friday. The three of us went out to throw a ball around," I said. Shit, that was a nice save.

Well, it would have been if Dad hadn't pulled the sleeve of my shirt up immediately and saw the bloodied bandage on my arm. He gripped my shirt tighter as I tried to wiggle away.

"Want to try again?" he asked, his tone suddenly angry.

"Dad, it's fine."

"Did that girl get you in some sort of trouble? Girls like that always mix with the wrong crowd," he growled, picking off the bandage as he inspected the cut.

I pulled away. "Girls like that? Seriously? This has nothing to do with Clara," I snapped. Actually, it had everything to do with her. I wasn't blaming her, but I also wasn't going to tell my dad the truth.

"Look," he said, shaking his head. "I get you haven't had a

girlfriend before, and this is probably just some phase, but first she breaks your heart and now this?"

I could see him start to puff his chest which only made me more upset. It was hard not telling him what was actually happening between Clara and I. He wouldn't understand our powers, and he definitely wouldn't understand our connection.

"Dad, she is not some phase. Can you please just let this go? It's not a big deal."

"If you tell me the truth about what happened, I *might* consider letting it go. Might."

As he folded his arms, I spit out the first thing that came to mind. "Some guys tried to pick a fight using Clara, and I fought back, but not before they got a cheap shot in."

There, that was sort of truthful. Richard and Aidan did use Clara, but the cheap shot was my own fault because I couldn't stick my landing.

My dad relaxed, but that wasn't comforting. I could see the disappointment in his eyes. "Look, I can't control who you hang out with or who you date. I guess I need a better chance to know this girl, but I hope you can make better decisions about this before it gets worse."

I didn't have anything more to say, and I had lost my appetite, so I turned around and headed up to my room.

After Dad had gone to sleep, I left a note on the table saying I had left early for school. That was at least something I could get away with unless he woke up to check on me in the middle of the night. It's not like I'd make much noise sneaking out. I grabbed my backpack and used the shadows to get to Clara's house. She had clearly fallen asleep waiting for me so I kissed her cheek and crawled over to the other side of the bed.

Your dad is going to kill you. Clara groaned and rolled over to face me, struggling to keep her eyes open.

"Worth it to see you," I replied, brushing the hair out of her face. "How was the library?"

"Messy. How was your dad?"

"Messy."

She smiled and rolled back over, scooting back into me so I could hold her. I played with her hands until her breathing got heavy as she fell asleep again. It wasn't long after that when I was back in the same nightmare. It was terrible watching Clara die from that mysterious wound in her stomach. Even if I caught her in the dream, she would still collapse; she would still die saying the same words.

"You're too late."

I woke up to the sound of rain against the window and an empty bed. I pushed up to see Clara sitting on her desk chair, her feet propped up on the windowsill. She had thrown on sweats over her pajamas and her hair was still in a tangled, beautiful mess. She swirled her fingers in the air as the rain danced in patterns along the window, obeying her command.

"C?"

She didn't respond but I noticed her headphones in so I got out of bed, stretching my shoulder as I walked over to her. I wrapped my arms around her from behind, resting my chin on her shoulder.

Clara leaned into me and placed her hand over mine. "Sorry. I didn't mean to wake you."

"You didn't. What are you thinking about?"

She pulled out one of her earbuds and handed it to me.

Grey Morning. FOXTRAX.

I frowned. "Are you making it rain?"

"No, I wish," she replied, her voice distant as she continued staring out the window. "Otherwise I'd make it rain all the time. This is my favorite weather."

"C, you couldn't have known about your dad, you know that right?"

"But I should have pieced it together. I should have trusted the previous version of myself. Every time I think I can get answers, shit happens." Clara flicked her fingers and the raindrops turned to ice.

I turned her shoulders to face me. "You can't help that your dad's a psycho, but I'm here now, so let me help you."

I changed the song on her iPod.

Take on the World. You Me At Six.

The house creaked around us as my eyes widened. Clara burst into laughter.

"I think House likes you now." She slid off the desk and made her way to the closet to change.

House? Like, it had a personality? I shook my head and changed into the clothes I had packed, prepared to make breakfast. I rolled my eyes as I made it to the kitchen. Yeah, I should have seen that coming. There was already a spread of food out, with extra sweets and a massive cup of coffee in front of Clara's space.

She came down the hall wearing my old sweatshirt and black jeans, her violet hair in a tangled bun on top of her head. Clearly in a better mood, she skipped up to the table and grabbed the sugar jar, turning the container over and dumping it into her coffee.

"What?" she asked as she leaned over the table for a donut. "I can feel you staring."

"Sometimes I can't believe I'm this lucky to have you in my life," I replied.

She sat down and threw her feet up on my lap. "You're just lucky I didn't run away after you shoved me into your closet."

"You can't hold that against me. I panicked."

"No, I'm absolutely holding that against you. Plus, you said that wouldn't happen again, yet here we are," she replied, sticking her tongue out.

I pushed her legs off my lap, holding in a laugh. "What can I say? You're just a phase I have to go through, according to my dad."

Clara smiled, reaching forward as she grabbed the leg of my chair and pulled me closer. How the hell was she so strong? She leaned toward me and kissed me hard, but pulled away quickly. "Wait, a phase?"

I laughed and kissed her again. "He'll come around. I just didn't have a good enough story for my shoulder."

"So he totally hates me, first for sleeping with you, and now for getting you hurt."

Glitch interrupted us as he honked from the front. We grabbed our bags and ran out in the rain, hopping in the back seat together.

"You both thought it was a good idea to sleep together after the last time?" he asked, watching us in the mirror.

I rolled my eyes. "We aren't sleeping together, dude."

"Yeah, sure you aren't." He and Clara exchanged a look after seeing my cheeks flush, laughing. Why was this stuff always funny?

"It's funny because you're nervous about it," she said, poking my side.

"Stop listening to my thoughts. Can we please change the subject?"

"Sure," Glitch said, pulling into a parking spot at school. "Let's talk about all the subjects we have midterms on next week."

"Huh, I kind of forgot we do schoolwork," Clara said, scrunching her nose.

"Just normal teenage stuff going on here," Glitch replied. "Powers, homework, Nate's overbearing dad, Clara's evil dad, midterms…"

28

Clara

Nate didn't risk getting caught sneaking out the rest of the week. We spent the afternoons studying for midterms and he went home before curfew. I still couldn't sleep much, and it was worse to wake up to those nightmares alone, even though I was dying in the dream. After almost four months of the same scene playing over, I thought I'd be used to it now, but this week it felt worse. Maybe it was the headache that came back in full force.

The voices were almost always present, but they picked my most vulnerable moments to get worse. Thursday was one of those days. I woke up already dizzy and nauseous, barely able to stand. After knocking everything off my nightstand, I managed to text someone that I had a headache and wouldn't go to school. I didn't know if it was Glitch or Nate, but they were the only two contacts in my phone. Actually, I didn't even know if I had sent something coherent since I just poked at the keyboard using muscle memory.

I could feel the pressure in my head building as the voices hissed and scratched at my skull. Having another outburst right now was not ideal, but I could feel it coming. Stumbling into the hall, I pushed through the door into the training room. If the outburst was inevitable, at least this room would require the least amount of cleanup.

I curled into the corner and pulled my knees into my chest, but something cold pinched my leg. I pulled the Blue Star marble out of my pocket, watching the blue lights swirl violently under the surface. If I had just woken up, how did it get into my pocket? The last time I had this thing, I had almost lost myself to its power, and now Nate wasn't here to pull me out. I chucked it to the other side of the room and buried my head into my hands. No matter how hard I pressed my palms into my forehead, the pressure wouldn't release.

There was only one way it had released before.

I screamed and pushed the voices out with all of my power. The wave of energy expanded out of me and sent everything in the room flying away from me. The weights and equipment crashed and tumbled across the floor, their sounds barely audible over the ringing in my ears. I felt the blood running down my arm again, but also out of my nose. I didn't bother trying to contain it because I didn't have the energy. I just let every inch of my body release the pressure until I couldn't focus any longer, numb to the pain of everything except what was left in my head.

The room slowly stopped spinning and the headache returned to the constant dull pain in the back of my neck. I didn't know how long I sat in the corner before I was finally able to push off the ground. Blue blood stained my old shirt and sweats I had slept in, but I didn't care. It felt like I was walking around in a fog, bumping into the walls and trying to ignore the banging sound in my head.

No, that wasn't in my head. Someone was banging on the front door. I wobbled closer and heard Nate's voice through the door.

"Clara! House won't let me in through a shadow. What's going on?"

Shit. I couldn't let him see me like this.

House tried to open the door but I held the lock with every ounce of power I had left in my body.

"Nate, I'm not going to school. Just come back later, please," I begged, pressing my head against the wall.

He stopped pounding as House creaked underneath me. I could tell he wasn't happy about keeping Nate out, but I held firm. No one should get in my way when I felt like this; I was a danger. But I also couldn't let him see what had happened to me.

"Clara, it's Saturday. I've been trying to get in to check on you for two days," he said, his voice more gentle this time. "Please, unlock the door."

My heart dropped and I lost focus. Two days?

House took advantage of my distraction and opened the door. Nate's face turned from concern to horror as he looked at me.

"C, holy shit," he said, stepping through the door as he responded to my thoughts. "You didn't know you were locked in here for two days? Why didn't you let me in?"

I let him guide me down the hall, even though his revelation had cleared the fog in my mind. "I didn't know what I was doing. I couldn't control it. I just… I didn't want to hurt you," I replied, avoiding his gaze.

"This is much scarier. Twice now? And getting worse?"

I left him in my room and turned on the shower, ignoring him. I couldn't deal with the truth. I grabbed a change of clothes from the closet and walked back toward the bathroom. Nate grabbed my hand before I could get inside.

"Clara, answer me."

"Yes, it's getting worse, but I can't do anything about it," I snapped. "Can I please shower?"

I didn't mean to be rude but I could feel the wave of nausea building and I didn't want him to know. He sighed and let go of my hand, not saying anything more. Careful not to turn around too quickly, I walked into the bathroom and leaned against the door to close it.

God, I looked terrible. Blue blood was smeared from my nose over my lips, like I had been attacked by a blue paint ball gun. My hair was in the same top knot I had slept in two days ago, matted with the blood from my hand where I had gripped tightly to fight the pain. No wonder Nate was so worried about me.

The cold water ran blue again, something that no longer freaked me out. At least I could concentrate again. I had spent two days with that headache and didn't even know about it. Nate was right; it was getting worse. The pain, the voices, the damage… I didn't want to think about what would have happened if Nate got caught in that path.

I could feel the remnants of my headache pain and stiffness radiating through my body as I changed clothes. I shoved my old clothes in a corner of the bathroom, ready to face Nate's disappointment in me.

He was sitting on the bed, waiting with the first aid kit, but he avoided my gaze. Somehow he was learning to block his thoughts from me so I just stood in the doorway waiting for him to say something.

He sighed. "I saw the training room."

"Nate, I—"

"I get it."

I shook my head. "I locked you out because you could have gotten hurt. I didn't even realize what I was doing, or that I had been in here for two days."

"C, I heard the voices. I get it," he said, lowering his head.

"What?" I felt my heart sink again as I slid forward and sat on the bed next to him. He picked up my left hand, careful not to touch the cut, and turned over his right palm to show me his scar.

"I could hear them because of this. It was nowhere near what you felt, but I could hear them shouting at you. To me, it was like a whisper in the back of my head. That's why I came over. When House was locked, I didn't know what to do. You scared me."

"But now you see what these headaches do to me; the destruction I'm capable of. Why are you still here? You should be terrified of me," I replied, pulling my hand away.

"Clara, I'm not scared *of* you. I'm scared of what you're doing alone. Don't you dare think that we shouldn't be together because of this," Nate said. He took my hand back in his and started wrapping my arm.

I shook my head. "I have to stay alone, otherwise I could hurt you. Do you have any idea what that would do to me?"

"Do you have any idea what that would do to me?" he snapped, securing the tape around my arm. His shoulders sank. "C, I'd rather be by your side through this than see you fight it alone."

There was no point in arguing with him. I had shut him out so many times before and look where that got me. Maybe he was right, and for the first time, I had someone on my side.

"So, now what?" I asked. "I don't really want to sit around waiting for my next headache."

Nate stood up and plugged his phone into the speaker before tugging me off the bed. "First, you dance with me. You just spent two days locked up."

Hopeful Romantic. This Century.

He pulled me closer as I rested my head on his shoulder.

"Third," he whispered, "you come to dinner tonight. My dad insists."

His voice caught, like he was nervous. I glanced up. "You skipped number two."

"Agree to number three before I tell you."

I scrunched my nose. "Fine. I agree to dinner."

Nate took a deep breath, ready to say something, but paused. I raised my eyebrow, waiting for him to continue.

He sighed. "Second, I tell you something I've been trying to say for a week now. C, it kills me when you shut me out because… I love you."

The music stopped and I realized it was because I stopped. I could feel Nate squirming in my arms as I stood in silence. It was unintentional, though. He really had taken my breath away.

I resorted to the only other thing that crossed my mind. I pulled in and kissed him, hard. There was at least one good thing in my life, even if the rest of it was crashing down around me. I lifted away from Nate's face, even though he resisted, and placed my hands around his neck as his remained locked around my waist.

"My fellow insomniac, I love you too," I laughed, pulling him onto the bed with me.

29

Nate

Clara picked up my hand and traced the scar on my palm as I rested my cheek on top of her head. Her hair was drying and sticking out in a tangled mess, but I didn't care. She was perfectly her, the girl I loved, and now I knew she felt the same way.

"We really should try to find out more information about the Blue Star," she said, sitting up as she adjusted her shirt and looked at me. Wait, not her shirt, my shirt. How did she always look so much better in my clothes than I did?

"You just went through a crazy two-day headache explosion. Can't you take a night off? Pretend to be normal for one night," I said, sliding my fingers across her thigh.

"The two day explosion is the reason I shouldn't take a night off. What if this happens again in a few days? What if it happens again tonight?"

"Then I'll be there to help you. Plus, you already agreed." I picked up the hem of my shirt hanging off her shoulder and poked at the tattoo on her side. I remembered it from the book she threw in her bag on our first day of school. "Purple hair, destructive, and tattoos. Maybe you are trouble."

I sat up and swung her around so she was in my lap. I kissed her neck as she giggled.

"Seriously," she said, pulling away. "If I could just figure out how to use my powers to stop these headaches…"

With perfect timing, my phone buzzed. I reached over to see the text from my dad. "Dinner in an hour." I set it back on the nightstand and turned to see Clara holding in a laugh. "Now what?"

"Do you think he's gonna know you were actually my overnight guest this time?"

She couldn't hold it in any longer and burst out laughing as my cheeks flushed. "Why is this always so funny? Also, it's the middle of the day. Also, also, please never use the phrase 'overnight guest' ever again."

Clara leaned forward and kissed me through her laughter. "Nope, that's the only phrase I'm using from now on." She rolled off the bed to change. "What do I need to be prepared for tonight?"

"Maybe talk about college? Dad kept telling me I would find a new relationship once I got there." I had one leg through my pants when my shirt hit me in the face. Clara leaned out of the closet, her nose scrunched in a frown. "Sorry, it was right after we broke up."

"Why do I have to go to college? Technically, I don't exist," she shouted from the back.

"At least pretend you have a plan to go," I replied.

I finished dressing and watched Clara pick through the knots in her hair. She had my old sweatshirt on again, her key necklace swaying with each movement she made. Eventually, she gave up on the last knot and walked out.

"Okay, one night of normal. Then library tomorrow, and we're hiring Glitch to help," she said, folding her arms.

"You know he's going to be paranoid about midterms next week. He's not going to be much help."

Oh, crap. Glitch, the nosiest person about our relationship, was definitely going to find out about this. He could always see right through me.

"Yeah, you get to handle that one," Clara laughed at my thoughts, sticking her hand out to me. "Come on. Your dad already hates me so let's not be late."

Thankfully I had driven the car so we made it back home in plenty of time. As we stood on the porch, Clara hesitated.

The last time I was here was after my outburst.

I stuck my fingers through hers. "C, it's okay. Normal relationship, normal life. I'm here now."

She sighed. "Nate, we are anything but normal." She gave me a kiss on the cheek before we walked through the door.

Dad was in the kitchen but heard us come in. He poked his head around the corner. "Oh, good. Glad to see you're feeling better, Clara."

I told him you had a headache. At least I didn't lie. I squeezed her hand.

"Yes, sir," she replied with a half smile. "They get pretty bad."

We walked into the dining room to see a plate of lasagna and bread already set out. My dad was setting down the last glass of water at the table and motioned for us to sit.

"You should get those checked out," he said, watching Clara as she fumbled to use her fork with her right hand. Crap, I forgot that she was left handed but had a bandage over her palm. That wouldn't help our case with my dad's suspicions about my injured shoulder. Plus, how could we explain the blue blood?

"Sorry, get what checked out?" she asked, finally settling on a grip that didn't look terribly awkward.

"Your headaches. Do they run in your family?" he asked, watching how clumsy she looked trying to pick at her food.

"Oh, I don't think so. Just me." Clara dropped her fork and reached for her water instead.

Another uncomfortable silence fell.

"Well," Dad said finally. "I'm sure you don't want to talk about headaches all evening."

If anyone couldn't stand uncomfortable settings more than me, it was my dad. At least I knew where I got that trait from.

The rest of the dinner went off without a hitch. Dad asked all about school and college and our shared interests. Luckily, Clara had an answer for everything without hesitation. Though she wasn't completely confident on calculus, she was pretty sure she could ace the rest of her tests. We rambled on about movies and music, which I think surprised my dad to hear she was a fan of Star Wars. As for college, she wasn't sure what she wanted to study just yet but figured there was still time. I think by the end of dinner, he was finally satisfied with the girl I was dating.

We cleaned up the dishes and I got the keys ready to drive Clara home. My dad stopped us before we made it to the front.

"Clara, if your parents wouldn't mind, I have a work party next Friday evening that I'd like to invite you and Nathaniel to."

I could feel her grip tighten in mine. She was barely tolerant of making plans for the next few hours, let alone a week away. We didn't know if or when her headache would come back.

I was about to think of some excuse when she straightened up.

"I would love to, thank you. My uncle will be delighted to hear I'm getting out of the house more."

I tried to hide my surprise at her description of House.

"Oh," my dad stammered, fumbling over words. "I didn't realize—"

"Don't worry. I never really knew my parents," she replied with a shrug. Wow, she was handling this perfectly.

"Well, then, I'll extend another invite to you and your uncle to come over for Christmas. Nathaniel's mother will be in town and I'm sure she would love to meet you."

"That sounds wonderful. I'll check to see what we have planned."

I closed the door behind us and wrapped Clara in a hug. "Thank you for tonight. I know it's been a long day for you."

She squeezed back. "Things are a lot easier with you around."

30

Clara

I invited Nate and Glitch over after I woke up, just before noon on Sunday. Even though the plan was to study, I figured I could rope them into helping me through the library for at least an hour. We needed to find answers before I had another outburst.

"It's about damn time you two figured out you loved each other," Glitch blurted as House opened the door.

"Whatever, man," Nate said, rolling his eyes as he pushed him through the door.

"Admit it! I'm the reason you got back together after Nate was an idiot," he said, a smug look on his face.

I shook my head. "How did you even find out?"

"It's written all over Nate's face. He gets so nervous around you," Glitch laughed as he hugged me.

I spun him around and pushed him toward the library. "Go. Study and research time."

"Ugh, do I have to?" he asked, sagging his shoulders.

"Yes, we both do. I owe her," Nate said, shrugging. The bruise on his shoulder peeked out from under his sleeve as he pulled his jacket off. I grimaced, knowing I had somewhat been the cause of it and a lot of drama with his dad. He saw me staring and leaned over to kiss me.

"Gross, get a room," Glitch groaned without turning around. How did he always know what we were doing? I twitched my fingers and flicked him in the nose using my powers. "Ow!"

Nate laughed as we headed off after him. The library had been cleaned up for the most part, but there were still stacks of papers for the books I couldn't find the match to. I had used my powers to mold the railings back as close to their original shape as I could, but it wasn't pretty.

Glitch sat down at the desk and threw his backpack on top. He must have been serious about studying because it was actually full of books.

After an hour, it was clear Glitch was going to pass all of his exams with flying colors while Nate and I settled on being slightly above average. Glitch kept quizzing us while he fiddled with the desk drawer until he got so frustrated that he gave up on the questions and started yanking on the drawer.

"Do you think I haven't tried that before? It's not budging. Even my powers can't get it open." I put down my study guide and picked up a library book instead as Nate read over the note I had pulled out of the desk.

"I don't get it," Nate said. "Glitch and I never went through these Trials to get powers. We don't even know how we got them."

I shrugged. "I don't think our cases are normal by any means. Maybe we found objects that The Complex didn't know about?" I sighed and tossed the book to the side, leaning back on the floor to stare at the ceiling. I needed a break from working my brain.

Nate stuck his head in my vision. "Do you think you could have gotten in contact with the Blue Star before the Trials?"

I shrugged again. All of my answers at this point were 'I don't know'.

"Hey, where is that Blue Star anyway? I've never seen it," Glitch said, finally slumping into the chair as he accepted defeat by the inanimate desk drawer.

"I threw it somewhere in the training room," I replied, pushing off the ground to look for it. But something cold pinched my leg. "Shit."

As I pulled the Blue Star out of my pocket, Nate frowned. "Why do you have that with you?"

"I didn't," I said, staring at the little marble in my hand. "I thought I left it in the training room... but wait. Those days I spent in there, I found the Blue Star in my pocket, but it shouldn't have been in there. I had just woken up."

Glitch snagged it out of my hand as Nate shook his head. "Maybe we should keep a closer eye on that thing. The voices and headaches get stronger around it."

I sighed. I wasn't trying to keep this thing around, it just kept following me.

"Got it."

Nate and I snapped our heads to look at Glitch as he leaned back in the chair, a smug look on his face as the drawer opened.

"What?" we said at the same time.

Glitch looked at me like I was an idiot. "The Blue Star opened it. Did you really not try that before?"

"Not since it was whole," I said, running over. I shuffled through the notebooks and papers, handing an old book to Nate who was right behind me. "Maybe the old me used this for protection, so no one could figure out what I was researching. Start reading."

I sat down on the ground and leaned against the desk to start flipping through the notes. They were all in my handwriting, all signed 'F'. I wouldn't care if I never saw or heard that name again, except that it would probably come back with my memories. Either way, this was a step closer to finding out who the old me was.

"Check this out," Nate said. He slid the book across the floor to me. It was in a different language but I had translated things in the margin. In big block letters at the top, I had written 'Power Sources' and listed the translations of about thirty different names next to each line. All but three of the objects were crossed out. The Golden Arrow was near the middle of the list while The Ruby was third to last. The final object was the Blue Star.

"I think these power sources are ranked by how much energy they have. Why are some of them crossed out?" I asked, pointing to a few at the top.

Glitch read upside down. "Maybe they ran out of power."

I flipped through the next few pages to read about the sources but none of them were translated. I kept scanning until I came to the page with the Blue Star. My handwriting was all over the page, filling every white space there was.

But something didn't look right with the words. The page blurred out of focus, making it hard to understand what I had written. Oh, god, another headache. I squeezed my eyes shut and pressed my palms into my forehead, trying to concentrate. It wasn't going to be long before I needed to get out of here to protect Nate and Glitch.

"What the hell was wrong with you?" Nate asked as I felt his presence next to me.

"I don't know," I grumbled. It felt like the room was starting to spin. "I can't read it."

Glitch's voice pierced my ears. "No one can. These aren't real words. You wrote complete gibberish."

"Guys," I blurted, my stomach lurching. "Headache. Get out now."

I shoved Nate away from me and tried to hold onto my powers as long as I could. I could feel the floor start to tilt and I instinctively threw my hand to the ground to keep from rolling. Someone grabbed the book off my lap as I curled into a ball, trying to hold the pain and voices as they screamed and clawed inside my head. I couldn't scream back. I didn't know if Nate and Glitch were safe.

I heard the book slam shut, as loud as a gunshot, and the headache started to dull. The room slowly settled into stillness... no, my senses were just returning. I could hear and feel papers falling down around me as I opened my eyes.

Nate and Glitch weren't next to me anymore and the desk was missing. I slowly pushed myself into a sitting position to see the damage. Nate was clutching the book in his arms, sitting against a bookshelf to my left and surrounded by the books that had fallen when he hit the shelf. Glitch was on the opposite side of the room in the same situation. The desk wasn't as lucky. It was splintered and scattered around the staircase.

I threw my hand over my mouth to hide a sob. Nate and Glitch had just gotten caught in my fire and it was a miracle they hadn't ended up like the desk. I couldn't keep them safe from myself.

"That was not fun," Glitch said, trying to joke as he rubbed the back of his head. He collected a few floating papers as he stood.

"I... I'm so sorry," I whispered, pulling my knees up into my chest as I buried my face. Every part of my body was suddenly exhausted.

"C, are you okay?" Nate asked, his voice getting louder as he hurried toward me. He pulled me into his arms.

"I'm so sorry. I'm so sorry." It was all I could say as I let him lift me off the ground and carry me out of the library.

31

Nate

"She okay?" Glitch asked, sifting through the papers and trying to sort them as I walked back in.

I shoved my hands in my pockets. "Yeah, she's sleeping now."

Glitch watched me carefully, a concerned look on his face. "Did you hear the voices then?"

My shoulders slumped as I nodded. "Yeah, but they're just whispers to me. It's so much louder for her. She couldn't even hear us when we were trying to get her attention."

He frowned and handed me one of Clara's desk notes. "You should read this."

I overheard my dad talking to Aidan. I think Aidan has been using his powers on me to throw me off their trail. They are getting close to figuring out how to extract the energy from people and replenish the objects, or worse yet, take it for themselves. I suspect they are trying to keep me under Aidan's spell until I use the Blue Star. They want the power, but they can't get it without me.

I can't use the power source. They can't be trusted with that sort of energy, and if they can take it from me, I don't know what will be left of me. I fear it only ends badly.

I am stuck with two terrible choices. Let the Blue Star consume me and see if the legend of the Cold Soul is true, or be driven mad as the Blue Star continues to scream at me. Neither ends well. The voices hiss at me during the night and haunt me during the day, making it hard to concentrate on anything. I'm already going crazy with the voices, and it's getting harder to hold onto reality.

I have set up an escape if necessary, I just hope I make it to that day alive.
-F

"So this really was her escape," I said, reading over the note again.

"And her dad and Aidan really are dicks. They want to use her for her powers," Glitch added as he returned back to the notes.

"Did you find anything about the Cold Soul legend? What does that mean?"

No wonder she thought she was going crazy. The Blue Star was already cold and calling her with the horrible voices. The Cold Soul didn't sound any more pleasant.

"Not yet," Glitch groaned in frustration. "I really wish she had dated these notes." I picked up the book that Clara had reacted to and played with the cover. Glitch raised his eyebrow. "Are you sure you want to try that again?"

I shrugged. "She's in the other room. I'll just flip through and see if we missed anything."

"Wait until I brace myself. I'm already sore from that first trip across the room."

I fanned through the book quickly, stopping only at the pages that had been translated and completely avoiding the Blue Star page. Nothing. When I shut the book again, I noticed a gap near the front cover. I opened it and pulled out a folded sheet of notebook paper that had been stuffed into the crease.

"Glitch," I said, unfolding the sheet to see Clara's handwriting.

Whispers.

Screams.

Fear.

A soul.

Replaced by the Cold Soul.

Erased.

Consumed.

Existing within.

Waiting.

The Blue Star.

Called into Darkness.

Called into Cold.

Dividing.

"Oh, shit," Glitch said over my shoulder.

So this is what was happening to Clara. Every voice she heard was calling her for this reason. Her past was erased by the Blue Star, but it hadn't completely consumed her. I flipped my right palm over to look at the blue scar I had.

The Blue Star hadn't become the Cold Soul because it still had power inside it. Clara hadn't taken it all in, and now I had some of it. I walked over and picked up the marble among the splintered desk. Soft blue light swirled inside, still visible despite the blackness it swam in.

That blue light was what still called for her; the reason it kept finding its way into her pocket. It wasn't her fault. It wanted her to take in all of the power, but she was resisting and it wasn't happy about it. How much longer could she stay strong?

Before Glitch left, he reminded me to make sure we showed up for class so all of his quizzing and tutoring wouldn't go to waste. It also reminded me to text my dad that I would be staying at Glitch's place so we could study some more. Hopefully he wouldn't see through that.

I went back to Clara's room, surprised to see she wasn't in bed anymore. I heard the shower turn on and relaxed. At least she was feeling good enough to walk around.

I sat on the edge of her bed and flipped through her nightstand, pulling out a small sheet of paper from her copy of *The Magicians*. I pressed out the wrinkles and laughed.

Clara.
18 on August 18.
Sarcastic.
Senior, West Hills.
The Magicians.
Music.
Headaches.
Left-handed.
Mind reading, telekinesis.
Volleyball?
Nightmares.
Marble— Blue Star?

It was a list of all the things she was discovering about herself. I smiled and put it back in the book as I heard the shower turn off.

"C, do you want anything to eat?" I called into the bathroom.

She stuck her head out of the door, purple hair dripping everywhere. "Cereal."

"Done."

I went to the kitchen and sat next to a big bowl of chocolate cereal, setting her two notes off to the side. House creaked unpleasantly below me.

"She wrote the notes," I said, grimacing as I realized I was talking into empty space. "I think she needs to know." I heard Clara's door open, and when I turned back, the poem she had written about the Cold Soul was folded tightly on top of the other note. "Got it, just the first one."

I slid the poem into my pocket just before Clara turned the corner.

"Are you mad at me?" she asked, leaning against the counter as she played with the sleeves of my old sweatshirt.

"Why would I be mad at you?"

"Because I got you into this mess. Because I launched you guys into the walls."

I shook my head. "I'm not mad. I hear the voices too, and they are not friendly. I can't imagine what that must feel like for you."

"I wish you didn't have to hear them too," she said, frowning.

"And I wish I could help you with them. Their screams and scratching must take their toll."

I kept an eye on Clara as she walked over and sat on my lap to hug me. She leaned over the table, reading the note that was still out.

"Shit," she whispered, biting her lip nervously.

"Look, we don't know if they figured anything out, but it looks like you knew they needed you to do it. I'm not sure how they were going to take that power, though."

Clara pointed at the note. "What's the Cold Soul?"

"We couldn't find anything yet. We're still trying to sort through all the papers that got thrown out of order," I replied, blocking my thoughts. I felt awful lying to her, but House didn't want her to know.

She sighed. "Okay, I'm too tired to worry about that, the fact that Aidan and my dad can steal my power, or that Finnley was convinced she was going insane. Speaking of dads, yours is calling." She pushed my phone closer as she slid into her seat to eat.

"Hey, what's up?" I answered with a shrug. It was the best I could do.

"Just making sure you have everything you need. Clara isn't spending the night, right?" he asked.

"No, she went home with a headache."

Dad let out a breath. "Okay, well, good luck with midterms. I expect you home tomorrow after school."

"Yes, sir," I said before hanging up. Clara just stared at me as I raised my eyebrow. "What?"

She narrowed her eyes. "Are you moving in with me or something?

Who says I want you to be my overnight guest?"

I cringed. "I'm not leaving you alone after that mini outburst."

"Fine, but I have rules," she said as she leaned back in her chair with a smirk.

I rolled my eyes. "Alright, what are they?"

"First, no morning breath kisses."

"No promises. Next."

Clara laughed and pulled my chair closer. How the hell did she do that so easily?

"Second, no getting between me and coffee. And no judging how I look when I wake up." She frowned and stuck a piece of wet hair behind her ear.

"C, I've never judged before. But that's two and three. How many rules are there?"

"One more, and it's important. I want a new song every time you stay over."

I smiled. "Easy, and you owe me one too. Now tell me, how are you so damn strong?"

Clara grinned and scrunched her nose. "I cheat." She pulled my chair closer without moving her hands. Of course she used her powers.

I wrapped my arms around her waist, letting my hands trace along her spine as she kissed along my jaw. We made our way back to the bedroom and held on to each other, focusing on the cool touch of our skin. At least for the moment I could ignore the scratching of voices in the back of my head that were probably yelling in hers. Clara turned on her stereo without leaving my arms.

Can't Get Enough. ROMES.

32

Nate

Our morning midterms went well. Thankfully Glitch was an excellent tutor or I absolutely would have failed history. It also helped that Clara and I were giving each other the answers every time we got stuck. There were definitely perks to reading your girlfriend's mind. And that she could also read the mind of our genius best friend. We were going to be screwed tomorrow for calculus.

"You guys owe me for your relationship and your grades," Glitch groaned, reaching across the lunch table to steal one of Clara's fries.

She smacked his hand away as I laughed. "You're just jealous we can't include you in our heads."

"At least I don't have to cheat to be this brilliant," he replied, sticking his tongue out at me.

Clara let out a forced laugh and pulled her knee into her chest. I knew she had the remnants of a headache after yesterday because I could feel it too, but she was trying to fight through it. I wondered where the Blue Star was hiding this time.

I tried to distract Glitch from bothering her. "We're getting A's in all our classes anyway. What's the difference between one-hundred points and ninety-two?"

A commotion in the middle of the lunch room caught our attention as we all turned. Some freshmen girls had decided to sit at Emma's table. Since the volleyball team hadn't made the championship tournament, they had been in a sour mood for the last few weeks. It was definitely not a good time to cross QB. She was shouting at them to move from her table, even though there were three open ones right next to it.

"I think I could make her skirt catch fire if I really concentrated,"

Clara said, tilting her head as she tried to figure out how to make it happen.

"Do it," Glitch encouraged, an evil grin growing on his face.

"Maybe something less dangerous?" I blurted quickly. I definitely didn't want Clara sending the whole room up in flames.

"Fine." Clara scrunched her nose and in the distance, Emma's soda exploded, covering her face and drenching her hair in a sticky mess. She screamed and ran out of the room while everyone laughed. The freshmen girls stayed in their seats, surprised at their good fortune, as Clara turned and rested her chin back on her knee.

As Glitch continued to laugh, Clara's face suddenly froze and she dropped her foot to the ground. I felt a hand grip around my right shoulder. The cut had healed enough, but it was still pretty sore as fingers dug into me.

"Hello there, darling Finnley. Oh, that's right, it's Clara now."

Shit. Aidan.

I tried to pull away but he pulled up a chair and poked my side with something sharp. Glitch gripped the table, knowing he couldn't do anything with his powers in the middle of a lunch room. Aidan wasn't using his powers yet, so Clara leaned forward, her eyes a fiery blue.

"What do you want?" she hissed, her face dark as the air around us got colder.

"Careful now, Finn. You try anything and pretty boy here bleeds out." Clara clenched her jaw but leaned back slightly at his threat. He nodded slightly. "Better. Now, let's have a friendly chat."

"Real friendly," I grumbled as I tried to slide away.

He just poked me harder as he growled. "I won't do anything unless you make me. Richard wouldn't like it if I killed you all right now."

"If you aren't going to kill us, why are you here?" Clara demanded. She flashed me a look as the sharpness turned to pressure, using her powers to protect me from getting stabbed. I could hear her mind spinning to find a better way to help but there weren't any options that didn't involve the entire school finding out about us.

Aidan let out a small laugh. "Just wanted to make you squirm a little knowing that you can't hide from us. We'll be coming for you one of these days." He pulled away from me so he could slide next to Clara. I instinctively shifted to dive at him but Clara held me back with her power as Aidan laughed at me. His gaze was dark as he slid his hand along the inside of Clara's leg, making my stomach churn. But Clara sat tall, defiant and unflinching as he ran his other hand through her hair. "Maybe that's the day I'll jog your memory about the two of us together."

He turned to smirk at me but Clara shot her hand up, grabbing his wrist as she dug her fingers into his skin.

"I will kill you," she hissed through her teeth. Her face was just inches from Aidan's face, but her victory was short-lived. Her fingers started to shake loose from his arm as the air thickened around us.

Aidan yanked his arm away from her and stood up, Clara remaining stuck to her seat as she stared into nothingness, still affected by his power.

"Oh, that's so cute," he growled, hate dripping from every word. "You think you can beat me."

He turned and walked out of the lunch room, releasing his grip on Clara. I let out the longest breath of relief, glancing to Glitch who looked like he had just seen a ghost. Now he knew the real shit we were up against.

Clara shook in her seat, her fingers still trembling in the cold air as a single tear ran down her cheek. We barely noticed when the bell rang.

33

Nate

The day flew by, and then the evening, and the next thing I knew it was Friday. Somehow we had to pull out of our trance long enough to survive my dad's work party. The events of the week were a complete blur, and none of us could talk much. It became mechanical as we sifted through the books and notes in the library, careful to avoid anything that remotely triggered a headache for Clara. Other than a few minor ones here and there, she hadn't had them much this week.

Clara and I spent the morning binge watching as many episodes of *Doctor Who* as we could fit in, trying to take a break from the library for just one day. The search for answers was starting to wear on her, and being stuck there all day and night was starting to mess with her sleep more than the nightmares. I'm sure she was in there long after I went home for the night. It pained me not to be there all the time for her, but now I needed her to help me get through my dad's work party.

I went home to change and kicked at the dress shoes my dad had set out for me. They looked stiff and uncomfortable compared to my Converse so I threw those on instead. Their stained fabric stuck out under the pants that were just a little too short for my legs. Even my tie wasn't long enough for my torso. Dad had clearly underestimated my height.

He had offered to drive Clara and I to the party, but it was probably best if he didn't see House with his knob-less doors and magical interior. In a surprising move, he let me take the car myself to pick her up. Unsurprisingly, Clara wasn't ready yet so I sat on the bed and switched out my tie for the gray one House had left sitting on the covers.

"Why did this have to be a suit and tie event? I feel ridiculous,"

Clara shouted from the back of her closet.

"You are ridiculous. Besides, I'm sure you look great in a suit and tie." I laughed but choked slightly as my tie tightened around my neck. Clara clearly didn't think it was funny. I shook my head. "I'm kidding. Would you hurry up already?"

She walked out, arms folded with a sour face on, but I couldn't understand why. Part of me expected her to walk out in my old sweatshirt but I was blown away by the dress she had on. She kicked out the silky gray skirt, the fabric shimmering and flowing from the waist down. It faded up into light gray sleeves that attached at her fingers, carefully covering her lightning scar.

"I miss my pants," she grumbled, her purple curls bouncing as she reached up and adjusted her key necklace.

"You are absolutely stunning. No words can describe how perfect you look," I replied, standing up so I could spin her around.

"Thanks, Nate. You look very hands—" she paused as she looked at my shoes, holding in a laugh.

I frowned. "Hey, don't judge my shoes. They go perfectly with my short pants."

"Right," she replied sarcastically. "About as much as my shoes go with this dress." Clara laughed and picked up her skirt to show off her Converse.

I wrapped my arms around her and leaned down to kiss her. "Glitch was right all along. You're definitely my type. I love you. Always."

"Always forever?" she asked.

"Always forever," I replied as I kissed her forehead.

Clara took the moment to slip the key off her neck and over mine, tucking it down my shirt as she pulled me closer.

"This definitely doesn't go with my outfit," she said, patting my chest as the key buzzed gently against my skin. Before I could kiss ehr again, she took my hand and dragged me out the door.

I pulled up to the venue, the Forest Hills Museum, and looked up at the sad structure from the front seat. It used to be so fascinating. All of the school field trips took place here. You could run around and look at all the dinosaur skeletons, see the little figures acting out the history of the town, and watch fish swim around in the large tank. Now that we were older, we started to find the flaws. Dinosaurs were mislabeled and missing bones, the figures had misshapen features or no faces at all, and the fish we had lovingly named Killer as children had eaten almost all of the other creatures in the tank.

A small crowd had formed outside the door, all older couples. We would easily be the youngest in the room by a minimum of ten years. As the line started to grow yet again, I realized something I should have all along.

"Shit, C. I didn't even think about this. All those people's thoughts."

"Nate, it's okay," she said, trying to reassure me. "I feel fine right now. Plus, I've been practicing something." Clara picked up my right hand and turned it over. The blue scar was gone.

"How did you do that?" I asked, poking my palm with my left hand.

"Well, Aidan gave me the idea." I grumbled as she shook my hand. "No, listen. It's like how he messes with my mind, but I'm doing it in a nicer way. I'm just making your brain think it's not there."

"Rude. Stop messing with my brain," I replied. She smiled at my comment but as she reached up to rub the back of her neck, the mark popped back up on my hand. I looked at her nervously. "Are you sure you can do this?"

She nodded. "Yeah, just not for too long. Hold my hand if you can't hide it easily?"

I picked up her left hand and leaned over to kiss her cheek. "I don't think I could ever let go."

"Ugh, you're so cheesy," she giggled, turning to duck out of the car.

The doorman took our invitation, observing the minimal space between us. I wasn't going to let Clara out of my grip so I didn't really care what the guy thought. He let us pas, condescendingly looking us over as we walked by.

I stood in front of the door to the ballroom, listening to the bustle happening inside. Maybe this was a bad idea; Clara with her headaches and both of us with our powers in a room full of government people. It hit me that I had completely forgotten what branch my dad even worked for, what they did, or who any of these people would be. Suddenly, I was nervous about everything.

Clara squeezed my hand and bumped me forward through the door and into the room. The tables were arranged carefully to allow more people to sit, but a cleared aisle stretched up the middle and led to a stage. Three men stood behind the podium, chatting and drinking happily. Cocktail tables were spread out around the sides of the room with people chatting mindlessly around them. This was not what I expected government employees to look like.

My dad spotted us and left some people behind to greet us. "I'm so thrilled you could make it, Clara. You look lovely," he said with a smile.

Clara nodded. "Thank you for the invite. A little fresh air is probably good for me." She shifted closer to me, locking her arm into mine a little tighter. My dad paused for a second, looking back and forth between us before he continued.

"I'm glad you're feeling better. Our table is up front to the left. You wouldn't mind if I had a quick moment with Nathaniel? I've hardly seen him this week."

Now that was adding more anxiety on top of my nervousness. Why did he want to talk to me? Could Clara really keep my hand hidden if needed? From far away?

Stop spiraling, I've got it handled. You'll be fine. "Not a problem, sir," she replied, squeezing my hand as she nodded to my dad.

I gave her a kiss on the cheek as her fingers slid out of mine. I shoved my hand in my pocket while I watched her silky dress flow around her. And I wasn't the only one staring at her either. Several eyes were locked on my blue-eyed, purple haired girlfriend. It added to her demeanor that even with Converse on, she was still a giant teenager in an event of older government employees.

"You've done it, haven't you?"

My heart jumped into my throat and plummeted to my feet as I looked back at my dad. Were we really going to have this talk in public? Holy shit, I had every reason to be nervous. *Clara, please come back.*

"Sir?" I asked, my voice squeaking.

"You've told her you love her, yes? I can see the way you look at each other," he replied, nodding in Clara's direction.

Holy... the pounding in my ears started to die down as I released my breath as quietly as I could.

"Uh, yeah, we both said it," I said. I was trying so hard to keep my face from getting red but he kept staring at me. There was no way he didn't see right through me.

"Mhmm." He raised his eyebrow. "Do I need to remind you to be safe?"

"Dad!" Too late. My face was a bright red now.

"Just making sure," he said through laughter. Why did everyone think this was funny? He sighed and set his hand on my shoulder. "Will you at least tell me the truth about where you're staying tonight?"

"If I ask to stay at Clara's, will you be mad?" The truth was that I was mad, as in crazy, for asking him that, but he seemed to be in good spirits tonight.

He shrugged. "I'm not entirely happy about it, but I trust you. Is her uncle really okay with having you stay over?"

"I think he likes me, and he trusts Clara."

My dad patted me on the shoulder and chuckled as he turned to go back to his coworkers. With the invisible weight lifted form my chest, I found myself suddenly out of breath. I hurried over to the table and sat down next to Clara who was tugging at the sleeves of her dress.

"Hey," I said, poking her to get her attention. "You okay?"

She looked at me, temporarily shaking off the distraction of her sleeve. "Yeah, the fabric keeps sticking to my arm. Did you have a nice chat with your dad?"

"Uh, I guess you could call it that," I replied with a shrug.

She looked at me with a calm, straight face. "Did you learn all about safe sex?"

"Clara!"

She let out a short laugh as she pulled my chair closer and rested her head on my shoulder. "Just asking."

"You are the worst," I grumbled sarcastically.

She shrugged. "Well, you're stuck with me because apparently my uncle likes you enough to let you be my overnight guest."

Now I could tell she wasn't okay. She was trying to convince me but there were no smiles or hand squeezes to her comments.

"C, do we need to go?" I asked. I focused and felt the slight tingling in the back of my head. The Blue Star voices were picking up, mixing with the voices of all the people around us and their thoughts, only higher volume in her mind.

Clara shook her head. "I'm good on the people in the building. I can block them out. I'm not close to anything bad yet."

"Keyword is 'yet'. Come on, let's go. My dad will understand." I pushed my seat back and got ready to stand when a man tapped the microphone up front.

"If everyone would please find their seats, dinner will be served."

We could have made it out through the crowd but two couples sat at our table before we could get up. Clara found my hand and squeezed.

It's okay. I'll be fine.

We ate and shared meaningless conversations with the people at our table. I made sure to finish my food as quickly as I could so Clara could stop using all her energy to hide my mark. When she slid ehr hand back into mine, it was freezing cold. We were going to need to get out of here soon, but she was surprisingly alert, participating and answering all the questions thrown our way.

"So, have you two been together since high school?" the younger lady who came with the man at least twice her age smiled at us. I probably should have listened when they introduced themselves, but I was too busy worrying about Clara.

"We're actually still seniors at West, ma'am. We met this year on the first day of school. I was new," Clara answered.

The older lady next to my dad smiled. "Only dating a few months and already so attached? Young love is so cute."

Only a few months? Wow, it didn't feel that short. I felt drawn to her the minute I saw her in history class. Maybe when you already love someone and then magically get connected even stronger than before, it messes with your sense of time.

I squeezed Clara's hand. "We've had a few bumps but seem to find our way back to each other."

"So, what's the story of how you met?" the young lady asked, wrapping her arm through her older partner's arm.

Clara jumped in. "Nate's friend actually got the ball rolling for us. I didn't get a very warm welcome but Nate walked me to school the next day. I think I overwhelmed him with my music, but I was nervous." She gave me a half grin as she sipped her water, but I saw the drops around her fingers turn to ice as she set it down. Luckily they were too small for anyone to notice.

"That's nice," the man with the older woman said in monotone. Apparently we were boring him with this conversation. "So, Nate, you must be proud of your dad."

"Sir?"

"Your dad's retirement? Today was his last day."

34

Clara

I felt everyone around me tense. Why didn't we know about this?

Oh, Tom didn't tell his son. That was the man who had been bored with our previous conversation. He flinched as his wife kicked him under the table.

Idiot. That was a surprise recognition. The younger lady with the older man definitely looked about as embarrassed as the guy who realized he ruined the surprise.

Crap. That was Nate's dad for sure. Clearly he wasn't prepared to be recognized tonight.

I mustered the strength I had left and focused my energy to quiet the voices in my head. I needed to make it through just a little longer, and I needed to be here for Nate. The trick was doing that without bringing the museum crashing down around us.

"We're honored to be here," I replied with a smile, luckily spared from any more questions as the man at the podium called someone up to the stage.

I didn't pay attention to any of the speeches. There were laughs and stories shared about Nate's dad, but I couldn't hear any of them. I was too concerned about my breathing and Nate's hand in mine, still unable to move. I couldn't even drink my water because my touch was turning the condensation into ice. I was breaking and I could feel it.

Nate, I can't hold it much longer.

The fork that I had been playing with in my right hand now looked like a bent and tangled mess. The headache was getting stronger and the voices were growing.

Nate snapped out of his trance and looked around. *I'm sorry.* He focused on something before his eyes rested on me. *There's a side door behind you. As soon as there's a break, we can get out. Just find my heartbeat and try to stay relaxed.*

I put the fork down and slid my hand to his wrist, focusing on his pulse through my fingers and using it to pace my breathing.

In, out. In, out. Shut up, voices. In… in…

Nate's dad finished speaking and everyone started to stand. Finally.

Nate jumped up in an instant, dragging me with him, but the closer we got to the door, the more people stopped him to chat about his dad. They blabbered on with the same fake conversation topics like "you must be so proud" and "you're going to see a lot more of him". Nate was clearly not in the mood as he mumbled his thanks and continued pulling me along.

He weaved us through multiple conversations until some short, old man stood directly in front of me, shaking his finger in my face while holding a full glass of wine.

"How dare you disrespect your husband with that hair, young lady. You should be ashamed."

I just stared at him… at three of him. I blinked, trying to figure out which one to look at. Nate panicked and grabbed my shoulders, pushing me toward the door while I tried to figure out which old man was the real one. I'm not sure if I meant to do it or if the headache was finally escaping me, but I watched his wine glass tip over onto a woman's skirt. Two of her now shouted at five of him as he fumbled for napkins.

Nate pushed me out the door as cold air rushed over me. Finally outside, I threw my fists into my temples and tried to press as hard as I could to stop the pain. The tears were forming in my eyes and I could feel every part of my body shaking. The headache roared to life inside me, the Blue Star voices hitting me full force as they screamed and pressed on the inside of my skull, begging to be released.

Nate wrapped his arms around me and guided me down against the wall of the building.

"Clara, you need to focus. You can fight it."

His sentence came through in seven different echoes, mixed with the hiss of the Blue Star. The voices were cackling, screaming, and scratching in my head. A loud crack drowned them out for a moment as the dumpster next to me began to crumple from my power. I was going to lose control.

"Nate, get away," I forced out, my teeth clenching as if I could grind away the pain that shot down my spine. "You have to get away from me."

"Clara, I'm not leaving. Focus on my voice, focus on me."

I couldn't fight the splitting pain in my head as the tears rolled down my cheeks. Pressure was building and thrashing at my insides but I had to hold it in. I couldn't do this here, not now, not with Nate in my line of fire.

Suddenly, Nate dropped down on his knees, wrapped his hands around my face, and kissed me hard. The surprise made me catch my breath and he pulled back just slightly to speak.

"Calm down, C. I'm here," he whispered. He pulled my hands away from my head, squeezed them in his, and kissed me again as he gently pressed my head against the wall. I could feel the voices ease up on their attack, but their echoes were still voilent as they tried to hold onto me. Somehow, the pressure was releasing. I took my hands out of Nate's and wrapped them around his neck, pushing my forehead into his as if I could get closer to his voice and thoughts.

C, I need you to fight back.

I focused on his voice in my head instead of the Blue Star. The more we pressed into each other, the lighter I felt. The scratching was still there, but it dulled with each passing second until only my heartbeat throbbed through my body.

Had I really just stopped an outburst? Nate finally broke away from me, his body lifting off of mine as he turned around. I looked up, confused as to why he was trying to get away, and snagged his sleeve.

"Nate?"

I yanked harder to spin him toward me just as he was wiping blood away from his nose. I gasped and threw my hand over my mouth.

He pulled his hand out of mine. "I'm fine, C. It's fine," he said, shaking his head.

I used the wall to help me stand as Nate balanced me on the other side. "I did that to you, nate. I hurt you. How is that fine? I can't control this and I hurt you. Again. And worse this time."

Nate reached over and grabbed my hands to keep them from shaking. "C, this wasn't you. The Blue Star voices... I can't explain it, but I think I was pulling them away from you. I don't know how, but they weren't happy about it. Clearly I'm not as strong as you."

I weakly threw my hand into his chest in frustration. "Why would you do that? Why would you let them in?"

"Why wouldn't I do that for you?" he asked. "I told you I'd find a way to help you, C. I love you. Why would I ever let you go through that alone?"

Now I really was crying. Still off balance, I stumbled into Nate, pressing my entire body into his as I kissed him with the rest of the energy I had. He walked us backward and pushed me against the wall, kissing my neck and collarbone as I hung onto him, afraid to let go. He paused as he pressed his forehead into mine, running his finger over my cheek.

I shook my head. "How did you even know what to do?"

He took a breath as he frowned. "I used to get panic attacks when I was little. I always needed something to ground me, and counting heartbeats was one of my tricks. After that, I really just wanted to get your mind focused on something else and I only thought to kiss you."

I sighed in relief. "I love you, always forever." I leaned forward and kissed him again, feeling both of our bodies grow heavier. Still, he helped me off the wall and I clung to his shoulders as he carried most of my weight with his arm around my waist. We made it halfway to the car before we both gave up and collapsed on a bench.

"I'm sorry about tonight," Nate said, his head leaned on my shoulder.

"You didn't know, and neither did your dad. I'm not sure why he didn't tell you about retiring, though."

Nate twitched his fingers in mine as his warm chest pressed into my arm. Weird, I could feel it buzzing against my skin, faster than his heart could have been beating. I reached around his neck and pulled out the key from under his shirt, sliding it off his head. The key glowed and vibrated but almost immediately faded back to stillness.

"Neat trick, kiddo."

My heart sank as I watched Richard about twenty yards in front of us. We both straightened, still unable to stand.

"What the hell do you want?" I growled.

"That's no way to talk to your father. Aidan said you still didn't have your memories." Lightning cracked in the distance, almost perfectly timed with his sentence.

My fingers dug into the bench in anger. "I'll say whatever I want. You and Aidan were luring me into a trap."

"Of course we were. You don't deserve the Blue Star's power, that's why it's eating at you. It erased half of what you were, and now I'm going to make sure it takes the rest of you so I can finally have that power for myself."

He flashed a crooked smile before the lightning struck closer. Holy shit, he had control over it.

Nate tensed. "You took down the gym that night."

Richard laughed. "Did it really take you that long to figure it out? I was trying to push Finnley's outburst along so she would give in to the Blue Star's energy. If she had become the Cold Soul, she would have let everyone in there die while she walked out unscathed. You see, I have to wait until she gives into it completely before I can take the power she stole. I was really expecting that to happen tonight."

"I'll die before I let you have that power," I snarled.

He just smiled wider. "Oh, I know. Hope you enjoy your *dreams*, darling daughter." Lightning slammed into the ground in front of him, and by the time our eyes adjusted, he was gone.

I placed my hand over my stomach where the mysterious wound continued to kill me every night in my dreams. Richard knew. How could he know?

A soft rain started to fall as Nate and I sat on the bench in silence.

35

Clara

While I had been up since the sun poked through my window, Nate was still fast asleep. After driving home soaking wet, we had been too exhausted to change and now I could smell that mistake. But every part of my body hurt so I just stayed still, focused on Nate breathing steadily next to me.

Hope you enjoy your dreams, darling daughter.

My dad's voice shook around in my head now that it was empty of the Blue Star voices. That didn't stop the soreness of the headache, though. I took an aching breath and rolled my head to watch Nate's chest rise and fall, lulling me back into the present. I felt a little guilty to see the cut on his arm had reopened last night because of me.

I made an attempt to roll over without waking him up, but a roar of nausea hit me as I stood. Ignoring all decency, I sprinted into the bathroom, barely shutting the door before I threw up in the toilet. The room spun around me as I crawled over to the shower, remembering that the cold water had worked before. I heaved my body over the side of the tub, dragging the skirt of my dress over the edge as I curled into the spray of water.

"C?"

I heard Nate tap on the door but I couldn't make the words come out of my mouth. Instead, I groaned as loud as I could and he came stumbling in. He looked about as crappy as I felt. He stepped over the edge and helped pick me up, but after that we were out of energy. We leaned on each other, using the shower wall to hold up the rest of our weight.

"I have a question for you," Nate grunted, taking longer than usual to spit out the words.

"Hmm?"

"Do you think the bags under my eyes match my outfit?"

We both laughed weakly, spending another few minutes trying to climb out of the shower. He guided me to the closet so I could change while he turned back to the bed, stopping every few steps to sway back and forth before continuing.

I leaned against the closet wall after changing and watched through the crack in the door as Nate tried to put his clean shirt on. He was trying to put both of his arms through the same sleeve, getting frustrated when it wouldn't fit. If someone had walked in on us, they would have thought we were drunk out of our minds.

I had enough of my bearings to walk over and help him get his shirt figured out.

He fell back onto the bed with a grunt. "Is this the headache you feel every day?"

I shrugged and sat down with him, leaning my head onto his chest. "No, this one is actually pretty bad. It's usually a daily dull ache, but you probably only feel that when the voices are screaming at me."

"Shit, no wonder you're grumpy all the time. This sucks."

"Rude."

We probably stayed there for another hour as I played with his hand, tracing the scar on his palm. When we finally had the strength to stand, House delivered plenty of junk food and caffeine for breakfast. I finished and pulled my knees up to my chest so I could rest my chin on top, lost in thought about the events of last night. It was a miracle we were sitting here right now.

"What's up?" Nate asked, poking my shin with his spoon.

"Thinking about what my dad said last night."

"Which part?" he groaned.

I frowned. "Well, two parts. He said that if I had become the Cold Soul, I would have let everyone in the gym die. Could I really become so cruel? That's the second time we've heard of the Cold Soul. What do you think it is?"

House creaked and the table shook as I looked around, confused. Nate just shook his head.

"*You* would never do that, but he does know more about the Blue star power source than we do right now. Those voices are evil, so maybe that's what happens if you take in all the power."

I chewed my cheek in thought. "Hold up. He thinks I'm the only one who has the power. That brings me to number two with the last thing he said. He knows I have the nightmares, so he knows I die."

Nate sighed. "You're not going to die, C. It's a nightmare, but that's all it is."

I shrugged. "I'm just saying, we have one advantage over him now. He doesn't know you have some of the power too, which means he can't take all of it from me while you still have some of it."

"So, he won't kill you. He said he was waiting for you to give in to the Blue Star before he made his move, but you can't fully do that if I have some of the power," Nate said, lifting his right palm up.

I pressed my forehead into my knees and groaned. "Then why does it still give me headaches? Why does it still call to me?"

Nate reached his fingers under my chin and lifted my head. "I don't have that answer, but maybe if we find out how he plans to take the power, we can be ready for him."

"If we want to be ready for him, we need to be ready to fight," I replied.

Nate looked at me nervously. "What does that mean?"

"It means we start training tomorrow morning."

36

Nate

It was official. I hated the training phase of our plan. I slammed into the wall for maybe the fifteenth time, and they were starting to not feel padded anymore. I can't believe I missed the library.

"Dude, you're getting your ass kicked," Glitch laughed as he sat on a wooden box in the corner.

"Says the guy who gave up after three tries," I groaned, pushing off the ground.

The name of the game was stealing the tennis ball in Clara's hand. It seemed like an easy task when she stood in the middle of the empty room, but I was proven wrong time and time again.

Clara flicked the air toward Glitch as she tipped his seat, tossing him to the ground.

"Ow," he huffed.

Clara shook her head as she glared at him. "Take this seriously, Glitch."

I tried to use her distraction to my advantage, running up behind her. I was about five feet away when my face smacked into an invisible wall.

She rolled her eyes as she glanced back at me. "I can hear your thoughts."

I just groaned, still sprawled on the ground.

Glitch folded his arms. "Why do we always have to steal the ball from you?"

"Because she can kick our asses before we even know what's happening," I answered, staring at the ceiling.

I don't know what happened next, but Glitch hit my side after sliding across the floor.

"You two aren't even trying," Clara groaned. I could see she was a bit annoyed at us, which was fair because we were terrible at this, but we were out of our league here.

Clara began throwing the ball against the wall, catching it as it bounced back. That gave me an idea. I concentrated on the ball's trajectory, creating a shadow on the wall just as she threw it. The ball disappeared into the hole and popped out of the next shadow I created on the ceiling above me, kind of like a portal. I caught it as it dropped into my lap.

"Yeah! I win!" I cheered, holding it over my head.

Glitch poked the ball to see if it was real as Clara cocked her head. "How did you do that?"

I shrugged. "No idea. It just happened."

She shook her head. "Seriously, that could be useful. Going into one shadow and hopping out of another adds an element of surprise. Do it again."

I tossed her the ball and she continued to throw it against the wall. I focused again and made a shadow to swallow the ball on her next toss. But as I opened another hole on the wall behind Clara, nothing came out.

Clara sank her shoulders. "Bummer. I'll be sure never to jump in one of those."

"Yeah, I'd hate to be floating around in nothingness for all eternity," Glitch said as he hopped up, glitching to the other side of the room.

Clara's eyes widened. "Hold up, do that again."

Glitch obeyed, popping up behind her. "Boo!"

She jumped, but seemed more excited than startled. "How quickly can you do that?"

"Instantly, why?" he asked.

"Do it again, but keep doing it all around the room."

Glitch shrugged but complied. I think I knew where Clara was going with the idea, because the more Glitch used his power, the more of him popped up around the room. It looked like a bunch of glitches around us.

"This is awesome," he said, his voice echoing around the room.

Slowly, they all started to disappear. I followed the one I thought was him, but it disappeared after a few seconds.

"Gotcha!" he said in my ear, popping away right before I could punch him. Clara had caught on to his pattern because she pushed him over with her powers just as he landed next to the wooden box. She laughed and walked over to help him up.

"Alright, now it's my turn," she said, fake punching the air toward me.

"You've already been showing off with the tossing me against a wall thing," I grumbled.

"Those are only brief surges. I want to try to hold it."

I raised an eyebrow. "You sure you're up for that? How's your head?"

"I'm fine," she said a little too quickly, throwing up a wall around her head before I could read her thoughts. She shifted to stand next to me and turned to face Glitch, holding her hands up. "Okay, bring it."

Glitch reached his hands out carefully, waving through the air so he wouldn't go crashing into another wall. When he found her shield, the air rippled around him.

"Trippy. It's cold," he said, his voice muffled from the outside of the shield.

He placed his hands against the wall and started to push against it. Only, one of him wasn't having much luck so he started glitching around the perimeter, using ten of himself to push against the wall in different places. Clara slid back a bit in her stance before planting her feet firmly underneath herself. Glitch made a few more of himself, filling up every gap as he continued to push against the wall. Ripples shook the air around us, distorting his figures. Watching this gave me hope that we might actually have a chance in a fight.

"Nate, what's up with her?" all of the glitches asked, a few of them starting to disappear.

I glanced toward her, my eyes drawn to the blue glow coming from her arm. Shit. The Blue Star had to be in the room, taking advantage of her surge of power. I patted my pockets, not finding the marble until I dug through Clara's pocket.

I pulled out the marble, the surface glowing the same blue as Clara's arm. I could hear the voices now, soft in the back of my head as they begged Clara to let them in. The wall Clara was holding broke and she dropped her hands to her sides, but she just stood there with her eyes glazed over. There was no outburst, just a constant pull and ache that she probably felt ten times worse than I did.

"Get this out of here," I said, tossing the Blue Star to Glitch. He popped out of the room in an instant.

As soon as he was gone, Clara dropped to her knees. I tried to catch her but ended up falling to the ground with her.

"I'm sorry. I'm so, so sorry," she whispered, avoiding my gaze. I reached to her hand but she winced, turning her palm over to reveal the fresh blue blood dripping from her reopened scar.

"What happened?" I asked, trying to get her attention as she avoided my eyes. "That wasn't like the other times."

She shook her head. "The voices were different this time. They told me they could protect me... protect you. They were offering a trade. I didn't have to die if I just let them in."

I pressed my forehead against hers. "They lied to you before. Why was this any different? Why would you believe them?"

"They showed me what happened when I ran away."

I sat back on my heels. "What?"

"I stole the Blue Star. I knew my dad and Aidan were waiting for me outside to take the power. My mom was running after me as I escaped with that man chasing close behind. He had the fire... he killed her, but the Blue Star told me it would keep me alive so I could save everyone else. So I let it in, but it didn't feel right. I got scared and dropped it before all of the power consumed me, but I still had an outburst. Now the Blue Star is angry I didn't take all of it, and it needs me to take in the rest so I won't die like my dreams. It's the only way," she replied, her eyes watering.

"Look at me, C," I said, lifting her chin. "You can't trust this thing. We can figure this out together, just don't give up yet."

She sighed and closed her eyes, pressing her face into my shoulder.

37

Clara

I sat on the edge of the bed, watching Nate do a better job wrapping my arm than I ever could. He hadn't said a word since we walked out of the training room. He didn't even say goodbye as Glitch left. He just walked me to my bedroom and got out the first aid kit like wrapping my arm had just become a normal thing to deal with.

I could tell Nate was mad at me without reading his thoughts. I had tried to listen to the voices of the Blue Star; the same ones I had promised I wouldn't follow. But this time they had been so much more convincing. I had a piece of my memory back with their promise. If I gave in, they'd protect everyone around me. I could hear those same promises in my memory, whispering to me as I ran away after stealing the Blue Star. That's why I had given in the first time, and that's why I wanted to give in now. I was so close...

His silence finally broke me. "I'm sorry, Nate. I was weak and I didn't listen. I didn't let you help me," I blurted.

Nate closed the first aid kit and put it back under the sink, still not speaking to me as he paced back and forth.

I shifted anxiously. "Please, Nate. I know you're mad at me, just say something. Yell at me, I deserve it."

He stopped and shoved his hands in his pockets. "I lied to you."

"What?"

"I'm not mad at you, I'm mad at myself. I lied to you about the Cold Soul." House creaked but Nate just raised his voice, speaking toward the ceiling. "She deserves to know. She's the one who left the note, and maybe it'll help."

"Nate, what are you talking about?" I asked.

He pulled out a neatly folded note from his pocket and handed it to me. I opened it to see my handwriting.

Whispers.
Screams.
Fear.
A soul.
Replaced by the Cold Soul.
Erased.
Consumed.
Existing within.
Waiting.
The Blue Star.
Called into Darkness.
Called into Cold.
Dividing.

Nate sighed. "C, this is why the voices are lying to you. It's your own warning. I promised House I wouldn't show you, but I can't keep it anymore. You have to know they are lying. They aren't going to protect you, they want to consume you."

I read over the words again. "The Blue Star and the Cold Soul are the same thing? They're replacing my soul?"

Nate nodded. "You didn't just forget your past. The Blue Star erased it."

I clenched my jaw. "It's consuming my soul so it can fill the space with the Cold Soul."

Nate just hung his head, thoughts of shame running wild in his head. But I wasn't mad at him, I was upset with House for hiding this from me. Did he think I would give up? Feel defeated? Or maybe I was upset with myself for believing the voices again. That's how I ended up in this mess to begin with. Protection? It was too good to be true.

I crumpled the paper in my hand, the desk behind Nate splintering under the weight of my mind. Nate didn't flinch, and House didn't fight back.

"Why the hell wouldn't you let him tell me about this?" I shouted up at House. He didn't respond.

I let my frustration spill out of me, screaming as the mirror in the bathroom shattered, followed by the light overhead. Glass showered down around me as I threw my fist into the bed as I stood. The legs cracked underneath, sending the frame crashing into the floor.

House still didn't respond. I spun to face Nate who hadn't moved from his spot. He didn't even look surprised.

I gripped my fists. "Why aren't you scared of me? Why aren't you afraid of what I'm becoming? You've read the note, and I've almost killed you twice. Why are you just standing there?" I spit as I yelled, hating every word that came out of my mouth.

Nate looked up at me, shaking his head. "What part of 'always forever' do you not understand? Regardless of what you think is happening to you, I'm not letting you do this alone. You are everything to me, and you can't keep pushing me out."

My shoulders sank. I knew he was right. It was so much easier to push him away, but it was so lonely.

"Nate, I thought I was protecting you. I can't lose you. Please don't give up on me."

He sighed. "I'm not going away that easily."

I surveyed the mess I had made of my room. I had been in control of the destruction this time. I had done this on purpose. What would become of me when I couldn't hold back? What would happen to the people around me?

Then I looked at Nate. He was grounding me from the Blue Star, and more than that, he was saving me from myself.

I stepped closer and wrapped my arm around his waist, leaning my head on his chest as his heartbeat filled my mind. Relief washed over me when he put his arms around my shoulders and pulled me tighter. Flicking my fingers, I turned on my iPod and let the song play through the stereo.

Soldier. Firewoodisland.

38

Nate

We spent the next couple of weeks between researching in the library and training. Clara was afraid of using any of her powers for too long, so a lot of her time was spent in the library. She stayed clear of the book we found in the desk drawer but went over all of her notes with meticulous focus, hoping she might find something we missed.

She did her best to let me in every time her headaches got worse, and nearly every time the Blue Star was somewhere nearby. Glitch even took it home once and it still ended up in her pocket.

Dad had gotten used to me staying over at Clara's every other night, but I don't think he was terribly thrilled about it. He did make sure to extent his invite again for Christmas when she came over for dinner one night. He was happy she agreed, reminding me that my mom would be home for the first time in a couple years and was excited to meet Clara.

Great, at least Mom keeps in touch with Dad.

Late Friday night, when most teens would be out partying or on vacation, Clara and I were still in the library. She was up on the second floor picking through another shelf while I sat on the stairs, flipping through a conspiracy-filled book about witches and supernatural beings.

I jumped as a book flew over my head and crashed into the wall across the room. I looked up to see Clara banging her head on the bookshelf.

"Headache?" I asked, standing up quickly. We had emergency procedures for that now.

She groaned. "No, I'm just frustrated."

I relaxed my shoulders, checking my phone to see we were well into the early hours of Saturday. Sleep was definitely needed at this point. I climbed the stairs to stand with her, running my hand over her shoulders. Ever since that first training day, things had been a little strained between us. She was still pretty upset with House, and I later found the poem crumpled underneath her pillow. I knew she was trying, but with her headaches getting worse and us not finding answers, it was weighing on her. Add onto that with nightmares every night. We had no idea when her dad would show up again and make things even worse.

"Come on, we need sleep," I said, tugging at her hand.

She pulled it back into her body. "No, I'm sorry. Just one more book," she begged, reaching for a different book.

I shook my head. "Seriously. The books will be here tomorrow."

It was hard to say no to her, but she reluctantly let me drag her down the stairs and out of the library. She tried to pick up a book on the way out but I snagged it and tossed it inside just as House closed the door behind me.

With sudden energy, Clara whipped me around and pressed me into the door of the library. House locked the door against my back, barely in time.

Clara leaned up, biting her lip. "Just one more book." Her lips pressed against my neck, trailing up my jaw to my ear.

Shit. "Are you trying to seduce me into going back inside the library?"

"Of course I am. Is it working?" she whispered, her breath sending a shiver down my spine.

I wasn't going to last long if this was her tactic, and she knew it. Her hands found mine and positioned them around her waist, making sure I was touching her skin underneath my old sweatshirt. I let out a soft noise as Clara just smiled and pressed more of her body into me, kissing my lips and wrapping her hands around my neck.

It took every ounce of my power not to kiss her back, but this was totally not fair.

"Not working," I replied, my voice strained. At least House was backing me up.

Clara tried one more time, moving my hands tighter around her back, but I had a different idea. I scooped her up and swung her over my shoulder as she squirmed.

"That's cheating!" she cried, biting my shoulder in an attempt to get me to drop her.

"Me? Cheating? How dare you accuse me of cheating," I replied with a laugh, carrying her into her room. "House, lock the door."

The door closed behind me and I heard the click of the lock.

Clara huffed. "You two are ganging up on me."

"Says the girl who tried to seduce me into letting her stay in the library."

House creaked as I tossed her on the bed.

"Rude," she grumbled, reaching over her head to throw a pillow at me. She sprawled out on the bed, taking up as much space as possible. I picked up the pillow and threw it back.

"Scooch."

"Make me," Clara replied, sticking her tongue out.

"You are ridiculous," I laughed.

She leaned up and rolled onto her knees, sitting at the edge of the bed in front of me. Her hands reached up and gripped my shirt, pulling herself up to kiss me.

"I love you, always forever," she whispered, leaning away just enough to speak before she kissed me again and pulled me down next to her.

"I love you, too. Always forever," I replied. I kissed the top of her head and watched her body rise and fall gently as she drifted to sleep.

Clara and I stood together, her left hand in my right with an icy touch. We weren't in the clearing... some sort of alley maybe, but I didn't recognize it.

Aidan stood in front of us, the haze he created making a cloud around us. It floated between us, but this time it wasn't working. His smug grin turned to anger as he dove forward.

Clara responded, pulling her hand out of mine as she pushed forward with force. A wave of energy exploded out of her, knocking Aidan away from us. He launched across the alley and slammed into the wall, cracking the brick and sending showers of dust and shards around his limp body on the ground.

I stepped forward to see through the cloud of dust, struggling to balance as the ground shook underneath me. When I turned back to Clara, she only had a blank stare on her face. I focused on her hands as they wrapped around a knife, held steady by Richard's grip.

"You're too late," he said, flashing his wicked smile. With a single, swift move, he shoved the knife deep into her stomach.

"No!"

Clara and I shot up out of bed. She clutched at her stomach as we both gasped for breath. I could feel the sweat rolling down my chest.

That's how she was going to die. Her dad was going to kill her.

"C, ar—"

She threw her hand over my mouth. "Shush."

I could feel her mind spinning as I replayed the nightmare myself. What about her dad was different? Had he stolen her energy? If her blood was still blue, did that mean he failed? But why would he kill her if he didn't have the power?

"Shush your thoughts too," Clara snapped, holding her finger over her lips. I did my best to clear my head, but it was spinning just as much as hers. She finally let out a breath. "I figured it out."

"Figured what out?" I managed to mumble through her fingers. Clara pulled her hand off my mouth, climbing out of the covers so she could face me.

"Aidan's powers don't work on you. When you were holding my hand, they didn't work on me either."

"Don't let go of your hand. Got it."

"No, you don't get it. Your right hand, my left," she said, lifting my right hand in front of us to show off the mark on my palm. She turned her left hand over to reveal the same scar. "This is where the Blue Star connected us; where the power is strongest. I think it really is trying to protect me this time."

I grimaced. "I'm still a little hesitant after the Blue Star's track record, but it could work."

"I also figured out the second part. The transfer of energy? I know how my dad is going to steal it."

"How?"

Clara pinched her lips together. "The Blue Star only reacts to me, right? When you and I held it together, some of the power transferred to you, hence the blue scar. The power source is a conduit and I juice and direct that power."

"Holy shit," I breathed.

Clara nodded. "If we keep the Blue Star hidden, he can't use it."

I frowned. How could we possibly keep the Blue Star hidden if it always found a way to our pockets? It wasn't letting Clara out of its grip, and it would do anything to get her to use it. Now, Richard was going to take advantage of that.

"C, he kills you," I whispered.

She placed her hand over her stomach, her eyes fading to a dull blue. "We just have to finda way to change that without getting consumed by the Blue Star. I'll keep ignoring the voices." Clara leaned back on the headboard, shifting slightly as I leaned back with her.

"Normal teenage worries, right? Don't fall victim to an evil blue marble and try not to get killed by my evil dad."

I reached around her shoulders and pulled her closer. "It must be so boring to have a normal life."

"I could go for boring right about now," she sighed.

39

Nate

Glitch had the perfect distraction.

"Laser tag?" Clara asked, uneasy.

"Exactly," Glitch replied. He started to put his feet up on the table but House creaked to deter him.

"Why laser tag?" I asked, poking the eggs on my plate.

"Exercise, for one. You two have been spending all your time in the library. Minus your extracurriculars, you need to run around a little." Clara rolled her eyes as he continued. "Second, we need to blow off some steam without literally getting thrown into the walls by Clara. There's minimal risk of physical injury. Third, there's a max of sixteen people in the game which means C doesn't have to block out a ton of thoughts. Come on, let's go shoot people."

"Fine, but no more than an hour," Clara replied, continuing the steady stream of sugar into her coffee.

I folded my arms. "I don't know…"

"Dude, you need to get out of the house," Glitch said, his mouth full of donut.

"I'm perfectly fine staying inside on a Saturday. That's what weekends are for."

My chair spun around as Clara pulled it to face her. She uncrossed my arms and put them around her so she could sit and balance on my lap.

"Come on, I can handle an hour. Normal for one hour." She scrunched her nose against mine and kissed me.

I groaned. "First you try to seduce me into the library, now you want to seduce me into laser tag?"

"Yup. Think of it like you're taking me on our first date."

"What?" Glitch blurted. "You haven't taken her on a real date yet?"

"We've been busy," I grumbled. "Fine, but no cheating with powers... for any of us." I held up my finger to Clara, knowing she would absolutely cheat to beat us. She grinned and kissed me again.

"Gross. Get a room," Glitch mumbled behind me.

Clara pulled away and stared Glitch down. "This is my house." She planted her feet and stood up. "Well, if we're going, I'm changing into darker clothes. I'm not giving either of you losers a chance to beat me."

~

We suited up and listened to the employee drone over the rules. Clara was too busy sizing up her competition to pay attention. With the first game a free-for-all, it was going to be a madhouse once it started. After we walked through the doors, we had less than a minute to find our spots before it started. Glitch took off in one direction while Clara took off in another, leaving me to wonder if they'd actually follow our 'no powers' rule.

I ran around and did my best to have fun. I nailed a few kids from a birthday party and one other high schooler, but every time I got a kill, someone would tag me from behind. Whoever it was did a great job of hiding. I dodged a few more shots from the birthday party kids before turning out of the maze. Glitch jumped out from hiding and tagged me.

"Sorry dude," he said with a shrug. "C! I got him!" He turned and ran away laughing.

Teaming up on me, that's what they were doing. I wound back through the maze, trying to find higher ground so I could pick off Glitch and get some payback. I snuck up a ramp, my sights set for the lookout corner. Out of nowhere, someone ran into me and pushed me against the wall.

Clara. She pressed her body into mine as she kissed me, hard. I forgot everything going on around us and let her take over, running my fingers through her hair and holding her close with my hand in the small of her back. I was getting dizzy when I finally remembered to breathe. She pulled her head back just slightly so I could see her blue eyes shining against the blacklight.

"Oh, good. It's you. The last guy I kissed was really confused, but he almost got to second base before I figured it out."

She leaned into kiss me again but I twisted away. "Wait, what?"

"Kidding!" she giggled. She jumped back and shot me.

"You little shit," I shouted, fumbling for my gun to shoot her back.

Clara let out a small shriek through her laughter and ran off, leaving me to chase her. She was just a few steps ahead of me when she turned the corner out of my sight. I slowed my pace to make sure she wasn't going to try a sneak attack, poking my head around the wall.

To my surprise, she wasn't running anymore. She just stood in the middle of the path, her back toward me. But someone else was there with her.

Aidan.

The haze was already surrounding her, looking fuzzy in the blacklight. Clara was swaying in her stance, clearly no longer in control of her mind. I lunged forward and grabbed her left hand, yanking her away from Aidan. She wobbled but regained her stance, realizing what had happened. But it worked. His powers couldn't affect her if we were connected.

"What the hell are you doing here?" she asked, her speech slurred.

Aidan brushed off his surprise with a smile, his teeth glowing. "Oh, Finn. I just want my girl back."

"Back off," I growled, trying to look around to see if Richard was here too. "What are you really doing?"

"Speeding up the process. Richard moves too slow. I'm going to bring Finn in now, and take the Blue Star off your bloody corpse later," he snarled.

"Not happening," Clara hissed. "I'd rather kill myself than let you have that power."

Aidan's grin curled again. "Don't you realize, stupid girl? You *are* going to kill yourself. I'm here to make sure that doesn't happen until you've transferred that power to me." I could feel Clara's hand get cold in my grip. Aidan continued, chuckling at our surprise. "Oh, did you not realize what was happening in your dreams?"

"How do you know that?"

"Because I tried to take the Blue Star's energy once and it denied me and stole my powers. I had to steal my power back from a different source. It only wants her and she doesn't even want it. She doesn't deserve it. Do you have any idea what you could do with that kind of power?"

A kid ran through the middle of us, shooting Clara and I before running off. I took advantage of the distraction.

"Glitch, run!" I shouted, pulling Clara down into the shadows.

I slid us out the side of the building and pushed Clara out onto a pile of bags as I slammed into the dumpster. I stood off and ripped my vest off, trying to get Clara to hurry with hers. She was moving slowly, still dizzy from Aidan's power. I looked around, trying to find the best exit, but the fences were all locked. We could use the shadows again, but we couldn't leave Glitch behind either.

"Nate..." Clara mumbled, struggling to get to her feet. I reached down and lifted her, balancing as her knees wobbled.

"Hey, we gotta find Glitch and get out of here."

"No, Nate. Look where we are."

I looked around again, realizing what I had missed the first time. The alley from our dream. Before I had a chance to get us out, Aidan popped up across from us with Glitch, using Glitch's power.

"What did you do?" I asked, grabbing Clara's hand again to protect her.

"I made the playing field even," Aidan hissed. The haze around Glitch thickened, his dull stare a sign he had lost control of his mind.

"Glitch!" Clara shouted at him.

He focused his eyes on her, a disgusted snarl on his face as he turned to me. "How can you be with her?"

"What?" I could feel my stomach clench. That voice... it was his, but so full of hate.

"She almost killed us," Glitch snapped. "She's weak, listening to the voices. They control her."

I shook my head. "Glitch, that's not you. Aidan is making you think these things. You have to fight it."

"Look at her arm!" he growled back. "She's already given in once. You can't stop her anymore. She is going to listen to the voices no matter what you do. She'll give in and kill you."

Aidan laughed behind him as I gripped Clara's hand tighter. We had seen a way out of this before.

Nate, you can't let go of me. No matter how hard I fight you, please don't let go.

I won't.

I felt our grip getting colder as Clara's hand tensed in mine. The voices hummed in the back of my head, sending shivers down my spine as I pushed their pain down.

Aidan picked up on our strategy, moving forward with Glitch following his command. Clara's grip was starting to numb my fingers, but I could still make out the trickle of blood between our palms. The faint voices in my head were getting louder, fighting against me which meant they were now shouting at Clara. I could see the pain in her face as she inhaled again.

And then she screamed, throwing her right hand forward as I used all of my strength to keep a grip on her left. The blast narrowly avoided Glitch as it connected with Aidan's chest, sending him flying backward. Just like the dream, his head slammed into the wall, the crack echoing in the alley as the wall was smashed. Brick pieces showered down with his body as he dropped into the shadow I created on the ground. As he disappeared, I closed the gap. Besides the crack in the wall, you would never have known he had been here.

Glitch dropped to the ground and clutched his head, groaning in pain. But he was alive, and that's what mattered.

Now the voices came roaring back through my neck, louder and stronger. I realized I hadn't heard them over the sound of Clara's scream, and now I could hear both. I guided her back against the dumpster, not letting go of her hand. I did what I had done the night of my dad's party. I kissed her and tried to give her my thoughts as I pulled the voices out of her head.

Clara, I'm never letting go.

I focused on the voices, allowing them to grow in my head. I lured them away from Clara, pulling her pain. The voices screamed and clawed through my head, begging to return to Clara so they could be released.

Keep fighting, C. Let me in. Let me help you.

I felt her tears on my face, but I didn't pull away. The pressure was growing in my skull and I could feel my nose bleeding, but I refused to let the voices win. I pressed harder into Clara, squeezing my eyes shut against the fading light. Maybe this is what blacking out felt like.

I gasped as the voices disappeared in an instant. It was easy to breathe now as the silence echoed through my head. I took my head away from Clara, looking around as she shoved her face into her knees. We were sitting in complete darkness.

"Clara." My voice stretched into the emptiness.

She picked her head out of her knees, looking around as she frowned. "Nate, the voices. They're gone. They're gone from my head," she whispered.

"How are you doing this?" I asked, tapping the ground. I could have sworn we were floating in the blackness, but I felt solid ground underneath me. The space looked like it would never end.

"I'm not doing it," she replied, her eyes wide. "You are."

"What?"

"Nate, I was stuck with the waves and the voices just like before. They were swallowing me, crushing me, but then you pulled it all away. You brought me here…"

"I don't know what I did," I replied, still lost in confusion.

"'Called into Darkness'," Clara whispered, running her right hand over my cheek. "The poem. I don't think the Darkness is part of the Blue Star… I think it's you."

"But… how?"

The darkness began to fade as the alley came into focus. In a way, I could feel it drawing back into me, but at the same time I had no idea what I was doing or how I was doing it. I looked around as it finally became light again.

Glitch was doubled over in the corner, throwing up. Aidan's body was nowhere to be seen. Clara was still staring at me, her thoughts spinning so quickly I couldn't follow him. Then again, maybe it was because my head was spinning too.

I think I wanted to throw up with Glitch.

40

Clara

For the first time, I was the one without the headache. We had just found a way to beat Aidan. Somehow, we had made it out alive and we had some answers. But I could only focus on one thing right now which was getting the two groaning and barely conscious boys to House.

I felt weak, but I managed to drag Glitch and Nate into the car so I could drive home. I threw Glitch on the couch as he mumbled on about an imaginary laser tag game he was playing against us. At least that was a pleasant memory. Hopefully he wouldn't remember what he shouted about me in the alley.

Nate was more awake than Glitch but completely incoherent. I tried to throw him on the bed but he pulled me down with him. He landed on my arm, leaving me pinned only inches from his face.

"Clara," he said, clearly trying to act serious while slurring his words. "Voices are bad. You should listen." He paused, deep in thought. "No, that's wrong... *don't* listen. Yeah, don't listen." He grinned and poked my ear.

I sighed, trying to hold my head over his. "Nate, you're on my arm."

He blinked quickly, trying to focus on me. "That's not important."

"It is if I want circulation in my hand," I groaned.

Nate scrunched his nose. "Aidan isn't nice. Don't date him."

"Nate, I'm not dating Aidan. I'm dating you."

He sat up and grabbed me by the shoulders, staring deep into my eyes. I pulled my arm out from behind his back before he could lay back down on it. He moved his hands to my face and held it closer to his.

"I don't want to be darkness," he whispered.

I sighed and shook my head before kissing his forehead. "Nate, you aren't darkness… it's different. And I won't listen to the voices."

He grinned wide. "Your eyes are pretty." I went to stand up but he reached out and held my hand. "Wait, please don't let go."

"Never again. I promise, always forever."

Nate was snoring before I had even leaned back with him. I should have been exhausted but my mind couldn't relax. Nate had to be Darkness, from my note, but it wasn't a bad thing. I went over the warning again. *Called into Darkness. Called into Cold.*

Did that mean I had a choice? Nate had called me *out* of the cold, just like he was always pulling me. I felt it even before we had the Blue Star connection. Could I really pick the Darkness over the Cold?

The more I thought about it, the more I focused on the feeling, the more it felt like the Blue Star was pushing us together. I had never found the other half, but Nate found it without trying. It connected us when we fixed it. Why did the Blue Star feel so conflicting? Why would something evil connect us in a way that kept the voices out? It was protecting me from Aidan when he would have given the power source a chance to take over me. Right?

Was Nate and I being together a good thing if this evil power source was driving us closer?

"Do you really think I'm Darkness?" Nate asked in a groggy voice.

I sighed and turned to face him. "Darkness doesn't have to be a bad thing. Whatever you did, you pulled me out of the cold. The darkness is what saved me. It was a good thing."

He frowned. "I don't know how I did that."

I reached down and lifted his right palm. "I think this extra power is how."

Nate yanked his hand out of mine and threw it over his mouth. "I'm gonna be sick."

I jumped up and pulled him into the bathroom. He rolled over the tub like I had once done and turned on the water. I pushed off the ground, drying my hands on my jeans.

"I'll go check on Glitch."

"Good luck. He's a pain when he wakes up, especially if he's sick," Nate mumbled, pressing his face against the tile to cool down.

Glitch was sitting up on the couch when I walked in, groaning with his head in his lap.

"Don't puke on House or you'll never be allowed back inside," I said gently, leaning against the wall.

"Ugh, don't shout. Can you shut off the sun?" he asked, squinting as he held his hand up to block the light. I flicked my fingers and shut all the blinds. Glitch sighed in relief and leaned back. "I should apologize."

I shook my head. "You don't have to, Glitch. Aidan was using you."

"No, I *need* to apologize. Aidan might have had his evil agenda, but those were all thoughts I'd had before. He just made them... real. I never wanted to say that," he said, hanging his head.

I walked over and sat next to him, wrapping my arms around his chest. "If our little family is going to work, we need to be in the business of forgiveness. I'm not mad, Glitch. We've all screwed up, me most of all, but we're under extreme circumstances."

"Are you cheating on me with my best friend?" Nate asked, leaning against the wall to steady himself. Somehow he'd managed to change and get a dry shirt on. Progress.

"Shit, he caught us," I said with a grin. I kissed Glitch's cheek and helped him stand as Nate balanced him on the other side. I groaned. "Glitch, stop singing 'we're the three best friends' in your head."

"I can't help it. My brain feels hungover."

Nate chuckled. "I hope you drown in the shower."

After a few minutes, Nate joined me on the couch. I leaned back and rested my head on his lap, staring at my bloody arm. It was a miracle I hadn't run out of blood.

"Okay, let's talk about it," Nate said, pinching my nose.

"Which part?"

"Aidan. What you said about killing yourself."

"Nate, I don't actually see that as an option. Plus, you saw my dad in the nightmare. He's the one..." I trailed off.

"Do you think Aidan was telling the truth about the Blue Star? That the power only wanted you?" he asked.

"He said the Blue Star took his power when he tried to use it. That's probably the only reason he got close to me... to Finnley, I mean. He wanted that power for himself, and I bet he tried to cut Richard out."

"He said Richard moved to slow, which probably means he has a plan," Nate sighed, running his fingers over my forehead.

"We're lucky he wasn't there, but if he's willing to wait, there's definitely a reason," I replied.

Nate nodded. "Our dream gave us a hint about Aidan's attack."

I traced my fingers over my stomach. "Which means those nightmares have been hinting my fate since the first day."

"But we changed it this time. Aidan is floating around in the shadows, not lying on the ground."

"But he's still dead," I whispered.

"The Blue Star gave us a chance to change the scene, though. We still can," Nate said, a new hope in his eyes.

I shrugged. "I hope so. The voices want me alone. They want me alive so they can take over, which means everyone around me is an obstacle keeping me from giving in... even Aidan. Even you."

"What do you mean?" he asked.

"I wasn't entirely in control back there. It was mostly them, or it. I was fighting back, barely enough to direct the blow. The Blue Star would have taken out everyone if I hadn't resisted. It wanted to kill Glitch. It wanted to kill you right next to me, even though you were helping."

But you fought back and won, that's what matters. Nate leaned down and kissed my forehead.

You got me away from the voices.

Nate leaned back, scrunching his nose. "So about laser tag... did you really kiss someone else?"

"I figured out it wasn't you because he was really good at kissing." I winked at laughed but Nate didn't humor my joke. "I'm kidding, Nate. I was tracking you the whole game." I poked his head to let him know I was following his thoughts.

His jaw dropped. "You were the one who kept killing me!"

I stuck my tongue out as Nate smiled. He leaned down and pressed his lips to mine. He slid out from underneath my head and rested his body on mine, kissing me deep. Chills ran down my arms and spine.

"Gross. Get a room," Glitch groaned as he ran toward the rood. "See you weirdos later."

41

Nate

Four days before Christmas, we decided to send Glitch off on his vacation with a Star Wars movie night, something we hadn't done in a long time. We even capped the night with a training session disguised as a lightsaber fight, using our powers and wooden sticks as weapons. It was nice to just be loose and have fun again.

We pulled the pads off the walls to use as beds, leaning back as we stared up at the ceiling. When Glitch left tomorrow, Clara and I were going to be left without help. There was no telling if Richard would try something, but we had to play the waiting game.

"I've been practicing something," Clara said, reaching her hand up toward the ceiling. It started to fade into darkness as the night sky appeared, the stars blinking and shimmering where there should have been a roof.

"How are you doing that?" Glitch asked, waving up at the sky.

"Making you think we're outside." Clara's hand continued to brush through the air as the stars followed her movements, leaving streaks of light behind them.

"Stop messing with our brains," I said, looking at her.

She winked and stuck out her tongue. "I mess with a lot more of you than your brain."

"Ugh," Glitch groaned. "You guys are so gross. I can't believe I wanted you to be together. I better not wake up to you two kissing."

"Nope, I'm pretty sure it'll just be the two of us yelling as I die again in our shared nightmare," Clara sighed as the night sky disappeared. I had noticed her gallows humor was getting worse the longer we went without answers.

"Joy," Glitch said as he rolled over and pulled his blanket with him.

"I shouldn't have agreed to this."

Clara laughed and slid closer to me, playing with my fingers until we both fell asleep.

Aidan was lifeless on the ground, the cloud of dust settling around him. I made sure not to let go of her hand this time, but she didn't fight against me. In fact, she didn't move at all. Her touch was limp.

"You're too late, boy."

My gaze shifted to Richard as he reached his arm into the air in front of him. I tried to focus on his hand that had a soft red glow spilling out of his grasp. But I didn't have long as Clara's free hand lifted up, a knife held tight in her grip.

Everything happened in a flash. Richard pulled the red object into his stomach as I dove for the knife in Clara's hand, but her movements followed Richard's precisely. She plunged the knife deep into her gut, blue blood spilling around her fingers as she screamed.

I fell face down into the empty space next to me, reaching for Clara. I scrambled forward, unable to find her until I ran into a sleeping Glitch.

"Ow, what the hell?"

"Where's C?"

The panic in my voice made Glitch sit up quickly. "I don't know. I just woke up."

I jumped up and looked around the room until I spotted her. She was standing with a blank face in front of the open door, staring out at nothing. My heart dropped when I saw the kitchen knife in her hand, extended out in front of her.

"Clara!" I stepped forward but her grip tightened on the knife handle.

"I got it," Glitch said. He popped over to her, wrestling the knife free. She didn't seem to fight back, but it still took him a second to yank it from her hand before he glitched out of the room.

Clara's arm dropped to her side as she screamed, sending out a blast of her energy around the room. Weights and padding went flying through the air, but not even the energy hit me. It was almost like she created a path. I moved forward cautiously, just in case there was another knife or sharp object I couldn't see.

She stood still, blue blood dripping form her fingers as she stared right through me. "The Ruby. My dad's plan. I'm going to die."

42

Clara

"Where'd you even find the knife?" Glitch asked. He continued to open every drawer in the kitchen, but it was useless. House was going to hide everything that had a sharp edge.

"I told you, I don't remember doing any of it," I replied, wincing as Nate cleaned around the lightning cut. I was going to run out of first aid supplies and blood if I wasn't careful.

"Did you have the same dream as me?" Nate asked, pressing a little too hard. I yanked my arm away as he cringed. "Sorry."

I shook my head. "I didn't have a dream. One minute I was falling asleep, the next I was standing there holding a knife. I was there, but not there. It doesn't make sense."

"The Blue Star did this?" Glitch asked as he sat next to me.

"Not this time," I said with a shrug. "My head was completely blank. No emotions, no fear, no voices, and no cold. I saw what I was doing, but I wasn't thinking or reacting. I was just... empty."

"What did you mean by the Ruby?" Nate asked, securing the wrap on my arm.

"Huh?"

He frowned. "You said 'The Ruby. My dad's plan. I'm going to die'."

"No I didn't."

Nate raised his eyebrow. "You definitely did. So you don't remember that?"

"No. I mean, I believe you, but I don't remember that," I answered.

"In my dream, I think your dad was holding something red. Maybe that was the Ruby. But he used it to make you..." Nate scrunched his nose as he trailed off. I guess I had died again.

"Wait," Glitch said, leaning forward. "Why does the Ruby sound familiar?"

I sighed and hung my head. I knew exactly what it was. Well, at least where we could find out about it. "The book when I sent you guys into the walls. It's a power source."

Glitch went to get the book while Nate stayed with me. I could feel him watching me, trying to see if I was actually in control of myself. This wasn't good. Now we had more than just the Blue Star to worry about.

Glitch dropped the book on the table and went to open the cover but I slammed my hand on top. "Not while I'm in here. Clearly the Blue Star is trying to keep me from reading this book. I don't know what the hell happened to make me go crazy last time, but I'm not about to test it again."

"Just turn your back and as soon as you feel dizzy, we'll close it. The Blue Star will never know," Glitch replied, motioning for me to turn around.

Instead, I walked away and planted my face into the couch cushions. I didn't have a headache, but I almost wanted one. It would make me feel less uneasy than this dull, empty feeling.

Nate spoke from the other room. "You translated half of it. Oh, wait, maybe not. It's still gibberish."

"Great," I mumbled through the cushions. "I don't date papers and I don't know how to write real words."

"Shit." Nate and Glitch said in unison.

I shot up off the couch, but as soon as I looked in their direction, I felt the nausea punch me in the gut. I dropped back to the couch as I heard them shut the book. The room slowed its spinning and the floor settled underneath me but I kept my eyes closed just in case.

"What did you find?" I asked. I felt them sit on either side of me as Nate wrapped his arms over my shoulders and Glitch took my hand in his. Neither spoke. "Would someone please tell me something?" Why the hell weren't they talking?

Glitch was the one to break the silence. "C, the only legible words you wrote were 'puppet master'."

My stomach churned. I was my dad's puppet now. That's how he killed me.

Focus on their hearts beating. Count them. Regain composure. I tried to reassure myself before panic set in. If my dad was going to try to control me, I had to be strong to fight him, or at least strong in front of these two. They were doing so much to help me. I stood up off the couch and spun to face them, pressing my shoulders back.

"C?" Nate asked nervously.

I threw up the walls around my head. "I'm fine. We can find a way out of this. My dad found the Ruby. So what? We have that book and a library and a magic house to figure this out." Glitch and Nate exchanged concerned looks as I gripped my fists. "Seriously, guys. Get out a translating app or find a book that can help us understand that thing. I'll be in the library away from it. Just keep an eye out and make sure I don't walk out the front door. At least I don't have traveling powers like you two."

I walked out of the room, trying not to speed up or give myself away. House opened the library door for me but I had to shut it after I walked in, collapsing on the ground. I leaned up against the door, flicking my fingers to lock it as I started to cry.

I knew my future. My dad was going to use the Ruby to control me. He would use it to make me juice the Blue Star for him before he killed me. That was it. My story ended there. I picked myself up off the floor and started digging through the books again, reading through all of my notes to see if I had ever been able to resist Aidan's powers. That's essentially what Richard was doing with the Ruby. Nate wasn't affected by Aidan's powers, so maybe I could find a reason why, or at least a way to protect myself from the Ruby.

What was the Blue Star's power besides those evil voices? The Ruby was the puppet master, but the Blue Star was just the Cold Soul. To me, it was just a headache with useless voices, hissing promises that only brought pain and destruction. They would claw and fight through me to get out and kill everyone. Blue Star or Cold Soul, it was evil.

Glitch left that night with no answers and no way to help until after the new year, assuming I made it that long. He picked me up in a hug and spun me around.

"You better be here when I get back. I can't go back to hanging with that loser alone."

I kissed his cheek and closed the door behind him. Back in the library, Nate was flipping through three different books at once and comparing lines between them. I picked him up off the floor, cheating a little bit, and hugged him. We shifted away from the desk, swaying slowly.

"You know," he whispered, "most people dance to music."

I flicked my finger and turned on the stereo.

All About Us. He is We ft. Owl City.

It played slowly in the background as I pressed my head harder into Nate's chest, listening to his heartbeat to distract myself from my twisting insides. I must have been distracted enough to sway the next song.

Sound of Your Heart. Shawn Hook.

Nate sighed and tried to lift away despite me holding him tight. "C, I'm not leaving your side. If that means I never let go of your hand again, I'll hold on forever."

"Nate, you are so important to me. You need to know that. I need you to know that."

He frowned. "Stop acting like this is the end. We'll figure out a way to save you. Just keep fighting a little longer."

I looked into his eyes, knowing that he would never let me give up. "Okay, I love you."

I flicked my fingers to change the song again.

Gold. Apollo LTD.

He smiled and pulled me back in. "Always forever."

43

Nate

Due to weather, Mom's flight home was canceled and she didn't have any options to get home. But she was still close enough for Dad to drive out and bring her home by Christmas. While I was excited to see her, it meant I could get away with Clara staying over for a few more days. We needed a break from the library and we desperately needed to relax. It didn't go as planned since I barely slept. Every time she shot up from the nightmare, I was there to catch her because I had already been awake for hours from the same one.

On Christmas morning, we were both awake before the sun. Being that tired, we couldn't even enjoy all the decorations around the house. It felt like fake happiness, and not even the tree could lift our spirits. We just sat on the couch and stared at it, not even turning the lights on.

I should have been happy that I could spend so much time alone with Clara, but the fear of it being our last moment together ate at me more and more. What happened if Clara had an outburst with my parents around? What if Richard showed up and my parents found out about our powers? Were we ready to fight him alone?

Clara shuffled back from the kitchen, her second cup of coffe steaming in her grip. She had on my old sweatshirt with the sleeves pulled over her hands. She set her cup on the table and dug under the tree to pull out a poorly wrapped present. Knowing her first aid skills, this was definitely her doing.

"Stop judging my wrapping. I know I'm terrible at it," she huffed, dropping the gift on my lap. "Merry Christmas, my fellow insomniac."

I flipped over the crumpled wrapping paper to pull a mound of tape off the small box. The lid of the box lifted to reveal a large key on a chain, just like hers.

"Are you asking me to move in with you?" I asked, playing with it in my hands. It buzzed just like hers had.

"No way, you're a terrible overnight guest. Just put it on," she said, rocking on her feet impatiently. What a weirdo.

I threw it over my neck, confused why Clara still looked at me with anticipation.

"I don't get it," I finally said. But as I turned my hands over to question her excitement, I saw my palms. My right had was blue-scar free. I looked up with a smile. "How did you do that?"

"I charmed it! I found a book in the library and did it to mine too. Now I don't have to hide it all the time," she cheered, lifting her sleeve to a scar-free arm.

I took her hand and rubbed my fingers over her forearm. There was still a bump I could feel under my fingers, but I couldn't see what it was.

"So it's still there, but now instead of you messing with everyone's brains, the key does it?"

"Basically."

"Well, my gift is complete shit compared to this," I groaned. Technically she had an unfair advantage using charms.

Clara switched places with me as I pulled her gift out from a drawer in the table. She frowned at me as she pulled at the gold ribbon. "You didn't put it under the tree?"

"If I had, you would have opened it early."

"Fair point," she replied with a shrug. She lifted the lid and slid the chain necklace out, resting it in her palm.

"It's a caffeine molecule for your coffee obsession. I guess we both stuck with the same theme for our presents. No charm on mine, though."

"Nate, I love it. Help me put it on?" she asked.

I nodded as she shifted in her seat, pulling her tangled hair off her neck. Half of it was still in the way as I wrapped the necklace around her neck. When I lifted the rest of it through the chain, bruised splotches peeked out from her hair line and down the back of her neck.

"Clara, what the hell is wrong with your neck?" I lifted the rest of her hair, running my fingers over the bruises.

"What are you talking about?" she asked, trying to spin around. She reached back and grabbed my hand. "Nate, you're freaking me out."

"How hard have you been digging into your neck when you get headaches? There are bruises everywhere."

Clara turned her body so she could look at me, sadness in her gaze. "I was using my powers to help with the pressure, but now I don't even notice when I do it. How bad?"

"Bad enough you'll need to keep your hair down for a while. It looks like a black and blue painting back there."

She sighed and pressed her cheek into my chest. Great, more depressing things right before my parents got home. We were going to be a buzzkill today.

Clara sniffed but stood up, pulling me with her. "No, I'm done letting the Blue Star win. I don't want to walk around like I've already lost."

I heard her iPod start playing on the table.

You Know Me. Air Traffic Controller.

She looked back up at me and placed her hands on my cheeks. "I love you, always forever, and I intend to be present with you for that whole time."

I could see her fighting back her emotions so I played along with the distraction, wrapping my arms around her hips to help her up as she kissed me. We swayed, listening to the music in the background until the front door lock clicked open.

"Merry Christmas!" my mom cheered, running in from the front and leaving my dad behind to drag in her bags. She looked as pretty as always, her long brown hair tied in a braid and green eyes shining behind a face that never seemed to age. I met her in a hug. She squeezed so hard I thought she was going to break a rib.

"Hi Mom. I missed you too," I grunted through her grip.

She leaned away and held my face in her hands. "Now, I've been waiting forever to meet this wonderful girlfriend of yours."

"Mom, this is Clara." I slid to the side, looking back at Clara. She had her sleeves wrapped around her hands again, tugging at them in her nervous habit.

"Ma'am," she said with a smile, shifting anxiously in her stance. She quickly lifted her hands to fix her hair again, but her smile soon changed to confusion.

"Finnley."

I spun back around in shock. My mom's face was pale and her voice echoed with surprise and… anger?

"What?" Clara and I said at the same time.

"You promised me. You promised you wouldn't get him involved," she snapped, her voice rising with each word.

"Mom, how do you know what her name is? What promise?" I asked, stepping back. I bumped into Clara's arm, the chill sending ice through me.

"Wait," Mom said, turning her head to me. "How do *you* know her name?"

"Okay, hold on a second," Clara blurted, sending her mug rattling on the table. "What the hell is going on?"

Everyone stood there, glancing awkwardly as we waited for someone else to go first.

"Let's try to get on the same page here," Clara said, breaking the silence. "I *was* Finnley, I lost my memory, and I clearly don't remember you so I have no idea what promise you're talking about. How do you know me?"

"This is Finnley?" my dad asked, shaking his head. He guided Mom to the chair. "Angie, your description was off."

Hold on, he was in on this too? Who the hell were my parents?

"Tom, not the time. I didn't know she was still alive," Mom sighed, turning to us again. "I know you because your mother was my best friend. Do you remember anything about The Complex?"

"Only what I've read in books, why?" Clara asked, shifting and bumping into me again.

My mom hesitated, glancing back and forth between us before finally breaking the silence.

"I'm one of the leaders.

44

Clara

"This whole time you've been an hour away and couldn't bother coming home?" Nate asked, his voice raising as he gripped the couch cushions. As anxious as I was to have my past filled in, this wasn't going to be easy for Nate either. His parents had lied to him his whole life.

"I was trying to protect you," Angie sighed. "Was it the best way? No, but it kept you safe. All of this started for you around the same time as Fi- I mean, Clara."

Both Tom and Angie glanced at me but I didn't react. In fact, I couldn't move. My entire body felt heavy and numb. I barely noticed Nate slide his arm around my waist and pull me into his side.

"Then start explaining," Nate demanded, breaking the silence as he glared at his parents.

Tom sat in the chair next to Angie and looked at me. "We found out about Finnley's powers just a few months after she was born, and a couple months before Nate was born. Ellie called us in the middle of the night saying Finnley was moving things without touching them."

"We had never seen or heard of anyone born with powers," Angie added.

"Why did my mom call you?" I asked.

"I told you. Ellie and I were best friends. She knew we would keep a secret." She looked down, fighting back her emotions. I could hear her thoughts twinged with sadness, but I couldn't understand the anger. "I did the only thing we could have done. People who tried to take the Blue Star's power usually lost theirs, or never got them in the first place. We did it to protect you, and to protect others. It wasn't your fault, but you couldn't control your powers as a baby."

We just made things worse. The thought ran through Tom's head as he glanced at Angie and then Nate. "When Nathaniel displayed powers, we used the Blue Star on him and he stopped showing signs of power. We thought it worked on both of you, but to be safe, I took Nate away from The Complex before anyone knew his name. We convinced everyone that we wanted a normal life for our son, away from The Complex and away from powers. Clara, you didn't have the same option, so your parents kept an eye on you there."

"You were okay leaving her with that psychopath Richard?" Nate asked.

"He wasn't always. Finnley liked to push his buttons growing up so we didn't notice it getting worse. No one knew she still had telekinetic powers... or telepathic ones." Angie looked back at me as her voice got quiet. "You came to me before The Trials. You were having nightmares about your dad using you to take the Blue Star's power and then snapping Nate's neck."

I frowned. "I knew who Nate was before all this?"

"Not exactly. The boy you described... with the power to play with darkness? I knew it had to be Nate." She took a breath. "You explained your powers and your dreams to me and I knew—"

"Okay, but why *you*? Why would I tell you all those things and not my mom?" I snapped, trying to shove down my anger. It wasn't fair that this version of me didn't know her. "I'm sorry. It's just hard to wrap my head around this because I don't know you... well, this version of me doesn't remember."

Angie nodded sympathetically. "I know this isn't easy. I don't think you wanted to worry your mom, or put her in Richard's path. What we did to you was terrible. Introducing you to the Blue Star as a baby had consequences. We knew it was rumored to show visions of the future to lure people into its trap; false promises in exchange for using the power source. All it ever did was steal powers away. That is until Finnley touched it. Clearly you still have your powers."

Yeah, there are a lot more consequences than that. I thought to Nate. I kept my mouth shut, knowing there was still a hint of anger behind Angie's story.

She sighed before continuing. "The energy of the Blue Star was too strong for a single person, but that's also how it could be emptied so no one else could use it. Finnley was supposed to take in the power and let it consume her so no one would ever use it again."

"You told her to kill herself?" Nate growled.

I wasn't bothered by that statement because I finally understood. I rested my hand on Nate's knee to try to calm him down.

"It was my plan, wasn't it?"

Angie finally nodded. "Yes. You wanted your dad or Aidan to make a move before you took all the power so The Complex could stop them. If you had gone to them before, they would have known about your powers."

"And I was a coward," I whispered, repeating the word that ran through Angie's thoughts. "I didn't want to die or become the Cold Soul, so I ran away instead. I pretended to die so no one would come after me. I set up a whole life for myself outside The Complex so I could live a little longer. I ruined everything."

"The Blue Star tricked you," Nate said, trying to reassure me that it wasn't my own failing.

"Hold on, the Cold Soul?" Tom asked.

I glanced to Angie, the same confused look on her. "I think the Cold Soul and the Blue Star are the same thing. The nightmares, the voices clawing in my head, the headaches and outbursts, the fact that I feel cold all the time... I have half of the Cold Soul in me already." I pulled my necklace off and showed them my scar. "I don't think it's going to kill me. I think it wants me to take in the power so it can turn me into the Cold Soul."

"Do you still have the same nightmare? Nate still dies?" Angie asked, her face turning pale.

"No," Nate snapped, surprising me. "Because of what you did to her, she's now the one getting killed by Richard. I have to see it every night too." He pulled off his key necklace to show them his palm.

"How is that even possible?" Tom asked, leaning forward to get a better look.

"The thing only responds to Clara," he replied, turning to me. "What did you call yourself?"

"A conduit. That's why Richard needs me to get the power. It only responds to me, and apparently I can channel it into others." I could see the look of horror on Angie's face. "I didn't mean to do that. I didn't know what was happening."

"You promised me you'd keep him out of this!" Angie's horror snapped to anger, spilling what had been running in her mind the entire conversation. "The Blue Star is tricking you so you don't destroy it. Now you've gotten my son into this mess!"

"Mom!" Nate shouted, launching out of his seat.

I fell into the dent he left in the couch but I didn't react. Maybe under other circumstances I'd be angry, but all I felt was guilt. Angie was right. Even if I couldn't remember Finnley's promise, I was the one who needed to be held accountable for her actions. She listened to the voices that continually lied to her and didn't take in all the power to destroy the Blue Star. It was my fault.

Nate swung around to look at me. "Absolutely not. You are not allowed to feel guilty because this is *not* your fault."

"What?" Tom and Angie said in unison. Shit. He had just responded to my thoughts.

He turned back to them. "The connection from this mark allows us to communicate in our heads. I think she transferred the Blue Star energy as a piece of her power, though I can only hear her thoughts." Nate sat down again and took my hand. "I've been able to use my powers to reach her whenever she's having headaches or outbursts so she doesn't destroy things, but it's getting worse. Now Richard has the Ruby and is using it to control her. He's going to make her transfer the Blue Star power to him and then he'll kill her."

"The Ruby was stolen," Tom said, glancing at Angie. But it shouldn't work like that unless he makes physical contact with you. Maybe because you're related he can have an influence over you."

"Great," I mumbled, sinking back into the couch.

"Do you have any other options?" Nate asked. "Maybe another power source that could protect her?"

Angie's voice was quiet as she thought. "Unless we find Richard before he uses Fi- I mean Clara, we have to keep the Blue Star hidden from her. Anything she knows, he will know if he takes control."

"What about you two?" I asked, trying not to let desperation bleed through my voice. "Don't you have powers that can help?"

"I'm afraid we don't have powers. As leaders, we are only supposed to direct those who pass The Trials and oversee The Complex," Tom replied, avoiding my gaze. "Clearly our last panel failed with your father."

Nate shifted closer to again so I was practically sitting on top of his leg. It felt like he was never going to let me out of his grip until all this was over. "So what do we do now?"

Angie frowned. "How have you hidden from your dad this long? If he knows where you are, he should have come for you already."

I shrugged. "I think House has been protecting me. He's charmed or magical or something. Richard hasn't bothered me there until he used the Ruby to control me in my sleep. Nate was able to help protect me from Aidan's powers through the Blue Star connection, but in my dreams it doesn't work against Richard."

"Let me guess," Angie said, raising her eyebrow. "You have a library in your house?"

Nate raised his eyebrow as he looked at me. "How do you know that?"

"That's a story for another time. There will be something in there to add to the protection, hopefully something against power sources." Angie stood up and reached out her hand. "I'll hide the Blue Star so Clara doesn't know anything about it. Tom and I will reach out to our contacts in The Complex for anything else that can help."

Nate reached into his pocket and pulled out the marble. Of course that thing was nearby. But how could Angie hide something that never took it's grip off me?

Tom gave me a sad smile. "Once we stop Richard, we will look for something to help with the headaches and resisting the Blue Star."

It surprised me that he wasn't mad about me getting Nate involved. Angie was full of unpleasant thoughts about me.

I winced and took a sharp breath as the voices hissed louder in my head, probably in response to Tom's comment about resisting them. Nate pulled my head in to rest on his chest as he looked up at his parents.

"Please hurry. Like I said, it's getting worse."

45

Nate

Christmas was ruined. My mom had sent Clara and I digging through House's endless and hopeless library for answers that were impossible to find. If they were here, House would have shown us the right place to look, and the more books we tossed aside, the more distracted Clara got. How could we be present with each other when we were only looking for ways to keep Clara from dying?

She sat at the window, pressing her forehead against the cold surface. I could hear her thoughts wishing for snow.

"Why do you want snow? It's cold and miserable," I said.

Clara frowned as she turned. "I've never seen it. I mean, I don't think I've seen it. Besides, it's not like you can tell if it's cold anymore since you have that mark."

I just shrugged and looked back at my book. "Well, it rarely snows, even if they call for it."

She snagged the book out of my hands and threw it behind her, yanking me off the ground. "Then we'll just have to make our own. Come on."

"You're crazy. Shouldn't we keep trying in here?"

"I'm done for tonight. I can't ready anymore," she replied, grabbing her iPod in her free hand as she dragged me into the training room and plugged in her music.

She's Out of Her Mind. blink-182.

"From the first day of school. Because you think I'm crazy," she giggled, spinning around as she danced.

"You are crazy. It's a fact." I watched her run to the other side of the room as the ceiling turned into a gray sky. Little white flakes sprinkled from the ceiling, falling to the floor that was suddenly blanketed in snow. I reached out to hold a snowflake, admiring that it didn't melt in my hand. It also didn't feel cold. I let it drop to the ground with the rest of the flakes.

Clara scrunched her nose. "I can change your perception, but I can't get the rest of your senses to respond."

"Don't you be messing with my senses now. Perception is far enough," I laughed, changing the song.

I Wear Glasses. Mating Ritual.

If she was feeling good enough to act carefree, I was going to let her. And I was determined to put my worry behind me too. I ran over and grabbed her by the waist to swing her around.

She smiled. "You don't even wear glasses," she giggled as she kissed me. She spun out of my arms and continued to twirl around as I watched.

"Just listen to the song, dork. How do you even know how to make snow if you've never seen it?"

"It's called binge watching TV, Nate. I may only have four months of real memories but I still know things." Clara skipped around me as the song started over. She must have set it on repeat. "Are you going to come dance with me?"

"I'm performing an experiment," I replied, thinking back to the first day of school.

Clara's eyes lit up brighter than I had seen in the last month. "What's your conclusion?" she asked, hopping up and down as she impatiently waited for my response.

"Hush, now. I'm still performing it." I swung her around by the hand and pushed her against the wall, running my hands through her hair until my figners found a knot. I pressed my lips into her neck as I slid my hand under her shirt and across the small of her back. As my fingers brushed along her skin, I could feel the chill run through her spine. Just before she caved and tried to wrap her arms around me, I stepped away.

"Okay, now I've analyzed the results and reached a conclusion," I said, smiling.

She shook her head, still waiting. "Well?"

"Oh, I'm done. I have to leave you wanting more, right?"

Clara rolled her eyes. "You're an ass."

"I just march to the beat of my own drum," I laughed, sticking my tongue out at her.

She laughed and ran up to me, jumping and wrapping her legs

around my waist as I walked her back against the wall. The snow around us started to fade but the music stayed on as I melted into her.

Whispers.
Screams.
Fear.
A soul.
Replaced by the Cold Soul.
Erased.
Consumed.
Existing within.
Waiting.
The Blue Star.
Called into Darkness.
Called into Cold.
Dividing.

Clara stood in front of me, wearing the same gray dress she had worn before, but the skirt and sleeves were shredded and covered in blue ink. No, blood. Blue blood. The first rip was along her stomach, the blood staining the front of her skirt. Then, the sleeve on her left arm was ripped off, revealing the glistening cut of the lightning scar tracing her palm all the way up to her shoulder.

"Clara?" I asked, my voice echoing.

She frowned and tilted her head before shaking it. "No."

She lifted her left hand toward me, uncurling her palm to reveal the Blue Star marble, completely black and lifeless.

"No." I felt my heart sink into my stomach. "You took in the power. You became the Cold Soul."

She smiled softly. "Nate, you misunderstand. I left you the poem."

"Clara, what are you talking about?"

"I'm not Clara," she replied calmly.

My fists clenched. "Then you're the Cold Soul. You replaced Clara's soul."

"Nate, you misunderstand. I am the Blue Soul. I replaced the Cold Soul, not Clara's soul." She paused for a moment, waiting for the shock to fade. "The poem was about more than just Clara's soul. It was about the Blue Soul too. I am power. I replaced the Cold Soul in Clara."

"Clara didn't have a Cold Soul," I replied.

"The Cold Soul was woven into Clara after she was born. My cage held two powers, myself and the Cold Soul. It took advantage of the child, but she was too weak to hold all of it. I tried calling to her throughout her life to protect her. To save her. On her eighteenth birthday, she used me again. I replaced the

Cold Soul and trapped it with the other half of me. The voices she hears are the Cold Soul trying to get back to her. It wants to be free. We can't destroy it while I'm still in the cage."

I shook my head. "I don't understand. The other half of you, the Blue Soul, is still in there, but she can't take all of your power."

"No, she cannot. I am too much power and I would erase her completely."

"Then what else can you do to help her? The voices are killing her. If she can't take the rest of you in, how can we save her?"

"I wrote the poem," the Blue Soul replied in the same gentle tone.

"That's not an answer," I groaned.

The Blue Soul smiled again and pointed to my feet. I followed her gaze to see my shadow creeping along the floor, stretching out of me like an elongated person. I watched it crawl forward, reaching its arm toward Richard who held the Ruby in his hand. He didn't notice the black arm lift from the ground as it wrapped around his ankle. In a swift move, the shadow sank back to the ground, pulling Richard into the darkness underneath.

"Clara!" I shouted, frantically looking around at an empty room. "Clara!"

I shouted louder, my voice echoing through House. He creaked and whined in response. Shit.

I threw my shoes on and ran around House, checking every place she might have been, but I knew the truth. She wasn't here.

Then I saw it. Hanging on the front door and held by a knife, a small sheet of paper fluttered against House's panic.

Blue Star. Clearing.

You're running out of time, Nate.

-R

It was Clara's handwriting, but clearly Richard was in control now.

But I was ready. I understood what I had to do.

I didn't have to look for the Blue Star, or Soul… whatever it was called. My mom might have taken it, but I knew it would find its way back. It had a different agenda. I knew why it kept coming back to Clara.

I patted my pocket, feeling the cold pinch of the marble, and ran out the door.

46

Nate

The morning light highlighted the trees and illuminated the clearing as shadows swayed along the ground. I burst through the tree line, skidding to a stop as I made eye contact with Richard, an evil grin on his face as his fingers dug into Clara's shoulder. She swayed slightly, her face blank. She was still in the oversized shirt and shorts she had worn to bed. At least she couldn't register the cold anymore because it was below freezing outside.

"Clara!" I shouted, my breath clouding the air.

Richard laughed as she didn't register my voice. "You think she can hear you? Oh, boy, you have so much to learn about us."

"About who? The Complex?"

"Of course, idiot. Where do you think you got your powers? Every once in a while, someone is bound to come in contact with a source we didn't know about. I'm still trying to figure out where yours came from. You're too stupid to have gotten into The Complex yourself."

Well, at least he didn't know who I really was. I could use it to buy time. I still had to figure out what exactly the Blue Soul wanted me to learn after that dream, but the priority was trying to use the new power it had showed me.

"What do you want, Richard?"

A bolt of lightning slammed down behind him, sending sparks and fire into the trees. Shit. If I wasn't careful, the next bolt would come down on top of me. I had no way to protect myself from that.

"You already know what I want," Richard snarled. "I assume you brought it? You wouldn't risk your darling *Clara's* life."

His hand lifted, brushing her cheek as he slowly trailed his fingers down her left arm. Clara didn't flinch, standing unrealistically still with dull and pale skin. Even in the yellow light she looked lifeless.

Clara, you have to fight back. I dont' know how yet, but the Blue Star can save you.

"So, what happens when I give you the Blue Star?" I asked, closing my fist so he couldn't see my palm. I needed a longer distraction while I focused on calling Clara and extending my shadow. I needed to know the Blue Soul wasn't lying about saving her.

"I'll use her to steal the Blue Star's power. She'll direct it into me and then you two can live happily ever after."

Clara, fight it, please. I'm trying to save you. "You're lying. What are you going to do with that power? Why do you need it?" *Damn it, Clara! Wake up!*

Hope surged in my chest as Clara's finger twitched. It was nearly indiscernable until I saw the single drop of blue blood fall from her hand. She was fighting back.

That energy ran through me and down my feet as my shadow grew underneath me, creeping slowly toward Richard. The Blue Soul wasn't lying. I could help her. And then I would help her defeat the Cold Soul.

Richard grunted. "Of course I'm lying, but I'm not spilling my plans to you. It's a waste of time. Tell you what. If you hand over the Blue Star without a fight, I'll kill you first so you don't have to watch me kill your sweet love. I'll promise you both a merciful death."

My shadow was only half way to him and moving too slow. I couldn't risk him seeing it coming toward him, especially because Clara's fingers were twitching more often. More blood splashed to the ground, her scar starting to shine as the lightning mark opened up. But she was fighting, and I needed to give her more time.

"I can't give it to you," I replied, trying to hide the effort it took to speak and use more power than I ever had before. *C, fight. Just a little longer, please.*

Richard laughed and raised his right hand up, the Ruby glowing through his fingers. Clara's right hand obeyed and lifted in front of her body, a knife gripped in her fingers just like our nightmare. But this time her grip was shaking.

"Want to try that again?" Richard asked, his smile curling again.

My shadow was still a few feet away but I was out of time. I had to make my move.

"Tell me, do you think this scar matches my outfit?"

"What?"

Just a few more inches, come on, hurry up. I held up my right hand, showing off the scar on my palm.

Richard's nostrils flared as his face contorted into pure rage. "That's not possible. You're going to suffer for that."

I heard the crack of lightning and shut my eyes. I hadn't been close enough to grab him. I had failed, and here was my punishment.

The trees behind me exploded, the force pushing me closer to Richard and Clara. Fire rolled through the branches before burning out into the sky. I turned back to Richard who was just as shocked as I was. He grunted again, a deafening crack piercing my ears from overhead. Light ripped from the sky but bounced away from me, just like before.

Clara.

Richard realized it at the same time I did. He looked over her shoulder to see her hand shaking, trying with every ounce of effort to release the knife. Richard turned back to me, his face hardened.

"You're too late."

But I had been thrown closer and my shadow was finally underneath him. I shoved into the ground with my energy, curling the shadow around Richard's leg. I yanked.

But I was too late. He pulled the Ruby into his stomach as I dragged him into the dark shadow and released my grip.

Clara's body jolted as she lowered her gaze, her hands clutching at the knife sticking out of her abdomen. Tears ran down her cheeks as she looked back up at me. She slid the knife out and dropped it to the ground, holding her hands over her stomach as the blood ran through her fingers.

"No!" I screamed.

I sprinted forward as she collapsed onto the ground, sliding forward in the last few feet to scoop her into my lap. I shook as I held her head up with one arm, my other hand pressing into her stomach to stop the bleeding. Her fingers twitched under my shaking hands. She opened her mouth to speak, but barely a wisp of breath escaped.

Nate, I'm sorry. I tried to fight it. I tried.

Please keep fighting the Blue Star isn't what it seems. It's a soul. It can save you.

I'm too tired, Nate. I don't want to hear those voices anymore. I can't do it. I'm sorry.

No, keep fighting, you don't understa—

I just want the voices to go away. I love you, always forever.

Clara stopped thinking but still held on as I pressed my forehead into hers. I couldn't keep the tears from falling with hers as she threaded her fingers through mine. She tapped the back of my hand, trying to stay with me longer.

Please, C. I love you. Don't leave me.

The last tap was weak as it hung on my hand, but her body sank into me as she fell limp.

Clara, you can't leave. Please don't leave.

I felt my body grow cold with hers. She couldn't be gone. The Blue Soul promised that it would save her from the cold.

I shot up, pulling the marble from my pocket. Light swirled and spun in my hand, banging on the edges of the marble as it tried to get out. I held it in my right palm and placed Clara's left hand over mine, squeezing my eyes shut.

Come on. You said you'd protect her. Tell me what to do.

Emptiness hung in the air, swallowing my hope and crushing my chest. But a bitter cold breeze lifted my chin. I opened my eyes to see the swirling blue energy again. Waves ripped around me... around Clara. She stood at the edge of the space with her back to me, her hair whipping with the wind and waves.

Clara!

She didn't answer. Her left hand lifted as her fingers slid into the waves.

No!

I dove forward and yanked her away from the edge before she could be sucked in. She frowned, blinking her bright blue eyes in confusion as I stepped away from her. The scar on her left arm had grown to her shoulder, blue blood trickling down her arm and dripping from her fingers. The wound on her stomach was worse, a river of blue flowing down and staining her shorts and legs.

If I could have gasped inside this place, I would have. *You're the Blue Soul now. She took all the power.*

Do you understand the poem now? She cocked her head.

I nodded. *You're more than just power. You're the soul. Called into Cold. That means called into Clara.*

She nodded. *She had the cold, yes. And now?*

And now you're called into me. Darkness.

A smile grew on her face as she lifted her right hand to my face. *It is time for me to do what I've been trying to do for years. The Cold Soul has to be destroyed. Take in the other half of me and destroy the source.*

What happens after that? I asked.

My soul is split, but the Cold Soul will never be used again.

She took her hand away from my face and motioned for me to lift my right hand. I opened my palm to reveal the black marble as she rested her left hand in mine. Energy rushed up my arm, digging into my veins. Icy cold power carved into my skin as the scar on Clara's arm receded and grew along my forearm. Blue light glowed as it traced lightning along my skin, illuminating the darkness that was surrounding us now. Everything around us emptied into blackness, like it had after we had stopped Aidan. Pain disappeared as the scar reached my elbow, but I could feel the marble shaking in our grip. Pressure built in our palms, rattling and shaking until it exploded into black dust.

I sucked in a breath and pulled my forehead away from Clara's.

"C?"

She didn't move in my arms.

47

Clara

"Clara?"

I rolled off something and hit the ground, pain rippling through my body with each cough as I struggled to breathe. My head felt like it was going to explode.

Clara! "Clara!" Nate continued to yell, his voice and thoughts echoing in my head.

"Stop... shouting... my... head..." I grunted each word.

He rolled me over and kissed me but I shoved him away, gasping for breath and wincing in pain at the same time. It felt like I had just taken a truck to my abdomen.

Holy shit.

I grasped at my stomach. No knife. No gushing wound. Just a raised scab where there should have been a knife. I picked at the hole in my shirt that was stained with sticky blood. Too much blood. Enough to kill someone.

"Nate, I died," I whispered, focusing on my breath. Why was my chest tightening so much?

"You're okay. You're back with me."

As his hands reached over to turn me around, blue caught my eye. I snatched his right hand away from me and studied the blue scar that traced up his palm and to his elbow. A lightning scar, freshly cut and dripping blue blood just like mine.

"Nate, what did you do?" I asked. I turned to face him but pain shot through my body and I shut my eyes to keep from passing out.

"The Blue Soul," he replied. "Do you remember anything?"

Waves. My arm. Nate. It all came rushing back and I leaned over, nauseous. "Yup. Yeah, I remember. Lots of calling into things. You're the Darkness, I'm the Cold, and the Blue Star is really a Soul."

It may have come out as a jumbled mess, but I knew what it really meant. The Blue Soul had saved me. Nate had saved me. He risked everything to protect me.

I blinked, the boy I loved coming into focus. But something was wrong.

"Nate, your eyes are blue."

"Really?"

He made an attempt to look at his own eyes but ended up going crosseyed. I tried to stifle a laugh but the pain shot through me again. Nate slid closer as I lifted his right arm, tracing the scar that was identical to mine.

"Thank you for saving me," I sighed.

"You saved me first," he replied. "The lightning from your dad? You were protecting me somehow. That's why you couldn't fight the Ruby. That's why you…"

"Why I died," I said, finishing the thought for him.

"Do you remember that part?"

I didn't really want to tell him the truth, but I was too weak to hold back. "Yes, kind of. I remember standing there, completely empty. But then I felt you growing in my head. It was either focus on you or the Ruby. I watched all of it, I *felt* all of it, but I couldn't do anything to stop it. You faded… and then the voices and energy waves and you know the rest."

"The Cold Soul voices?" he asked.

I nodded slightly. "Trying one last time. A final plea, I guess. But now they're gone."

"Are you sure about that?

A pair of familiar voices spoke in unison, startling us both. Nate shot up with ease while I struggled to push myself up. Across from us, a black energy cloud was growing, spinning and swirling without a breeze. From within the dust and smoke, two figures walked out.

Us.

Well, sort of us. They were wearing the same clothes as we were, but everything was wrong. The version of me had the same tear in her shirt, but the blood around it was black. In fact, both of their arms were dripping the same black blood from lightning scars that matched ours. Their green eyes narrowed on us as they smiled.

"What?" Nate asked, sliding his arm around my back as he helped me stand. I lifted my hands carefully, ready to fight if needed.

"Oh, honey," the weird version of me said as she rolled her eyes. "You really believed us in your dreams? Pathetic."

"Now, dear, love is blind," the black-blooded Nate replied.

"What the hell are you?" I asked, leaning closer to Nate.

"Darling Clara, you poor thing," the green-eyed me mocked. "You were so close to defeating us, but your idiot pet pulled you away and saved us."

Nate stiffened next to me. My Nate. "You're the Cold Soul."

"Souls," she corrected. "You made two Blue Souls so we became two Cold Souls. We tricked you into taking the rest of the Blue Soul, leaving our cage unprotected. If Clara had kept going, we wouldn't exist, though, neither was she. That's why it was so easy to make you believe you were talking to the Blue Soul. Anything to save your precious girlfriend."

"You became us? But..." I lost my balance slightly, Nate flinching as he steadied me.

The other me snarled. "I didn't *become* you. I'm what should have existed in the first place. Clara isn't real, but Finnley is. That's the girl I lived inside for eighteen years. The Cold Soul has been stealing every evil thing from anyone who tried to take in the Blue Soul's power. Then *little baby Finnley* came along and that Blue Soul became so obsessed. I used the chance to sneak part of me into you, waiting for years until you were strong enough to take me in. But you kicked me out the night of your Trials and the Blue Soul replaced me to protect you.

That's why it was so easy to trick you into setting me free again. Nate's only option to save poor, helpless Clara was leaving that prison without a defense. Now I get to be everything you were too afraid to become." She licked her lips and winked at my Nate. "You're just an added bonus. Two different powers to play with now."

My mind was reeling. "There were two powers inside the source," I whispered. The green-eyed me seemed interested that I was finally catching up. "It was two powers the whole time, a Blue and Cold Soul. Before the Trials, the Blue Soul was going to save me, but the poem and the dreams? It was always you, tricking me and drowning out the Blue Soul that was trying to protect me. You manipulated us into this moment."

The Cold Souls grabbed hands and started to slide into the shadows. "Maybe you are smart after all. See you around, lovebirds."

They were gone before either of us could react.

48

Clara

"What the hell happened?"

Angie's voice stirred me out of my distraction. When had we gotten back to House? How did Angie and Tom get inside?

I readjusted my hands over my stomach as I zoned out again, feeling empty and overwhelmed at the same time. Their thoughts ran rampant through my head, bouncing around in empty space. The voices that once overpowered my head were gone, which gave every thought more volume. I couldn't keep track of it as Nate explained what happened because the thoughts felt out of order. While Angie focused on one detail, Tom was focused on something else, and Nate was in a completely other part of the story.

Instead of following them, I tried to find my own thoughts in the mess. Why did I feel wrong? Why did my mind feel so empty... lonely? What did the Blue Star do to me?

Not one Blue Star. Two powers. A Blue Soul and a Cold Soul, split.

I died. It split because I died. Richard emptied my head when he used the Ruby, just like the Cold Soul stole my memory. My mind was as empty as it felt now, every noise reminding me of losing control. I had no power to stop Richard as he commanded every move I made. He lifted the knife, he drove it deep into my stomach.

I nearly yelped in surprise as Angie's voice rang through my ears. "We need to go explain this to The Assembly."

Tom shifted his nervous glance toward Nate and away from me. "You both need to clean up." He turned to Angie. "Let's call and give The Complex a heads up that we're bringing them."

I willed my legs to move, but I couldn't make the commands work. Why couldn't my legs move?

Nate slid his arm around my back and nudged me. I should have fallen, but his touch sent warmth through my body and my legs caught my weight. I let Nate guide me to the bedroom, instinctively stepping over the tub with my clothes still on.

For a minute, I stood there without moving, letting the warm water run over every nerve. At least now I could only hear Nate's thoughts in my head. He focused in the mirror, studying the new blue eyes that had come from the Blue Soul. That's how mine had changed; all because of the scar on my arm from taking in the energy.

I glanced down at my arm, trying to avoid looking at my stomach. As if blue blood wasn't enough to make me sick… that was going to be a challenge. I moved my fingers around the lightning mark, watching the stained water swirl down the drain under my feet.

I sighed and moved my hands to my stomach, brushing over the raised bump as I cleaned around the wound. There was so much more around the scar, the slick feel only getting worse. No matter how much I scrubbed around it, the blood never stopped and the water only turned a darker blue. My chest tightened, constricting my throat as I finally gasped.

"Nate!"

My vision blurred between black and white spots. Just before my knees completely gave out, the shower curtain tore open and Nate dove underneath me, catching me before I hit the tub.

"Hey, hey, it's okay, I've got you," Nate whispered as he pulled my body into his. He released one arm to shut off the water before curling it around my cheek. "Breathe with me. Count my heartbeats."

I steadied my body on his, focusing all of my mind on the pounding of his heart on my cheek. With each breath, the tightness lifted until only the echo of his heart in my head was left.

"I'm so sorry," I whispered.

"Don't be sorry. I was here. Can you explain what happened or will that trigger you?" he asked, gently tracing his fingers over my skin.

"Blood. So much of it…"

"From your arm?"

I shoved my face harder into his chest as I shook my head. I didn't want to think about my arm lifting the knife, my body trying so hard to fight the movement. It plunged, in slow motion, deeper and deeper… I breathed and found Nate's heartbeat again.

His hand slid down my arm and found the hand that I didn't know was still pressed against the wound. In slow movements, he lifted each finger before pulling my palm away. I squeezed my eyes shut as he sighed.

"I think you reopened it. Can I help you?" he asked.

I nodded, letting him steady me as we got out of the shower. Nate was deliberate with each move he made as he peeled my shirt away from the cut. As he worked to clean the wound, I tried to focus on his touch to keep my mind occupied. Each gentle brush of skin felt... better than it had before. Was that feeling returning to my body or something new?

As he finished securing the wrap, his hands shifted to my arm, tracing around the lightning scar. Was this finally the last time it would cut open? Without the Cold Soul fighting me and digging through my head, I might never deal with an outburst again.

Nate lifted my chin. "I'm going to shower. Will you be okay?"

I blinked, glancing to my arm to see I had completely missed him finishing the bandage. I looked back to Nate, locking my gaze onto his new blue eyes as my muscles relaxed. Energy seemed to buzz to life inside my body, circulating through every inch that had felt so empty just moments ago. I leaned forward and kissed him, feeling a surprised smile grow on his lips.

I stepped back. "Do you feel okay?"

His smile turned to contemplation. "What do you mean?"

"You took in half of the Blue Soul," I replied.

"If you're asking if I have new powers or something, none that I know of or can feel. But if it's possible, I think I feel a stronger connection with *you*," he said with a smile, kissing me again. I let him pull me in tighter, trying to press our entire bodies together. He dropped his chin, pressing his forehead into mine. "I thought I lost you."

As he kissed me again, I finally understood what he meant about a stronger connection. That energy was running through our touch, like electricity. It was beautiful; a pull together that sent goosebumps over my skin. My muscles eased even more, so much that for a moment I felt my pain release. I wasn't cold, I wasn't empty... I was whole.

All those feelings crashed back over me as we separated. It was like my insides had been violently thrashed around, shredded, and put back in the wrong places. I hid my reaction by leaning into the sink, brushing off my discomfort with a forced smile.

"I love you, always forever." That was still the truth.

It took an unnaturally long time to change but I finally peeled my clothes off, all while avoiding looking at my stomach. If taking off loose clothes was a challenge, there was no way I could pull on jeans. I found some leggings and a loose shirt and sports bra to put on instead.

Tom and Angie weren't in the kitchen when I walked in, but House had prepared a feast of junk food. I should have been hungry, but something about the smell and idea of eating made me nauseous. Even the coffee was overpowering my senses.

I gripped the back of a chair and convinced myself to at least get some coffee to settle the feelings. I picked up the cup and dumped my normal mound of sugar in before taking a half-hearted sip. I spit it out. It was like drinking mud or tar straight from a mug. I swirled the liquid around, wondering how something so smooth could feel like I was drinking paste. One more sip and I just dumped it into the sink. Staring at the table, nothing looked appetizing. I tried the toast, plain, forcing myself to swallow a single, scratchy bite before tossing it. That was enough food for today.

Nate's parents had somehow convinced House to let them into the library. I don't know why it made me uncomfortable to see them walking around like they owned the place. Tom moved around upstairs, pacing between bookshelves while Angie read over my notes at the desk. I guess at one point in my life I had trusted Angie, but did she have to go through my stuff?

She gestured around after seeing me walk in. "You've replicated The Complex library. I'd ask how you did it, but I'm guessing you don't remember."

I shook my head. It made sense, though. If I replicated the library, I could study the Blue Star-Soul without drawing suspicion.

"Did you ever find anything?" Tom asked, coming downstairs to join us.

"Nothing that helped," I answered. "Just general and vague stuff about The Complex and Trials."

Angie gave a small shrug. "We keep a low profile." She narrowed her eyes. "So you really don't remember *anything*?"

The way she said it and her suspicious thoughts of me boiled anger inside me. I was already on a short fuse.

"No, we already established that. You know, I really don't appreciate you digging through my stuff," I growled.

"You were busy," Angie replied, brushing off my snap response. "Still sharp-tongued, I see. Some things don't change. Your mother always loved that about you."

My emotions flipped in an instant, my heart sinking. Angie was one of the only people who could tell me about my past, all my lost memories including my mother, and I was treating her like garbage. After the Blue Star-Soul this morning, my last chance at knowing my past escaped in the form of Cold Soul Finnley. Now I felt guilty.

"I don't even remember what she was like," I whispered, taking a ragged breath to keep from crying. That only sent sharp pains running through my body.

"Brilliant, strong, and kind," Angie replied softly. "You were the light of her life, and she helped instill those same traits in you. You were definitely more fiery. In fact, much of your personality now is similar to who you were before."

I frowned. "Some of it is different?"

She shrugged. "Let's just say you didn't socialize well with others, except your mother. You were quite the troublemaker, but I guess I can see how the Cold Soul might have affected that behavior. Actually, a lot of things make more sense now, including your interactions with Richard. Even as a baby, you would fuss when he was near. Oh, and it explains your relationship with Aidan."

"I hated that guy," Nate groaned from behind me.

Angie chuckled. "Everyone did, but two troublemakers together didn't seem all that surprising to us."

I grumbled at her comment. I never wanted to think about that again. But the more he manipulated me, the more my dad got involved, the more I fought back. What if they had done the same to my mom?

"Did my mom know?" I asked. Everyone in the room stilled as I gestured toward myself and the room. "Did she know about me? About my dad? About any of it?"

Angie pinched her lips together. "I don't know. She went after you when you ran... I'm sorry."

Nate moved next to me, sliding his fingers through mine. I wanted the buzzing energy to swallow my sadness, but it wasn't enough. At least now I could find answers to my past, and maybe that would help all of this get easier. All it required was facing everything I had run away from four months ago.

It was time to go back to The Complex.

49

Nate

Besides my mom furiously typing away on her phone, it was quiet in the car. I couldn't help but feel annoyed that she was clearly staying in contact with people, just not me. What sort of place made her think that cutting me off completely would keep me safe? Was The Complex really good in all this?

After thirty minutes, we drove past the the exit for Richard's house. I could feel Clara's grip tighten in mine, and even my parents glanced back at her. Just another half a mile down the road, my dad turned off on a deserted exit and drove several miles on an unpaved road.

Holy shit, did I run this far that night? Clara kept her eyes glued out the window, studying the surroundings. Dense trees lined the path and clipped the car every once in a while until we finally pulled into a wide space that came out of nowhere. At least twenty parked cars lined the edges of the lot.

Just in front of a large incline sat a plaza-looking space, with buildings that looked like they belonged in a small town setting. Situated neatly between the aisle of buildings was a city-hall-like structure. For such a secretive place, all of this felt bright and open. How many people were actually involved here? And how did no one notice this place?

Mom turned around in the front seat and looked between us. "It's best if you don't draw any more attention to yourselves than you already will. People were already on edge after Finnley stole the Blue Star. Now we're bringing both of you back into The Complex."

I nodded and slid my key under my sweatshirt before getting out of the car, but Clara stayed planted in her seat, fiddling with the caffeine charm I had given her for Christmas. My parents waited patiently at the front of the car, talking quietly between themselves while I moved around the car to help her out. It took a lot of my strength to get her out of the seat, partly because she was injured but more because she was reluctant to face the community she ran away from.

My feelings were significantly different. The Complex felt like a life I had been denied from living. What would I have been like if I had grown up here and known about powers? I could have learned so much about myself and the powers I was born with. Would any of the Richard and Blue Soul drama have happened?

Then I thought about what it would have been like to grow up with Clara. Our moms were best friends so we would have known each other... but we also wouldn't know Glitch. I'm not sure I'd ever have the courage to ask her out if it weren't for him.

Even with my parents leading the way, Clara kept trying to pressure them to walk faster, her hands clutched around her stomach. She curled into herself to appear smaller, holding her head low and avoiding every glance from strangers. But people were noticing us, pointing fingers and speaking in hushed tones. Anyone in our path moved aside and stared; no, glared. I couldn't imagine what awful things they were thinking.

They don't like me, but at least their thoughts are uncensored. I need answers. Clara bumped into me as she shuffled her steps to avoid stepping on my dad's heels.

Are you learning anything?

I'm not popular, and even more hated after stealing the Blue Soul. They think your parents caught me and are bringing me in for punishment.

I frowned. *They won't actually punish you once they know the truth, right? You were protecting the power source from Richard. You had to run away.*

They don't see it that way. I stole a powerful source and disappeared for four months. Psycho dad or not, I broke their rules and I should have spoken up sooner. Besides, from what I gather, this was not the first time I got in trouble here.

Now I understood why Clara was trying to walk so quickly. We walked past a small group and pushed through the doors. The city hall building had the same capabilities as House. Inside the doors, two long hallways wrapped around the outside of a large, guarded room. The oak doors were at least ten feet tall with intricate carvings that made the guard outside look tiny, but as we got closer, he came into perspective. He was at least my height and age, but twice my dad's build. He eyed us suspiciously before focusing on my parents.

"The Assembly is waiting for you. These two," he said, gesturing to Clara and I as his voice switched tones, "will have to wait outside."

"Understood," my mom replied, nodding. She turned and put her hand on my shoulder. "Nate, stay inside the building and avoid others. Except maybe you can take Clara to the library. I think at least one person will be happy to see her." She pointed down the hallway to our left but I was too busy watching the guard react to her calling Finnley 'Clara'.

As my mom spun back around, the guard snapped to attention and opened the door just wide enough for my parents to slide through. He pulled the door closed before I could see anything inside and crossed his arms, staring at Clara.

"Finnley," he growled, unable to keep his composure as he glared at her.

Clara hesitated, looking nervously between him and I before grabbing my wrist and dragging me down the hallway. When we were out of earshot, I stopped walking and tugged her back toward me.

"What was that about?"

Her cheeks flushed. "Um, don't be mad but I heard his thoughts. Apparently I flirted with him and stole his keys so I could sneak into the library at night. He got in a lot of trouble."

For a moment, I think I might have been jealous but then I found myself laughing. "Trying to seduce someone so you can get into the library after hours? Sounds familiar. At least you didn't actually like him... right?" Now I wasn't laughing.

She rolled her eyes. "I was *clearly* using him. Besides, he's not my type."

"Really? And what is your type?" I asked.

Clara grinned. "Shut up." She leaned up to kiss me but we were interrupted.

"Finnley dear?"

A small, wiry-gray haired woman poked her head out of the door behind Clara. She looked every bit like the stereotypical librarian; small glasses on a chain around her neck, a long-sleeved dress that floated just above her ankles, and a bony body that looked like it would snap if she picked up a book.

Clara turned around and the woman smiled big, jumping forward to hug her. In a stunning move, she picked Clara up with ease and swung her around as Clara winced. When the woman finally set her down, Clara grunted and wrapped her arm over her stomach.

"This is awkward, but I don't remember you," Clara said, trying to catch her breath.

The woman didn't seem bothered. "Of course you don't. The Cold Soul took your memories, but... something changed. You shouldn't be here." The woman frowned before making eye contact with me, another smile growing on her face. "Nate!"

Now it was my turn to get squished in a hug far too strong for such a small woman. I lifted off the ground just slightly before she set me back down.

"Uh," I mumbled, straightening my sweatshirt. "I don't think we've met, ma'am."

She held her finger up at me. "Now don't you go calling me 'ma'am' or I'll go around calling you Nathaniel. I'm Jeanie, and no, we haven't met."

Clara and I exchanged looks of confusion as Jeanie grabbed our hands and pulled us into the library behind her. "I know a lot about you two, and I'm so happy you are still together, but it looks like we have a whole new future on our hands."

50

Clara

Nate and I froze as soon as Jeanie pulled us through the doors to the library. It was an exact replica of the library in House, only bigger. Or, more appropriately, mine was just a smaller scale version of this one. There were more desks around the lower level and rooms between each bookcase. And, obviously, this place was much cleaner than mine.

"I assume you go by Clara now?"

Jeanie's voice startled me. She stood only a few feet away and craned her neck to look up at me, her eyes sparkling with her smile.

"Yes... how did you—"

"My power is knowing," she replied.

"You can read minds?" Nate blurted. My surprise reaction was similar.

Jeanie laughed. "No, dear. I believe that power is exclusively Clara's... wait, you have it too, now that the Blue Soul has connected you. Very dangerous. You shouldn't have done that." She wagged her finger and frowned at Nate.

I shook my head. Why would I have told a librarian, not my own mother, about my plans to run away? "How can you *know* about us? Did Finnley tell you about her dream?" I asked.

"*You* didn't have to. You trusted me because I read people, not minds. Past, present, and future, I know. You came looking for answers in the middle of the night, but that's how you met me. I delivered your punishment for breaking in after hours, though really we just talked. I knew about the two powers that were stuck inside you, the Blue and Cold Soul, but it wasn't my place to tell you. You had to find out on your own, but I gave a few nudges in the right direction. I'm afraid I got a little attached and might have... made some mistakes," she said, patting my cheek.

"You might be the only one who likes me around here," I grumbled.

"Wait," Nate interrupted, his tone harsh. "You knew she was going to die?"

Jeanie nodded her head slowly. "Just because I knew didn't mean I wanted it to happen. Her future was set, but she didn't have to die alone. I set up House, as you like to call him, and helped give her a life to run to. That's four more months, and true love, otherwise you two never would have met. But I can see that was a mistake... I can't read Clara's future, nor yours."

I scrunched my nose. "I have a good idea as to why."

Nate glanced at me nervously. "I can think of two."

Jeanie ushered us into her office and pulled out a wooden chair for me while Nate sank into the soft couch. It took a moment to sit but I finally found a comfortable enough spot as Nate filled her in about the Cold Souls escaping. My thoughts filled the empty space in my head, and with no real thoughts to think, they turned back toward my death. I died. This morning. There was a giant stab wound in my stomach from where I bled out. And I was still sitting here.

Nate's hand slid under mine as he turned his wrist under my fingers. Heartbeats. He offered a sad smile as Jeanie pulled out a book from her desk drawer. She scribbled something onto a notepad and stuck the sheet into the pages of the book.

"I should have seen this coming. I made all of this worse," she sighed and handed the book to Nate. "Under no circumstances do you tell anyone about this book or what I'm about to tell you."

He frowned and glanced back at me to see what I thought. Really, I had no idea what to think with all this space in my head. This woman, whom neither of us really knew, had changed our futures by pushing me in Nate's direction. The Cold Souls never would have escaped and we wouldn't be in this situation. Then again, I would be dead if she hadn't, and now we were on our way toward answers. Nate looked back at her and nodded.

Jeanie clasped her hands together and pointed at the book. "This is the only book about the Original Complex. An account of its history *and* its destruction. All I can see is that I'm supposed to send you there. You can find the address for a cabin on that paper as a safe house. Don't tell anyone where you're going and learn what you can."

My fingers gripped into Nate's arm and the chair underneath me as my voice raised. "That's it? You can't tell us anything more?"

Jeanie lowered her head. "I'm so sorry, but that's for you to find out. I can't intervene any more than I already have. This is my role." She got up and opened the door. "Nate, your parents are looking for you."

He got up and tucked the book under his sweatshirt before heading out the door. I stood up gingerly, prepared to follow, but Jeanie stopped me.

"Clara, I really do want to help. I'm giving you as much information as I can… but please know I never wanted you to die."

I sighed. "I'm sorry. I know you were trying, it's just…" I felt the tears building as Jeanie slid her hand into mine.

"It's just you can't remember life here," she replied, squeezing my hand. "Your mother wouldn't like you dwelling on the past. She would be so happy for the life you get to live. Now, I broke all the laws to get you and Nate together, so don't you dare hide those panic attacks from him. He can help you."

I chewed my lip for a moment before gently leaning over to hug her. "Thank you for Nate. I promise we will find a way to stop the Cold Souls."

"I know you will, dear. And again, I am so sorry." Jeanie pulled away and rested her hand over my stomach, frowning. "Take care of yourself, and protect that boy. He needs you too."

I wanted to pull her into another hug but I could hear Nate calling for me. Jeanie smiled again and nudged me out of her office. I could have sworn I saw tears in her eyes before she shut the door behind me.

51

Nate

The Assembly room felt like a giant conference room, complete with dull white walls and a white floor. A long table stretched down the middle, with seating on either side. Dad walked behind us, guiding us to the head. Fifteen middle-aged and older men and women lined the table, my parents taking seats at the farthest end of us.

I shifted my grip in my sweatshirt pocket to help hold the book up. It was big enough to sit tightly in the waistband of my jeans but I was still nervous someone would notice the block shape underneath my clothes.

For a third time, we recounted the events of this morning. My parents had filled them in on our past already, and Clara did her best to explain what we had discovered from her notes and visions. Then, of course, it came time to explain what happened in the four months after she disappeared. The worst was when they forced her to recount every detail of this morning. I tried to help, but they demanded it from her perspective.

Mom had warned us not to interact with each other. They were already concerned about the two teenagers who were born with their powers, but now we had an additional power source shared between us. No one had ever been born with powers and no one had ever contained so much power and survived. It was no wonder they looked frightened of us, despite trying to remain stoic.

Clara's breath came out in harsh bursts. I could see her struggling and all I wanted to do was reach out and calm her.

"The first thing I remember was hearing Nate in my head, trying to pull me away from the Ruby's hold. Everything in my mind was empty, but I could see all of it happening. I could see what Richard was doing." Someone in the middle of the table shifted as she said Richard's name. "As he held out his hand, so did I, without question. I tried to fight against it, but when he tried to kill Nate, I shifted my focus to protect him. That's when…"

As she stopped talking, I felt her mind flash through the back of my head. She was picturing the scene, and I could see everything from her perspective. The knife, the fog around her vision, the shift in emotion as she fought to protect me instead of herself…

"I died," she said after a moment. "Somehow the Blue Soul connected us and I woke up. But then the Cold Souls escaped. They looked like us, but with green eyes and black blood." Clara shut her eyes and I felt her again in my head. *Please be done. Please be done.*

"They didn't say anything else about the Blue Star before disappearing?" the oldest woman asked, folding her hands on the table in front of her. Her outfit and posture made me think of a snooty rich woman, the pale pink coat highlighting the massive pearls she wore.

"No ma'am," I replied, trying to hurry the conversation along for Clara's sake. "They just called it the Blue Soul, not Star. We think it was two separate powers inside the source."

The man next to my dad leaned forward. "You two are a very peculiar case. So much power for two people, not to mention from a source that was unresponsive to everyone else."

Several others nodded before a woman my mom's age spoke. "Finn — pardon, Clara. Despite your previous record, under these new circumstances we have decided not to punish you for your actions. We do ask that you both report to the doctor immediately so we can understand a little more about your powers and the Blue St—Soul. This could help understand the Cold Soul as well."

"Until they are stopped, you are required to stay here at The Complex," the oldest woman said.

"What are we doing about the Cold Souls?" I asked.

My mom flinched in the background as I bit my tongue. That was definitely not the right thing to say.

"That is for us to take care of," the man at the end said, standing up. "You've done enough here."

My parents walked us out as the guard frowned. He must have thought she wouldn't be coming out without punishment or shackles or something. Normally, I would brush it off, but then I remembered all of the glares we got walking in. The Complex people would be just as frustrated to see her walk free if they didn't know the truth. How much of our story would be shared with them?

Luckily, we slid out a side door and moved around the backs of buildings before we ducked inside one. The same trick as House and the Assembly building was being used inside the hospital. On the inside, it felt like we were in a normal doctor's office. Why did that make me uneasy? Were we about to get handed off like lab rats?

My parents walked up to the counter and spoke with a younger lady in a hushed tone. Clara shifted closer and I gave up trying to hide us from sight. I pulled my arm out of my pocket and wrapped it around her waist, pulling her closer.

"Nate, I don't like this," she whispered.

"I don't either."

My dad turned around and walked back to us, a sad smile on his face. "I know this isn't ideal, but your mother and I don't have a choice in this. I'm sorry." He paused, chewing the inside of his cheek. "Because of our decision to hide you two, we were forced to step down from The Assembly."

"What does that mean?" I blurted, squeezing Clara tighter.

"Nothing, you're going to be fine. They just want to understand what makes you two different. Look, this is something we wanted to protect you from, but we had to make a deal. If we step down, they don't ask any more of you two."

My mom walked up, the doctor following closely. The woman was the same height as my mom but with short black hair. She smiled softly.

"I promise you will be fine. Come back with me," she said. The four of us started to follow her but she hesitated. "I'm sorry, only Nate and Fi— Clara."

Mom wanted to protest but Dad spun her around and returned to the waiting room. We followed the doctor as she wove us around hallways before finally stopping at the last room.

She glanced between us, still holding onto. "Who would like to go first?"

Clara tensed and I shook my head. "Nope. Together or not at all."

The doctor thought about it for a second before letting us both walk in the room, closing the door behind her. She fiddled around the drawers for a minute as I helped lower Clara into the chair.

"I just need to take a blood sample, nothing more. Please don't hold this against me, these are just my orders."

Clara let out an audible growl. "Oh, so if you were ordered to make us lab rats, you'd do that too?"

The doctor frowned. "Honey, I do have a code. I would never do such a thing."

She held out the needle, waiting for one of us to volunteer. I wasn't happy about it, but I stuck out my left arm. She waited for a second, thinking I would roll up my sleeve, but I couldn't do that without letting go of the book I was hiding. Eventually she caved and did it herself.

I watched her carefully as she pricked my arm, seeing the shock on her face when my blood came out blue. Clara grumbled and held her right arm out, refusing to lift her sleeve either. Now the doctor looked fascinated by the strange blood.

She labeled the samples and put them in a dark, strongly sealed container before pulling off her gloves. She spun her chair to look at us.

"Okay, my orders are done. Off the record, Clara, do you feel okay?"

I looked down at Clara who was still glaring at the doctor. She hugged her arms tighter into her stomach.

"None of your business."

The doctor let out a soft laugh. "Ah, same personality. You used to come to me about the headaches. I just thought you were cranky." She sighed. "I am being serious, though. As a concerned friend of your mother's, is there something I can help with? I can't imagine what you've gone through."

Clara hesitated, flashing me a look before lowering her head. "I don't know. I feel like I'm in a constant panic attack and I can't eat. Everything tastes... wrong."

"What?" I blurted. "C, you haven't eaten anything?" If my always-hungry-for-junk-food girlfriend wasn't eating, something was wrong. How could I have not been thinking about that? I should have been better for her.

She shook her head. "It's only been since this morning. I'm fine."

The doctor leaned forward and placed her hand on Clara's knee. A bold move considering Clara wanted to bite her head off thirty seconds ago.

"Listen, I know what happened. Can I check to make sure there isn't any more damage?"

Clara pinched her lips together and stood up slowly without arguing. She removed her key necklace and lifted her sweatshirt just enough for the doctor to pull off the bandage. This morning when I had wrapped it, there was just a large gash. Now, purple and blue bruises splotched her stomach and the cut. It looked significantly worse than the back of her neck had.

The doctor pressed around the wound and Clara's hand shot out to steady herself on me, groaning.

"Sorry," the doctor whispered. "There's a lot of bruising. I think I should run some scans—"

"No," Clara snapped. She tried to lower her sweatshirt but the doctor held it up.

"I strongly suggest—"

"I said no. Just wrap it so we can leave."

Clara didn't let me protest, digging her fingers into my upper arm as the doctor took out another bandage and wrapped it around her stomach. The woman walked us back out to my parents who jumped out of their seats to greet us. After sharing a few words with my mom, my parents guided us out the front door.

52

Clara

I stood at the window, looking out at the plaza lit by a fading sunset and street lamps. Most of the lot had emptied, but there were still a few people walking around outside. Angie and Tom had taken us up the stairs of one of the buildings which turned out to hold a lot of apartments. Their apartment only had one room so Tom was busy trying to get me the apartment across from theirs while Angie went back to House to grab clothes for Nate and I. Nate was busy cooking something for dinner but I couldn't stand the smell so escaped to the bedroom to open the window and breathe fresh air.

So many things felt wrong now. Without the Cold Soul, I expected my temperature to return to normal. The winter air should have been bitter against my face, but it felt normal. And though I should have been exhausted, I couldn't imagine laying down to sleep. For four months I had watched myself die in my dreams. Now that it had actually happened, I was terrified of what might come next. I felt like I was in a constant panic attack that never went away, the scene with Richard replaying in my head on a loop. The people here hated Finnley — hated me — and now so did I. This was all my fault.

Someone knocked on the door but I didn't respond.

"Are you trying to freeze us?" Angie asked as she slid past me and shut the window, shivering.

"Sorry," I mumbled, rubbing my eyes as I tried to erase the image of the knife in my stomach. It was too late. I felt my chest tighten, crawling up my neck as I tried to pull my collar away to breathe. Tears rolled down my cheeks as Angie grasped at my hands.

"Hey, now. Easy." She finally grabbed me in a hug, pinning my arms to my sides so I wouldn't thrash. I buried my face into her sleeve and just gave in. For a good five minutes, she held me, running her hand over my shoulders trying to comfort me. When I finally stopped shaking, she lifted away and held my cheek. "Sweetie, talk to me."

I swallowed the lump in my throat. "I keep seeing it... the knife, the blood. Now everything is just wrong and I have to see how much everyone hated Finnley and I'm just alone."

Angie guided me into the chair and knelt in front of me. "Clara, I've known you your whole life. First as Finnley, and now as Clara. I need you to listen to what I'm about to say." She waited until I nodded before continuing. "Finnley was not awful, she was brilliant and misunderstood. You fought against your father since you were born and kept that all inside. No one understood what that was doing to you. You had to suffer because of what we did with the Blue Soul when you were a baby, constantly fighting the voices and your dad. Your mother raised a fierce and amazing young woman and she would be so proud of you."

I sniffed. "I wish I could remember her."

Angie took my hands and helped me stand up again. "I will tell you everything you want to know, about Finnley and your mother, but you need to eat something first."

I let her lead me out into the dining room, the smell of roast and potatoes hitting me hard as I tried to hide my gag. Food sounded terrible right now, but I was somewhat impressed with the spread that Nate had set up. When House did all the chores and cooking for me, I never realized that Nate could make something like this.

"Wow," Nate said as he walked over and kissed my forehead. "Don't act so surprised. When your parents leave you to fend for yourself, you learn a thing or two."

"Watch it," Tom grumbled.

Angie just laughed. "We deserve that. Looks like we'll both be home for good now." Angie sat at the head of the table next to Tom who had already dished up his food.

Nate pulled out the chair for me, helping me down. "Are they kicking you out completely?" he asked, sitting down.

"No, just removing us from The Assembly, but not because of you. We lied to them for years about you two and now we have to face those consequences," Tom said with a shrug.

For spending all their time here, I was surprised they were so casual about the situation.

Angie reached over and patted my hand. "Clara, you need to eat something."

I took another look at the food but shook my head. Nate frowned and pushed away from the table.

"Alright, C. Chicken noodle soup and crackers. You're not allowed to say no," he said, dishing it from a pot on the stove. I guess he had been prepared for me to reject the food. I accepted the bowl and dunked a cracker, forcing myself to swallow.

Nate seemed to relax as Angie leaned forward. "Since I never got the chance to hear about it, tell me about your relationship. The only thing I know about is the morning your father caught you sleeping together."

Nate choked on his food as his mom stared across the table at him. Tom winked at me as I held in a laugh.

"I don't get why this is always so funny to you people. Nothing happened!" he stammered, his cheeks a bright red.

"Ah, but that face tells me otherwise. Maybe just not that night." Now Angie turned her gaze to me. I threw my hand over my mouth in shock as she nodded. "That's what I thought."

"Mom," Nate groaned, pressing his forehead into the table.

"Okay, okay," Angie said, holding up her hands as she surrendered. "I'm just trying to lighten the mood. Where'd you go on your first date?"

Seeing as Nate was still recovering, I answered. "We actually haven't really had one. Glitch is pretty much with us all the time."

"Nathaniel Beckett," Angie blurted. She threw her roll across the table at Nate as he caught it without flinching. That clearly wasn't the first time she'd thrown food at him. "You haven't taken her on a date? I did not raise you like that."

"We've been busy," he grumbled.

The rest of the night went along like that. It was strange to finally have a normal evening where I didn't have to hide anything. With each passing minute, I could feel my chest loosen as I finally started to relax, but that's also when the exhaustion hit me. Nate looked tired too, but he kept his eyes on me as I finished eating, worried I would stop if he looked away. That was accurate.

I thanked Tom and Angie and picked up the keys to my apartment across the way as they cleaned the dishes from the table. Nate grabbed his sweatshirt, wrapped tight to hide the book Jeanie had given us, and followed me.

"Where do you think you're going?" Tom asked as he stepped out of the kitchen.

"Uh," Nate stuttered, glancing between me and his dad.

Tom waited a moment before cracking a smile. "I'm kidding. Come over when you wake up." I could hear Angie start laughing in the background.

Nate grabbed my shoulders and nudged me out the door. "Oh my god, go before he changes his mind."

The apartment had the same set up as theirs, but instead there were two twin beds, our bags sitting on each of them. Now I understood why his parents were okay with us sharing the place. Nate laughed when he saw me standing and staring at the beds.

"Ah, now I see." He dropped his sweatshirt on his bed before stepping to the side of it, pushing it against mine. "Joke's on them. These beds are easy to move."

I unzipped the bag that Angie had packed for me and grabbed my toothbrush. Right on top was Nate's old sweatshirt. I pulled it out along with a pair of shorts and went into the bathroom.

My hair was a complete disaster. It had air dried since the shower this morning and was a knotted mess, but I also couldn't lift my arms to brush it out. It was a struggle enough trying to change into my shorts so I didn't even attempt to get today's sweatshirt off. I brushed my teeth and went out to find Nate flipping through the book.

"What does it say?" I asked, walking past him to read over his shoulder. It must have been another book like the one I had found in my desk because the pages looked blank, probably some trick to keep me from reading it. "I can't see any words."

Nate looked up at me, confused. "There aren't any words to see. The whole thing is blank except for the note Jeanie wrote."

"What?" I pulled the book out of his hands and flipped through it myself. He was right, it was completely blank. Just an address inked onto the notebook paper Jeanie had shoved in the cover.

"I don't get it either. Why would she give us a blank book?"

I tossed it back on the bed. "She must have had a reason. She told us to find this place and learn what we could. But if the place was destroyed, how are we supposed to figure it out?"

Nate shrugged. "Maybe we just go and see what happens. But we should probably give it a couple days. The Complex is already angry with us and I don't want my parents to get in more trouble."

He stood up, wrapping his arm around my waist as he pulled me into him. Buzzing surged through my body as I squeezed harder, locking my arms around his back as I pressed my cheek into his chest.

Do you feel that buzz? I asked in his head so I wouldn't have to lean away.

Yeah, I do. Should we be worried about it? Or tell my parents?

No, or they'd never let us touch again.

Nate pulled away and I groaned as aches creaked through my body again.

He sighed. "I'm not going to tell them, at least tonight. I just need to change so we can go to sleep." He tugged at the sweatshirt sleeve I couldn't get off myself. "Clearly you need help."

I scrunched my nose as he helped pull my arms out of the sleeves. He lifted the jacket over my head, taking my key necklace with it. Despite my left arm being hidden by a bandage, blue splotches appeared on the cloth. I had been so focused on my stomach, I had barely noticed the sting in my arm. Nate hesitated when he saw the blood, worried that I might get sick or panic again, but I reached forward and started to pull off the wrapping. He grabbed my hand.

"Are you sure?"

I sighed as I picked up his hand, sliding his sleeve up to reveal his bandaged arm. He had already taken his key necklace off so the blue stains were visible.

"I'm not okay, but I can't be weak forever." I let go of his hand and kept unwrapping my arm, determined to get over the nausea. Nate reached his hand to my cheek and held my chin up.

"C, you're not weak. You are anything *but* weak."

"I need to get over this," I said, finally pulling the rest of the bandage off. I started at the lightning shaped scar that had hopefully reopened for the last time. Nate reached out, expecting to have to steady me, but I wasn't dizzy. It was almost a relief to see it. I sighed. "See, I'm fine."

Nate raised his eyebrow. "Really? So you're ready to see your stomach."

"That's not fair. It's different," I grumbled.

"Okay, sorry."

I nodded toward his arm. "I showed you mine, now you show me yours."

He smiled and lifted his shirt over his head, sticking his arm out so I could unroll the wrapping. If there hadn't been such powerful repercussions, I would have thought his scar was beautiful. Strange. I hated mine so much before, but now that Nate and I shared the mark, it didn't seem so bad anymore. I played with his fingers until he finally wrapped them around my hand and held it up to his chest. His other arm slipped around my waist and pulled me in tightly as he leaned down to kiss me. My pain melted away again, the energy running through my body. He carefully picked me up before lowering me down on the bed. Just when I thought he was going to stay, he stood up. I groaned but he just laughed.

"Go to sleep. I'll join you in a minute." He reached into his bag and pulled out his toothbrush as I tried to focus on the soft bed underneath me. The aches were back, but the relief of finally getting to lay down almost drowned it out. I didn't even try to pull the covers out from under my body.

I vaguely remembered Nate sliding in next to me as my body started buzzing again.

"Nate?" I mumbled.

His arm rested over my body. "Yeah?"

"Aidan and Richard…" I forced a breath. "They're really gone, right?"

I felt Nate's lips press into my neck. "Yeah, they're gone. Anything else we have to face, I'll protect you. Always forever."

"I love you," I breathed, finally letting sleep take over. I didn't have to worry about my dreams if Nate was with me.

53

Nate

I woke up to a loud crash and blinding light. I shot out of bed, squinting in the sunlight as I threw the covers off me. Clara sat up just as quickly, her hair tangled in a knot in front of her face. I blinked away the light, focusing on the source of the noise. The lamp by the window had fallen over and taken the curtains with it, shattering the lightbulb across the carpet.

"Did you do that?" I asked, my voice cracking with sleep.

"No, did you?" Clara mumbled, curling back into the bed as she pulled my pillow over her face.

I rubbed my eyes, trying to wake up. "Why would I ask you if I was the one who did it?"

"I don't know. Shush. I wanna sleep," she said through the pillow. Just a few seconds later, she shot up again, launching my pillow flying as her eyes widened. "Nate, holy shit."

"What?"

"I'm not sore. Nothing hurts," she said, her eyes suddenly sparkling. She lifted her arm in front of her, running her fingers along the cut that had healed over and become a scar. I lifted my arm and saw the same thing.

"What the..." I poked at it, trying to see if it was just a trick my mind was playing. I had just woken up from a coma-like sleep.

Clara reached out, feeling my arm too. "Do you think the buzzing energy we feel could do this?"

I shrugged. "That's the only thing it could be." My fingers twitched as she traced my palm, her smile growing. In a swift move, she rolled over me, pressing me down into the bed with her lips. *What happened to hating morning breath?*

Before I could wrap my arms around to flip her, I heard a knock on the front door.

"Wow, great timing," I grumbled as she jumped off me, but I quickly smiled. It was good to see her with energy again.

Clara laughed as she skipped to the bathroom. "I'm not hiding in the closet this time."

"At least put a shirt on," I shouted back into the bedroom as I moved to the front.

My parents stood at the door, a panicked look on their faces.

"We heard a crash. Are you okay?" Dad asked, hesitating when he saw I wasn't dressed.

Oh, right. The lamp had fallen. "Yeah, our lamp fell over. No big."

Dad pushed past me as Mom tried to stop him, her eyes locked on my healed arm. I think she was putting the wrong pieces together seeing that I was healed with no shirt and knocking furniture over. Ugh, I had the worst luck. I moved to the side so she knew it was okay to come in.

Dad got to the bedroom door and turned around immediately. I didn't have time to warn Clara before she ran out of the bathroom, still in her sports bra and shorts, but her bandage was pulled off her stomach.

"Nate, look," she said. She froze as she looked up and saw my parents but shrugged it off. "Okay, everyone look, I guess."

The bruising around her stomach was completely gone, with just a thick blue scar that had healed over.

"How is that possible?" Mom whispered, sitting on our couch. Dad joined her, still looking embarrassed about what he walked in on.

Clara spun around to her bag and grabbed my old sweatshirt, tossing me a shirt on her way out. "We didn't mention this before, because we didn't fully understand it, but with the new connection we have this buzzing feeling when we touch."

I quickly clarified. "We were just sleeping. We didn't even notice our scars until the lamp broke and woke us up."

Clara looked back at the broken fixture, cocking her head to the side. "I'm pretty sure I didn't do that…"

My mom glanced between us, deep in thought. "This is a little concerning. We don't know what you two are going through or what this means. We're in new territory."

"You can't tell anyone about this," my dad said, snapping out of his embarrassment. "Keep those scars hidden. This is dangerous."

My stomach twisted. "Dangerous?"

Mom nodded. "You two share the strongest power source known to The Complex, and we have no idea what it does. You might not even notice things that you do. If you don't know your own strength, you could hurt someone... or yourselves."

Clara looked at me nervously. *Nate, what if these are my headache outbursts all over again? I could have done that without knowing it.*

I reached my hand out to pull her closer, ignoring the reluctant groans from my parents, and laced my fingers through hers. "See, nothing happened," I said. Well, nothing except the rush of energy I felt run up my arm.

My parents weren't convinced as Mom stood up. "Just be careful. Now, get dressed and don't ruin your appetites. Dinner is in a couple hours."

"Dinner?" Clara and I asked at the same time.

Dad hurried toward the door faster than he came in. "Yes, dinner. It's half past three in the afternoon," he said over his shoulder.

Mom hung back, and when Dad was on the other side, she closed it behind him and spun around to face us. "I love you both dearly, but I'm serious about being careful. Not just about your powers."

I groaned. Clara squeezed my hand and bumped my side. "Don't worry. I think *that* buzz was sufficiently thwarted by your entrance."

I let out a forced breath as Mom left. "My life is one embarrassment after another."

I rolled my head back to groan as Clara ran into the other room and pulled out her iPod.

Healing. Oh Honey.

I snatched it out of her hands and picked a new song.

Someone Like you. The Summer Set.

She giggled as I kissed her cheek, moving my hands around her back. "What happened to being careful?" she asked.

"She said we had a few hours before dinner. You're alive, full of energy and healed, so we can celebrate," I replied, moving my lips down to her collarbone.

Clara slid her hands around my waist and spun me around, tossing me back on the bed with ease. She climbed on top, pressing her body into mine as she continued to slide her lips along my jaw. I slid her sweatshirt over her head and tossed it to the side, unintentionally throwing it on the lamp. Clara paused and frowned.

"What if I really did that?"

"Nope. We're not worrying about that until later," I said, tipping her off of me so I could swing on top.

"You're the worst," she said, grabbing my collar as she pulled me down to her face.

I know. And now you're stuck with me, always forever.

54

Clara

Nate's parents were preoccupied during dinner, their thoughts racing about our powers and the consequences of having the Blue Soul shared between us. I had to agree with most of them, but at the same time, they didn't understand what Nate and I felt when we touched. I was used to the Cold Soul feeling that was dangerous and nagging. The Blue Soul was the opposite.

One thing they were definitely right about was our new strength. Using my powers was easier, and was barely any effort to block everyone's thoughts at dinner. With that ease, it was entirely possible I had knocked over the lamp, not to mention the strange events that healed our cuts overnight. I finally felt good.

Nate convinced his parents to let us walk around The Complex once it was dark enough. Plus, no one could judge us because it was absolutely frigid outside. Though they almost changed their minds when the only layers we put on were our light sweatshirts, but I pulled us out the door before they could stop us.

The bitter air felt good on my face as we walked along the path. The night was still and quiet, only our footsteps making noise as we shuffled along. It hit me that I had never known what silence felt like. Both Finnley and I had always heard voices, and I was always drowning them out with music. Right now I didn't mind that emptiness. Silence felt beautiful. Neither Nate nor I needed to talk to enjoy each other's company, and it was even stranger that our third wheel wasn't chirping our ears off.

Nate froze. "We forgot about Glitch," he blurted.

I stopped him before he pulled his phone out. "He'll still be there in the morning. Plus, what are we going to tell him?"

"Uh, that you're still alive?"

"Not about that. I meant about your parents and this place," I replied, pulling Nate back into a walking pace.

"Should we tell him about Jeanie and that book?" he asked.

I shook my head. "I don't think so. Jeanie was pretty adamant about us not telling anyone. Besides, it's blank, and Jeanie sees the future. She probably knows what she's doing."

Nate shrugged. "At least he can't read our minds ot know what we're hiding."

"Let's just see what we can find first. There really aren't any more answers than before, just more questions."

We continued in silence again, weaving through the open spaces between buildings. It was nice to be out in the open, and the cloudless sky gave me more constellations to recreate on the ceiling. It was my favorite trick, even more than using my powers to make Nate think I was stronger than I actually was. I wonder what new things I could do with the extra power I had.

After we had circled the buildings twice, we walked back to the apartment building. Coming from this direction, Nate and I paused at the same time as we saw a path running into the trees. It had clearly been trampled often. As he turned his gaze up, I noticed his parents watching us from the window.

"You know how they said Finnley was always a troublemaker?" he asked, his eyes still turned up.

"Uh, yeah?"

"Let's get into trouble."

He spun and pressed me against the opposite wall, running his hand through my hair until his fingers got caught in the tangles. He pressed his face into mine and kissed me.

Your parents are watching. Not that I was complaining about him kissing me, but even I was a little uncomfortable knowing his parents were watching us.

I know. Tell me when they stop.

He moved his hands up my back as I wrapped mine around his waist, pulling his body into mine. As Nate moved his lips down my neck, Angie pushed Tom away from the window and they closed the blinds.

Did they give up yet? Nate's thought startled me.

What? Oh, yeah. Wow, I had been really distracted.

"Come on then, sexy," Nate laughed, grabbing my hand as he

pulled me off the wall and toward the path.

"Are you quoting Doctor Who to me?" I asked, jogging to keep up with him until we were out of sight in the trees.

"Yeah, I am. Is that a turn on?" he asked, a clear smile on his face even though it was dark.

I chuckled. "Absolutely. You know what would be better?"

"What?"

I nearly ran into him as he stopped in the path, his face just inches from mine. I tapped his nose and whispered. "If you had brought a flashlight."

He laughed. "You know, they have this brilliant invention called the cell phone, equipped with a weak, but still useful, flashlight."

Nate clicked the light on and stretched his hand toward me. I slid my fingers through his as we continued walking.

"What do you think is down this way?" I asked, pulling myself a little closer to Nate. Even if my boyfriend was the king of shadows, I couldn't help but feel uneasy to be out here.

He shrugged. "Complex secrets, strange worship relics, a naked cult, a magical river that gives you everlasting life..."

His list faded as we came up to a fallen tree trunk that came up to my chest. Nate turned to me, holding his hands out as he prepared to boost me over. Instead, I grabbed his hips and lifted him to sit on the trunk. Placing my hands on top, I pushed and jumped, launching myself over to the other side.

"Need help?" I asked, smiling as Nate swung his legs over to my side. He flashed me with his light.

"Only because you asked," he replied. I grabbed his hips again and brought him gently to the ground. He smiled but stuck his tongue out. "Showoff."

"I think the term you're looking for is 'badass'," I teased.

We walked along for several more minutes until the path started to open up. I realized the trail had weaved us around to the other side of the hill that was behind the city hall building. A small opening, designed like an old mining entrance, was directly in front of us. The trees were completely cleared from around the area, with small stone benches sitting around the entrance.

"Whoa, what is this place?" Nate asked, moving forward.

But I stayed stuck to the ground. Something didn't feel right.

I didn't feel right.

My knees gave out instantly and I dropped to the ground. Nate was still looking around but I couldn't make a sound. It wasn't a headache, but I still had that metallic taste in my mouth as my eyes blurred out of focus. Nothing hurt until a wave of nausea slammed into me and I rolled onto my side.

The last thing I heard was Nate shouting my name.

I was standing in the same spot where I had just fallen. Voices were growing behind me as I spun. A large group of people were walking through the trail. I shifted to the side as they walked closer without stopping, but they didn't see me at all. Then I saw why.

Finnley was in the middle of the group, holding her mom's hand. My mom. I was watching myself — my past. I focused behind Finnley, catching the glares from Richard and Aidan. Anger swirled through me as I launched forward, trying to strangle Aidan, but I just floated through him. No matter how much I swatted at them, they never noticed me.

Angie walked through me, taking up the rear of the line as everyone took their seats. No one here had any idea what truths Angie and Finnley knew. Not even my mom. They were all completely oblivious to the two men who were obsessed with killing me and taking an evil power source. Angie thought Finnley was about to absorb all of that power and die. My mom just thought I'd walk out without powers.

Finnley rubbed her hands together nervously as I focused on her left arm, free of any scars or blue blood. Her black shirt, jeans, and Converse were clean as well. In a few hours, all of that would be ruined. She had no idea what was about to happen, but I knew. I was going to watch Finnley steal the Blue Soul.

She walked into the opening alone, but I ran after her. I weaved through the rocks, ducking and sliding through some of the narrow pathways. Finally, the mouth of the tunnel widened into a small cave. Built into the rocks in front of us were about thirty different power sources, but only three of them were glowing. The Ruby, the Golden Arrow, and the Blue Soul.

Finnley sat down on the ground and closed her eyes as I walked around, brushing my hands over the objects that had all lost their light. I couldn't feel them, but somehow I thought I could see little lights spark inside them. The closer I looked, the less I saw. Just emptiness.

'Mom, I know this is surprising, but don't speak. Don't let anyone know you can hear me.'

I turned around, but Finnley hadn't moved her mouth with the last sentence. She was thinking.

'Finnley? How?'

I closed my eyes. This was the first time I remembered Mom's voice. Tears ran down my cheeks.

'I've always had these powers. I've been hiding them, and I'm so sorry I didn't tell you earlier, but I'm scared.'

'You fought the Blue Star. You didn't let it steal your power, just like I asked. Why are you scared?'

I watched a tear run down Finnley's cheek. 'Dad and Aidan are planning to use me for the Blue Star's power. I need you to do something for me, though.'

'They what? Oh… anything, baby girl. I'll do anything.'

'I'm going to steal it.' I heard Mom gasp as Finnley continued. 'Don't question it, please don't argue, and under no circumstances can you follow me. I have a plan, and when I'm safe, I'll come back for you.'

'Finnley…'

'Mom, there's someone I have to save. His name is Nate. I see him in my dreams. I don't know how, or why I see it, but I have to find him.'

'I knew you two were meant for each other.'

Finnley shot up off the ground, shoving her fist forward as power exploded from her arm, cracking the wall behind me. She ran forward, slamming her fist repeatedly into the stone as shards of rock scattered the ground.

Noise grew from the mouth of the cave as Finnley scrambled to pick up the Blue Soul. Her hands pushed forward as she ran toward the entrance, a shield of energy weaving just in front of her. I chased her, only a few steps behind.

When Finnley reached the opening, the energy spread and launched everyone flying backward. Benches knocked over, sending everyone out of their seats. Angie lifted her head off the ground.

"What are you doing?" she screamed as Finnley ran and created a new path through the trees.

The closest man to her path jumped up and followed. Shit, I knew that outfit. That was the man who controlled fire, the man who was dead in the clearing.

With my next step, my feet stuck into the ground, dragging me down so I couldn't follow. My memory fogged around the edges of my eyes. I know what was going to happen, but I couldn't stop it.

Still clear to my right, I saw my mom push off the ground and start running toward Finnley's path.

"No!"

55

Nate

I wrapped my hand around Clara's mouth as she shot out of bed. She thrashed and yelled under my grip as I tried to calm her down in a hushed tone.

"C, quiet, quiet. It's just me, it's okay. You need to be quiet, it's two in the morning," I whispered.

Her eyes were wide as tears ran down her face and through my fingers. She looked around in a panic, slowly putting her surroundings together. Finally she stopped fidgeting, still breathing hard as she reached up and pulled my hand away from her mouth.

"How did we get back?"

"I carried you through the shadows to avoid my parents. What the hell happened?"

Clara wiped her face with her palms, her body still shaking. "I remembered the day I ran away. When I stole the Blue Soul." She swallowed through a sob. "I warned my mom. I told her not to follow. I spoke to her through her mind and she still didn't listen."

Clara shoved her face into my chest and sobbed. I wrapped my arms around her and held her up, powerless to pull her pain away. All I could do was hold her.

~

Clara had been asleep for a while now but by six, I couldn't stay in bed any longer. I rolled off the edge, taking a stack of clothes out of my bag and into the bathroom to shower.

The fact that the cold water didn't bother me should have, well, bothered me. If the Cold Soul wasn't in Clara anymore, why didn't the cold bother us? Was it because they were still running around doing who knows what?

After two days, I wasn't as startled to see blue eyes in my reflection, but they still looked weird. My arm didn't bother me either, maybe because I had gotten used to seeing Clara's scar and mine was identical to hers. I pulled my shirt over my head and heard Clara talking in the other room.

She was still laying in bed, her eyes puffy from sleep and crying. My phone was on the pillow next to her, Glitch's voice coming through loudly.

"Yo, Nate, I can hear you breathing. C, please tell me I'm on speaker."

"You're on speaker," she mumbled as I sat down on the bed.

"Dude, your girlfriend is cranky in the morning."

"Says the guy who could sleep until four in the afternoon," I replied, trying to keep from laughing. Clara did not look in the mood.

"Well, I'm finnled in. The Complex? Your parents? Crazy."

"Yeah, man. It's been interesting to say the least," I said.

He laughed on the other end. "Break out of that prison and come home to see me before they send you off to a research lab or something."

"Not funny," Clara grumbled and rolled away from the phone, planting her face in the pillow. I picked up the phone and took if off speaker.

"Glitch, this whole place is seriously messed up. And now with the Cold Souls out…"

"Yeah, Clara warned me not to trust any versions of you two that have green eyes and black blood. Speaking of weird stuff, do you have any awesome new powers from the Blue Star?"

"Blue Soul," I corrected. "No powers that I know of, just a stronger connection to Clara."

"Gross, get a room."

I rolled my eyes but thought harder. "Actually, it was a lot easier to stick my landing last night through the shadows. And Clara's ridiculously strong now. She puts us to shame."

"Clara cheats, so that's not fair."

"You ain't cheatin', you ain't tryin'," Clara mumbled through the pillow. I chuckled.

Glitch let out a groan. "I take it C just made a snide remark. Just remind her that you were my best friend before she even came along."

"Yeah, yeah. I'll call you if anything else comes up or if we need a rescue."

"Good luck escaping your family cult!" He hung up before I could groan.

Clara didn't move out of her face-plant as I slid under the covers with her. After a few minutes, she couldn't stand breathing into the pillow and rolled over to face me.

"We really do need to escape to go find that old Complex. Or at least see if The Assembly found anything on our evil Cold Souls."

"My parents getting kicked out doesn't help our situation. We need to trick someone into telling us something."

Clara frowned and sat up. "Wait, no we don't. You took me through the shadows last night. Was it easier?"

I nodded. "Yeah, it actually was. I even got us out with ease. What's your plan?"

"Do you think you could sneak us into The Assembly room and stay in a shadow?"

"Probably. I guess if I have any issues we can just slide out in a different room," I replied with a shrug.

Clara stared into space, thinking. "If you get us into the room, we can hear them talking. Or better yet, if I'm in the same room I can pick up the thoughts they don't want me to hear."

"You are brilliant and I love you." I slid her closer and kissed her forehead. "Are you okay after last night?"

She paused. "I'm fine. Remembering my mom for the first time was hard because I knew what was going to happen. I couldn't stop it." Clara lifted her hand to my face. "But when Finnley was talking to my mom, she wasn't surprised that I was going to look for you."

"Finnley said she was going to look for me?"

Clara frowned as she nodded. "Yeah. Angie didn't know I was running away to find you, but then my mom said she knew we were meant for each other."

I shrugged. "My mom told Finnley about me, though. And Jeanie pushed us together too. Why is this surprising?"

"Jeanie thought we only had four months together. Angie tried to keep us apart. My mom said we were meant for each other. It's just interesting, given the other accounts we have of my past."

"Well, if it's any consolation, your mom was more right than Jeanie, who literally knows the future. My mom is just a downer," I said, pinching her side as she relaxed.

"You're right," she mumbled, sticking her nose up.

"I'm sorry, what was that?" I joked back at her as she pushed off of me.

"I said I'm going to take a shower."

Clara grabbed her bag and dragged it along the floor to the bathroom. I heard the water start and rolled onto my back. I could probably fall back asleep in a few minutes if I closed my eyes. Suddenly, something hit me in the face. I pulled her sweatshirt off my head and looked up.

"Are you joining me or what?" she asked, poking her head around the door frame.

"Wait, yes." I jumped up but she locked the door before I could get there.

"Too bad. Now that you're up, will you make me coffee?" she laughed through the door.

"I could literally use a shadow to get in. A locked door won't stop me." I felt my nose pinch. "Ow, rude."

"Save your energy. We have a lot of trouble to get into today."

56

Nate

"Are you two not sick of each other yet?" Dad asked, eyeing us suspiciously. I was sitting on the couch while Clara was on her back, her legs resting on my lap.

Clara shrugged. "Not really."

"Maybe it's the connection," my mom said, still scribbling furiously in her notebook.

I leaned forward, squishing Clara's kees between my legs and chest. "What are you writing?"

"Documenting," she replied. "Writing down as much as I can remember about your childhood and everything from the last few months."

"That's not weird or anything," Clara said, tilting her head to look at my mom. "What's the point?"

My mom looked up, frowning. "The point? You two are the first individuals born with powers, and the only ones to interact with the Blue Star — Soul. I think that's worth keeping track of."

"We're also the idiots who released the Cold Souls into the world. I'd rather not be remembered for that," Clara grumbled, sliding her legs off me as she sat up.

Dad leaned back in his chair. "The more we can understand, the better chance we have of figuring out what they are up to. Maybe we can also figure out what's going on between you two."

"I thought we weren't supposed to intervene," I said, poking Clara discreetly to signal the start of our plan. I needed to get my parents to think about the right things so Clara could read their minds. "Isn't that The Assembly's job?"

"I'm just gathering all I can," Mom answered. "If they find anything from their lab tests, it could help this information make sense. You do want them to find the Cold Souls, right? The faster they stop them, the faster you get out of here, and this info could help. You still have another semester of school to worry about."

Clara huffed and leaned back into the couch. "I thought sitting here all day was boring, but now you're making us go back to school?" *Nate, I know where to go. We need an excuse to leave.*

"Seriously," I said, leaning back just as dramatically as Clara. "We've been cooped up in a library for months and now here with nothing to do. Can we at least go walking around or something?"

My parents looked at each other nervously. "That might not be a good idea for Clara..." Dad hesitated.

"Please, I'm antsy," Clara pleaded, clasping her hands together. "I promise we will avoid all people and stay on the sidewalks."

Damn, she was good at this. I think my dad was convinced. Mom not so much. She narrowed her eyes. "No snooping, stay on the paved paths, and don't go into any buildings."

Before she could change her mind, Clara grabbed my hand and stood up. "Deal."

The cold afternoon air rushed inside the hallway as we left the side door. I could feel my parents watching us from the window so we started our path toward the plaza, trying to look as normal as two teenagers with light sweatshirts on in below freezing temperatures could look. There weren't many people walking around, and most of them were just rushing to get back inside, so they didn't pay much attention to us.

Your parents think the lab tests are coming back today, or at least that's what the doctor told them. Clara bumped me so we could turn across a different path and away from The Assembly building. *I think I remember a small paved park over here. It's out of sight so we can disappear without raising any suspicions.*

The path extended to the left of the parking lot, lined with thicker trees. Their shadows didn't move in the still air, but I could feel them stronger than before. It was like a new flow of energy, and that connection filled me with power. I played with a few of them as we walked further on the bath, pulling and pushing them to make it look like the trees were swaying without a breeze.

"Could you do that before?" Clara asked, watching where she stepped with a smile on her face.

"I don't think so. They feel different in the sunlight," I replied.

"Cool." She stopped walking and glanced around. "I think we're good now. You ready?"

"Let's snoop."

I wrapped my arms around her and slid easily into the shadow I was playing with. We wove through the trees and along the rear of the buildings, pausing whenever someone walked by. In a place that was full of people with powers, they'd be more suspicious of a moving shadow.

As we slid into The Assembly building, the same guard stood at attention in front of the doors. The only problem was the gap in the hallway between shadows. He would easily see us.

Create a distraction. I expected to wait for her to come up with something but Clara already had a plan.

One of the light fixtures down the opposite hallway shattered, causing the guard to jump away from the door. As soon as he turned, I jumped across the gap and slid through the door easily. The left wall was dark, which made it easy to relax and hide. The Assembly was gathered around the table, but the doctor wasn't there yet. My parent's seats at the end of the table were left empty.

No one spoke, so it was Clara's turn to dig through their heads. She started reporting thoughts back to me.

They haven't found the Cold Souls. That fat man is digging through Finnley's file. Apparently I got in trouble a lot with them.

More than just stealing keys for the library?

Yeah. Destruction of property, trespassing, oh, and I blew up a building.

Holy shit. Because of headaches?

No, I think I literally just mixed a bunch of chemicals I wasn't supposed to. Damn, Finnley was a genius. For being a little shit, she got perfect scores on all their tests, including The Trials. I think I like her now.

That didn't surprise me, but at the same time I was impressed. Clara continued as she moved to the next person.

That old woman... she thinks we should be separated and locked up.

What? Why?

I didn't catch enough. She's suspicious of what we can do together.

You have a bunch of mind powers ad all I can do is hide in a shadow. What's so suspicious about our telepathic connection?

The door swung open and the doctor walked in, clutching a file folder to her chest as she moved across the room and stood at the end of the table. The Assembly waited patiently.

"There's nothing out of the ordinary."

The doctor's statement was met with several confused looks.

"How is that possible?" the fat man asked, tossing Finnley's file on the table.

"They have the same levels of energy as everyone else who has taken the power from a source. Maybe the Blue Soul wasn't as powerful as we once thought."

"The Blue Soul had never reacted to a person before. How certain are you about these findings?" the old woman asked, not convinced. I could hear Clara growl at her.

"As certain as I can be with a blood sample. Perhaps the Blue Soul was just selective, but with the same energy levels, it's impossible to track the Cold Soul signature." The doctor flipped through her notes one more time but shut the file.

She's protecting us. I could feel Clara's heartbeat pick up.

Protecting us from what?

From them. She knows someting is up with our powers and she's trying to keep us from becoming test subjects.

"This can't be a dead end," a slender, balding man snapped. "They were already a danger with their powers before, and now they have a power source. Not to mention the Cold Souls have the same power as they do, and significantly more dangerous."

He thinks we're working with the Cold Souls. Actually, a lot of them think we are the Cold Souls and are toying with them.

I was about to respond but felt something slide along my ankle. I kicked, but only waved into empty space. Could that feeling have something to do with staying in a shadow too long?

"Assembly," the doctor said, trying to keep her composure. "I can assure you that their energy levels show no indication that they are any more powerful or dangerous."

She's lying. She faked the report to protect us. Something is going on between us.

The old woman knocked her chair back as she stood. "There has to be more. Go get the two of them and run whatever tests you can think of."

"Ma'am, you promised Angie and Tom—" the doctor stuttered.

"Those two are responsible for releasing a powerful and evil force into the world, which now threatens our existence," she shouted. "Until we can get conclusive evidence of their power and how they got it, they will submit to our request. I'll do it myself if I have to."

The same feeling around my ankle now slid up the back of my leg.

This time when I kicked back, I felt my foot connect. My stomach twisted.

Clara, we need to get out of the shadows. Something is in here with us.

What?

I moved as fast as I could out of the building and launched us into the trees. I turned my body to cushion our exit, crashing into a stump as Clara slammed on top of me. In front of us, I watched the shadow we had just left shake and extend out of the ground and toward us before snapping back into stillness.

"That wasn't me," I stammered, scrambling out from under Clara. I looked around, unable to see any other moving shadows.

"Nate, we have to go. Now," Clara said, grabbing my hand as she yanked me toward the apartments.

57

Clara

I was busy shoving our clothes into our bags, carefully hiding the blank book in the bottom of mine when Nate hurried in with his parents.

"You did what?" Angie shouted at him.

"Mom, I don't have time to justify what we did, but we have to go. They're coming to get us," he replied, out of breath. He tried to push her out the door so they could start packing their things.

"Hold on," Tom growled. "What did the doctor say *exactly*."

"She didn't tell them the truth. She gave a false report. Clara heard her thoughts, though. The doctor knows we have more power thans he led them to believe. Now they want to keep us as lab rats because they think we're dangerous," Nate said, tapping his leg nervously. Tom turned and hurried back to their apartment.

"Dangerous?" Angie asked, wide eyed.

"Mom, we aren't dangerous, but until they run their tests, we aren't safe. I get it, we have a lot of power, and that scares them. Please, just let us try to figure this out. If we can find the Cold Souls, we can make this right."

Tom returned and held out the car keys. "You stole them from us before you went out on your walk," he said, slowly and deliberately. "We never heard you come back and assumed you were still out walking around. Don't use your powers until you're far away from this place."

I stopped zipping our bags and looked up to see Nate frozen.

"Hold on, you aren't coming?" I asked.

Tom shook his head. "If we're here, we can calm the waters and keep you updated on their plans. We'll be okay and this is far safer for you."

He had a point. They were our last connection to this place. If The Assembly discovered something, or if the doctor contacted them, we could get more answers.

Angie lunged forward and pulled Nate into a hug. I heard him grunt as she squeezed him. Tom patted him on the shoulder and nodded to me.

Keep him safe, please. Keep yourself safe.

I nodded and he pulled me into a quick hug.

"Okay, get going," Angie said, stepping back as she sniffed. "Be safe and check in when you can."

"We'll get answers and come back, promise," I replied.

Angie gave me a half smile and slid to the side so we could get out the door. Nate and I picked up our bags and started jogging down the hallway.

The plaza was still empty as we ran toward the parking lot. Every few feet, I would turn back to make sure no one was following us. Nate kept watching the shadows around our feet, trying to see if something moved. We made it to the car without trouble and drove off.

Nate hesitated as we reached the highway before turning in the opposite direction of Forest Hills. "Get that address and map from the glovebox. We need answers so we can keep them from dissecting us."

According to the map, we had about two hours of driving. Most of it was spent in silence as we worried about what we might find. Jeanie said the old Complex was destroyed and then gave us a blank book. If she could see the past and future, shouldn't she have been able to see what happened? Why couldn't she tell us?

And that word 'dangerous' kept popping up. Jeanie said it, the doctor thought it, and The Assembly believed it. Our future had changed, according to Jeanie, and now she was directing us to find the Original Complex. There had to be a connection somewhere. We needed answers before the Cold Souls made their move. They were the dangerous ones.

By the time we reached Jeanie's cabin, the sun had ducked under the horizon and very little light was left to illuminate the rocky path up to the door. We wouldn't be able to search tonight.

The fireplace burst to life as we walked in. I could see a tiny bathroom behind a cramped kitchen. The old fridge whirred loudly, completing the picture of a worn and outdated place.

"Wow, Jeanie made House and her library so nice. At least she got us a fire," I said. I turned my nose in disgust as Nate sat on the bed, hearing it creak. Actually, I'm pretty sure dust puffed out of the comforted.

"Better than an operating table," Nate replied. He dropped back and sent more dust flying. He coughed and sat back up, waving his hand through the air.

"Why do you think it was so important we come here?" I asked. I joined him on the bed and pulled the book out of my bag. The pages were still blank, but I guess I sort of expected that.

"Maybe there will be something to sue against the Cold Souls. Assuming they just have our memories, they probably don't know about this place," he said before laughing to himself. "My mom is going to have a field day with all this if we find answers."

I frowned. "Do you think they are okay back at The Complex?"

"Probably. My mom can talk her way around almost anything." He stood up. "Come on. Help me shake out these blankets. We have to get up early."

58

Nate

The morning light made the cabin look even more pathetic from the outside. We were out the door just as the sun started to rise, mostly because neither of us had slept well on the lumpy mattress. It didn't help that the fridge started to make a clanking sound in the middle of the night.

Dried and cracked trees scattered the rocky ground. Some were completely splintered while others were bent and tilted, facing away from where we were walking. The farther we hiked away from the cabin, the more damage the trees seemed to have taken. Jeanie was right about the old Complex being destroyed. Whatever did this was insanely powerful.

After about forty minutes, we stumbled into an opening. Trees had been completely uprooted from the rocks, littering the ground around our feet. The blast seemed to originate in the center of the clearing. We climbed and scrambled over the rocks until we stood in the middle, observing the mess around us.

"What the hell happened here?" Clara asked, her mouth hanging open as she looked around.

"How could this have been a Complex? There's nothing left," I said. What sort of answers were we going to get from a place that looked like this.

"There's no proof that there was ever anything to begin with. What are we supposed to write in the book? 'All that's left is absolutely nothing'?" Clara growled, throwing the book down in anger.

The spine hit the rock at an angle, popping the cover open as it settled on the ground. The pages were still blank as they started fluttering in the breeze.

Wait, there wasn't a breeze.

Clara's eyes got wide and I saw her knees buckle. I didn't have time to make it over to her before mine did the same.

"I swear, if I pass out again—" Clara heaved and slapped her hand over her mouth, stopping her sentence before she threw up. The same nausea punched me, spinning the horizon until I couldn't figure out which way was up or down. I gave up trying to steady myself and just shut my eyes.

Something brushed against my nose. I flinched my hand up as a reflex, grabbing grass between my fingers. My eyes opened to the bright sun, but it didn't blind me. Sitting up, I tried to put the pieces together. I was in a meadow, scattered with trees, but none of it was familiar.

I felt a hand press into my shoulder and I spun, grabbing the wrist of the person and twisting them to the ground. Clara wiggled under my grip, pissed. I tried to open my mouth but nothing came out. Not even my thoughts could get through to her.

She yanked her hand away and pushed me off of her, annoyed. I tried to mouth 'sorry' to her but she just rolled her eyes and picked herself off the ground. She rubbed her wrist while her eyes focused on something behind me.

I turned around to see a small village in the distance. People were walking around, going about their morning, but it was anything but normal. We watched an old woman lift an entire wagon of fruit off the ground and over her head with incredible strength. A father picked up his child before turning invisible, letting the child squeal as it looked like he was flying off the ground. Another young man entertained a group of children by shapeshifting into different animals, letting them chase a cheetah, a monkey, and then a dog through the buildings. These people all had powers.

Clara stepped in front of me so I could see her face. 'Complex' she mouthed, nodding toward the village as she started walking. I followed closely, letting her lead because she looked like she knew what she was doing. Maybe this was what her memory was like back at the cave. It explained why she didn't want to pass out. That wasn't fun.

The village people didn't notice us as we walked directly up the aisle of their buildings, though they were all acting strange. Some looked nervous, their eyes dodging between the people around them and back to one of the buildings. Standing at the head of the plaza, similar to how our Complex was designed, was a large stone structure, tall and threatening against the meadow backdrop.

Clara stuck her arm out and I followed her finger. She was pointing to the side of the structure where a boy our age had stuck his head around the back.

He looked about as nervous as the rest of the village. We moved toward him, but as we made it to the front, his head yanked back like he had been pulled away. I took off running, dragging Clara behind me.

I skidded to a stop after turning the corner. The boy was pressed against the back of the building, making out with a girl. Clara leaned her head on my shoulder and watched them, squeezing my hand. Of course she thought this was cute. I just felt uncomfortable watching two people kiss who didn't know we were there. The girl pulled her lips away and pressed her forehead against his.

"Don't be nervous," the boy whispered, reaching his hand up as he held her cheek.

"Right, why would I be nervous?" she groaned. "They're only asking me to completely recharge all the power sources. No big deal." She rolled her eyes along with her mocking tone.

Clara and I stiffened.

"Kins, you know what to do. It's not that big a deal."

"Of course it's a big deal, Isaac. All I've been told my whole life is 'Kinsie, you won't get to have powers because it's your job to make sure everyone else gets to have them in the future.' It's bullshit," she snapped, folding her arms.

"But you do have powers," Isaac said, pulling her arms away.

Clara hit my side to get my attention, as if I hadn't just heard what they had said.

"Yeah, and so do you, but neither of us have gone through The Trials. It doesn't make sense," she replied, pulling her hands out of Isaac's to rub her temples.

"Look, all you have to do is use the Soul to power the rest of the sources. They said the object would tell you what to do when you touched it."

Kinsie shook her head. "Isaac, I'm telling you. I've been hearing these voices and I'm not sure it's a good idea. No one has ever done this before."

Isaac slid his arms around Kinsie's waist and pulled her close again. "Kins, you play with shadows and darkness. I'm sure there are all kinds of monsters hiding in there, saying things. It's probably nothing."

"If you can read minds, why can't you hear the voices in my head? Please, Isaac, you have to believe me."

Clara shot her hand over her mouth in reflex, even though we couldn't make sounds and they couldn't see us. These two had our powers before The Trials. They were us.

"I'm sure you're just nervous. Come on, they're going to be looking for you," Isaac said, picking up her hand. He pulled her through us and walked around the corner.

Ouch. At least I believed Clara. Poor Kinsie.

Clara yanked my arm and chased after them. They had been stopped at the front of the building as an older woman pulled a reluctant Kinsie toward the entrance. Isaac stood still as Clara studied his face, standing directly in front of him. She looked upset at him, shaking her head as he looked right through her, watching Kinsie disappear into the structure. I pulled Clara away and followed Kinsie and the woman inside.

The building was just a giant stone room, each of the three walls in front of us a tall monolith. Small cracks in the walls let sunlight creep in, scattering the reflections of the power sources that sat on a stone table against the back wall.

"The Soul will tell you what to do," the woman said, lettin ggo of Kinsie's arm as she turned to leave.

"Wait!" Kinsie said, wringing her hands together. "If no one has used it before, how do you know what it does?"

She smiled. "It's written in the stars." The woman slipped out the front as the door shut behind her.

"Great, that's not vague or anything," Kinsie groaned and turned back around, stepping up to the table.

Clara and I walked closer. Power sources scattered the table, glinting with faint color in the sunlight. I saw The Ruby in the corner, a weak red glow lighting the surface, the only source besides two marbles that had light left in it. The Blue Soul sat on the right of the table, shining bright blue without the sun.

Clara leaned in closer for the same reason I did. The Soul Kinsie was looking at wasn't actually blue. The light was black somehow, humming and rattling gently on the table. It wasn't the Blue Soul she was going to pick up. It was the Cold Soul.

Kinsie shot her hand out as I tried to grab the source to stop her. My hands slipped right through hers as she gripped it between both her palms. Clara and I watched in horror as the black light crept up her arm, shaping and forming in slivers just like our lightning scars. Kinsie realized what was happening and started to fight back. The mark sank back toward her palms, shaking as she started to push her hands closer together as light around us started to fade.

No, the entire room was fading into blackness. Kinsie was creating the darkness that I had once made by accident.

But the Cold Soul was too strong. The black light exploded back up Kinsie's arms, the blast sending the other power sources slamming into the stone wall in front of us. The other walls crumbled and crashed to the ground, dust clouds blanketing our surroundings. Even though Clara and I didn't feel the rock falling around us, we lost sight of everything.

When the rumbling noise finally dulled, faint screams could be heard echoing. The dust cleared slowly, revealing where we were standing... right where we had fallen when the book opened. This was the center of the destruction we saw.

Kinsie stood facing the wall that had caught the objects. They were all glowing again, embedded in the stone and full of power. She smirked and turned around, revealing her arms dripping black blood onto the rocks under her feet. She was the Cold Soul now.

The village around us had been completely decimated. Screams came in louder as we saw the people who were crushed between the rocks and ground that had just been uprooted. Their voices faded into the sky as their lives left them. The old woman we saw earlier pushed in vain against a rock that had pinned her down before finally slipping into death. The young man who could shapeshift dangled from the branches of a tree, unable to change form before the branch snapped and sent him falling into the crevice below. Their powers were gone, and they were helpless against the Cold Soul.

I turned as movement caught my eye. Behind the Cold Soul, Isaac, covered in blood, dug through the rocks and stone. He must have been using what little strength he had left ot move the large rocks as he finally pulled a body out from the rubble. It was Kinsie, the real Kinsie.

She struggled to keep her head up as Isaac wrapped his arm around her waist to hold her up. The Cold Soul was busy observing her mess, not noticing Kinsie and Isaac limping over to the wall of sources. He picked up her bloody palm and pressed it into the empty Cold Soul marble as his fingers ran over the identical blue one. He was channeling the power of the Blue Soul for Kinsie to use.

The Cold Soul finally noticed, spinning around in fury, but Kinsie had her own trick with her newfound strength. We watched as the Cold Soul stumbled, unable to stand as Kinsie pulled its shadow from under its feet. It hissed and clawed forward, trying to fight against Kinsie's power, but tripped and slid deeper into the black shadow. It crept along the ground and into Kinsie as she guided it back into the marble.

When the Cold Soul was back in its prison, Kinsie collapsed, her hand smearing blood down the wall. Isaac was using the wall to keep himself, slowly sliding down as he lost consciousness. He sucked in a breath and swung his arm back before slamming his fist into the Cold Soul. His force rippled through the air before getting sucked into the marble. Blue light swirled and spun, filling the marble as the black light disappeared. The original Blue Soul was emptied, now swallowing the Cold Soul completely in *the single cage.*

Isaac sank toward the ground, his head pressing into Kinsie's chest. The heavier his eyes drooped, the more I started to get dizzy. Clara started to sway as we felt the pull of gravity. Our knees finally gave way and we crashed to the ground.

59

Clara

The best description for how I felt was sleep paralysis. It felt like my mind was awake but the rest of my body wouldn't respond. There was no feeling.

Nate and I had just seen exactly what we needed. The marble given to me as a child had both the Cold and Blue Soul, and that's what the Cold Soul Finnley had meant when she said the Blue Soul liked me. Isaac had the same power as me, and maybe the Blue Soul remembered that. The only problem was that the Cold Soul went into me instead, waiting for me to turn eighteen so it could recharge the rest of the power sources like it did before. The Blue Soul was waiting to react to my power, and it did that the night I ran away.

But when Nate rescued me, he took the rest of the Blue Soul and left the Cold Soul unguarded. It shattered the cage, but if we could find the original Blue Soul power source, we could lock it inside. We could stop it. Kinsie and Isaac had shown us how to trap it.

Feeling crept back as I felt the weight of my body pressing into something soft, but that couldn't be right. Nate and I had passed out on the rocks.

I jolted upright from a bed. The room was dimly lit, but it definitely wasn't the cabin Jeanie had sent us to. The bed wasn't lumpy and the sheets were dust free. The lamp on the nightstand was the only light, barely strong enough for me to see a chair in one corner, opposite from a closed door. The crack around the frame was lit from the outside, seeping light over the carpet.

Something kicked under the blanket and I felt a figure move next to me. I quickly identified Nate's groan as he reached his hand over his face. If Nate was just now waking up, who had gotten us here? And where the hell was *here*?

"Nate, get up," I whispered harshly, trying to shake him.

"Rude. I'm trying to sleep," he groaned. He tried to roll away from me but I grabbed the collar of his sweatshirt and yanked him up, holding him in front of my face.

"Nate, I didn't get us here and neither did you."

"Shit," he blurted, his eyes widening.

"Yeah, exactly."

We scrambled out of the bed and crept up to the door. Nate pressed his ear against the door but shook his head. "I don't hear anyone. Should we use a shadow?"

"Not if you think something else is in there. I'll defend if we have to. Grab the book and let's go."

He looked around the room, unable to find it. Whoever had brought us here must have had it. I opened the door slowly, peering out into the empty hallway. The walls were bare, just a small lightbulb hanging from the middle. A few feet to our left was a dead end, while the right hallway turned a corner with another light shining.

I stayed in front of Nate as we shuffled quietly along the wall. The closer we got to the corner, I started to vaguely hear someone's thoughts, whispering in the back of my head. I pushed my finger up to my mouth as I looked back at Nate.

I hear someone.

Nate held up his fists, unsure if he'd need to fight without using his powers. I hoped whatever we were about to find wasn't strong enough to fight my power. Leaning against the wall, I inched closer to pick up more of the person's thoughts. They were still quiet but the voice... it was familiar.

I spun around the corner and stood in the open. Nate's eyes widened as he tried to reach out and pull me back but I knocked his hand away. I dug deeper into her thoughts, letting the voice echo in my head. The woman stood over the table, leaning over the book and flipping through the pages that were now full of text. She didn't seem to know any difference, and I had learned not to be surprised by anything going on now.

Nate tried to grab me again but I walked forward to dodge his grasp. As he spun around the corner behind me, the floor creaked. The woman straightened just as Nate grabbed the hem of my sleeve. His grip released as soon as the woman turned around smiling.

"Mom," I whispered.

Suddenly I lost the ability to move. My legs wouldn't move forward as I stared at the woman I only knew from the police report of her death and the brief memory I had seen when Finnley stole the Blue Soul. How could I tell her that I didn't actually know her?

"Baby girl, your eyes are blue," she said.

My mouth opened but no words came out as she glided forward. Her hand reached up to my cheek, running it down my neck to pull my necklace chains out. I was still frozen as she played with the charm Nate had gotten me, followed by the large key that hung lower.

"You were always obsessed with keys." She smiled up at me again but her face turned into a frown. "Baby girl, what's wrong?"

Tears were rolling down my cheeks as she reached up again, using her thumbs to brush them away as she held my face.

"I lost everything, all of my memories. I lost every piece of you," I choked, trying to stay composed. She wrapped her arms around and pulled me close.

"It's okay. It's okay. Come now, we both have a lot of explaining to do." She tried to let go of me but I hung on and she laughed. "Sweetie, I think it's time to introduce me to your boyfriend. He looks a little uncomfortable right now."

I straightened and let go of her, sniffing and wiping my sleeves over my face. Nate was quiet as he stepped forward, his left hand sliding around my back.

"Mom, this is—"

She cut me off. "Oh, honey, I was kidding. I know exactly who Nate is." She jumped forward and hugged him. For a second Nate was confused but eventually reached his arms around her. She leaned back, holding his shoulders. "Sorry, maybe that wasn't the best time to play a joke. I hope you put up with hers too."

Nate smiled. "I see where she gets it now."

"Mom. How?" I mumbled, still trying to wrap my head around all of this.

Her dark green eyes stared back at me as she motioned for us to sit at the table. She placed three cups of coffee on the table, pushing the sugar jar in front of mine. Nate chuckled at the gesture as I slid my chair closer to him. My mom, who was definitely not dead, sat down across from us and didn't take her eyes off me.

"So, my story. I guess you won't remember that my power is healing. Jeanie warned me of your plan, and that she had changed your path so you'd have a few more months to live happily. But I was afraid that the man who followed you would get in the way. Long story short, I healed and went missing from the morgue." She paused and took a sip of her coffee. I was shocked that she casually brushed over her death. I was already feeling the panic building, knowing I'd have to explain mine too. "I didn't know you survived that night. I thought that either the man or your father had killed you."

"Why did you come here?" Nate leaned back in the chair.

"Because when you two were both born with powers, I did what I could to find the answers. I found this place several years ago, but that's where the information ended. I knew the who and where, not the how and why. Will the rest of the book tell me more?"

I glanced at Nate. She didn't know about Isaac and Kinsie's powers yet. And she didn't know about the Blue Soul and Cold Soul.

"Mom, how did you know we were meant for each other?" I asked, looking back at her.

She looked confused. "You two were born with powers, that's never been heard of. When you told me at The Trials you were looking for Nate, I realized it was fate. That's what Jeanie meant when she said you would be happy. That's why I chased after you, because I wanted you to have that. Or is there something more?"

Nate nudged me and I knew what he meant. We reached up at the same time, pulling off our keys and sliding our sleeves up. She gasped and yanked our arms across the table, spilling coffee over the edges of all our cups.

"You should probably read the rest of that book," Nate said, shifting up in his seat as my mom pulled our arms closer to her.

"Why don't you give me the cliff-notes?" She said as she released our wrists and we slid our sleeves back down.

"There are no cliff-notes. It's a full-on, one hundred page thesis." I shrugged.

I recapped as much as I could, starting with the returned memory of The Trials and then my actual four-month-long memory. Nate and I meeting, all of my headaches and outbursts, putting the Blue Soul back together and our new power, all the information we started to find, how Nate used his powers to keep me from destroying things, Aidan and Richard, up until meeting Angie and then...

My chest tightened and I gripped at the table. I could never forget the scene burned into my mind. The knife, my hands, the blue blood. Nate pulled my hand off the edge of the table and slid his wrist under my fingers. My mom watched our interaction carefully because I couldn't talk anymore, even with the buzzing energy I felt through Nate's skin. He was prepared and continued for me.

He recounted his dream, how the Cold Soul tricked him into letting it out. He reassured my mom that he would do it all over again to save me, even if he let two Cold Souls out. But now we knew how to stop them, thanks to the book and our discoveries at The Complex.

I released my grip on Nate's wrist and he flexed his fingers. I had been holding on a lot stronger than I realized. He saw me staring at the red hand mark I had left on his skin and slid his fingers through mine.

It's okay.

I leaned my head on his shoulder and focused on my mom. She was looking at us but deep in thought. "I have a theory." She scrunched her nose just like I did when I was deep in thought. There were so many mannerisms that were like mine and it pained me that I couldn't actually remember her.

"Theories are welcome," Nate said, rubbing his thumb over the back of my hand.

She ran her finger over her chin. "Why do you think people called it the Blue Star before now? Don't answer, I'm going to continue. A blue star, in the real stars, is bright and hot and has a short lifespan. The explosions are violent supernovas and often turn into black holes."

I looked at her like she was crazy. "They said it wasn't the Blue Star, they called it a Soul. Two different powers, two different souls shoved into the same source. Where are you going with this?"

"Black hole." She pointed to Nate. "Absorbs everything around it. Kinsie trying to contain the Cold Soul. Nate pulling your headaches and pain away." She pointed to me now. "Supernova. Explosions. Violent, powerful shockwaves. Isaac's punch, sending the power back inside. Your outbursts."

"That's nice. I'm violent and explosive," I groaned.

"No, C, I think I get it," Nate said, looking at me.

"C?" Mom questioned Nate, but he continued.

"The extra power we have isn't the Blue Star. The *power source* is the Blue Soul. We, *together*, are the Blue Star. In broad terms, I contain your explosions and you counteract so I don't pull everything in with me. We keep each other grounded, constantly. That's what we feel when we touch."

"Yes, that's where I was going with this. You called her C?" My mom leaned forward but we ignored her question.

I frowned. "Mom, why would the Cold Soul want to recharge the objects?"

She looked disappointed that we were avoiding her question but she responded. "A soul, Cold or not, is essentially life. But you can't just create that energy to recharge the sources out of nothing. It has to come from somewhere."

It clicked in my head. "The Cold Soul wanted Kinsie to create the black hole. Isaac couldn't contain it if he wasn't there. It absorbed the powers back from everyone in the village. If they took any power, it got returned, and if no one had powers, no one could put the Cold Soul back." I turned to Nate, excited that we finally had answers.

He was putting it all together too, his eyes widening. "But Kinsie and Isaac survived, not part of the Cold Soul's plan. They still had their powers because they were born with them. They used their powers, an explosion and a black hole, to contain the Cold Soul inside the power source. They had to use the extra power source because they were about to die and it was the strongest available."

"You said the source was destroyed. How can you contain the Cold Soul without its original power source?" Mom asked.

"We use the one that Isaac left empty; the Blue Soul's original source. We know we need our powers to hold it, but it should be a lot easier for us since we are basically extra strength right now." I stood up at the same time as Nate and he joined in on my next sentence.

"We need to get back to The Complex."

My mom stood up across from us and leaned over the table. "First, one of you better explain why Nate keeps calling you 'C'."

60

Clara

My mom drove us back to the dingy cabin, knowing Nate's parents would be pissed if we left their car out in the middle of nowhere. On the way there, I had to explain my new name. I suppose I could have gone back to Finnley, but it just didn't feel right to me when I still didn't have those memories. Mom didn't seem to mind that I wasn't using the name she gave me but she admitted it might take some getting used to.

"I suppose you picking the name Clara Rivers shouldn't surprise me. You chose the best two *Doctor Who* characters to model yourself after." She turned to look at me in the passenger seat. "Wait, you do remember *Doctor Who*, right?"

So she was the one who showed it to me. I shrugged. "Yes. Well, no. I don't remember it, but Nate made me watch it, so kind of."

Nate poked me from the back seat. "Made you? You loved it."

"Alright, yes. And Star Wars," I laughed.

"Oh, that one was your obsession alone. I'm surprised you didn't choose the name Quinn. Quentin was always your favorite character from *The Magicians*. I could never pull you away from that book." Mom smiled as she looked over at me. "You still seem like you... I know that probably doesn't mean much when you have nothing to compare it to."

"Yeah, tell me about all the trouble she used to get into. She still seems to have a knack for that," Nate said, leaning forward between my mom and I.

"You mean besides sneaking out after dark to break into a library? I suppose there are worse things, like blowing up a building," Mom laughed. "I used to think she did all those things to piss her dad off, but I guess that was more of the Cold Soul fighting in her head. Still, there was no stopping my little rebel."

"You weren't mad at me?" I asked, surprised.

"Of course I was mad at you. You blew up a building as a 'scientific experiment' in the middle of the night. But you also never did anything that put anyone else in danger. You were strange, and no one understood you, but you were never evil."

"Like dad was?" I asked, folding my arms.

Mom sighed. "He wasn't always. I think he was a little jealous of you being born with powers. His power was the only thing he had worked for and you got it without trying. I think he probably tried to use you to get more, and he roped Aidan into helping him."

Nate groaned in the back seat at the mention of Aidan. As we pulled up to the cabin, I turned around to kiss him before he got out.

"I love you." I smiled at him.

"Always forever." He winked and slid out, letting me stay so I could keep talking to my mom.

We pulled out behind him and followed as he drove out toward the highway. We still had another two hours before we got back, and it would be well past midnight. The night was clear and the stars sparkled as I leaned against the window. I could see my mom's reflection looking at me, dimly lit by the dashboard.

"What?" I asked. It was easy to block out thoughts now but it didn't mean I wasn't interested in listening in on them.

"Lots of things. Your eyes for starters."

"The power source did it. I don't know why my key doesn't hide them. I did the same charm for Nate and it worked on his." I frowned but I didn't actually mind the blue. It was the only color I knew.

"I wouldn't know either." She reached her hand out and held mine. "So tell me about Nate. I didn't see him grow up. Angie sent him and Tom away from The Complex shortly after he was born, thinking he didn't have powers. I was the only one who knew about him."

"He grew up with a normal life. I mean, besides his parents not really being around. He and his best friend both had powers but they kept it secret. The three of us were doing fine until we met Richard and Aidan."

"Oh, please tell me Nate is better than Aidan."

"Even without my memories I can tell you he absolutely is. It's not just the connection we share," I said, smiling as I watched the taillights of his car. I wondered if he was listening in. Sometimes I couldn't block my thoughts from him, even if I tried. "He has done so much for me, and I almost feel terrible that I dragged him into this."

"Sweetie, he was in this long before you both knew it. All you can do now is stay together." She paused. "You do want to stay together, yes?"

I looked at her, surprised she would ask that. "Of course we do."

She laughed. "I'm just checking. You've only been together for four months. That must be one powerful connection."

"Kinsie and Isaac had the same one. You were right, we were meant to be together."

Mom shared some of her favorite stories and filled in more of my past. Even without my memories, I could still picture everything she described since I had seen The Complex and I could easily see myself doing the things Finnley did.

Apparently when I tricked that guard so I could steal his keys, I forgot to shut off the building alarm. They caught me climbing out a window on the second floor. No one could explain how I reached it, and I wouldn't tell them either. They had to get a ladder to force me down off the roof because I kept climbing up and away from Richard as he tried to wrangle me in front of a crowd of people. I had to help out in the library for two months as my punishment. That's probably how I met Jeanie.

Then, when I blew up the building in the middle of the night, everyone ran up to see me just sitting in the middle of the rubble, scribbling in my notebook and laughing like a total psycho. Not only was I performing a scientific experiment, I was documenting every reaction that came as a result of my crazy actions. Those notes probably included everyone's thoughts too.

I was clearly fueling my dad's hate for me. I may have been defiant of him because I watched him kill Nate in my dreams, but I was only making it worse. The older I got, the more trouble I got into and the worse I was to the people around me. I had no more friends and people started to hate me, pitying my parents for having to deal with the actions of a crazy child. Even the doctor, who ran a brain scan to see if my headaches and behavior were a result of something, concluded that I was just a pain in the ass and somehow a brilliantly functioning insane person. The brain scan was probably where Richard got the idea to use a tumor to trick us the day we went to his house.

We followed Nate off the exit and through the rocky path. Without light, it was hard to see anything except what was directly in front of the cars. But as we got closer to The Complex, my stomach started to churn. There was an eerie orange glow in front of us, getting brighter through the trees and Nate started to speed up.

Clara, my parents.

He slammed on the brakes as he entered the parking lot. His door flew open and he jumped out without turning off the car. I didn't wait for my mom to stop the car before I had done the same, sprinting to catch up with him.

The Complex buildings were engulfed in flames, smoke billowing and blocking out the night sky. There were no screams, no people around, just the sound of fire cracking around us. The Assembly building was already crashing to the ground, sending creaks and roars through the night.

"Angie! Tom!" I screamed as I gained ground on Nate. He was running toward the apartment building like he was going to run inside. But something else caught my eye as I finally snagged the back of Nate's sweatshirt to stop him from running. He fought me for a second before he saw the figures in the middle of the plaza.

The Cold Souls stood over his parents, Finnley pressing her hand hard into Tom's shoulder while the evil Nate had the same grip on Angie. Black blood dripped down their scars and over Angie and Tom's shoulders. They watched as we got closer, not moving or releasing their grip. When we got too close, Finnley stuck her other hand out and I walked into an invisible wall.

"Hey there, cutie," Finnley said, winking at my Nate as a smile creeping over her face. I saw the black now, creeping over Tom's shoulder. It wasn't blood, it was some sort of energy. No, it was Evil Nate using a shadow.

"Aw, babe, do you have to flirt with him in front of me?" Evil Nate groaned. "Look how nervous you make him."

"What do you want?" I spit in anger, squeezing my hands into fists. I looked for something, anything, to separate the Cold Souls from Nate's parents.

"Oh, I'd be careful with those powers of yours, sister. I'd hate for someone to get hurt in your blast. We all know how you can't control your tricks." Finnley's fingers dug deeper into Tom's shoulder and he winced.

C, what do we do? I heard Nate in my head, panic in every word.

"'C, what do we do?'" Evil Nate mocked him before his face turned cold. "We can hear you, idiot."

"Oh, would you look at that! Hi there Mom, nice to see you're alive." Finnley actually looked surprised for a second as my mom ran up next to us before her eyes locked on the book my mom was holding. Her eyes narrowed. "Good, we were looking for that. I guess poor Jeanie died for nothing. She refused to tell us where she hid it. I propose a trade."

"What are you going to do with the book?" Nate asked. He shifted, bumping into the wall Finnley was still holding up.

"The book for your parents." Evil Nate didn't answer the question. I could tell we weren't going to get their answer.

I took the book out of my mom's hands and stepped forward through a gap in Finnley's wall. Finnley popped it back up quickly to separate me from my mom and Nate.

"Let his parents go and I'll give you the book," I growled, glaring at Finnley.

"Why would we trust you to hand it over? These two are our leverage," Evil Nate hissed.

"Because you can read my mind and you know I'm not lying." I let the wall down around my thoughts, letting them know the truth. I was going to trade, no tricks.

The Cold Souls lifted their grips as Finnley pushed Angie and Tom forward with force, pulling the book out of my hands with her power. She caught it and the Evil Nate dropped them down into the shadows before I could fight back.

Nate ran forward, sliding on the grass as he grabbed his mom in a hug. My mom stepped up behind me, her hand resting on my shoulder.

"Why would they want the book?" I asked, shaking my head.

"They probably don't know how to empty out the people with powers. The Cold Soul doesn't know how to create a black hole. They need the book to see how it was done."

"Now they know we can stop them. They'll find out Nate can make a black hole and use him before we can trap them. Worse if they can make the black hole themselves." Our plan was ruined, but my mom didn't seem as worried as she should have been.

She shrugged. "Joke's on them. The book went blank as soon as we left the Original Complex. They can't read it."

61

Nate

The New Year came with no Cold Soul appearance. Then another week passed. Then another two weeks.

Ellie kept the empty Blue Soul power source protected in House. We couldn't risk the Cold Souls destroying it before we had a chance to trap them, and House was the best protection.

It was somewhat relieving to have a name for our powers. The Blue Star. Things just started to make a little more sense. Now the strange part was going back to school and pretending like nothing from winter break had actually happened. Ellie was back, Clara was alive, and Glitch was overjoyed that we were all together again.

Middle January weather got colder and darker, but never cold enough for snow, much to Clara's disappointment. Our lives pretty much returned to normal. We walked to school, did our homework, applied to college, and annoyed our parents incessantly when we tried to sneak out of the house to see each other at night. I mean, if they were worried the Cold Souls would kidnap us or something, we had a better chance of fighting them together. But they could also potentially use me to create a black hole if we weren't careful, and I was starting to suspect they couldn't do it themselves or they would have done it already.

I rolled over and stared at the clock. A few minutes past midnight, and I had been trying to sleep for the last two hours. I missed turning over to see Clara next to me. Our connection made it so much easier to relax. That buzzing from our touch calmed the nerves of the Cold Souls. We were right back to playing the waiting game, just like we had done with Richard when he used the Ruby to kill Clara.

In the darkness, the window creaked. My heart clenched, picking up the quiet click as the latch unlocked. I had no time to be afraid, I just had to act. I shot out of bed as someone slid inside, but before I could run into it, the dark figure grabbed me and spun me around, slamming me into the wall.

"Wow, you ass," Clara growled, flipping on my desk lamp without moving. Her face was just inches from mine, her blue eyes sparkling. She readjusted her body to keep me pinned to the wall. "That's no way to greet your girlfriend."

I let out a half groan. "You climbed through my window in the middle of the night with the Cold Souls still running around. How did you expect me to react?"

She shrugged. "I can leave."

I rolled my eyes. "You could also tell me when you're coming over. Or come in the front door like a normal person," I said, reaching up to tuck a strand of purple hair behind her ear. She had colored it again, which meant it was brushed and free of knots. A rare sight.

"Then it wouldn't be a surprise. Also, your parents are still awake and watching TV in the front room," she replied, hopping up to sit on my desk as her feet planted in the chair. She tugged at the sleeves of my old sweatshirt, gripping them in her fists. "Happy birthday, by the way."

My shoulders finally relaxed. Clara watched carefully as I set my hands on either side of her and leaned forward.

"If it's my birthday, where's my present?"

She raised her eyebrow. "I snuck out of House, walked here, and climbed through your second-story window so I wouldn't get caught. Where was I supposed to hold a present in all that?"

In a swift move, Clara kicked her feet out, tripping me so I dropped into the chair with a thud. She slid off the desk and sat on top of me, pressing her lips against mine. Her hands reached around my neck as I moved mine under her sweatshirt, feeling the buzz swirl around my body. I could feel the tingling through my fingers, aided by our cool touch.

Clara didn't pull away, whispering softly in my head. *Wanna play hooky from school today?*

Of course I do. I smiled as she moved her lips down my neck.

No parents, no Glitch. Let's run away for a day, just the two of us.

The TV downstairs shut off and we pulled away from each other as my parents started shuffling downstairs. I reached over and shut off my lamp quickly while Clara held in her laugh. The stairs creaked, probably them coming to check on me. Clara hadn't exactly been quiet coming in.

Clara's breath was warm as she nuzzled her nose in my neck again.

Would you cut it out? There was silence outside but Clara didn't listen. Her hands slid down my chest, moving under my shirt and around my back.

They aren't coming up here. Your mom is turning around.

Great. You're listening to my mom's thoughts while making out with me.

Sure enough, the stairs creaked again and I heard their bedroom door close. I felt Clara smile into my jaw as she kissed me again. My hands slid to her hips, picking up the hem of her sweatshirt, but she stopped me.

"First, we have to run away," she whispered as she stood up, dragging her hand slowly along my arm as she moved toward the window.

"We're sneaking out the window?" I asked, snagging her hand.

She yanked me up. "You can hold onto my back as I climb us down, or you can use a shadow. Your choice," she said, a grin growing on her face.

"Shadow," I replied, shaking my head. "Are you sure about this?"

Clara patted her jeans pocket. "I have the Blue Soul cage just in case we need it."

I sighed. "Fine. Do I need a change of clothes where we're going?"

She leaned up, biting her lip. "Nope."

I smiled and picked her up, dropping into a shadow as Clara directed me away from the house.

Burn It Up All Night. Sweet Talker.

Clara danced her hand through the air, playing with the stars she had made on the ceiling. The sleeve of my shirt hung loosely over her arm, drifting with each movement she made. If I wasn't careful, she'd steal all the clothes from my closet.

She had found the treehouse we were in just beyond House. The hatch in the floor didn't have a handle, but it opened for her without any effort or powers. It didn't have the same 'bigger on the inside' magic that House did, but it still had plenty of room for us giants. I wouldn't mind spending the day locked away in here with her.

The night sky started to fade from the ceiling as she dropped her hand back to my chest. "One day, when this is all over, we should run away for real," she sighed.

I slid my fingers through hers. "There's no more Complex so no one will come after us. We really could get away."

"Think you can put up with me?" she asked, clearly smiling even though I couldn't see it.

"Only because you have great tasted in music."

Stay with Me. Sweet Talker.

Her head pressed harder into my shoulder as she fell asleep. The gentle energy buzz lingered on our touch as I drifted to sleep with her.

"Nate! Wake up!"

I expected to be blinded from the sun when I opened my eyes but it was still dark. In fact, it was completely black, only it was like a bubble around us. Clara had her hands pressed on the surface of something, pushing hard and grimacing from the strength she was using.

"Nate! What are you doing?" she shouted, her eyes wide in fear as she waited for me to do something.

I sat up and realized that Clara was creating a shield to protect us from... a shadow? But that wasn't me. I threw my hand out, easily connecting with the darkness, or at least most of it. The part that responded melted away and the room filled with sunlight.

Clara continued to shove, a black figure outlining a body pushing back from the foot of our bed. I tried to push again, unable to connect with the shadowed figure. Finally, Clara sucked in a breath to shift her strength into her left arm, grabbing me with her right. I felt her power surge as she punched forward, knocking the black figure and pinning it to the wall.

"The cage!"

Shit, this was the Cold Soul. Back in The Assembly room, I hadn't kicked *something* in the shadows, I kicked *someone*. I rolled over the side of the bed and picked the empty marble out of Clara's pocket.

As the figure squirmed under Clara's strength, I focused on the power instead of the shadow. I just had to pull that into the cage. I picked through the energy I could feel, connecting with something as it started to respond. The blackness sunk into the ground, sliding toward my outstretched hand.

The power slid through my fingers as I pulled it through my body and into the cage. It was metallic tasting, and it pulled like a thick liquid through my chest and down my arm as it filled up the cage. But the light that started to swirl inside wasn't black.

It was red.

I looked up at the figure Clara still had pinned against the wall. The blackness was gone, revealing the thin, hollow frame of a man. His eyes sunk into his face, pale and weak against Clara's power as she continued to grip harder.

Richard.

He thrashed and tried to yell, weak raspy moans escaping his mouth. As Clara pressed him harder into the wall, I could hear the wood cracking against his back.

"Clara!"

She didn't listen, her nostrils flaring as her eyes narrowed. Swinging one arm back, she loaded and punched her fist forward. The wood exploded and splintered behind Richard as he dropped out of the tree. There was a loud crack as his body hit the ground below.

I scrambled forward to confirm what we had just heard. His body was tangled and crushed in a mess of wood from the treehouse wall, no longer moving.

My eyes were wide as I turned to look back at Clara. Her body was shaking as she gasped for breath, one hand pressed into her forehead with the other against her chest. It sounded like she was choking back tears as I jumped back on the bed to keep her from having another panic attack. I pulled her hand away form her chest so I could help her but I froze. A light red mark was already fading into a blue bruise, creeping out from the neck of my shirt that she still had on. The bruise looked like fingers.

Clara looked down as I ran my hand over the mark, stretching the collar as I found the entire handprint on her chest. She coughed and pulled my hand away, rubbing her thumb over my wrist as she stopped shaking.

"I woke up because I couldn't breathe," she said, her voice raspy and strained. "The blackness was crushing me and I thought you might have been having a nightmare. How did Richard do that?"

I lifted my other hand, white from how tightly I was gripping, and opened my fingers. The little marble glowed with red light.

Clara coughed again. "He was using the Ruby to control the shadows? He didn't die."

"He is now," I replied, wrapping my hand back around the marble as Clara pressed her head into my shoulder.

"Now we don't have a cage to trap the Cold Soul. None of the other power sources are strong enough to hold it," she said, her voice full of despair. Even the energy through our touch changed.

We sat, stunned and silent in a half-destroyed treehouse while Richard's lifeless body was down below.

62

Clara

My mom was quiet as she sat on the couch. Nate was in the training room, probably getting ripped to shreds by his parents for sneaking out and skipping school. I'd almost rather my mom yell at me too. Finnley always got in trouble, but she never put anyone in danger. Clara, on the other hand, did both.

I knew what I did was stupid and reckless. Who else would think it was okay to sneak away with the power source cage and skip school? Now that it wasn't empty, we had no way of stopping the Cold Souls. They were free to continue their rampage of destruction, and that meant Nate was an even bigger target. It was all my fault.

"Could we use another power source to hold the Cold Souls?" she asked, not looking up from the floor.

I shook my head. "I doubt they are strong enough. Kinsie and Isaac only used those two sources."

I picked at my caffeine charm as Mom sat still. It was only a matter of time before she yelled at me. She should be furious with me, but instead she just sat there.

"And your father..."

Oh.

That's why she wasn't yelling. I had only known Richard as a psycho, hell-bent on stealing my power and killing me. Mom had loved him at one point. I should have realized that sooner. I should have known what I had really done. I killed my dad. I really killed him this time. Was that something I did now?

"He was using the Ruby to control the shadows. He must have been learning, or maybe getting stronger. The lamp that knocked over without us touching it, Nate kicking something when we were spying on The Assembly… he was following us."

"But you're okay, right?" she asked, finally looking up at me. Even if she had loved him once, I saw the anger in her eyes. The green eyes that I used to share with her. Richard was trying to kill me, and that was enough to make any mother furious. I brushed my hand over my chest, making sure that the bruise was still hidden. I didn't want her to see the second failed attempt Richard had at killing me.

"I'll be fine," I swallowed, hoping she didn't see my hesitation.

"Then what the hell were you thinking?" she screamed.

There it was. "I know what I did was dumb. We just wanted a day to be us again."

"You can't afford that luxury right now! What if that had been the Cold Souls?" she yelled, her hands gripping the couch cushion.

"Then we would have trapped them. We were prepared. If they need Nate to create a black hole, wouldn't it be better if I was with him so I could contain it? They want us separated. They want to use him when I'm not there to stop it," I replied, trying not to raise my voice.

"This isn't about that. How could we ever know if you were in trouble if we didn't know where you were or what you were doing? You can't do this alone."

"You both have a point," Angie said as she walked in, Nate and Tom following close behind. "It's true, the two of them are probably better. If the Cold Souls try to use Nate's black hole, Clara would be able to stop it. Even if they can't trap the Cold Souls, they could at least keep them from recharging the power sources until we can find a new way to trap them."

"See?" I snapped, glaring at my mom. She just glared back.

"She said you were both right," Tom said. "You're just teenagers. You shouldn't be doing this alone."

Don't do it. I heard Nate in my head, trying to keep me from opening my mouth again, but I did it anyway.

"What do you want us to do? None of you have powers, or any power you can fight with. We could get Glitch involved, but he's just a teenager too. We let the Cold Souls out. They look like us and they have our powers. It's our job to stop them"

"Really?" Mom said as she stood up. "And how do you plan to do that? The last time you did this on your own, you got stabbed."

I could see the regret wash over my mom as soon as she said it, but it was too late. The image flashed back through my head. The long walk to the clearing with the knife in my grip, knowing I could do nothing to stop it. My hand lifting, shaking, but unable to respond to my commands. Red tugging at my vision, emptying my mind and my body as I watched in slow motion. The blade dug deeper and deeper, and I could feel it slide through me, the sharp pain piercing my spine as blue blood spilled through my fingers.

Clara, you have to listen to me. Let me in.

I opened my eyes. Nate had my arms pinned around my stomach as his body wrapped around mine. We were kneeling in the middle of the floor, shards of glass from the shattered mirror scattered around us.

My mom looked down at me in guilt and horror while Tom and Angie were still ducking away from us.

Nate picked me up off the ground, glaring at my mom. "We're done here."

I was shaking, completely horrified as flashes of that scene crawled back through my head.

"Why are you walking away?" Angie shouted after us.

Nate growled. "None of us have answers, so I'm going to actually try to help the one situation we can help right now — Clara — because you sure as hell don't know how to handle this."

I don't know if it was Nate or House that slammed the door behind us.

63

Nate

"Oh hell yeah I want to get involved." Glitch spoke a little too loudly. Mrs. Roberts looked up from her desk but decided to ignore us. The TV was still blaring in the front of the classroom, playing some history documentary that no one was watching. He lowered his voice. "You've had to kill Richard twice now. I want in on the action."

Clara pulled the collar of her shirt back up to hide the handprint bruise as I shook my head.

"We don't even know what action there's going to be."

The pencil I was bending finally snapped in my hand. I set it down, annoyed that I couldn't keep my fidgeting under control. We were in over our heads, with all of it. Our parents were right, we were just teenagers and we were in no way equipped to handle this situation.

Glitch shrugged. "You can absorb powers, dude. Just steal the Cold Soul back."

Clara sighed. "It's not that easy. We have nowhere to put that power."

"Didn't you have the whole Cold Soul in you once?" Glitch asked, leaning closer.

"That was before we had half of the Blue Soul power in us. The Complex said that much power would kill someone, and I believe it. This guy is packing a lot of punch," I said, pointing to my arm to remind Glitch that we already had too much power in us to begin with.

"Plus, the Cold Soul literally drove Finnley insane. She was absolutely crazy," Clara added.

"So we just sit around waiting for them to use Nate as a black hole?" Glitch asked, finally seeing how helpless our situation was.

"And hope that Clara is around to keep it from happening," I replied as I picked up the broken pencil and went back to bending it.

"I hope you guys like each other. You can't break up ever again," he laughed.

Clara found my hand without looking and I felt the power shoot up my arm. "Insomniacs united," she said as she laced her fingers through mine and squeezed.

Glitch leaned back, smug. "I told you she was your type."

"She's out of my league," I corrected.

"No, I'm out of my mind," Clara clarified.

We laughed before several glares shut us up, one from Mrs. Roberts. That first day of school seemed so long ago. Now that everything was in perspective, I could smile about how much everything made sense. The headphones when Clara had walked in, the cold air as she pulled herself into the desk, the volleyball 'experiment' she had run, the smoothie and scar reference after Queen Bitch Emma tripped...

Clara's eyes got wide as she slapped her hand over her mouth to keep from laughing. Glitch looked at us confused.

"You tripped her, didn't you?" I whispered, a huge smile on my face.

"Of course I did. You wouldn't let me punch her."

I pulled her hand away from her face and kissed her as Glitch scrunched his nose.

"Gross. Get a room."

~

Clara didn't want to go back to House so she could avoid her mom. Our parents had decided to take turns keeping an eye on us. We would spend two days at my place, one for my mom and one for my dad to stay up, and one at House so Ellie could watch us. Clara decided she would wait the full two days before going back to House.

I was sitting at my desk, finishing our calculus homework while Clara sat on the bed, staring at the ceiling. She had finished her homework faster than me. I knew she was brilliant, but now that she didn't have voices in her head, she didn't get distracted and could breeze through her assignments.

The last question was driving me insane. I had burned my pencil eraser to a nub trying to figure it out. As I scrubbed the paper again, the poorly taped pencil I had fixed from this morning snapped again. I groaned and planted my face into the desk.

"Here." I jumped as Clara slapped her answers next to me.

"Complements of Finnley's brain."

"You remember Finnley taking calculus?"

I had been using the completely wrong formula to try to solve the question. No wonder I couldn't figure it out.

"No, your thoughts were making me dizzy and I'm really smart now that I don't have Cold Soul voices distracting me." She slid around behind me and kissed the top of my head as she wrapped her arms around my neck. I leaned my head back against her stomach as she continued. "I still don't know if I remember anything about Finnley or if I can just picture my mom's stories happening."

"Do you want to remember things?" I asked as I closed my notebook.

"I think I kind of like Finnley now. Even if she was a pain in the ass, I understand why. The Cold Soul drove her absolutely nuts. You saw what it did to me. I wouldn't mind learning a little more about her, from my own perspective." She pushed my papers to the side and sat on the desk to face me, her eyes a dull blue as she looked at me. "I just don't know how to get the memories back."

That gave me an idea. It was a bad idea, but it was an idea. "Well, House and The Complex didn't trigger anything, but going back to that power source cave did. I hate to say it, but maybe going back to Richard's house would do something?"

"We're under house arrest on a Friday night. We should probably just wait until we figure out what to do about the Cold Souls. It's not like those memories will help us stop them."

I shot up, sliding the chair back away from me. "Clara, yes it could."

A smile crept over my face in excitement while Clara just looked at me like I had grown a second head. "What are you talking about?"

"If we can trigger a memory of Finnley, you'll remember what it was like to have the whole Cold Soul inside you. Maybe you can find a weakness or figure out how to stop them?"

Now Clara shot up, inches from my face. "Holy shit. Screw Finnley being brilliant, you're a genius." She kissed me hard, forcing me back against the wall and knocking the chair over. Just as quickly, she pulled back. Her blue eyes started to shine as she grabbed my hand, dragging me out the door. "Come on, we have to tell your parents."

64

Nate

Our parents actually agreed it was an idea worth trying. Saturday morning, Ellie met us to drive up to her old house. I had forgotten at one point she would have lived there too. She seemed just as hesitant to go as Clara did.

Clara and I sat in the back seat with her, my parents in the front. It was an extremely uncomfortable silence as Clara leaned into me hard, avoiding touching her mom. My parents looked just as uncomfortable as when they had walked in on Clara and I back at The Complex.

"Good, you should be sorry." Clara's harsh tone startled everyone as her head snapped to face her mom. Ellie had probably tried to apologize with her thoughts.

"It was an awful thing for me to say and I should have been more careful," Ellie murmured as she hung her head. "I'm worried about you."

Clara folded her arms and leaned back into me. "Just be glad Nate was there to stop me. It could have been worse."

"Is that what your headache outbursts used to do?" Ellie asked.

Clara faced forward, avoiding eye contact. "No. That was weak in comparison."

"Your panic attacks have never done that before," I chimed in. I looked over at her but she just elbowed me, angry that I had spoken up.

"Panic attacks?" Ellie said, her face going pale.

Now Clara sat up and glared at me before facing Ellie. I shouldn't have opened my mouth because even my parents looked nervous.

"Yes. I used to get them because of the headaches. Those were much more destructive. Now I'm getting them because…" Clara trailed off.

"We keep it under control. It's done and over with," I said, trying to end the conversation.

"You two together are always going to be a handful," my mom grumbled as she glanced back at us. "There is no controlling you."

I knew our parents had never been able to control Finnley's antics, but I had never been in trouble before in my entire life. I'm pretty sure I'd never broken any rule of theirs. Well, at least until Clara came into my life. Of course they thought she was a bad influence on me. I didn't have a chance to argue as we pulled into the driveway.

Ellie hesitated while the rest of us climbed out of the car. My dad made it up to the front door and wiggled the handle before Ellie had opened her car door.

"Locked. Ellie, is there a key?"

Clara walked up on the porch and flicked her fingers. We heard the lock click and my dad pushed it open.

My dad shrugged. "Right. Should have known better."

Nate, if I start to remember something, can you come with me? Clara kept her eyes locked on the inside of the house.

How?

I'm letting my wall down. Maybe you can read my thoughts?

I stuck my right hand in her left, connecting the scars on our palms. The energy felt stronger that way, and the buzzing feeling always made me feel closer. Our parents followed us as we stepped into the house.

The living room was dustier than the last time we had been here, probably because no one had been inside for a couple months.

"Your room is upstairs to the left," Ellie said as she leaned against the wall, looking around at her old house. Her fingers slid over a framed photo of her with baby Finnley peering up into her face. Their dark green eyes were identical as both of them smiled.

"I'm sorry, mom," Clara whispered as she bit the inside of her cheek.

Ellie gave us a weak smile. "I am too. I'll just be a moment." She sat down on the couch as my mom went to join her. Dad seemed uncomfortable so he just stood still.

Clara turned to walk up the stairs but paused, looking at another framed photo. I had missed all of these things when we were first here.

Finnley looked barely younger than Clara was right now. Her purple hair was tangled in the branches of the tree out front as she leaned against the trunk, her legs resting on a thick branch. She had climbed just out of reach of Richard, his arms folded as he looked up at her. Finnley was smiling, holding *The Magicians* open as she read, probably ignoring Richard. I nudged Clara who broke out of her trance and started walking up the stairs.

The bedroom door creaked as it opened. It was definitely her room because it was in complete disarray. Clothes were thrown all over the floor, sticking out of the closet that couldn't close all the way. The gray comforter and pillowcase were stained in pink and purple splotches, probably from her wet hair. Even her desk was stuffed to the brim with notebooks and loose papers. Pens and other random items had been stuffed into the pages as bookmarks.

Clara just stood there, looking around. Her walls were down but her mind was blank. She didn't know what to think. Slowly, she pulled me into the room, dragging her right hand against the white walls as she made her way to the bed. As we passed her desk, I snagged one of the notebooks on top. She sat down on the comforter that was bunched up at the foot of the unmade bed.

"Anything?" I asked as I sat down next to her and started flipping through her notes with my free hand. Her lettering was neat and clean but didn't stay on any of the lines. The handwriting slanted across the page and filled every white space, written at different angles or completely upside down. The sentences were clustered in groups that didn't make any sense.

"No," she groaned and rolled onto her back. "What did I write about?"

I chuckled. "This is from when you blew up the building. Everyone's thoughts and reactions."

"Nate." Clara squeezed my hand and pointed her free one up. I looked up at the ceiling she had painted a blackish blue, speckled with white and pale yellow. She had literally created a night sky on her ceiling.

Then I felt it, the punch of nausea knocking me back next to her. I was either going to feel her as she went through her memory or get sucked in with her.

"You've got to be joking me," Clara groaned as the stars started to spin on the ceiling. I had to shut my eyes to keep from throwing up. Soon, I felt a cool breeze running over my face.

I opened my eyes, still staring up at the ceiling. No, that was the actual night sky. The ground underneath me was rough as I sat up. Clara leaned up too, holding on to my hand tightly. I still couldn't talk or think to her but I don't think she was going to let go for fear that I wouldn't be there anymore.

We stood up in the middle of The Complex plaza. It must have been late at night because none of the lights inside the buildings were on. Movement caught our attention to the left.

In the building where all the apartments were, the screen of one of the windows pushed out. Hands tried to reach out to keep it from falling but they only knocked it hard to the side. The screen dropped, bouncing off an awning before crashing to the ground.

Finnley stuck her head out the window, grimacing as she looked down, her purple hair swinging in the breeze. I wanted to laugh but no sound came out.

Clara and I watched as Finnley climbed out of the window, dangling with her hands as her Converse skidded against the wall, trying to hold her up. I could see her starting to slip as she swung her legs to the side. She let go of the window and flung herself toward the awning. As she hit it, she lost her balance. Her legs scraped the awning but she tumbled and rolled off, dropping down to the ground with a loud crack.

She groaned as she lay sprawled on the sidewalk below. Clara yanked me along with her as she started to run over. I don't know what we would be able to do if Finnley was actually hurt, this was just a memory.

As we approached, Finnley sat up laughing, her hand pressed to the back of her head. She pulled it away, looking at the red blood on her fingers. There was a small amount on the sidewalk where her head had hit the ground, but she didn't seem bothered.

Holy shit, Finnley was a psycho.

She just shrugged and jumped up off the ground, taking off running toward a building near the parking lot. That building hadn't been there when we were there. Clara and I chased after Finnley as she ran up to the front of the building. With a swing of her fingers, the door unlocked and she ducked inside.

When Clara and I got through the door, Finnley was in the process of ripping the alarm system off the wall.

"Fool me once..." she mocked.

The chirping sputtered out as Finnley ripped the cords apart and tossed the device behind her. This must have been after the alarm got her caught in the library.

We followed Finnley through the hall of the school building as she skipped along, making a lot of noise as her shoes squeaked on the floor. She didn't seem to care. Every few skips she would hold her hand back up to her head, seeing if the bleeding had stopped before wiping her hand on her jeans. Finally, she turned into a classroom.

Finnley had already started collecting all sorts of chemicals from the shelf of the lab when we got inside. As she surveyed her findings, she noticed something was missing. She spun around and walked up to the lab table at the front of the room. Her hand yanked at the locked cabinet a few times before she ripped the entire door off the table, sending the screws scattering across the floor. She laughed again, tossing the door to the side with ease.

Clara wobbled next to me as her grip tightened, her other hand shooting up to her temple. Finnley did the same thing in front of us, grimacing.

"Shut up. Shut up. Shut up," Finnley growled, smacking the heel of her hand against her forehead.

Voices. The Cold Soul and Blue Soul fighting in her head. Clara could hear it, just like Finnley.

Finnley shouted into the empty room. "What other explosion do you want? If I do this for you, you need to get out of my head."

The Cold Soul was trying to get Finnley to create a blue star explosion. They thought she could create the black hole herself. Finnley didn't understand what the voices were really asking her to do.

We watched Finnley mix her concoction, referencing the notebook she had pulled out of her jeans pocket. It was the same one I had been holding back in her room. She measured out the last chemical before gathering her hair into a bun on top of her head. She stuck her pen through the tangled mess and shoved the notebook back in her pocket.

"No one is here to get hurt, that was our deal." Finnley winced again. Clara did the same.

"No, stop." Finnley's arms shot around her head, squeezing hard. "Stop, please stop."

Clara's hand gripped mine tighter as she shoved her head into my chest. I didn't let go of her hand but wrapped my left arm around her to hold her close. The headache outburst. The Cold Soul was going to use her outburst, thinking it would create a black hole. The shelves and lab equipment started to shake as Finnley dropped to her knees, clawing at her head. Everything in the room started to rattle, creaking and scraping noises echoing around us.

The last chemical sitting in a beaker shattered as Finnley screamed. A gas pipe burst out of the table and mixed with a small flame that seemed to come out of nowhere, igniting the explosion.

I expected to be blinded, even if we couldn't feel the explosion, and dug my face into Clara's hair. But the roaring sound of fire muffled and died down. I looked up.

Finnley was standing again, her arms in front of her as her hands created a shield around the explosion. She was struggling to keep it held together, trying to press tighter around the force. Every time she twitched from the *headache, the explosion grew and spit flames out of her shield.*

Clara looked up and watched as Finnley tried one last time to squish the fire, but the Cold Soul won. Her hand shot over the back of her head where she was bleeding and the fire engulfed the room.

As the building crumpled around us, Finnley sat down in the rubble, covered in dust but otherwise unaffected by the blast. She yanked out her pen and notebook and started furiously scribbling notes. Her thoughts echoed around us.

'Explosion. Black hole. No. Blue Star. Screaming. Erased.' People started running out of the other buildings but Finnley didn't look up. 'Go away, your thoughts are distracting me. I have to know what the voices are afraid of. I have to know who the boy is. The Cold Soul is upset we can trap it. We can make the voices go away.'

The old woman from The Assembly pushed through the crowd in her nightgown, stepping over the mess. She tried to yank Finnley up out of her seat but Finnley pulled her arm away and dropped her back against the ground, laughing into the sky like a crazy person. Clara and I fell back with her as the memory faded, staring back up at the stars in the clear night.

65

Clara

The back of my head was throbbing, sending aches down my shoulders and through my back. Finnley's memory was painful. I could even feel the knot where she had fallen and hit her head on the sidewalk. Could I get a concussion from a memory?

I wasn't quite ready to get up yet, but Nate clearly was. He pressed his lips into mine, his body resting gently on top of me. I kissed him back, sliding my arms around his waist to keep him close. As his hand slide around my neck to lift my head, pain shot through my spine. I lost my breath, choking from the pain, but Nate just dug his fingers harder into the back of my head, holding his face tighter against mine. Finally, I squirmed enough to throw him off of me.

He started laughing as I rolled over, gasping for breath. My head spun in pain as my hand shakily moved to the back of my head.

Soft and sticky.

I tried to look at my fingers but watched three of my hands dance in front of my face, my fingers stained with blue blood.

"Stop making out with that bitch." It was my voice, but it didn't come out of my mouth.

Nate kept laughing. "Oh, come on. It's funny. It's not like she can do anything."

I scrambled back, trying not to throw up as the room kept spinning. As I pushed up off the ground, dizzy and stumbling, I crashed into a hard wall and fell back down.

"What the hell?"

My speech was slurred as I leaned against the wall, trying to use my other senses in between the throbs of pain in my head. The ground underneath my hands was rock. The wall I leaned against was rock too. I could smell the winter air, so we had to be outside. And there might have been an echo, but that could also be the headache. I focused my breathing and opened my eyes again.

Everything was blurry, but I could make out two figures, one squatting next to me and another standing behind it. As the closest one to me leaned forward, I started to make out Nate's features. His green eyes hung inches from my face as he studied me.

"Told you she couldn't do anything," he said, leaning back to stand up as the other figure moved next to him.

My vision finally focused. The Cold Souls.

"Where's Nate?" I groaned, feeling the weight of every word in my mouth.

"I'm right here, babe," the Cold Soul Nate laughed.

"You should have hit her harder," Finnley grumbled, crossing her arms as she glared at me.

I tried to push out against them with my power but missed completely. Rock cracked and showered dust to my left, a significant distance away from where I was aiming. But it finally revealed where we were; the cave at The Complex.

"Pathetic," Finnley said. "We should have just killed you." She leaned down, too close to my face. I slammed my forehead into her nose, feeling nausea punch every part of my body. As if that didn't hurt me enough, Finnley screamed and threw my head back against the wall with her power. The crack echoed through my brain as pain vibrated down my spine again. Warm trails of bood started running down the back of my neck.

"Where's my Nate?" I managed to slur the sentence together, fighting the tug of blackness around my vision. I couldn't black out now.

"Still out. We're keeping you alive long enough to get him to make a black hole. I want to watch the life slip out of you, slowly and painfully," Finnley hissed, wiping the black blood dripping from her nose. "I'm sick of you."

I heard a groan from across the way as Finnley smiled and turned around. I located Nate laying in the corner, slowly shifting as he woke up. Above him, all of the empty power sources remained planted in the wall, ready to be recharged. The Cold Soul Nate dropped down next to me, his hand wrapping around my mouth so I couldn't yell. I couldn't think straight enough to get my thoughts out to Nate either.

Finnley did what I assume the Cold Soul Nate did to me, pressing her lips into Nate's as she wrapped her arms around his neck. I wiggled helplessly in my corner as Nate moved his hands over her shoulders. She must have been messing with his head because the room started to darken. With all four of our minds connected, I could feel her tricking Nate into using his power. He had no idea what he was doing.

The Cold Soul Nate shifted just enough for me to shift my chin away from his hand. I bit down with all of my strength, causing him to yelp and pull his hand away.

"Nate!"

My scream was hoarse but the room snapped out of darkness. Evil Nate tried to reach for me as I scrambled forward but my foot connected with his jaw. It wasn't strong, but it was enough to stun him and knock him back.

Nate threw Finnley off of him but she kept herself from rolling. She popped back up as Nate jumped to his feet, eyes wide. He saw me crawling away from the Cold Soul and tried to make a dash for me.

"C!"

He slammed into an invisible wall and fell back. I was helpless too as the Cold Soul Nate wrapped his hand around my ankle, yanking me back across the rock. My hands slid, clawing at the ground to try to stop him. One of his hands snagged my arm, fingers digging into my skin as the other hand gripped my hair near the gash in my head. Searing pain shot through my body as he dropped me to my knees.

Nate pounded against his invisible cage as Finnley started laughing. "Oh, this is going to be so much fun." She shoved Nate against the wall with her force. "We really thought taking your forms would help us create the black hole. Seems we need you after all, hot stuff."

Finnley stepped closer, her fingers digging into Nate's chest as she pushed him harder into the wall. I could feel her digging into his head as his face strained, the nagging pull growing in the back of my neck. Around us, blackness started to grow again, reaching out from Nate and growing up the walls.

"Nate, take their power!"

I inhaled and threw myself forward, launching the Evil Nate over me and into the wall across the way. My last push of energy sent Finnley flying away from Nate. He collapsed off the wall, scrambling toward me as the room returned to light again.

As Nate wrapped his arms around me, I felt our connection burst to life. The buzz was strong, coursing through my body and filling me with new energy. The Cold Souls stood, walking toward us as they cornered us into another wall. Our exit was blocked and we had no way out. All I could do was give Nate the rest of the energy I had left in me.

"I'm done with you," Finnley growled, her green eyes blazing with rage as she focused on me. Her fist loaded back and I winced in preparation for the blow.

She punched forward... but nothing happened. Stunned, she threw her fist forward again, but no power left her body. Next to her, the Cold Soul Nate stumbled, trying to grip her as he fell to his knees. He pulled Finnley down with him, their eyes looking to the ground in horror as their shadows slid out of their bodies.

Next to me, Nate had his hand pressed into the ground, his other gripping my wrist tightly as I stood next to him. He was using our connection to pull in their power, but none of it was channeling into me.

"Nate, you have to give me some of the power," I pleaded, wiggling my hand so I could try to hold his arm.

He grunted. "No. I'm not sticking the Cold Soul in you again." He was still focused forward, watching Finnley and Evil Nate slide deeper into the darkness as they screamed and hissed.

"You can't hold all of it!" I shouted over the final cries of the Cold Soul.

The rest of the power slid into him and he let go of my wrist. Nate pressed his forehead into the ground, his fingers digging into the rock below him as it cracked under his power. The Cold Soul was still trying to get out, and it was going to bring the entire cave down around us.

Blackness started to seep out of his fingers like water. Shit. The Cold Soul was trying to control him from the inside. The cave snapped into darkness in an instant, empty and hollow surrounding us.

"Nate!" I shouted, gripping his shoulders as I turned him to face me.

He refused to open his eyes. "I'm trying! You have to get out of here!" he grunted through the clenches of his jaw.

I pressed my forehead into his, trying to pull the power out of him like he had done once for me. I worked my way around the walls he had in his head, giving him my strength.

Nate, you and me. We are the Blue Star. We can contain it, just let me help you.

He opened his eyes, the blue locking with mine as he finally let me in. I moved my left hand down his arm, forcing my hand into his as I squeezed as hard as I could. Now I could feel his power expanding around us, but the tighter I held him, the more I could feel the edges of the blackness he was creating. I wrapped my energy around the black hole, tugging it back into us. The energy fought against me, but I was making progress. With every tug against the shadow, cold shivers of wind whipped through us. It grew around our hands, pulling, pushing, and stinging my skin as I refused to let go.

Until suddenly everything was still.

I was afraid to pull away from him. Our hands were still pressed together, and our faces couldn't get any closer. Nate blinked, his left hand reaching up around my face and neck. His fingers slid across the blood that was still rolling down the back of my head. As he connected with the wound, my nerves cried out and I yelped. He tried to keep my head still, concerned about the gash on my head, but I was too focused on the wall of power sources across from us.

It worked. They were all lifeless on the wall. We had just stopped the Cold Souls.

I glanced down at our hands, seeing that my left hand was still gripping Nate's right, our fingers turning white from how tightly we were holding each other. But I was going to need to let go soon because something cold was burning my hand.

We peeled our fingers apart, blue blood smearing from our palms as we saw the Cold Soul. Pressed into a perfectly smooth black marble, black smoke and light swirled, fighting against a blue light that got stronger and picked up speed. The blue twirled and swallowed the black light, finally resting into a still blue glow.

But we still had our scars. We still had the Blue Soul. We created the little marble from our power. This was the real Blue Star that contained the Cold Soul. The cage would constantly be exploding in a supernova and collapsing into a black hole, keeping the Cold Soul trapped.

Nate dropped to the ground in a loud exhale. The world around us might have returned to stillness, but my head was spinning again. I crumbled down, my face pressing into Nate's chest as I closed my eyes. I could still feel the blood rolling out of my head and soaking his shirt underneath my face.

I love you. His words echoed in my head as his heartbeat took over my senses.

Always forever. I felt his hand rest over my back just before I lost consciousness.

66

Nate

Clara rolled over, stealing all the blankets as she woke me up shivering. Without the connection to the Cold Souls, we were no longer immune to the chill of winter. Even in my old sweatshirt and sweatpants, I could see her shivering under the covers. My layers weren't doing much for the cold temperature.

Now that we stopped the Cold Souls and had nothing to worry about, our parents tried to enforce strict 'no overnight guest' rules since we were still just teenagers in high school. It worked for zero days because here she was, sleeping in my bed. She had climbed through my window in the middle of the night, and I had no idea how my parents didn't hear her as she crashed to the ground laughing. She was Finnley-level psycho now that she didn't have any worries in the world.

I pulled the blanket back over my head which brought Clara rolling over to face me underneath the covers. She groaned, hair matted over her face.

I'm not Finnley-level psycho. I'm just normal psycho.

You climbed in my second story window in the middle of the night... again. I replied, brushing the hair out of her face as she squinted, struggling to wake up.

You didn't seem to mind when I did it. Either time. She gave me a tired smile, leaning forward. Finnley-level psycho didn't seem to care about morning breath as her hands wrapped around my face. She shivered as I slid my hands up her sweatshirt so I moved them back on top, dragging her body closer to mine to stay warm. Suddenly she pulled away, eyes wide, before scrambling off the bed.

Your mom.

Clara dove into the closet just as my mom walked in. I threw the blanket off my head and groaned. "Why can't you ever let me sleep?" I asked, hoping she hadn't just heard Clara crash into the back of my closet.

She shook her head. "It's a Monday morning. You have school."

"Ugh, can I take a sick day? I just prevented my massive black hole from absorbing everyone's powers and trapped the Cold Soul." I watched her shift the laundry basket to her other arm, full of the clean clothes that had been stained with blue blood from Saturday. I panicked as she reached for the closet door. "Hey, never mind. I'll wear that to school today. No need to put it away."

She spun to look at me, her eyes narrowed. "I thought you wanted a sick day?" She sighed and shook her head. "Nathaniel Beckett, where is that girl hiding?"

Clara fell out of the closet behind her, tripping before catching her balance on the wall. She leaned against it like nothing was wrong. "Hi there, Angie. Nice morning," she said sweetly.

My mom was not amused. "Clara, you have a concussion. And you shouldn't be here anyway."

"I don't know what you're talking about," Clara replied. "I'm perfectly fine, and as far as you know, I just got here."

Yup. Finnley-level psycho. Clara shot me a look as my mom dropped the clothes basket on my desk.

"Ellie is going to kill you," she sighed, shaking her head as she walked out the door. Clara closed it behind her and cheered silently.

"You're out of your mind," I laughed as she jumped back into bed.

"I know, and you're stuck with this Finnley-level psycho. Now tell me..." Clara said, holding her face just inches from mine. "Do you think this concussion matches my explosive supernova power?"

I snagged her collar and pulled her into my kiss before leaning my chin back just enough to speak. "I think it complements my black hole power perfectly."

I barely finished the sentence before she pushed me back down to the bed. I heard the speaker click on.

Electric Love. BØRNS.

Thank you for reading! If you have a minute, I'd appreciate if you left a review on Amazon.

The story continues with Soul Remembered and Soul Obscured.

Be sure to join my tribe at

sendfox.com/laurawinter

I'll send you a chapter that was cut from this book. Plus you can read a retelling of this story from opposite perspectives. Clara's scenes will be told from Nate's perspective and vice versa. I'm always adding new things so stay tuned!

Perfect for fantasy, sword and sorcery lovers

Warrior Series: Ten epic tales weave together across three perspectives, testing loyalty, duty, and love. A life in the balance, a great city on the brink of collapse, and a magic that could restore peace to their world... if it doesn't fall into the wrong hands.

The Shadowed Assassin: Haellen, the shadowed assassin of Napiron, has killed the rebel leader. But when a small band fights back, Haellen must trade stealth and infiltration to defend and protect the High Priestess. As the new rebel leader, Cyrox, comes to avenge his lover's death, Haellen is forced to question her duty to the High Priestess and Napiron.

Perfect for romance lovers

If Found, Do Not Return: Remy ran away for an adventure, but life punched back. After eight years of trying to escape her small town, she's forced to return home, defeated. Pulled in two different directions, Remy has to make a decision. Neither comes without a cost. Will she and Lucas make their second chance work, or will she run away on an adventure with Maddox that could burn the last bridge she has to her home?

Short Stories: find a collection of short romances with HEA at **laura-winter.com**

Made in the USA
Las Vegas, NV
28 February 2021

18758056R00163